THE LOOK OF LOVE

Grace looked up into Noah's eyes and seemed to get caught there for a moment. He was *such* an intense man, hard and lean and ragged. It seemed he was constantly on edge, as if he might break apart any second.

Truth be told, Noah Partridge frightened her. He made her nervous. She felt funny inside, as if she'd stood up too fast and her head was swimming. His powerful gaze made her remember how it had felt to be treasured, protected, loved. Mr. Partridge's gaze made her long to feel those things again.

Good heavens, what was the matter with her? With an effort, Grace broke eye contact and turned away. She rubbed her hands up and down her arms where gooseflesh had sprung up. She felt foolish.

"I won't hurt you, ma'am."

Noah's soft assurance startled her. She whirled around. A response danced on her tongue. She wanted to tell him that she hadn't thought he'd hurt her, but the declaration died before she could speak it because she got trapped by his eyes again. His intense, brooding, beautiful green eyes.

As if of its own accord, her hand reached out to him. He caught it in his and drew her to him.

When he kissed her, Grace felt as if a firecracker had been shot off in her veins.

Land of Enchantment:

Enchanted Christmas

Emma Craig

LOVE SPELL BOOKS NEW YORK CITY

LOVE SPELL®

December 1998

Published by

Dorchester Publishing Co., Inc.
276 Fifth Avenue
New York, NY 10001

ISBN 0-505-52287-X

Printed in the United States of America.

This series of three books called "Land of Enchantment" is dedicated to two people. The first is my mother, Wilma Wilson Duncan, who was born and reared in Roswell when New Mexico, although barely a state, was still wilder and woollier than any place I've ever been. She's told me amazing stories about life in those days, which was darned near as perilous as life in the late 1800s in this hard place.

Roswell has been christened a "tree city" (the only one in New Mexico) now, but back when Mom was growing up here, there weren't any trees at all. There were only the incredible empty plains, the sky above them—and the wind.

My mom's the one who told me about wagon yards. I'd never have known they existed but for her. I figured McMurdo's Wagon Yard is located on what is now the corner of Second and Union, where Nellis's Wagon Yard used to be. There's a Chinese restaurant on that corner now.

The second person to whom this series is dedicated is my agent, Linda M. Kruger. When I asked her what she reckoned Leisure wanted next, she told me—and she was right. She's right more often than not, in fact, and I appreciate her a *whole* lot!

Land of Enchantment

Enchanted Christmas

Chapter One

Once upon a time, on a fair October day in 1869, a little girl and an old man worked side by side. The two lived in the tiny community of Rio Hondo, which squatted between the Spring, Hondo, and East and West Berrendo Rivers in the southeastern corner of the New Mexico Territory,

An old rag doll, clad in a dress made of the same material as the little girl's, sat on a stump beside them. Her jolly embroidered face had an amiable expression, and she seemed to be supervising their activities. She looked as though she'd been loved quite hard during her days on earth.

A sound caught the little girl's attention, and she glanced up from the rope she'd been coiling into a tidy stack. "Listen, Mac. Somebody's comin'."

Alexander McMurdo, proprietor of McMurdo's Wagon Yard—a favorite stopover of cowboys trailing herds from ranches in the Pecos Valley and Seven Rivers country—took the old briar pipe from his mouth and looked. He smiled when he saw a solitary man, slumped slightly in his saddle, riding across the plains toward them. Mac had been expecting him. About time, too.

"Looks like we got us a visitor, Maddie, m'lass."

Five-year-old Maddie Richardson jumped with joy and clapped her hands. Visitors were a rare and welcome experience for the girl. She lived, after all, in the only—and very small—oasis of civilization within a two-hundred-mile radius. The land stretching between Rio Hondo and other seats of society was as barren and unspoiled as her own heart but much, much harder.

Rio Hondo sat in the middle of the southeastern New Mexico Territory like the hub of a spoked wheel, with trails leading east and south into Texas, west toward the Arizona Territory, and north to Albuquerque, Santa Fe, and the Colorado Territory. The forts Sumner and Stanton were within that two-hundred-mile radius as well, and provided what passed as protection for the citizens in this part of the territory. There weren't many of them. The army had rounded up most of the Indians in the early sixties, so that nowadays the most trouble settlers and ranchers could expect came from one another.

Maddie shaded her eyes and squinted through the harsh, cold sunlight at the stranger, now slowly making his way through the wide-open wagon-yard gates. "He's on a pretty horse," she said, her voice vibrating with excitement.

"That he is, lass. Let's you and me go see what the fellow needs. He's lookin' a little trail-worn."

"He's all dusty," Maddie agreed.

"So's his horse."

Maddie grabbed up her dolly and clasped the gnarled old hand Mac held out to her. Mac peered down at her, clucking softly when he noticed she wasn't wearing her sunbonnet. That meant she'd slipped outside in spite of her mother's vigilance. He grinned around his pipe.

She was a charmer, Maddie was. Almost as charming as her mother, but a great deal less bowed down by life. But that figured, as the wee lass had scarcely had time to collect any burdens. With luck and his own help, Mac trusted that Maddie would grow up to be as fine a woman as her mother—and that her mother's heart would heal at last. He matched his stride to hers, and they walked over to where the stranger had reined his tired horse to a stop and was dismounting.

Mac shook his head as he studied the newcomer and felt a little sad. It appeared to him as though the poor fellow had made it here just in time. Another year or two, and not even Mac's magic could have touched him.

Noah Partridge was almost as tired as he'd ever been in his life. He was sure sick of riding. This was the place for him, though; he knew it in his bones—all of which ached as if he'd been in a brawl. The countryside around Rio Hondo seemed as barren as Noah's soul, as bleak as his past, as desolate as his future, and as hard as his heart. The wind tore across it like a demon from hell, sometimes so stiffly that the dust and grit could rake a man's skin off his face. Noah shook out the bandanna he'd worn over his mouth and nose to protect them from the blowing dust. The cloth was stiff with dirt.

The only sign of life Noah had seen for at least twenty miles—until he rode into Rio Hondo—was low-growing grama grass and a few scrubby bushes. Greasewood, mesquite, yucca, and cactus dotted the landscape here and there. Every time Fargo, Noah's horse, had stepped on a clump of greasewood the tangy odor of creosote had nipped at Noah's nostrils. He'd decided he kind of liked the smell—as much as he liked anything, which wasn't much.

As he'd neared the community of Rio Hondo, he'd noticed a stunted shinnery oak that had been sculpted by the wind. It leaned to the northeast, bowing against the prevailing winds as if it had given up the struggle to stand upright. The very air Noah breathed here was hard, the water was harder, and Noah had a gut feeling he and they belonged together. He was harder than both of them put together.

Hell, even the animal life out here was sinister. Scorpions, rattlesnakes, coyotes, cougars. Wild Indians even, he supposed, unless the army'd gathered them all up. He'd seen about a million buzzards too, although he imagined they'd be gone soon. They'd all fly south to winter in the sunny climes of Mexico and wouldn't show up again until springtime. Which only went to show that Noah Partridge was tougher than a buzzard. He gave a small internal grin that didn't make it to his lips. Yup. This was the right place for Noah, all right.

He turned when he heard footsteps. The greeting he'd been about to pronounce withered and died when he saw a child walking with the old man whom Noah presumed was McMurdo. Hell, Noah hated kids. He hated kids almost as much as he hated adults.

"Howdy, stranger," the old fellow said.

His voice was cheerful and faintly tinted with a Scots burr. It grated on Noah's nerves like a metal file. He tipped his hat. "Hello. You McMurdo?" His own voice was leathery and cracked with disuse.

"I am Alexander McMurdo." The proprietor's eyes twinkled like stars. Noah didn't appreciate the effect.

"I understand I'll have to put up in your wagon yard while I take care of business here. You have room for me and my horse? I don't have anything but what's on the old boy's back." He gestured to his bedroll and saddlebags, which carried all his earthly possessions. Everything else he'd ever owned was gone now. Bitterness twisted through him as he thought about it, so he stopped thinking.

"Oh, aye, I expect we can handle you and your horse." The old man chuckled. His teeth were as white as pearls and were clamped around what looked like the oldest pipe in the universe. Because Noah could no longer tolerate the man's merriment, he turned and took longer unfastening his pack than he needed to.

When he turned around again, he found that the little girl who'd walked up with Mr. McMurdo had let go of the old man's hand and now stood about a foot away from Noah himself, her raggedy old doll dangling, evidently forgotten, in her right hand. She peered up at him as if she were looking upon something strange and foreign. Which she probably was. She undoubtedly hadn't met up with too many hollow men in her day.

Since he didn't know what to do with her, he resumed his work. He glanced at her once or twice out of the corner of his eye and wished she'd go away, or that Mr. McMurdo would do something with her. The kid made him nervous.

After a couple of very long moments, McMurdo did as Noah had wanted. "Maddie, me wee lass, allow me to introduce you to Mr. Noah Partridge. Mr. Partridge, this here sweet bairn is Miss Maddie Richardson."

"Partridge?" Maddie broke into a huge smile. "Like in the pear tree?"

She was just a kid. Noah reminded himself of that when he felt the urge to holler at her. How could a little kid understand that while Noah hated men, women, and children, he abominated Christmas and everything associated with it, including the blasted songs. Christmas was a season of sentimental hogwash, filled with sappy music, perpetrated by greedy merchants, and geared to pacify fools. Christmas was the season during which Noah's own personal life, which hadn't been a whole lot of fun to begin with, had gone straight to hell. He'd loathed it ever since.

He said, "Yeah," in a voice as hard as the local water.

McMurdo seemed unaffected by Noah's aloofness. He put a hand on the little girl's bare head. Noah knew his eyes were suffering from the territory's harsh light when dots of diamond-like sparkles seemed to flood from McMurdo's hand and diffuse in the air around them. "Maddie is turnin' six years old next month, Mr. Partridge."

"In November, eh?" said Noah, for the sake of saying something.

Wait a minute. When had he told McMurdo his name? He couldn't remember saying anything at all except that he wanted a place to stay in Rio Hondo while he conducted business. Noah's eyes narrowed, and he watched McMurdo closely. Something was odd here, but he couldn't put his finger on what it was.

Whatever expression he had on his face seemed to amuse the other man. McMurdo grinned like Father Christmas himself and said, "Give Mr. Partridge a curtsy, Maddie, like your mama taught you, and shake his hand to welcome him to Rio Hondo."

"All right." Evidently as happy as the proverbial lark and much more obedient than any kid Noah'd ever known, Maddie executed a curtsy that would have looked charming to anyone but himself. Then she looked up at him and gave him the sunniest smile he'd ever seen. He grimaced before he could stop himself.

Then because he figured he should—after all, even though he hated kids on principle, he didn't necessarily want to wound one of them—Noah smiled back. It had been so long since his last smile that this one damned near fractured his cheeks. He took off his worn leather glove and shook her hand. It was as soft as silk and as undamaged as a fresh peach. Noah hadn't been around anything undamaged in a month of Sundays.

Maddie released his hand and stepped back. She looked up at McMurdo, and her small face took on a confiding, somewhat sorrowful expression. "Mr. Partridge isn't used to smiling, Mac. His insides must hurt, like Mommy says hers do sometimes."

If he hadn't been holding his gear, Noah might have stuck a finger in his ear to clean it out. Had that kid just said what he'd heard?

He didn't have time to rethink his astonishment. The patter of running feet caught his attention, and he turned to see a woman racing towards them, her skirts

15

caught up in her hands, her apron ribbons flying, headed away from what looked like a small mercantile establishment. Good. He needed supplies. He ignored the woman, again on principle.

"Oh, Maddie! There you are. I was looking all over the place for you."

The woman was breathless. Noah tried to continue ignoring her, but it was tough when she breezed right past him and knelt before her daughter. At least he assumed Maddie was her daughter. They had the same honey-colored hair and blue eyes; the girl's hair was a little lighter and brighter than the woman's, but not by much. As she passed him, a faint scent of something sweet, like roses, assailed his nostrils. He turned his head brusquely away from it. Damned woman was wearing some kind of perfume. It reminded him of home, and he hated it.

He set his gear on a stump McMurdo indicated. Now how the hell had such a big stump managed to get itself out here, in Rio Hondo? Near as Noah could figure, there wasn't a tree as big as that within seventy miles of the place. He didn't ask, because he didn't really care.

"Me and Maddie were just meeting Mr. Noah Partridge, Grace. Mr. Partridge plans to stay a spell in the wagon yard whilst he takes care of business."

"In Rio Hondo?" Grace looked up at Noah, surprise written all over her face.

Her eyes were clear and wide and as blue as the sky, and framed by dark lashes. Noah noticed them. He hadn't noticed a woman's eyes for a long, long time. But Grace Richardson's eyes were very like Maddie's. That's the only reason he'd noticed, he was sure. Most women's eyes didn't have such an unspoiled quality. At least the women back home in Virginia didn't. Of course, they'd lost everything, including their innocence, during the war that had ripped their homes to pieces and killed their men.

Anyway, he was probably wrong about this female. She most likely only appeared unspoiled and was rotten underneath. Lots of women had that look about them, and used it to beguile. Too bad for this one that Noah was no longer capable of being beguiled.

"Yeah. Thought I'd look for some land to raise cattle." His voice cracked again. He'd have to oil up his vocal chords since he'd probably be doing a lot of jawing until he found what he wanted. Then he could shut up again and stay shut up. Good thing, too.

"Well, there's lots of that around here, I guess." She stood and took up her daughter's hand. Noah had a feeling she did so because she was nervous and needed something to hold on to. If so, she was being foolish. If there was one thing Noah didn't have any designs on, it was a female. Any female. Of course, she couldn't know that.

"Grace Richardson, please allow me to introduce you to Mr. Noah Partridge. Mr. Partridge comes to us from the grand old state of Virginia."

Noah's gaze sharpened upon McMurdo again. Dammit, he *knew* he hadn't told this old devil where he was from.

"How do you do, Mr. Partridge?"

His gaze slid to the woman. She was holding out a hand as if she expected him to shake it. He looked at it for a second, before he took it and said, "How do you do?" It was automatic. He didn't really care how

17

she did. Or how anybody else in the world did for that matter.

"I hope you find what you're looking for in Rio Hondo, Mr. Partridge."

Noah let go of her hand when he realized she was exerting some pressure to get it back under her own control again. Jesus, what was wrong with him? Sparkles in the air, people knowing things he hadn't told them, him holding a woman's hand. Maybe he was losing his mind. He might as well. God knows, he'd lost everything else. Sure as hell, his mind hadn't been of any use to him for years now.

"Yeah," he said. "Thanks."

Grace gave him a puzzled look and a faint smile and peered down at her daughter. "Come into the mercantile with me, Maddie, and let's not bother the men. You can help me stack the canned goods, all right?"

"All right."

Noah'd never seen such an obedient child. Of course, he was no expert on children. He remembered Julia's younger brother, though, and he'd been a real brat. A spurt of fury shot through him when he thought about Julia, and he slammed the door shut on his memories.

"It was a pleasure to meet you, Mr. Partridge. I hope you enjoy your stay in Rio Hondo." Grace seemed almost shy.

Noah didn't believe her. He nodded but didn't feel obliged to speak.

"Bye, Mr. Noah," Maddie said with another one of her sunny smiles.

He nodded at her too.

The two females turned towards the little store.

"You forgot your sunbonnet again, Maddie. You know I want you to wear a sunbonnet outside so you won't get sunstroke in the warm weather or frostbite this time of year. That's why I made you and Priscilla matching sunbonnets."

"I'm sorry, Mommy."

Noah shook his head. They looked like a couple of animated statues to him, one a miniature of the other. For a split second, he was almost curious who Priscilla was. The doll, he supposed.

As Maddie and her mother walked away from him, he heard Maddie say, "Mr. Noah looks just like the man in my dream last night, mama. The one who brought you the reed organ for Christmas."

"Does he? My goodness." Grace gave a little laugh and didn't look back.

As for Noah, he stared at the kid's back and experienced an urge to rush over to her, pick her up, shake her hard, and ask her what the hell she meant. How the devil had she just happened to pick a reed organ out of the air as if organs were as common as dirt and people dreamed about them all the time?

He shook his head again, hard, and turned to Mc-Murdo, frowning. The man gazed at him like some kind of benevolent gnome, as if he understood the source of Noah's unhappiness and confusion and pitied him. Noah resented him for it.

He decided to skip the reed organ issue. "How the hell did you know I was from Virginia?" The question was probably too sharp, but Noah hadn't had to use company manners for a long time and was out of practice.

19

McMurdo winked at him. "Accent, Mr. Partridge. Accent."

"You recognized my accent as being from Virginia?"

"Sure. We get us lots of folks from different states back east. 'Cause of the war and all," he added as if imparting a confidence.

The coldness that had engulfed Noah several years before suddenly turned a degree frostier. "Yeah," he said. "I'm sure that's true."

"Well now, Mr. Partridge, let me show you where you can stow your gear, and where to stable your horse. The two of you could use a bath, I reckon, even though the weather's nippy."

"I reckon."

"That's the washhouse." McMurdo gestured to a small shack. "There's a pump in there, and Mrs. Richardson keeps it supplied with soap and towels. She changes 'em every week, too, so we manage to stay pretty clean here. You know women." He laughed a jovial laugh.

No. Noah didn't know women. Not any longer. The only women he'd ever known were dead. Even Julia was dead now, and so was the baby she'd been trying to give birth to. Not that Noah cared about that. Hell, it hadn't been his kid. She hadn't bothered to wait for him. Not that there was much to wait for by the time he got back from the war. He gave himself a shake, irritated that he'd allowed bitter memories to crowd into his head. He thrust them out again, feeling vicious.

He said, "Yeah."

McMurdo led him to the back of the yard where the stable stood, protected by corrugated tin roofing material. Its row of stalls looked like stout, sturdy soldiers, standing side by side at attention. "Now, here we have a grand stable for your horse, lad. There's curry equipment, a grain bin, and a water trough, so the poor beast can recuperate from ridin' out here. I'll bring ye some oats if you're low on horse fodder."

Noah frowned, and wondered if McMurdo expected him to apologize for putting his horse to the use God— if there was a God—had intended for horses. The old fellow was smiling as if he found life a grand joke, so Noah didn't snap back at him. Noah considered life a joke too, but he didn't find it an amusing one.

"Looks fine," he muttered. "I'll take the oats. Thanks."

"Aye. I'm sure old Fargo will be right as rain in no time at all."

Noah tried to recall when he'd told McMurdo his horse's name, then gave it up. The old fellow just seemed to know things; things Noah'd doubtless forgotten he'd mentioned. Hell, he sure was unused to talking to people. His silent thoughts and his spoken words were probably getting all mixed up since he was accustomed to the one and out of practice at the other. Besides, he really was crazy; he'd known it for some time now, although the knowledge no longer bothered him.

He grunted to show McMurdo he'd heard him.

"You can sleep in this stall next to your horse if you're of a mind to, Mr. Partridge. We don't have any other visitors at the moment. They mostly come in the spring and fall, you know, when they drive the cattle to Fort Sumner or up north. Don't get us too many strangers this close to Christmas." His merry blue eyes

21

took on a confiding sparkle. "Folks like to be with their families at Christmas time, don'tcha know."

Yeah. Noah knew. His guts felt like somebody'd tied a knot in them. He grunted again, not trusting himself with words.

"Now it hasn't been awfully cold lately, but I expect it'll begin to frost any day now. If you get too cold out here, you just knock on the door of my house." McMurdo gestured to another tidy building, situated right next to his store. "Ye can bed down on the floor of the parlor in front of the fireplace, if it starts to freeze."

Because he figured he should, Noah said, "Thanks." In truth, he looked forward to the cold. It suited his temperament.

"And if ye get tired of fixin' your own grub, I always have a pot of stew bubblin' on the stove." He winked again. "My own recipe, and it's tasty stuff. Ye can get yourself a bowl of my famous stew, a slab of my famous corn bread, and a cup of coffee or a glass of beer for a nickel."

Noah nodded. He wondered how McMurdo's stew had come to be famous. Hell, there couldn't be enough people living out here to make anything famous. Which was encouraging.

"Of course, Mrs. Richardson cooks for little Maddie and me, and I'm sure one more mouth to feed wouldn't be a burden on her. She and Maddie would welcome the company, too, I reckon. It's mighty lonely out here, especially for a lady with a little girl to care for."

Yeah. Sure. Noah would perish fifty ways from Sunday before he'd be taking meals with Mrs. Richardson and her daughter. The mere thought made him tense up like a spring.

"And if ye ever get a mind for the company of another feller your age, and maybe a drink or two, there's the Pecos Saloon across the way."

Noah didn't bother looking where McMurdo pointed. If there was one thing he couldn't imagine a use for, it was company. Whiskey he could buy and use on his own if he ever got snake-bit. Otherwise, he didn't care for whiskey any more than he cared for the company of his fellow man.

Another one of McMurdo's chuckles brought Noah's thoughts back to his companion. "Aye, there's whiskey over there, and one or two pretty girls, too. The Pecos Saloon is where the cowboys go to have a drink after they've bought their supplies from me and before they go back to the ranches where they work. Poor souls. It's a solitary life out there on the plains."

This time Noah looked—in the direction of the plains. His tension lessened a bit. "Yeah." That's exactly what he'd hoped for. He craved solitude like other men craved money, whiskey, and women.

McMurdo went on, his voice friendly, as if he were in the presence of somebody who cared. "Got several ranchers in the area, though. There's the Blackworth spread, and a couple of lads recently come here from Texas—Cody O'Fannin and his cousin Arnold Carver. Chisum, of course, has the biggest spread hereabouts and runs the most cattle."

Noah had heard of Chisum. "Sounds like a lot of people," he murmured. He hoped all the good cattle land wasn't gone already. Hell, the territory had barely opened up; it couldn't be settled already, could it? Damned humanity always horned in where nobody wanted it to. Sometimes Noah wished he'd been born a cougar or a coyote. Out here, where there was nothing for hundreds of miles.

McMurdo's laugh rang out, hearty and loud. "A lot of people? Bless your soul, Mr. Partridge, there's land enough for thousands out here, and not a one of 'em would ever bump into another one unless he was of a mind to."

Thousands. Cripes. Noah hoped not. He tried to smile at the old man, but couldn't get his mouth to perform the unfamiliar exercise. "Know of any unsettled parcels of land hereabouts that I might buy or settle on, Mr. McMurdo?"

"Call me Mac, laddie. Everybody does."

Although he didn't want to get on nickname terms with anyone, Noah conceded. "Mac." It was easier than arguing.

The old man chuckled. It must be Noah's imagination that made this chuckle sound particularly canny, as if Alexander McMurdo knew Noah through and through—had known him for years, in fact—and, therefore, knew exactly what it cost Noah to unbend enough to call anyone by a pet name. He examined the old man keenly, but couldn't detect anything familiar in his face or manner. He was sure they'd never met before. He shook his head again, chalking this latest fancy of his up to exhaustion—or his soldier's heart. And what a fancy name for lunacy that was.

"Aye," McMurdo—Mac—continued. "I reckon I can take you out and show you all sorts of properties that might appeal to ye, laddie. Best give yourself and your horse a day to rest up, and we can set out the day after tomorrow."

That sounded all right with Noah. Although he

wasn't keen on having the chatty old man for company as he looked at land, his aims could be achieved with greater facility if he had a guide to show him around. He nodded. Since Mac wasn't looking at him and couldn't see his nod, he was forced to say, "Thanks. Appreciate it."

"Glad to help, Mr. Partridge. It will be my pleasure."

He sounded like he meant it, too. Noah didn't understand that, so he didn't respond.

"Ye can build a fire here." Mac gestured to a small, soot-blackened, sheltered fire pit that had been dug in front of the stall Noah'd be sleeping in. It had been lined with rocks, and boasted a corrugated tin shield on three sides and above it, and a serviceable iron spit upon which a man could roast meat or hang a pot. "But don't forget ye're not obliged to take your meals out here by yourself."

By himself was exactly the way Noah wanted it. He only nodded again. This wagon yard of Mr. Mc-Murdo's was a right nice place, just in Noah's line. It sounded as if Mac could help him find a place to settle, too. In the meantime, he could camp out in this little stall in Mac's wagon yard and still have the solitude he craved. He hoped that little kid wouldn't turn out to be a nuisance.

"Need any help getting yourself settled, lad?"

Noah's imagination—an item that hadn't been called upon to work much in recent years—made Noah believe he heard compassion in the old man's voice. He shot him a sharp, quick glance. "No." That sounded too curt a response to a civil question, so he added, "I'm fine, thanks."

Noah was positive Mac was taking stock of him. The old fellow, pipe clamped between his teeth, a grin on his face, looked him up and down as if he were inspecting a side of beef. It made Noah uncomfortable. Damn it, what was the matter with this old man, anyway? He looked away and pretended to study his sleeping stall again. There wasn't much to study. At least the straw looked clean.

"Aye, laddie," Mac said after a moment that seemed to crackle. "I expect ye'll be fine one of these days, at any rate. I'll leave ye to your horse and your own thoughts now. I'd surely like to know where ye expect to find a reed organ for Mrs. Richardson out here, though."

And, while Noah gawked after him, Mac walked away, leaving a trail of smoke rings and chuckles in his wake.

Chapter Two

The next day dawned as cold as ice, as silent as death, and as clear as crystal.

Disoriented at first, Noah had to sit up and look around before he remembered where he was. Then he sank back down on his bedroll as a feeling of peace, as foreign to him as any exotic language, stole through him.

He breathed deeply of the morning's freshness before he rolled out of his bed, hurried on his clothes, and jammed his feet into his boots. He'd slept pretty well last night—couldn't recall a single night vision, and he hadn't heard any voices. No shrieks or moans or groans. Not a single plea for help that he couldn't give. Maybe this place would be his cure. He doubted it.

He picked up his kit and headed for the washhouse. The clean, pure air seemed to call to him, though, and no sooner had he taken a step or two toward the washhouse, than he discovered himself veering over to the wooden fence encircling the wagon yard. The fence only stood about five feet high, and Noah, being a shade over six feet himself, could see over it quite well. He was even able to fold his arms, rest them on the top rail, lift his face to the sun, and shut his eyes for a minute.

The sun's pale autumn rays beat against his closed eyelids. Noah fancied that a few of them were leaking into his brain and burning the bad parts out. He even grinned a little at his whimsical thought before he opened his eyes again and gazed out into the plains. He knew he should be washing up and seeing to old Fargo, but he couldn't seem to stop staring at that great, stark landscape.

The plains weren't flat, exactly. Noah saw where the land rose and dipped briefly, almost gently, here and there, but nothing dramatic happened on those rises. They looked as bleak as the rest of the countryside. One lone mountain rose off to the west, and three wispy clouds hung over it like puffs of smoke. He wondered if the mountain was an extinct volcano. It looked like one to him, although what he didn't know about volcanoes could fill volumes. He liked the idea of something violent and once capable of immense destruction now looming over the countryside, its energy spent, a silent observer of the world's follies. It reminded him of himself.

Lord, this place was empty. For as far as his vision stretched, Noah didn't see a single other person. Mac's wagon yard sat at the edge of what passed for the town. Rio Hondo. Noah gave a small snort. Pretentious of its settlers to call it a town. That was the way of men, though. Seemed impelled to give themselves airs. Noah knew better. Men were weak—mere floundering, peacocking babies—compared to other forces.

But, oh my, these plains were empty. Almost. As he watched, two deer—startled by something only they perceived—bounded off, catching his eye. He hadn't known deer lived out here, and was pleased to have found out. At least he wouldn't have to look far for food. Noah allowed himself a brief fantasy of hunting on his own place somewhere out there in that gigantic nothingness.

Surely he could afford enough land on these plains to start a small business. He didn't want much. Only enough to support himself and Fargo. Maybe he'd get a dog. He didn't hate dogs the way he hated people, although he hadn't wanted the responsibility of one for a long time. But if he settled here, he wouldn't mind having a dog. Dogs weren't any trouble. And they were loyal. Noah could appreciate some loyalty at this point in his life.

He'd plant some trees. Not enough to interfere with the view, but a few to act as a windbreak. He understood it snowed out here occasionally, and he already knew there would be some fierce winter winds to contend with. So a windbreak would be all right. Maybe some poplar trees. They were hardy. Any tree'd have to be hardy to survive out here. Anything weak wouldn't last a month.

Noah was strong. He'd survived a lot worse than the New Mexico Territory and any winter winds it could throw at him. He'd get along fine here. Fine.

With Mac's help, maybe he could find himself a parcel of land with a river running through it. Even though much of the land looked as if water hadn't touched it for a hundred years or more, Noah knew, because he'd done his research, that there were rivers all over the place, and underground streams from which a man could get plenty of water if he dug himself a well. He'd find himself a river and some land, and build himself a soddy—he didn't need a regular house—and squat there with his dog and his horse and his cows and his poplar trees until his time came to die.

It was the first refreshing thought he'd had in days. He sucked in another breath of air so cold it nearly froze his lungs, and went to take care of his morning ablutions and Fargo.

Noah thanked his lucky stars that little Maddie Richardson didn't seem to be a nosy child. Although she waved a cheery greeting, she didn't pester him. He waved back and nodded and didn't guess he had to smile.

He noticed Grace, too, as he took stock of his supplies and made note of those he needed to buy at Mac's store. She'd evidently come outside to do some chore or other, and gave him a brief smile and a wave as she returned to the porch. There she paused to fiddle with something Noah couldn't see from where he sat.

He nodded at her, looked down again, then found his gaze drifting up from his list and fastening on her. She was a slender woman, and her movements were fluid and lithe. For all the harshness of the air and the naked sun that even now, as winter approached, beat down on the plains like a fierce Indian god, her complexion seemed clear and unwrinkled. He wondered how old she was. Probably no older than he, although she looked much younger. Of course she hadn't gone through the things he'd gone through. Everybody looked younger than Noah Partridge did.

Noah, who hadn't a romantic bone in his body, decided her name suited her. Grace. She was definitely full of grace; there was not an awkward thing about her. Then he wondered where that thought had sprung from.

Lord, he really was crazy. With an impatient shift of his shoulders, he wrenched his mind away from Grace Richardson, licked the end of his pencil, and went back to his list.

Mac had been right about the well-stocked nature of the horse stalls and the usefulness of the fire pit in the wagon yard. Noah'd given Fargo a good brush-down, then fed and watered him, using the oats Mac supplied and the water from the pump in the washhouse. Fargo had appreciated both the brushing and the food.

The washhouse, too, was a luxury Noah hadn't expected. Last night he'd given himself a good all-over bath, donned clothes that were clean, if not as fresh as they might be after having spent a couple hundred miles in his saddlebag, and felt almost human again afterwards.

Almost.

Noah had known for several years that his humanity had been all but starved out of him during the war. Any remaining spark had been doused when he finally made his way back home to Virginia. Or to what was left of his home. In what was left of Virginia.

Angry that he'd let his mind wander, he shrugged irritably and stood up from the stump upon which he'd been sitting. Hell, his mind hadn't dwelled this much on old times for years now. What the devil was the matter with him?

He was suffering from a lack of useful work to do, he reckoned, and aimed to remedy that problem right away. He took another good look at his list, tried to think of anything he'd missed, couldn't come up with a thing, and walked over to McMurdo's mercantile establishment.

Grace couldn't stop thinking about that man, Noah Partridge, and she wished she could. The first time she'd looked into his eyes and seen the stark pain they held, she'd felt a strong compulsion to put her arms around him and rock him like she rocked her daughter when Maddie stubbed her toe.

Why, his eyes had looked as tormented as hers had right after Frank died, only colder. Much colder. She wondered if the poor man had lost his wife.

She gave herself a shake and told herself to stop thinking about Noah Partridge. There were lots of wounded men wandering around out west these days— wounded both in body and in soul, if Grace was any judge. Poor things. She couldn't take care of all of them. She couldn't take care of *any* of them, actually. Besides, she had enough to do in tending to Maddie and keeping Frank's dream alive.

The front door of the store opened, and she looked up from sorting thread. Her chest gave an uncharacteristic spasm, and she told herself to calm down. Mr. Partridge might look a little frightening because of his air of remoteness and repressed violence, but Mac seemed to like him, and Grace would trust Mac with anything—even her daughter's life. In fact, she did.

With a small effort, she managed to smile in a friendly way. "Good morning, Mr. Partridge. Did you sleep all right out there in the cold?"

He didn't smile back. Grace got the impression he used his smiles sparingly. "Yes." After a moment, as if he'd only just then remembered his manners, he added, "Thanks."

Mr. Partridge was definitely not a friendly man. Grace sensed that his detached manner sprang more from unhappiness than antagonism, although she had nothing upon which to base her feeling. Nevertheless, she persisted. "I'm sure Mac has already told you this, but if you get too cold out there, please feel free to come in and sleep by the fire in the front parlor. It can get perishingly cold here in the winter, even though we don't get the snow and freezing weather some places do."

It took him a minute, but he finally said, "Yeah. He did mention it. Thanks."

Grace cocked her head to one side as she studied the man. He didn't look awfully old—maybe somewhere around thirty—but she sensed something almost ancient about him. With a little shake of her head, she decided she was only being fanciful.

"Please let me know if you need help finding anything, Mr. Partridge." She gestured to the jumble of thread on the counter. "We got a shipment of goods from Saint Louis. The package of sewing notions fell out of the wagon and broke open, and now I have to sort it all out." She laughed softly.

Noah stared at her as if he'd never heard a woman

33

laugh before. Grace wondered if she'd done something wrong.

He said. "Yeah. Thanks. I will," and went back to inspecting the goods displayed in the mercantile.

She wondered if he was a normally taciturn man, or if she'd annoyed him somehow. She hoped not. With a small sigh, she decided that if she had, it couldn't be helped. She couldn't be anything but herself; she knew, because she'd tried. Every time she'd attempted to live up to someone else's expectations, she'd failed. Eventually, she'd stopped trying, and now she only endeavored to be the best Grace Richardson she could be. She still failed sometimes, but not nearly so dismally.

That was one of the reasons she'd loved Frank so much. He hadn't wanted her to change. With a little shiver; she yanked her thoughts back from where they seemed determined to wallow in memories, and went back to her task.

"Where's your kid?"

Grace looked up quickly and found Noah Partridge watching her from in front of the shelf of canned goods she and Maddie had arranged last evening. Strange question—yesterday she'd gotten the strong impression that he didn't care for children.

She gave him another smile, because he looked like he hadn't been given enough of them in his life. "She's outside with Mac, pestering the chickens."

He nodded and didn't smile. "He's got chickens here, does he?"

"Oh, yes. Mr. McMurdo is extremely self-sufficient."

He nodded again. His face remained stony. Grace wondered if he rationed his smiles out one by one—if he had counted them and feared he'd run out.

With a gesture that looked jerky, as if he were unused to such spontaneous actions, he said, "He's got a pretty well-stocked store here, for such an out-of-the-way place."

Grace's grin was genuine and entirely spontaneous—she wasn't used to anything at all calculated, herself. "Yes. He certainly does. And quite frankly, I have no idea where he gets everything."

"Saint Louis?"

She let out another soft laugh. "Some of it. But he has other sources that remain a mystery to me. Frank—my husband—and I were astonished when we first set foot in McMurdo's Wagon Yard. I'm still astonished."

He grunted and turned away from her. Grace stared at his back for a moment, then returned to her thread.

An interesting man, Mr. Noah Partridge. Grace would like to hear his story, but she knew better than to ask. Especially out here in the territory, people were apt to be touchy about revealing too much of themselves. She knew that many of them had suffered ghastly losses in the war. Still others were running from things—the law, families, responsibilities, sorrows. Grace wasn't about to rub the scabs from old wounds.

Mr. Partridge looked particularly weighed down to her, although she knew her own soft heart often gave people the advantage of benefits they hadn't earned and didn't deserve. Still, there was something about him. . . .

Physically, he was lean and hard and haggard. His features were fine, almost classical. His nose was straight, his chin firm, and his eyes quite—quite beautiful actually. Green. They had looked green to Grace yesterday. They were probably hazel.

But his face had a drawn look about it that she'd seen before in people who had recovered from bad accidents and illnesses. She wondered if he'd once been terribly ill. Perhaps he still was. He wouldn't be the first consumptive person to come out to the dry heat of the high plains for his health. She understood doctors were moving out here all the time, hoping to cash in on the white plague by offering clinics to its sufferers.

Studying him from under her lashes, she decided his gauntness looked more as if it had come from an old injury or illness. Like Uncle Henry. She remembered how Uncle Henry had looked after he'd almost died during the war. It had taken him months and months to recover, and he'd borne the look of it afterwards— that emaciated tightness Grace thought she detected in Mr. Partridge's face. She wondered if he'd fought in the war and been wounded.

Poor Uncle Henry had suffered even after his physical wounds had healed, too. He'd had terrible nightmares. Grace understood that wasn't uncommon among soldiers who had been through the horrors of battle.

How sad. She didn't understand why people couldn't solve their differences in a manner less devastating than war. And this last one, with families torn apart, brothers fighting brothers, entire states ravaged—well, Grace couldn't comprehend any of it. She realized her eyes had begun to leak, and wiped her tears away impatiently.

For heaven's sake! If she didn't stop being so

blessed sentimental, she didn't know what would become of her.

Of course, she didn't know what was going to become of her anyway. With a sigh, she tucked the thought away. She'd survive. And she'd make sure Frank's dream survived, too. Thanks to Mac, she had a way to do it, if only there was time enough.

"Do you have any whiskey, ma'am? For snakebite. I don't want to go to the saloon if I don't have to."

Noah's voice penetrated her murky thoughts and made her jump. He spoke in a gravelly baritone, a little rough, as if he didn't use his voice much and hadn't worn the edges smooth. She gave a self-deprecating laugh to show how silly she was to have let him startle her.

"Yes, we do, Mr. Partridge. Mac keeps it here behind the counter—just in case, you know." She smiled.

"Yeah. Reckon I do."

She got the impression he didn't know at all and was merely humoring her. She asked kindly, "Would you like a bottle?"

"I suppose I'd better. Reckon it keeps."

Either Mr. Partridge wasn't a big drinker, or he was going to pains to make her believe he wasn't. She took a peek at him and decided he wasn't the type to pretend. Maybe he was making a joke. Another look told her he wasn't. She gave him another smile, because she sensed he needed as many as he could get. "I'll fetch it for you."

He nodded and resumed his examination of the leather goods. Harnesses and leather strapping hung from hooks. Two neat piles, one of leather chaps and one of vests, lay on a table next to a pile of shirts.

Mac had several good saddles on display, a couple of them used, and several pairs of shoes. Several odd boots, too. Most of the cowboys in the area would wear their boots until one or the other needed to be replaced. Then they'd buy one boot, wet it, and wear it until it conformed to the shape of whatever foot they needed it for. Grace shook her head as she opened the cabinet built into the counter, thinking how painful breaking in a new boot must be. She emerged with a brown glass bottle and a big smile.

"Here you go. Guaranteed to cure snakebite."

"Yeah?" He took the whiskey and set it on the counter alongside two heavy blue flannel work shirts he'd collected.

Was it her imagination, or did his mouth twitch slightly, as if he might be the tiniest bit amused by her medical opinion? His mouth seemed to have reverted to what looked like its permanently grim expression. It had probably been her imagination. She went back to her thread.

The only noise in the room for several minutes was the sound of Noah Partridge's heavy boots as he made a slow circuit around the store, and the rustle and click as Grace sorted spools of cotton twist. They were a mess, but at least none of the spools had unwound. The colors were a jumble, though, and there were at least a hundred different spools. The main problem was that when the package had broken open, several papers of pins had managed to get themselves mixed in with the thread, and Grace had a time of it not to prick her fingers on the sharp points of the pins as she gently pried the thread away.

From time to time, her attention wandered from her

work to her customer. There was something about him that intrigued her. The good Lord knew, men weren't exactly scarce out here. Except for her, Maddie, Susan Blackworth and those poor females who had to work in the saloon, the only people anywhere near Rio Hondo were men.

Grace had never had eyes for any of them. The only man she'd ever loved had been Frank, and she figured that was it for her. There were plenty of men out here who'd marry her in a minute if she'd give them an ounce of encouragement. But she wouldn't. She couldn't bear the thought of another man in her life now that Frank was gone. Frank was the one man she wanted, and he was dead.

Not, of course, that she had eyes for Mr. Partridge. Yet she couldn't deny there was something about him. It didn't attract her, exactly. It was more a feeling of intrigue. Grace discovered herself curious to hear his story, even though she was almost certain it would break her heart, if her heart hadn't already been shattered beyond repair by Frank's death.

The thought of her dead husband sent Grace's mind spinning back to the happy days of her marriage, and she sighed heavily.

"Anything the matter, ma'am?"

Again, the sound of Noah's voice startled her. She pricked her finger and muttered, "Ow!" Like the little girl she'd once been, she sucked her sore finger until she realized what she was doing and yanked it out of her mouth. "Oh, dear. I'm sorry, Mr. Partridge. This is such dull work, my mind wandered and I didn't pay attention to what I was doing."

He gestured at her finger. "Hurt yourself?"

"Not really. Just pricked my finger a little on a pin."

"That's quite a mess you have there, ma'am."

She sighed again. "Yes, it certainly is. It wouldn't be so bad without the pins mixed in."

"Reckon not."

With that, he set two pairs of heavy socks down next to the whiskey and shirts and wandered off again. Grace looked after him, and her sore finger found its way to her mouth once more. What was it about him? She wished some of the friends she used to know back home were here. They'd have a delightful time gossiping over tea about Mr. Noah Partridge.

She shook her head. She really didn't mind living out here, even though there weren't any other women nearby. But without Frank . . .

Grace told herself not to start dwelling on *that* again. Frank was dead; that part of her life was over; she was alone with Maddie. She loved her daughter more than life itself, and she owed Maddie her very best efforts. Frank would have expected no less from her, and she'd not fail him. She couldn't help the way her heart ached, though, or the way she couldn't get over missing him.

Which was nothing to the purpose. At last, the final spool of cotton twist was freed from the last pin on the paper, and Grace muttered a satisfied, "There! Finally!"

The door burst open, and little Maddie dashed in, hands cupped in front of her, a huge grin on her piquant face. Grace's heart lit up.

"Mama! Mama! Mac and me, we seed a roadrunner, and looky here. I found a horny toad all by myself!"

Maddie could barely reach the counter. Grace leaned over and saw the horned toad—it looked like a runt or

40

a baby, although it was awfully late in the year for babies—resting in her daughter's two grubby hands. Maddie held her hands together as if she were offering a gift to the gods.

"My goodness, what a beautiful horny toad, Maddie! Are you going to keep him?"

Maddie's braids bounced against her back as she nodded. "Yes. And then after winter goes away, you can put him in your garden, and he'll eat the bad grasshoppers that ate your carrots last year."

"What a clever fellow!"

"Mac built a box to keep him in, and I'll feed him flies and keep him alive real good."

"I'm sure you will, sweetheart."

Grace heard Mac—she would recognize the old man's step anywhere—and looked up. She did love him so much. He was like a grandfather to Maddie, and he'd been better than a father to Grace. She gave him the best smile in her repertoire. "Thank you for taking Maddie with you this morning, Mac. I appreciate it."

He winked. Mac was always winking. It was a charming trait, and Grace loved it almost as much as she loved him. "Ah, Grace, m'lass, Maddie was a big help to me."

"Were you?" Grace eyed her daughter and doubted it.

"I was, Mommy, honest! I feeded all the chickens, and then Old Pete runned away, and I peeled my eye and looked and looked."

My goodness, that sounded perfectly ghastly. Grace glanced at Mac, a question in her own eyes.

He chuckled. "Aye, that ye did, lass. Ye kept your

41

eye peeled real well, and you spotted that old runaway mule before I did.''

Ah. Grace understood now. Peeled eyes, indeed. She didn't laugh because she didn't want to hurt Maddie's feelings. ''I'm glad you were such a good helper, Maddie.''

In truth, Mac had kept Maddie with him so she wouldn't try to help her mother detach thread from pins. They both feared she'd end up stuck full of pins if she did.

Maddie whirled around. ''See my horny toad, Mr. Noah?''

Grace took note of Mr. Partridge's startled expression, and grinned. ''Poor Mr. Partridge is doing some shopping, Maddie. I don't think he has time for horned toads right now.''

He glanced from Maddie to Grace, and Grace was shocked to her toes to see that he was actually smiling. Almost.

''That's all right, ma'am. I've always been partial to horny toads.'' He looked at the toad.

The neck ruff of Maddie's bonnet, intended to keep the sun's rays from burning the back of her neck, squashed against the little girl's back as she tipped her head back far enough to look Noah in the face. ''Wanna hold him?'' she asked brightly.

''Um, well, I seem to have my hands full right now, Miss Maddie, but he's sure a fine looking horned toad.''

Maddie tipped her head to one side. ''You need some more practice, Mr. Noah.''

Noah blinked down at her. ''Beg pardon?''

Grace, who anticipated her daughter's next words—

which she'd never keep to herself because she hadn't learned anything about the world yet—hurried to intercept them. "You take your nice horny toad outside now, Maddie. Mr. Partridge is quite busy at the moment. You need to look for grubs and bugs for your toad, to get him big and strong for his work in the garden."

But Maddie, who had no playmates and was therefore unused to being sidetracked, continued staring at Noah. Noah stared back and looked nervous.

"Mac says if you practice anything, you'll get better at it. He says that sometimes even if you practice you won't be bestest, but practice always helps. I practice my letters and numbers every day."

"Is that so?" A muscle jumped in Noah's jaw.

Grace, who could see plainly that the man longed to escape, tried again. "Maddie, take your horny toad outside *now*, and leave Mr. Partridge alone."

Maddie turned, and Grace saw that she'd managed to offend her. She sighed.

"I'm not pestering him, Mommy. Honest, I'm not. Mac says that sometimes people don't know how to go about things. I'm only 'splaining to Mr. Noah that if he practices smiling, he'll get betterer." She peered up at Noah once more, her face a picture of earnestness. "Honest, Mr. Noah."

"Thanks, Miss Maddie. I'll keep that in mind."

It looked to Grace as though the infinitesimally small smile he bestowed upon her child was a mighty effort. She wondered what had happened to the man that smiles were such an effort for him. Maybe Maddie was right; he did seem to need practice.

She shook her head when she realized her child

wasn't done with the man yet. She glanced over at Mac, knowing he'd nod or something if he thought she should scoop Maddie up and haul her off before she could disconcert Mr. Partridge further. Mac winked again, and Grace knew he would solve the problem. God bless Alexander McMurdo.

"Why, I do declare!" Mac's exclamation drew everyone's attention—even Maddie's, and she was as persistent as a bulldog with a bone once she got started.

Grace knew Mac well enough to know what her next line should be. "Why, whatever is the matter, Mac?"

"I do believe I found me a licorice whip in my back pocket."

Slick as a whistle, Mac reached a hand behind him, and produced a long black twist of licorice. Grace looked from his hand to her daughter, and smiled when Maddie's eyes grew huge with wonder.

"Ooooh!"

Grace's daughter had been drilled too well in proper manners to ask if the licorice whip was for her, but her soft exclamation left no doubt of her hopes. She left off staring at Noah, who almost sagged with relief. In spite of herself, Grace grinned.

"And, since one little girl I know ate a good breakfast, and since dinner is a fair ways off, I reckon her mama wouldn't mind if I were to give this gift from heaven to her."

"My goodness," said Grace, playing the game. She tapped her chin with the finger she'd recently stabbed with a pin and tried to look as if she were pondering one of life's deeper mysteries. "I wonder what little girl you could possibly be talking about, Mac."

"Let's see, now. How many little girls are there in here?"

"Me!" cried Maddie. "There's just me!"

"Well, now, ye never know about these things, child. Want to search behind the counter, Grace, my lass? I'll take a peek under that stack of blankets over there. Never know where these little tykes will turn up, y'know. Why, when I was a wee lad in Scotland, we used to find children everywhere."

Grace made an obedient search behind the counter while Mac lifted blankets and pretended to peek under them. Maddie watched the two adults with eyes that had gone as round as grapefruit, her horned toad almost forgotten during this new game. Grace noticed Noah watching them, too. He looked even more puzzled than Maddie, and that made her sad. It was as if he'd never played a game with a child before and wouldn't have any idea how to join in if he wanted to, which she was sure he didn't.

She popped up from behind the counter, making Maddie jump and then squeal with delight. Noah looked first at Grace and then at Maddie, as if they'd both lost their minds. Grace experienced another pang of empathy for him.

"Well, there's no little boys or girls in amongst the blankets," Mac announced solemnly. "Unless—yes. I'd better just shake this one out. It looks a mite lumpy to me."

He lifted the top blanket—it did look a little lumpy—and gave it a quick shake. A dove shot out from underneath it, precipitating another squeal of delight from Maddie. Even Grace was surprised. Noah's mouth fell open for only a second. He closed it again almost before Grace had seen how surprised he'd been. No one could tell by his expression, though which remained as stony as Capitan, the mountain looming off in the distance.

Mac opened the door and the dove flew straight outside. Grace didn't have any idea how he did these things. She'd had experience with his magical expertise before, and wondered if he'd worked as a magician before he moved to the Territory. She'd asked him once or twice, but he'd only chuckled and given her enigmatic answers. He remained a puzzle, but the most kindhearted puzzle Grace had ever encountered.

After the dove had left, Mac planted his fists at his waist and frowned. "Well, Grace, I do declare that I don't see a single other child in this room but that one there." He pointed at Maddie.

By this time, Grace was almost used to the effect of the sparkles in the air that Mac seemed to be able to produce whenever he wanted. This time, as always, however, they startled her at first. She'd never seen another magician produce the same effect. It was quite lovely, and never failed to astonish her.

Sparkles danced in a cloud that slowly dissipated and then sprinkled down on Maddie. She looked at them, wide-eyed, as though she were too stunned to giggle or shriek.

Recalling that they weren't alone, Grace looked at Noah, who was frowning heavily and staring at the shimmering air as if he wanted to erase it, as if he didn't appreciate magic or sparkles or anything else the least bit out of the way of his own experiences.

Suddenly Mac clapped his hands, breaking the spell even as another shower of sparkles shot from his hands as they met. Everyone in the room jumped.

Then he threw back his head and laughed.

"Ah, me. 'Tis a grand life when an old fellow like me can make two grown people and a little girl stare in wonder at a wee bit of magic."

This time the spell was really broken. Grace gave herself a mental shake and smiled at her daughter. Noah blinked several times, peered down at the two tins of peaches he held, and then jerked toward the counter.

Mac held out his hand, Maddie transferred her horned toad to one hand, took Mac's with her other, and they left the store.

"Ye'll have to wash them hands before ye eat your licorice whip, Maddie m'girl."

"I will, Mac." She skipped outside with the old man, and Grace thanked God for at least the millionth time for having brought her and Maddie into his good orbit.

Chapter Three

"How the devil did he do that?"

Realizing what he'd said, Noah thought, *Aw, hell.* He stopped staring at the door and turned to Grace. "Sorry, ma'am. Didn't mean to swear."

She gave him an understanding smile. She'd been doing that ever since they'd met, and Noah wished she'd stop. She didn't understand a damned thing. Couldn't. And she was better off for it.

"That's all right, Mr. Partridge. I'm used to worse language than that, I can assure you. Life isn't full of tea parties and polite conversation out here."

"Reckon not," he muttered.

"As for Mac and his magic, I have no idea how he does it, but he's the most entertaining fellow I've ever met. I have a theory, of course." She turned and gazed at the door through which Mac and Maddie had just exited.

He waited, but she didn't continue. Faintly annoyed, sure she was playing some feminine game with him that would involve his begging her to enlighten him, he said, "What's that, ma'am?" Then he wished he hadn't.

He realized she hadn't paused only for effect when he saw her give a tiny start and gaze back at him. It was as if she'd forgotten he was there. His frown deepened.

"I'm sorry, Mr. Partridge." She gave a soft laugh. "I suppose I should be used to Mac and his ways by this time, but whenever he does his magic tricks, he surprises me all over again. At any rate, I've always speculated that he used to work on the stage or something, as a magician."

Acquitting her of subterfuge, Noah condescended to nod. "Sounds logical."

Grace's eyes narrowed and her brows knit, as if she were still bemused. "But he's so good at his tricks. I used to enjoy watching magicians back home, yet I never saw one as good as Mac. You—at least I—can never figure out how he does what he does."

"Mmmm." Noah felt a small tug of attraction to Grace Richardson, and frowned. Hell, if there was one thing he needed less than to have any truck with a female, he didn't know what it could be.

"My Uncle Henry used to do a few magic tricks, but you could always tell that they were tricks. I can't tell with Mac, he's so good."

Noah let out another "Mmmm," because he didn't know what else to say. He wasn't used to talking to people, especially women. This woman seemed unaffected, not at all like most of the women he'd known.

Noah was sure it was all a sham on Grace's part, and resented her for it. His level of resentment didn't quite reach his level of attraction, and he gave himself a mental kick in the butt.

"I mean, take that dove," she went on. "How in heaven's name did he get that dove in that blanket? For that matter, where did he get a dove at all?" She looked up at him, and he was struck once again by how pretty her eyes were. Damn, he was crazy. "And how could he have known he'd need it?"

Good question. "Couldn't say, ma'am."

"No? Me, neither." She'd left her thread in tidy rows on the counter top, and piled the papers of pins next to them. She picked up the pins now, gingerly. "It's certainly a riddle to me."

And she laughed again, at her own choice of words, Noah presumed. He tried to be annoyed—ever since the war, he'd loathed the sound of women giggling—but he couldn't be. In fact, he found himself wishing he could listen to Grace Richardson giggle for an hour or three. Lord, what an ass he was.

"Yeah," he said. "Me, too."

She went to the notions shelf, put the pins up, and returned for her thread. Noah realized he was staring at her, and tapped his peaches, trying to look as if he were pondering canned goods and not her. She couldn't carry all that thread.

Out of nowhere, he found himself saying, "Here, let me help you."

She shot him a glorious smile over her shoulder. It pierced his rhinoceros-thick hide and landed somewhere in the vicinity of his ribcage. He didn't like it. It made him feel something—vulnerable, maybe. Or wishful. To combat the effect of her smile, he scooped up a handful of thread and frowned harder.

"Thank you very much, Mr. Partridge. You really needn't help, you know. My job here in Mac's store isn't very difficult, after all, and I like to think I at least partially earn my keep."

"I'm sure you do, ma'am."

Where the hell was her husband? Why did she have to earn her keep here in this unlikely place? Noah got mad at himself for wondering. She was no business of his, and he didn't want her to be. God, that's all he needed. The idea of a woman in his life was so appalling, he shuddered.

"Are you all right, Mr. Partridge?"

"Yeah," he said. "I'm fine."

As soon as he rid himself of the thread, he paid for his goods and left the store, thanking his stars that he could now return to his solitary little stall in the back of McMurdo's Wagon Yard and be alone again. Women and kids. And horned toads. And doves and magic. Good God.

The following morning dawned as clear and chilly as the prior one, and Noah liked it every bit as well. In fact, after he'd been awake for a half-hour or so, he discovered there was a tune swimming around in his brain. He tried to recall the last time he'd thought of music, and couldn't.

He shook his head, and wondered if this new development meant anything. For twenty-some years of his life, music had been about all he lived for. And then music and Julia. They'd both been gone for years, however, and he couldn't account for this sudden reemergence of one of them.

Then he thought about Grace Richardson, and realized the title of the tune that had taken possession of his imagination was "Hard Times Come Again No More." A smoky, black curl of cynicism snaked its way through him. As if he should be so lucky.

On the other hand, music had always had the power to soothe him in the old days—until he'd run up against powers even bigger than music. Still, if this move to the Territory proved salutary, perhaps Noah might find himself actually breaking out in a whistle or a hum someday. Shouldn't take more than another fifteen, twenty years at the outside, if he worked at it.

He hoped like hell it wouldn't take that long to dislodge the picture of Grace Richardson that seemed to have tacked itself up inside his mind's eye like a reminder of everything he could no longer aspire to.

With a little too much force, he jerked his pack up from the stump where he'd been filling it. It nearly flew over his shoulder. He jumped back, but it still hit him in the chest.

"All ready, laddie?"

Rubbing the sore spot where his pack had hit him, Noah turned around and saw Mac walking toward him. The old man had a grin on his face, a twinkle in his eye, and his pipe in his mouth. Noah tried to dislike Mac for being amused at his expense, but couldn't find the energy.

"Yeah. I just finished loading my pack. I'll strap it on Fargo now." He gestured at his horse, who had been watching his antics and looked almost as amused as Mac. Noah shook his head, convinced his mind had bent too far this time.

"Good. Good. Got my horse all saddled. Samuel, I call him, and he can go for miles. Not much to look at, old Samuel, but a good horse for all that."

Noah glanced at where Mac gestured with his pipe and saw a sagging, flea-bitten gray hitched to a post. It looked about a million years old. But so did Mac, and Noah judged Mac could handle pretty much anything. Maybe Samuel could, too.

He unhitched Fargo's reins and led him over to the other horse. The two animals eyed each other benevolently. Noah had a funny feeling they were saying howdy. He decided it was a damned good thing he'd be out of the company of men soon, or somebody'd probably try to lock him up. He didn't think he could stand being locked up again.

"Maddie's bringing our food out in a minute. Grace packed a good supply for us this morning."

"That was nice of her." Noah spent a moment being surprised before he realized she'd naturally have packed the food for Mac, not him. Still, it would be pleasant to eat something besides hard biscuits, dried beans, tinned peaches, and sardines smashed on bread. Although Noah wasn't fussy about food, he was mighty tired of those particular commodities. He did have a sinking feeling he'd think of Grace with every bite. Hell.

"Here's your food, Mac!"

Both men turned at the cheerful, high-pitched announcement. A sudden smile lit Noah up inside. The smile didn't make it to his lips, but the sight of little Maddie Richardson hefting that huge bundle of supplies was one to behold. It was all she could do to keep the pack from dragging on the ground as she staggered towards them. She was a game girl, though, and even when the parcel knocked her sideways, she didn't falter from her goal, nor did her happy expression change.

"Looks like enough for a week or more," he murmured.

Mac nodded. "I expect it is. It's big country around here, and it'll take a while to see it all."

"Mmmm." Noah fought his urge to run and help the little girl. She looked so proud of herself. He sensed she didn't want help from anyone, and he admired her grit. He wondered if she'd got it from her mama, and sighed inwardly. Damn, he wished he'd stop thinking about that woman.

Taking the bundle from Maddie, Mac leaned over and kissed her cheek. "Thank'ee kindly, Maddie m'lass. And thank your mama, too."

"Mommy put lots and lots of food in there, Mac. There's ham and beef and beans and potato salad and bread and biscuits and bacon and coffee and pickles and sugar and salt." She ran out of breath.

She looked extremely proud of her mother. If he did such things, Noah might have thought she was real cute.

"My goodness, child. We'll have ourselves an entire restaurant on the backs of our horses."

"That's what Mommy said."

"Mac! Maddie! I forgot to pack the pies."

Noah looked up and saw Grace running toward them. She looked much as she had the first time he'd seen her, with her skirts caught up in her hand and her pretty hair flying. No. He meant her apron strings.

That's what was flying out behind her. Although her shiny blond hair was, too. Not that Noah paid attention such things. He looked away and fiddled with Fargo's cinch, which didn't need fiddling with, and wished he hadn't seen her this morning. The sight of her made his mental picture of her brighten and solidify.

"Oh, my, I'm glad you haven't left yet!" Grace skidded to a stop and her breath came out in little gasps.

Noah dared to peek at her, and was sorry he had. Her cheeks were pink with exertion, and she'd slapped a hand over her bosom as she held out another bundle—smaller than the first—for Mac to take. She had a nice bosom. Noah wished he hadn't noticed. He feared he'd never get rid of his mental image of her if this kept up.

"I made several little pies for you, some raisin and some dried-apple. They're folded over like tarts so they'll be easy to carry and eat."

"Ye're a good lass, Grace." With the license endowed upon him by old age and abiding friendship, Mac kissed Grace's cheek just as he'd kissed Maddie's.

Noah found himself envying the old man, was shocked by it, and growled, "Better be getting on, I reckon."

Mac's smile was the slyest thing Noah had ever seen. "Aye, we'd best be off, lad. Won't do to stand around out here bein' sociable or anything."

He chuckled at Noah's sharp frown.

Grace took up Maddie's hand. "I hope you'll find what you're looking for out here, Mr. Partridge." She had the nicest voice Noah had ever heard, even if she did have a back-east accent. Damn it, this admiring

Grace Richardson every second had to stop.

"Thanks." Noah swung himself up onto Fargo's back before he dared look at Grace again. Even then it was too soon. She held her daughter's hand and looked up at him with the most open, pink-cheeked, friendly expression on her face he'd seen directed at him in six years or more. He couldn't maintain eye contact with anything that innocent, but directed a brief nod at the two females, wheeled Fargo around, and headed toward the double gate.

Mac had evidently thought of a really funny joke by the time he caught up with Noah, because he was laughing fit to kill. Noah didn't look at him because he had a pretty fair notion that the joke was on him.

"Bye-bye, Mac and Mr. Noah!" Maddie's voice chirped from behind them.

Noah hunched his shoulders as if in that way he could deflect the good cheer being aimed at him.

"Bye-bye, Maddie-lass. Take good care of your mommy."

"I will."

"Be careful, Mac. Take care, Mr. Partridge."

That was Grace. Her voice settled into Noah's consciousness like a chorus of the song he'd been thinking earlier. Although he knew it would hurt, he turned slightly and waved. Damn. He wished he hadn't done that.

Maddie and Grace Richardson still held hands. The hands not occupied with each other were waving at him and Mac as if they honestly wished them well. Noah guessed they probably did, and the knowledge was so unnerving, and so completely contradicted everything that he'd come to expect out of life, that it threw his thinking all askew. Not that *that* was anything new.

Shoot. He'd be really glad when he'd found a piece of land, built some kind of shelter on it, and headed out of Rio Hondo for good. Being around those two females for any length of time was apt to make Noah forget that he no longer belonged in society. It wouldn't do to get to missing company again. He shivered, thinking about it.

"Cold?" Mac asked genially.

Cold? Noah couldn't remember a time when, he hadn't been cold, although his cold was internal and had nothing to do with the weather. In truth, his outsides were warm as summer. He said, "Yeah. A little."

"Ye'll warm up pretty soon, laddie. I guarantee it."

Because he had the oddest notion Mac wasn't talking about his physical well-being, Noah glanced at him from under his hat brim. The old fellow appeared to be as innocent as little Maddie, and was peering around at the landscape as if he hadn't seen anything so interesting in years.

They rode in silence for miles. Noah found himself intensely grateful that Mac seemed to be comfortable without conversation, because he knew himself to be deficient in the skill. Occasionally the old man would indicate a point of interest, but that was all.

In truth, the points of interest were few and far between and consisted mainly of the region's odd fauna.

"See those birds over there?"

Noah looked where Mac gestured with his ever-present pipe. "Yeah." He squinted at them, and realized that, although they were small and perched on the ground, they were owls. He'd never seen owls on the ground before. He wondered if they accounted for the noises he'd just heard. What were owls doing there, sitting on the prairie as if they belonged there?

"Burrowing owls," Mac said, as if he'd heard Noah's question. "No trees in this area, so they dig holes and live in the ground, like the ground squirrels and prairie dogs."

Noah had heard of prairie dogs.

"Aye, I expect you have heard of prairie dogs, lad."

When Noah whipped his head around to gape at Mac, he found him looking as artless as a baby and staring up into the sky. Noah looked, too, and forgot to ask Mac if he could read minds.

"Sandhill cranes, I think," murmured Mac, still staring overhead.

A V of migrating birds cut across the sky. They looked real pretty up there, Noah decided. When he tried to remember the last time he'd appreciated nature, his memory went blank.

"Unless they're geese. We get 'em both out here this time of year, and these old eyes aren't as keen as they once were." Mac chuckled happily, as if his failing eyesight were a grand joke.

"So that's where those sounds were coming from," muttered Noah, glad to have the mystery cleared up.

"Aye. Noisy devils, I reckon. I like 'em, though. Friendly birds, I've always thought."

"Yeah," said Noah noncommittally, thinking, *What the hell's a friendly bird?*

And that seemed to be it as far as wildlife went. On his own, Noah spotted a herd of antelope. He didn't point it out to Mac, because he couldn't get his jaw to work.

Once, after Noah had nearly dozed off from the quiet and the gentle rhythm of Fargo's plodding gait, Mac's voice jerked him awake again.

"Come springtime, you'll see the desert bloom, laddie."

"Yeah?" Noah squinted around once more. He had a hard time imagining this grim land in flower.

"Aye, lad. Wildflowers. Every year I find 'em surprisin', since a body'd never expect such soft, sweet offerings of God's mercy out here where life seems so harsh."

Noah stopped squinting at the landscape and peered at Mac for a moment instead. The man had the oddest way of expressing things, so that Noah felt as if he were speaking metaphorically, and that everything Mac said about the countryside could be twisted just a little bit and come back to be about Noah himself.

In any other man, Noah would have begrudged it. In fact, he wouldn't have tolerated it. He'd have left Mac and his picturesque manner of speech, and taken off by himself. There was something so benevolent about Mac, though, something so perfectly guileless, that Noah couldn't manage to take offense no matter how hard he tried.

As if he hadn't a single inkling what Noah's thoughts might be—which, of course, he couldn't— Mac went on. "Aye, we have us purple verbena and white bindweed and little yellow daisy-like flowers, and bigger yellow daisy-like flowers. I don't know what they are, but they're pretty."

He sounded as if he were offering an apology for his lack of knowledge about the local flora. Noah shrugged.

"And we have us Mexican hats, too. They come in all sorts of colors, and feel like velvet. Little Maddie likes to pick 'em and play games with them. She pretends they're people, you see."

Thinking he should say something, Noah murmured, "Enterprising of her."

Mac laughed as if Noah had uttered the cleverest bit of wit he'd heard in years. "Oh, aye, lad. A little girl has to be enterprising if she's going to live out here, where there are no toys and no playmates. I expect more settlers will head out here before too long, though, and then maybe she won't be so all alone."

"More people? You expect a big migration out here?" Noah didn't like the sound of that, whether it would benefit Maddie Richardson or not.

"Well, not so many as a lot of other places. It takes a certain kind of person to want to settle here."

The old man's eyes glittered and sparkled, and Noah got the impression he was being laughed at again. A prickle of irritation bloomed briefly in his chest but died. Mac was just too damned nice to get mad at.

"I mean," continued Mac, "no matter how you look at it, this is a hard land. A fellow has to be willing to live rough to tame it."

Immediately Noah thought about Grace. Evidently her husband wanted to tame some land around here. But where was he? *Who* was he? Maybe he'd gone out to build a place somewhere in the area, and Grace and Maddie had stayed in the comparative comfort of Rio Hondo while he accomplished it.

Something savage churned in Noah's stomach when he thought about Grace Richardson and her husband and their daughter, but he couldn't account for it. So he said not a word and rode beside Mac in silence as the old fellow, with good cheer and an ironic glint in his eyes, expounded on the types of settlers who might brave the territory, the types of wildflowers that would surely bloom in the springtime, and the amazingness of God's handiwork.

"Why, lad, just think on it. Right here in the Territory, He's created a land most folks would consider rough, if not downright hostile. Yet He's also given us flowers to pretty it up, and gentle women to smooth the harsh edges away."

Feeling beleaguered and not a little hostile himself, Noah grumbled, "I wouldn't know about that." Mac went into a gale of laughter that seemed likely to carry him off entirely, unless that was only Noah's own unkind interpretation of the dratted old fellow's hilarity.

"Ah, laddie," Mac choked out at last. "Ye're a welcome sight for these old eyes, ye are. And a balm to this old soul."

Noah eyed him shrewdly for several seconds. "Am I?" His voice couldn't have gotten any dryer if he'd left it out in the New Mexico sun for a week.

After another robust laugh, Mac wiped his eyes and said, "Oh, aye, lad. Aye, ye are." He took note of Noah's sour expression "There, lad, I won't be teasin' ye anymore right now. I'll shut me old trap and leave ye be."

Noah considered thanking him, but thought it would be impolite. After all, Mac didn't know anything about him and couldn't be faulted for assuming Noah was a man like any other—one who still had the capacity to love and hate, laugh and cry. Noah did nod his gratitude, though. He couldn't help it.

Mac grinned around his pipe, a grin the likes of which Noah had never seen. Then he shut his mouth, and didn't say another word until they pulled their horses up several miles later.

They had headed to the north and east of Rio Hondo. After an hour or two of dull, beige desert, the landscape began to look slightly more interesting. At last they'd come upon one of the rivers that had prompted folks to call this area the Seven Rivers country.

"That there's the Pecos River, m'boy. The very river that's given the place its name. The Pecos Valley, folks call it."

"Heard of it," muttered Noah. His voice had gotten used to resting, and cracked again.

He thought he heard Mac chuckle, but when he turned to look, the old man was sitting silent on his horse, as sober as a judge. Noah got the distinct impression—although he couldn't have said how—that Mac's sobriety of demeanor was for Noah's benefit alone, and that it was hardly heartfelt.

The Pecos River snaked through the plains like a sluggish, silvery-gray ribbon. Some gray-green scrub bushes hugged its banks, but there was nothing colorful about it. Noah eyed the river critically and decided he liked the effect. It didn't rush along in a hurry like the rivers back east. The Pecos was peaceful. It looked as if it took every ounce of its energy to move at all. Noah saw a fish break its placid surface and turn a somersault in the air. Sun glinted off the water droplets thus produced, as if the fish had brought a net of diamonds out of the water along with it.

"Looks quiet now, but when the spring rains come, it'll be roarin' along like a banshee. Ground's hard hereabouts, and rain water doesn't soak in like it does in more civilized places.''

Noah glanced at Mac. This was far from the first time the old fellow had seemed to have read his mind. On the other hand, there was very little to observe around here; maybe it was only logical that people's thoughts traveled along the same paths.

He grunted to let Mac know he'd heard and understood, and went back to contemplating the river. Unless he'd seen it himself, he'd never have known a fish had just turned a somersault there; the water had reverted to its former placidity, its surface unbroken.

If a fellow had a piece of land out here, he might plant himself a couple of willows and a cottonwood or two, and have a nice shady chunk of peace for himself if he didn't watch out. In fact—Noah squinted into the distance—by damn, somebody already had planted some trees. He wondered if whoever it was had found life too hard here and wanted to sell the land. Or perhaps something less savory than a move—an Indian attack, flood, or illness—had prompted whoever it was to give up the stake. He didn't ask.

Mac cleared his throat. In his contemplation of the river, Noah had almost forgotten he was there.

''Reckon this is the first bit o' land I wanted to show you, Mr. Partridge.''

That was encouraging. ''Yeah?''

''Aye, lad. This is a prime piece of property, all right, and a perfect place to settle, if you ask me.''

After taking another look around, Noah nodded judiciously. He tried to convey the impression that he was withholding a final judgment, but wasn't sure he achieved his aim. He did say, "It looks all right," because it was the truth.

"Aye. It's a pretty place." Mac began to repack his pipe. "Belongs to Grace."

Noah, who had been contemplating the river and deciding whether to build his house right on its banks—on stilts, like he'd seen in other places—or on a rise some little distance from the water, jerked his head around and scowled at the old man. "Mrs. Richardson? She owns this land?"

"Aye." Mac twinkled at him, as blithe as an angel. "Willed to her by her late husband, Frank."

Noah's thought processes scrambled like eggs in a frying pan. From contemplating his home on the range, his mind's eye threw an image of Grace Richardson into his brain: pretty, soft, womanly, kind. Widowed. He stammered, "Her—her *late* husband?"

"Oh, aye. Poor lad died two years ago. Struck by lightning whilst he was ridin' home one evenin'. Grace like to died, too, poor lass. If not for havin' to care for little Maddie, she might have. On account o' grief, y'know."

She might have died of grief. That was one scenario Noah'd had no experience of.

Mac shook his head sadly. "She's been true to her Frank ever since. Won't even look at another man."

"Yeah?" True to a dead man, was she? Well, wasn't that something? Hell, Noah's fiancee hadn't even been true to Noah as a live one. He found himself envying the dead Frank Richardson for having so irrevocably secured the love of a woman like Grace.

"Aye. Poor lass."

Poor lass, my ass, thought Noah bitterly. He looked

64

at the land again, then at Mac. Maybe Mac was trying to tell him something in his own convoluted way. He pushed his hat back on his head and scratched an itchy spot.

"So, you say she wants to sell this place? Wants to get rid of it?"

Mac's eyebrows shot up into two telling arches. At least they told Noah something. He'd begun to frown even before Mac enlightened him.

"Sell this land? Grace? Nay, lad, she won't sell. This was Frank's dream, and Grace means to see it through."

Then why the hell did you bring me out here? Because he anticipated only one more of the old man's cryptic excuses to account for the odd things he did, Noah didn't ask. Instead, he pulled his hat down again, stared for several long moments at the land he now wanted and couldn't have—because it was a dead man's dream—then squinted at Mac.

"So, now that you've had your little diversion, you want to show me some land that's for sale?" The venom in his heart seeped into his voice.

Mac only chuckled. Noah found himself unsurprised.

"Oh, aye, laddie, I'll be happy to show you some land for sale. First, though, let's eat this fine lunch Grace and her little Maddie made up for us."

Noah sucked in a deep breath. He felt like hollering at Mac that he didn't want anything to do with Grace or her little Maddie, and that included lunch. He restrained himself. For one thing, he sensed Mac would only laugh at him again. For another thing, he was hungry. Besides, he knew damned good and well such a declaration would be a lie.

* * *

"I like Mr. Noah, don't you, Mommy?"

Grace glanced up from the letter she'd just received from her sister Eleanor back home in Illinois. The letter had been posted only three months ago. The mail service out here was getting faster every day.

She grinned to find her daughter covered head to toe with garlands made of paper rings they'd cut out and pasted together. The garlands were intended to serve as Christmas tree decorations, but Maddie had evidently found another use for them. She held her arms out as if she were modeling a fur piece, like the ladies in the five-year-old fashion magazine her mother let her look through if she was careful with it.

"Mr. Partridge seems like a nice man, yes." Even as she spoke the words, Grace wasn't sure she meant them. To her, Mr. Partridge had seemed as remote as the stars in the sky. Either he was a naturally cold man, Grace thought, or life had battered him around more than his humanity could tolerate, and he'd removed himself from it. Although she had nothing on which to base her feeling, Grace suspected the latter.

"Do you suppose he'll bring you the reed organ pretty soon, Mommy?"

Maddie twirled around, and the garland floated in the air beside her, reminding Grace of angels' wings. Which reminded her of Frank. Which made her heart ache.

Oh, my, she missed Maddie's daddy. Especially now, as Christmas approached. Frank had adored Maddie. Often, as he and Grace had lain in bed at night, spent from love, Frank had wrapped his arms around Grace and talked about the Christmases they'd share in years to come. He had looked forward to watching their little girl grow up into a young woman. He'd even anticipated grandchildren someday.

And now Frank was dead. And Maddie was pretending to be an angel in a paper Christmas garland, and Grace was fighting tooth and nail to keep Frank's dream alive. And to keep from crying.

She wiped away a tear. "The organ, dear?" Her voice broke, and she was ashamed of herself for showing her daughter this weakness.

Maddie, however, didn't seem to notice. As she carefully unwrapped herself from the paper garland, she said, "The reed organ. The one he's going to bring you."

Grace cocked her head and was sure she looked as puzzled as she felt. "Mr. Partridge isn't going to bring me a reed organ, sweetheart. I don't even know him."

Maddie looked at her mother as if she'd just said something unutterably silly. "Yes, he is. Remember? I dreamed it. Just yesterday." She frowned and picked at a paper loop that seemed to be stuck in her hair. "Or maybe it was the day after yesterday."

"The day before yesterday, sweetheart?" Grace smiled at her daughter's careful but determined efforts to disentangle herself from the garland.

"Yes. The day before yesterday. I dreamed it. He's going to bring you a reed organ. An' then we can sing Christmas carols like you said we did when Daddy was alive."

Grace's eyes smarted with tears again. *Oh, dear Lord, why did you visit this on us?* With an effort, she pried her heart out of the morass of sucking grief it wallowed in. She knew she and Maddie were luckier than thousands of women and children in the country. At least she had a little bit of money—and a job. And Alexander McMurdo, who'd been as kind a friend as a body could wish for. At least she'd known Frank's love for several years. And she'd been with him at the end, too.

She glanced down at the letter resting on her lap. Eleanor's husband's body had never been found, although it was presumed he'd died at Shiloh. Eleanor had never been given the chance to say good bye to her Charles. At least Grace hadn't had to go through that misery and uncertainty.

Although Eleanor never said so in her letters, Grace knew—because she'd have done the same thing herself—that Eleanor secretly, in her heart of hearts, hoped that Charles would come home someday. It was too hard to imagine his bones resting in an unmarked grave in the South, where everybody had hated both him and what he'd been fighting for.

Eleanor had written a letter to Miss Clara Barton's Office of Missing Soldiers, but so far, she'd heard nothing. The closest Eleanor had come to her Charles through Miss Clara Barton was when she'd received a letter from a man who'd met him once. It hadn't helped much.

Grace shuddered and heaved a heavy sigh, then put the letter aside. "Here, darling, let Mommy help you."

Maddie obediently stood still and suffered her mother's assistance in detaching her from the paper loops. All at once she smiled.

"I know!"

"You do?" Grace kissed her head.

"Yes. It's going to be a Christmas present!"

Grace looked down into Maddie's upturned face. The little girl was beaming from ear to ear, and her freckled cheeks were as pink as summer roses. "What's going to be a Christmas present, Maddie?"

"The reed organ!"

Oh, dear. Grace rolled the garland into a coil, laid it on the table, picked Maddie up, and settled her on her lap. Then carefully, trying very hard not to bruise her daughter's tender spirits, she told her that a dream was a dream—and reality wasn't.

She got the feeling Maddie was only humoring her when the little girl nodded.

Chapter Four

"We'll just visit for a few minutes, lad. Can't pass by a neighbor without saying howdy. Not out here, ye can't, when neighbors are so few and far between."

Noah's nerves writhed under skin that felt too tight to hold them. He was strung as taut as a fiddle string, and it was all he could do to keep from bellowing at Alexander McMurdo to quit playing games with him and show him some land for sale.

Mac glanced at him and those damned eyebrows of his arched again. Noah was sure the old man could read his thoughts—this time they were transparent. Ever since the war, Noah's emotional reserves weren't strong enough to hide his nervous disorder. Of course, before the war, he hadn't had a nervous disorder. He knew Mac could see that his lips were pulled tight against his teeth, that the muscles in his jaw were working convulsively, and that the tendons in his throat bulged with barely suppressed anxiety.

The old fellow's face went as tender as that of a woman looking upon her own newborn babe. He pulled his swaybacked gray alongside Fargo, who nodded amiably to the other horse.

Then he laid a hand on Noah's clenched fist. It was all but strangling his saddle horn. "Ah, laddie, take a care for yourself. There's naught to be worried about now. This here territory's a new place, a land of promise and opportunity, where a man—any man—can start over again without his old life gettin' in the way."

In spite of his very best efforts, Noah knew he was going to explode. He hated it when his nerves bested him and he erupted into the chaotic fury that had been driving him these past several years. Yet it seemed he was powerless to control his condition. It was as if a demon had been set loose inside of him. Most of the time, if he stayed away from people, the demon slept.

Sometimes—now, for instance—the demon got free and, like Mr. Rochester's mad wife in *Jane Eyre,* it created blazing havoc. Noah was going to lose control now and yell at this kind old man who was only a little frustrating, really, and then Noah'd be humiliated and embarrassed—and there wasn't a thing he could do to stop himself. He opened his mouth. . . .

And saw the air around him bloom with sparkles. His rage vanished, taking his demon with it. Suddenly it was as if the very word *anger* didn't exist in Noah's world.

He blinked at the sparkles. They were transparent at first, like infinitesimally tiny diamond chips. Then, as

71

if the diamonds had become bored with only their own kind for company, ruby sparkles appeared. Soon sapphire- and emerald- and topaz-colored dots joined the others and flickered in the air. He rubbed his eyes and blinked some more.

He looked down at Mac's hand resting on his own, which had gone slack. The sparkles seemed to be emanating from where their hands touched. How strange. A sensation of peace invaded him. This was the weirdest thing that had ever happened to him in a life that lately had been filled with weird things.

"Ah, lad, ye'll be all right. Ye don't know it yet, and ye've had a harder life than most, but ye'll heal. Ye will. And this here's the place to do it."

Too befuddled to think, Noah turned to stare at Mac, his mind blank. Even his demon wasn't there anymore. It had gone away. Vanished. Exorcised by this strange old man's touch.

Nonsense. He tested the word. "Nonsense." It came out in a croak, like a frog trying to whisper.

Mac grinned. "Aye. The whole thing's nonsense, laddie. And here we are at the Hugh Blackworth spread. Old Hugh's out ridin' his range and tryin' to get himself richer. His wife, Susan, is inside, and she's a regular Tartar of a female. She's worth knowin', is Susan, and she'll be pleased to meet ye, although she won't show it."

Noah glanced to the right and to the left and even up into the sky above his head. The sparkles had gone away. He looked at Mac again and realized the old fellow'd been talking to him. "Um, I beg your pardon?"

Laughing, Mac withdrew his hand from Noah's,

turned his horse through the gate to the Blackworth spread, and guided Samuel down the beaten path to a big white house.

Noah watched Mac's back for a minute, and then decided meeting Susan Blackworth wouldn't be as bad as all that. He nudged Fargo into following the other horse. Fargo, who'd evidently become bored watching the hind end of old Samuel heading away from him, seemed pleased to obey.

"When will they be back, Mommy?"

It was, by Grace's count, the thirty-fifth time Maddie had asked the same question this morning. She glanced up from where she was rolling out a piecrust and sighed.

"I'm not sure, sweetheart. They may be away for several more days, you know, because Mac was going to show Mr. Partridge some parcels of land."

"How come?"

"I believe Mr. Partridge wants to establish a cattle ranch out here, Maddie."

The little girl took one last peek out of the window and wandered back to her mother's side. When Grace had the pies in the oven, she was going to roll out the remaining scraps and let Maddie help her sprinkle cinnamon and sugar on them, cut them into strips, twist them into curlicues, and bake the strips. Cinnamon sticks were, for Maddie, the culmination of the culinary art. Grace wished everything in life could be so simple.

"Why can't he live where Daddy wanted to live? Out by the ribber, where you said?"

When Grace glanced down at her daughter, it seemed to her that all she saw were eyes—big blue

73

eyes that were so innocent it hardly seemed possible that Grace herself might once have had eyes like that. "That land belongs to us, Maddie. Your daddy bought it for us. Mr. Partridge wants some land of his own."

"But we live here with Mac."

"We'll live by the river someday, sweetheart." At least Grace hoped they would.

The big blue eyes narrowed in thought. "But why can't we share? You said sharing is p'lite."

A grin caught Grace by surprise. "Yes, dear, sharing is very polite. But people don't usually share land and their homes. They share things like, oh, chores or food. Things like that."

"How come?"

How come? Oh, dear. Grace knew she was supposed to know the answers to these things, but children asked the most awkward questions. "Um, you see, dear, people buy their own land. It's just the way we do things. That way everyone can have his own little piece of the world to live on." She gave Maddie a tiny piece of raw dough, hoping to distract her.

It didn't work for long. "Indians don't," Maddie said after she'd swallowed her treat.

"Indians don't what, Maddie?"

"They don't live on their own little piece of the world. Mac says they don't think of the world like we do. They think that it belongs to everybody to share."

"The last time I looked in the mirror, we weren't Indians, sweetie." Feeling a little exasperated, Grace added, "You want to go look and see if you've turned into an Indian overnight?"

Perceiving a new game, Maddie nodded and skipped into the other room. Grace imagined her climbing on the little footstool Frank had made for her, and squinting into the mirror. She smiled as she pressed the first crust into a pie plate she'd brought with her from Chicago.

She heard Maddie tripping lightly back into the kitchen and looked up, still smiling. "Well?"

"I'm not an Indian," her daughter announced.

"Well, then, I guess you'll just have to be content in thinking like a little white girl instead of like a little Indian girl."

"I guess."

Grace could tell she wasn't altogether happy about it.

As for Grace, she imagined she would be happier about things if she could stop her mind from dwelling on Mr. Noah Partridge. She was, however, as powerless to stop her mind from that idle pursuit as she was powerless to solve her own problems. With a sigh, she decided to pay attention to her daughter. She was all that Maddie had, after all, and she loved her.

The first thing Noah saw when he stepped into the Blackworth's front parlor was the old lady, sitting ramrod straight in a wing chair. Clad all in black and propping her hands on a cane, she glinted at him out of eyes that looked, in the poor indoor light, to be as black as onyx, as cold as winter, and as glittery as those damned sparkles that outside had just knocked the demon out of him.

The second thing he saw, shoved into a corner of the Blackworth's parlor, was the reed organ. The sight of that organ brought Noah's demon rampaging back as if it had only gone away to recruit its friends and now had an army at its command. He sucked in a sharp breath and let it out only when Mac laid a hand on his shoulder. The demons vanished at once.

Damn, Noah wished he knew how the old man did that.

"This here's Mr. Noah Partridge, Susan. Mr. Partridge comes to us from the grand old state of Virginia." Mac's voice reminded Noah of a master of ceremonies, introducing an attendee at a ball.

"Is that so?"

Mrs. Blackworth's voice sounded like a rusty hinge. At first Noah thought she might be crippled, because she didn't move, but only watched him like a hawk. He sensed a fierce intelligence behind black-olive eyes. Then she rose in a rustle of crisp bombazine, and marched at him as if she were a general and he a private who'd just spilled the general's tea. He shuffled uncomfortably when she stopped dead in front of him. She was damned near as tall as he was, and he stood a shade over six feet.

"Noah Partridge, are you?"

"Yes, ma'am. Pleased to meet you." He wondered where that lie had sprung from. It was a remnant of his lost youth that he hadn't uttered in a decade or more.

"From Virginia?"

Maybe she was deaf. "Yes, ma'am."

"You wouldn't happen to be related the Partridges of Partridge's Pianos and Organ Works, would you?"

Noah opened his mouth. Nothing came out.

"In Falls Church?"

He still couldn't get his tongue and teeth and lungs coordinated. Astonishment held him speechless.

"Well, speak up, young man. Either you are or you aren't. It's not as if I asked you to parse a sentence."

"Yes," popped out of Noah's mouth. He licked his lips, decided he'd didn't relish being considered a fool, and tried to redeem himself. "Yes, ma'am. My grandfather started the business back in the twenties, and my father took it over. I—ah . . ." His voice trailed off. He couldn't bear to think about it, much less say it.

"I expect you lost it during the war," said Susan Blackworth, obviously not one to get mealymouthed over so trivial a thing as a war and the loss of a family business.

"Yes," said Noah, and shut his teeth with a click.

She nodded once sharply. "Tragic, that. Tragic. I lived in the nation's capital, you see. Hugh and I were married there."

She swept an arm out, and Noah understood that the gesture was meant to indicate the reed organ.

"My father bought me that organ at Partridge's when I was just a girl. We brought it out here on a wagon, believe it or not. I didn't care about anything else, but I wouldn't leave my organ behind, or my piano, either."

Noah hadn't even noticed the piano. He scanned the parlor. Oh, yes, there it was. It looked about as unhappy as the organ. The organ intrigued him, and he glanced back at it.

She chuckled dryly. "Of course, my rheumatism is so bad now, I can't play very often, but I'm not sorry I made Hugh haul it out here. He deserved the trouble."

Somewhere in the back of Noah's brain, the strangeness of her declaration registered. He didn't take time to think about it. At the moment he had eyes only for that old organ sitting like an orphaned child in the corner of Mrs. Blackworth's parlor.

It looked like it was a good forty years old. Or a bad forty, depending. His hands itched and his fingers curled, and he realized they wanted to be investigating the organ. They wanted to be running over the elaborately carved cherry-wood box. They wanted to dust it off and polish it up so that the wood gleamed again.

They wanted to run themselves over the keys. They wanted to open the box up and investigate the organ's guts, to see how the reeds were holding up out here in the perishing dryness of the desert. They wanted to oil everything, to test the stops and tune it, to clean it up and repair it.

Noah could see from where he stood that the poor thing was in dire straits. Hell, that organ looked like its insides might be almost as withered as his own. He forced himself to glance away from the organ and back to Susan Blackworth, and suppressed an impulse to lecture her on the proper care of reed organs and to scold her for neglecting this one. It could be a beauty if it were only cared for properly.

She grinned at him with almost as much irony as he'd seen Mac do. "Go ahead, Mr. Partridge. Feel free to investigate the instrument. You can let me know if you think it can be repaired."

He cleared his throat. "You want to repair it?"

"I've been thinking about it. Of course, I only have sons, and they're all about as musical as their father."

Noah got the impression that neither Mr. Blackworth nor his sons were musical, and that Mrs. Blackworth wasn't fond of any of them. "I'd, um, like to look at it, ma'am.'' He wanted to lift the lid and read the label.

That instrument looked like one of his grandfather's first efforts. Grandpa Partridge had begun the business with pianos, and moved on to organs in the late twenties. Noah's father had been partial to the piano side of the business. Noah himself had never been able to resist a reed organ. Until the war. He could resist pretty much anything these days.

Except Susan Blackworth's organ . . .

''Well, Mr. Partridge? Do you plan to stand there staring at it for the rest of your life, or do you want to examine it?''

Mac touched Noah's elbow. It was a gentle touch, but it propelled Noah forward as if Mac had shoved him.

Lord, it was a beautiful instrument. Noah's hand hovered over it for several seconds. He wasn't sure he really wanted to bring back all those old memories— they were older even than the ones that haunted him— but at last he lowered his hand, which settled on the warm wood like a nesting dove.

In the space of seconds, his heart filled with music. It began softly, a lilting waltz that grew louder and louder until it thundered through him like a pipe organ in a church, and then grew louder still, and sharper, until his brain reverberated with the noise of cannon fire and Gatling guns. He drew in a loud, rasping breath and covered his ears.

Mac's hand brought him back to Mrs. Blackworth's parlor again. It was gentle, barely perceptible, on his shoulder. Noah wasn't sure if he groaned aloud or not, but his breath sounded like fingernails on a slate.

''Here, lad, it's a fine old instrument, isn't it?''

Noah opened his eyes and stared at Mac. The old man smiled as if Noah hadn't just made a thundering ass of himself. In fact, Mac's expression was benevolent, almost good-humored. Noah remembered his grandfather looking at him like that when he'd fallen and scraped his knees and was trying not to cry because he was a boy, and boys didn't cry. Like hell they didn't.

"Yes, it is a fine instrument." Susan Blackworth's tone rang with satisfaction, as if she thought a fine instrument was only what she deserved.

"It's—" Noah had to stop and clear his throat again. "It's one of my grandfather's first reed organs." His hand lightly caressed the keys. When he looked at his fingers, they were dusty. "You should keep the protector down, ma'am."

"Yes, I know."

Noah heard the rustle of Mrs. Blackworth's skirts as she walked over to stand beside him.

"Of course, it needs work. It's sadly in need of oil and repair. And it's probably out of tune. There isn't a piano tuner within two hundred miles of Rio Hondo."

Noah wondered if she was as resentful as she sounded.

"There is now."

Mrs. Blackworth and Noah both turned to look at Mac, who beamed at them like a cherub.

"There is what?" Mrs. Blackworth's voice was as crisp as her bombazine skirt.

"Why, a piano tuner, of course." With his black briar pipe, Mac gestured at Noah. "This lad here can tune a piano to beat the band, and he can build a reed organ from the ground up. I expect he can fix this one.''

''Can he now?''

Mrs. Blackworth eyed Noah keenly. He twitched his shoulders and felt uncomfortable. ''I, uh, haven't done that kind of work for several years.''

''What exactly happened to your grandfather's business?'' Mrs. Blackworth asked curtly.

He turned away from the scrutiny of the two older people. He wasn't sure his voice would work. It had taken to drying up on him years before when he tried to talk to people—and he hadn't had to say anything this painful for ages. He decided to keep it short. ''It burned down.''

After a moment of silence, Mrs. Blackworth said, ''What a pity.''

''Yeah.'' A pity. That was one way of putting it.

''So many people lost so much in the war.''

Noah eyed her and decided she didn't mean it to sound sarcastic. He didn't give her another *yeah,* and couldn't manage anything else, either. Nor did he elaborate. The truth of Noah's life seemed worse to him somehow than what she obviously thought had happened. It was one thing when an invading enemy burned you out. It was quite another when your own townsfolk did it because they hated you.

''Tell you what, Mr. Partridge. I'll give you that organ if you'll repair my piano.''

Noah jerked around and stared at her. She had an odd look in her eyes, as if she'd just issued him a challenge.

''What the hell do I need an organ for?''

81

Her smile was as brittle as Noah's nerves. "As to that, I couldn't say."

Noah and Mac were away from Rio Hondo for a week. When they returned, Noah found himself in a quandary. After Mac had shown him Grace Richardson's property and Hugh Blackworth's ranch, he'd led Noah to several parcels of land that would work for his purpose—and that were for sale.

Unfortunately, Noah discovered he didn't want those other ones. He wanted Grace Richardson's land. The other properties were all right. Her land was perfect. But, according to Mac, she didn't want to sell it. Noah pondered and pondered, trying to think of some way to make her do it anyway, whether she wanted to or not.

The only way he could think of to find out was to ask her. Maybe he could talk her into it. Noah didn't want to spend that much time with anyone, much less Grace Richardson, whom he thought about too much to begin with. Lord, if he spent any time with her, he might get to wishing for things, and then where would he be? Hell, his life was bleak enough already without unlikely hopes. And he sure didn't trust in his powers of persuasion. The few powers he'd once possessed were long since withered from lack of use.

As hard as he tried, though, he couldn't think of another way to get that land. Hell, this was a United States territory. No matter how much he wanted that land, it belonged to Grace Richardson. He couldn't just squat on it and claim it as his own. Dammit. Civilization was a blasted nuisance sometimes.

They'd been riding in silence for two or three hours

and were only a mile or so away from Rio Hondo when Noah asked, "Do you suppose she'd reconsider if I asked her about it?"

"Do I suppose who'd reconsider what if you asked her about it?"

Mac's eyes twinkled like blue stars, and Noah had a gut feeling the older man had only asked his question for form's sake, that he already knew exactly what Noah was talking about. Noah was getting used to it.

"Do you suppose Mrs. Richardson would consider selling her property if I asked her? If I came up with a good, firm offer?"

Mac pondered the question for a moment. It looked as if he were studying Noah's face and finding the occupation an amusing one. Noah tried not to fidget, although Mac's scrutiny made him feel as if the old man could see through his skull to his brain and read his thoughts.

"I think it would be a fine idea for you to chat with Grace, m'lad. A fine idea."

"About the property," Noah said, then felt foolish. He'd received the distinct impression that Mac hadn't been talking about the property, but about something else entirely—as if he were talking about something Noah was incapable of.

Hell, he didn't want to have to talk to the woman at all. But there was something about that land of hers that appealed to a need way down deep inside of him. He wanted that land like he hadn't wanted anything in years.

"Aye. Of course. About the property." Mac chuckled so hard he bounced in his saddle.

Noah felt crabby.

* * *

"Look! Look! They're back! They're back!"

Maddie bounded down from the kitchen chair upon which she'd been kneeling, and raced for the front door. Grace laughed out loud and shook her head. Then she finished peeling the potato she'd been working on and plopped it into the bowl of water standing on the table. She didn't want the potatoes to get brown; she had plans for them.

She wiped her hands on her apron as she followed her daughter out onto the porch. Maddie quivered with excitement. To keep her from caroming down from the porch and spooking the horses—although these two mounts looked as if they were far too tired to spook—Grace put her hands on her daughter's shoulders.

"They were gone for so long, Mommy! I wonder if Mr. Noah found some prop'ty."

"I expect you'll just have to ask him, Maddie."

Maddie nodded. Grace looked down at her shiny hair and wondered if Maddie sensed the same reserve in Mr. Partridge that Grace did. She doubted it. Children seemed to have the ability to see past people's exteriors. She wished her own heart would stop battering at her ribs with excitement, particularly seeing as her excitement stemmed from seeing Noah Partridge again. This was no way for a grown woman—a grown *widowed* woman, who still loved her late husband—to feel.

They watched quietly until the men dismounted at the hitching rail and began to tend to their horses. Mac, of course, waved at them and called out a merry greeting. Noah did not.

"C'n I go say hi to Mac, Mommy?" Maddie

squirmed, trying to get away from her mother's grip on her shoulders.

Before releasing her, Grace warned, "Be careful of the horses' hooves, Maddie. You remember what Mac told you."

"I remember."

So Grace let her go, wishing she could run over there with her. She could tell Maddie had taken Mac's warning to heart because she gave a wide berth to the backs of the horses, then ran the rest of the way into Mac's arms. The old man swung her up and twirled her around, and Maddie squealed with delight. Grace's heart melted like butter in the summertime.

She closed the distance between the porch and the two men with more dignity than her daughter, but with every bit as much eagerness. No matter what she tried to pretend to herself, the strange new man fascinated her, and she couldn't wait to hear the results of his expedition. She rather fancied having him in the neighborhood. If the several hundreds of miles surrounding the dot of Rio Hondo could be considered a neighborhood.

She shared a warm smile with the two men. Mac returned her smile with one equally warm. Noah Partridge seemed to stare right through her. Then he nodded sharply once, and turned back to his horse.

Grace suppressed a sigh. She was willing to grant him a lot of slack on the grounds that he'd been a soldier in a dreadful war and had probably seen horrors she couldn't even imagine, but she did wish he'd say something so she'd know how to act around him. Ah, well. At least she had Mac. She gave him a big kiss on the cheek, and refused to admit to herself that she wished she could kiss Mr. Partridge, too.

"We've been everywhere you can imagine, Grace, m'lass. From Rio Hondo to Fort Sumner and all the way up to Capitan."

"My goodness! You covered a lot of ground."

"Aye, that we did. And we saw us about a hundred places where a man could build himself a nice, tidy ranch."

Grace decided to speak to Noah Partridge. Since she didn't know what was wrong with him, she reckoned she should probably just treat him the same way she'd treat anyone else. As she was a friendly woman with a lively curiosity and an interest in her fellow man, she asked him outright. "Did you find a piece of land that appealed to you particularly, Mr. Partridge?"

He glanced at her without lifting his head. She got the impression he wished she hadn't asked. Well, that was too bad. She couldn't be anything but herself. She hugged herself because the impulse to put her arms around him was so intense it shocked her.

"Yes, ma'am, I did," he said after a long couple of moments.

"That's nice. I'm glad for you." And she was, too. She hoped that getting settled would make him happy. Or at least happier. She squeezed her middle more tightly. Good Lord, these urges were most unseemly!

After another moment of silence, he said, "Thanks." His glance slid back to his horse.

So much for that. Grace sighed, dropped her arms to her sides, and turned to Mac again. "Maddie and I will go get a couple of apples, Mac. I expect your horses could use a treat."

"Aye, I expect they could. Thank'ee, lass. That'd be right nice o' ye."

So Grace went back to the house, Maddie skipping cheerfully at her side. They returned a few minutes later, bearing two quartered apples. Maddie ran up to Mac again.

"Can I feed the horses, Mac? Please?"

"Why, I expect you can, lass, if your mama says it's all right."

"We'd better ask Mr. Partridge if he minds, Maddie."

Maddie walked right up to Noah Partridge and tugged at his duster. She was a lot braver than her mother, Grace thought with gentle irony. Grace would be afraid to touch that man without asking permission first. Which was probably a good thing, given the outrageousness of her impulses whilst in his presence.

"Mr. Noah, can I give your horse an apple? I promise to do it right."

Noah turned his head and looked down at the little girl. He might have peered upon a creature from another planet in that same puzzled way, Grace thought. At first his expression amused her, then it made her sad.

He cleared his throat. "Sure."

Maddie lit up like fireworks. "Oh, *thank* you, Mr. Noah!"

He might have granted her three wishes like a fairy-tale genie, to judge by the elation in her voice. Grace smiled at her daughter, loving her for her bright disposition. Frank had been happy like that. Nothing ever got him down for long. It was one of the reasons Grace had loved him so much and missed him so terribly.

"Remember how I told you to hold food for the horses so they won't bite your fingers, Maddie-lass." Mac stood behind her and rested his hands on her shoulders.

As careful as careful could be, Maddie held out an apple quarter to the flea-bitten gray. It nuzzled the quarter up from her open palm, and she giggled. Then she turned and held out another quarter to Fargo, who nuzzled it up in the same way.

"He's such a pretty horse, Mr. Noah. I like him."

Noah cleared his throat again. Grace got the impression he was unused to conversing with children—or anyone else—and she pitied him. She wanted to run her fingers lightly over his troubled face, to smooth the furrows of worry and strain away. She sighed again.

"Yeah. He's a good horse, all right."

"Can I pet his nose?" Maddie looked up at Noah as if he held the answer to the most important question in her life. Which it might well be at the moment. For a second, Grace allowed herself to envy children their uncomplicated view of the world.

"Er, yeah. Sure. Go ahead." Noah made a gesture of permission. It seemed awkward. He wasn't used to children, Grace could tell. She wrapped her arms across her middle again, wishing these dratted hankerings would go away and leave her alone.

Maddie stood on her tiptoes so she could reach, and gently ran her hand down Fargo's velvety muzzle. The horse seemed to like the attention. He gently nuzzled her cheek, and Maddie's smile might have lit up the darkest night's sky. It certainly lit up her mother's insides.

"He kissed me, Mommy. Did you see him kiss me?"

"I sure did, sweetheart."

"What a nice horse."

"Yeah," said Noah. "He's pretty friendly." His voice sounded strained.

Maddie gave Fargo a second apple quarter and then, in the interest of fairness, offered another one to Samuel, who gobbled it down.

This was the sort of scene Grace had always expected to share with Frank. She shouldn't be out here laughing and feeling tender about her daughter with an old man and a taciturn stranger. She should be doing this with Frank, the only man on earth who could appreciate it the way she could. Grief welled up inside her. As had become her custom, she didn't let it show, although her arms did tighten over her ribcage, and she had a sudden sharp wish that Noah Partridge would hug her.

"I'm fixing a good potato-and-onion soup for supper, Mac. It shouldn't take too long to cook it up, if you and Mr. Partridge are hungry." As soon as she'd said it, she remembered that Mr. Partridge hadn't seemed inclined to partake of meals with them. She glanced at him quickly. "That is, if you'd like some too, Mr. Partridge. It will be a simple supper. Just potato soup and cheese and bread." She was proud of herself for keeping the strong yearning she felt out of her voice.

Noah seemed to be engrossed in watching Maddie feed apples to the horses. Grace wondered what he was thinking. As usual, his face was as unreadable as a mask. When he looked from Maddie to her, she realized his eyes weren't unreadable at all. In fact, she'd never seen such raw pain in a human being's eyes. She took a step toward him, startled, then recovered her composure. She hoped he hadn't noticed.

If he had, he gave no indication of it. After staring at her—almost blindly, it seemed to her—for a moment, he gave a tiny, abrupt nod. "Thanks. I'd like that."

Chapter Five

For all Noah's reluctance to cultivate it, conversation blossomed around the supper table like spring flowers after a rain. He watched Mac and Grace closely without seeming to. And Maddie. He watched her, too. After he'd been eating and watching in silence for several minutes, he realized he was studying them, trying to figure out how the dynamics of a family worked. He used to know a long time ago, but he'd forgotten.

When a gap opened up in the happy chatter, a fierce urge to belong to this little made-up family group seized him. He couldn't account for it any more than he could resist it. In spite of suspecting he was about to make an ass of himself again, he joined in.

"This is very good, ma'am," he said to Grace, indicating his potato soup. It was a bold step for him. No one else seemed to recognize the significance of the moment.

Her smile was as warm as a summer breeze. It harkened Noah back to the soft summers of his boyhood, when he used to laze in the tall grass with his dog Flip, a fishing line tied to his big toe, and dramatic tales of derring-do running through his head. He and Flip would talk to each other for hours, Noah spinning yarns, Flip yawning. Sometimes Noah's best friend Pete would join them, and then Noah would talk to Pete. Sometimes, they'd even catch a fish.

Grace's voice jerked him back to the present.

"Thank you, Mr. Partridge. I'm partial to potato-and-onion soup myself, even if it isn't a very elegant meal."

What was he supposed to say to that? He couldn't think of a thing, yet Mrs. Richardson was smiling at him as if she expected him to add something to the conversation. Damn, he wished somebody would say something and take the burden off of his shoulders. They weren't broad enough for this. Suddenly he thought of something else he could say.

"My mother used to put cheese in her potato soup sometimes." He glanced around the table to gauge reactions. Was that a stupid thing to have said? Was it appropriate? Noah wished he'd stayed away from the supper table and these people this evening. He wasn't ready for this.

"Look, Mr. Noah," Maddie said suddenly. "I can put cheese in my 'tato soup, too." She dropped a piece of her cheese into the soup and fairly glowed across the table at him.

Noah wondered if the little kid was making fun of him, then realized with a shock that she was trying to please him. It was as if his opinion mattered to her. He licked his lips nervously and scrambled for something to say to her.

"How does it taste?"

She dipped her spoon into her soup bowl—she did it the right way, he noticed, and aimed the edge of the spoon toward the far rim of her bowl—and took a bite. She cocked her head to one side while she chewed as if seriously contemplating the merit of cheese in potato soup. Noah discovered himself almost smiling. She was a nice little kid.

"I like it," she announced at last.

"Well, then, I'll just have to grate some cheese into my soup the next time I make it."

Damn. Had he offended Mrs. Richardson? Noah looked at her, but she didn't seem at all put out. She looked happy as a lark, in fact. He contemplated telling her that her soup was good without cheese in it but didn't want to muddy the waters any more than he already had. He was grateful when Mac spoke next, because he wasn't up to it.

"When I was a lad in Scotland, we put a lot of leeks in the soup."

"Leaks?" Maddie laughed at the absurdity of such a thing. "How could you eat it if it leaked?"

Even Noah nearly laughed. He was glad he didn't when he realized the adults' laughter had hurt Maddie's feelings.

Out of nowhere, he found himself saying, "I think leeks are like onions, Maddie. They're spelled differently than the way water leaks."

She cast him a grateful glance. "Oh."

"Aye, lass," Mac said. He, too, gave Noah an approving look. Noah was embarrassed. "We had plenty of leeks, but we didn't have potatoes."

"Really?" Grace seemed surprised.

Maddie's eyes grew wide. "No *'tatoes?* What did you eat?"

It tickled Noah that Maddie looked as though she felt sorry for the poor deprived child that Mac had once been. If he judged correctly, potatoes were one of Maddie's favorite foods. He wasn't surprised. He'd loved them when he was a kid too.

He remembered that his mother had served riced potatoes once for supper. Soon afterwards she'd served something that looked the same, and he'd been bitterly disappointed to discover those small rice-shaped kernels were *rice.* They had seemed so dull and flavorless compared to the potatoes.

In fact, when he thought about it, he guessed he still did love potatoes. He tested the admission and was surprised to find it true. He hadn't considered himself in terms of loving anything at all in recent years, much less an item of food. The discovery tickled him.

A minute passed, full of Mac's descriptions of the comestibles available in the Scotland of his childhood, before Noah realized he hadn't felt this humorous tickle in his innards for eight years. He was so shocked, he couldn't speak for another five minutes or more. No one seemed to consider his silence unusual. Well, why should they? Silence had become a way of life with him. It would probably shock them more if he suddenly began to chatter.

They included him, though. Without making a production of it, both Grace and Mac directed questions at him, most of which he could answer with a nod or a shake of his head. Even little Maddie's innocent banter, peppered here and there with questions and exclamations, seemed to be directed at him as much as at the other two adults at the table. After a while, Noah was stunned to realize that he no longer felt on edge. He didn't experience the impulse every three or four seconds to jump up from the table and run outside that had plagued him throughout the first ten minutes or so of this meal.

The thought occurred to him that if he hung around with these folks long enough, they might, without knowing it, guide him back into the human race. Although, he acknowledged sadly, that would be a mighty large job, even for such hardy specimens of humanity as these three.

Besides, he didn't think he was ready for such a formidable task; he wasn't sure he wanted to rejoin humanity. He'd have to gird his loins, prepare himself to tackle it. He would have to talk to Grace Richardson, though, whether he wanted to or not, whether he was prepared or not, if he expected her to sell him her land.

The knowledge that he'd rather bed her, in silence, and go away again before either of them could say a word, gave him a melancholy feeling in his gut. Sexual gratification for its own sake and without human love seemed such a cheerless thing. Yet he knew himself to be incapable of human love. He had been once, maybe. Not any longer.

Nevertheless, after supper, as he and Mac helped Grace and her daughter clear the table, he mentally braced himself and said, "May I talk to you for a minute, Mrs. Richardson?"

She jerked her head around and stared at him as if

he'd grown another head. "You want to talk to me?"

Oh, Lord, he'd known this was going to be hard. She already looked suspicious. "About your land, ma'am." He didn't want her to get the wrong impression, or to think he was going to try to seduce her or anything.

Her expression changed to one of puzzlement. "About my land?"

"If you wouldn't mind."

"Aye," Mac said, breaking into their strained silence. Noah silently blessed the old man, and hoped he'd be able to explain what Noah wanted. "Mr. Partridge took quite a fancy to your land, Grace. Talk to the lad. Maddie and me, we can clean up these dishes." He chuckled, and looked happy, and the tension in the room dispersed.

"Well, all right." She didn't sound eager. "Let me fetch my shawl. We can talk in the parlor, but until the fire gets going it will be cold."

Noah nodded and watched her leave the kitchen. Cold didn't bother him, so he didn't fetch a warm jacket for himself. He went to the parlor and poked up the fire, hoping the room would warm up some before she got back. He didn't want her thinking about being cold as he tried to persuade her to give up her husband's dream.

"Thank you, Mr. Partridge. I could have done that."

He'd been kneeling in front of the fireplace. When he heard her voice, he rose slowly and saw that she was hugging a woolen paisley shawl around her shoulders. The gesture looked more like one of self-protection than one meant to ward off the room's chill. Maybe she anticipated what he was going to say.

She sure was a pretty woman. Her cheeks were pink from having been in the warm kitchen, and her eyes looked big and dark in the dim atmosphere of the parlor. She looked much too appealing in the semidarkness. Elusive. Alluring. To help himself concentrate, Noah took a sulfur match from his pocket, struck it on a stone from the fireplace, and lit an oil lamp standing on a table.

When he looked at her again, the faintly mysterious aura clinging to her had vanished. Thank God. It didn't occur to him to ask her to sit down. He was too nervous.

"Like Mac said, ma'am, I liked your land."

That was too abrupt. Damn. Noah shut his eyes for a second, regrouped his resources, and backtracked.

"That is, Mac took me all over the Seven Rivers country and even up into the mountains, ma'am, and I think you've got the prettiest piece of land in the area."

A tentative smile flickered on her lips. "Thank you. My husband bought it the year before Maddie was born. We'd always intended to build a house on it. In fact, Frank had ordered lumber from Santa Fe, but died before he could begin building." She looked away quickly, as if she had a hard time talking about her late husband. She added weakly, "I still have the lumber."

With a nod, Noah said, "Yeah. Mac told me." That didn't sound right. He tried again. "I mean, he said something like that." No. That wasn't right either. He finally realized what he should say. "I'm real sorry about your husband, ma'am." There. That was it. Why did he want to stomp over there, wrap his arms around her, and kiss her until thoughts of her dead husband were driven from her memory? Lord, he was crazy.

He raked a hand through his hair, wishing he could reach into his head and untwist the kinks in his brain at the same time. This was so damned hard.

She graced him with another small smile and murmured, ''Thank you.''

''Well, um, it seems to me that a single lady with a little girl to raise might have a hard go of it on a place that far away from town, ma'am, and I wondered if you'd ever considered selling it.''

''Sell my land?''

''Yes. It would be hard for you to live out there, and I've been looking for a plot of land. And all that.''

He was getting better at this. Maybe, if he could keep her talking long enough, he'd—

''No.''

His thoughts stopped abruptly, as if they'd been lopped off by an axe. He swallowed. Had she said *no?* Just *no?* Without even a polite explanation attached? He mentally released her from his hug, took a step backward, and scratched his head. ''Um, beg pardon, ma'am?''

Grace turned away from him and went to the table with the lamp on it. Light from the lamp lit her face, and Noah could see the traces of weariness and sadness there. She'd loved her husband, he could tell. His lips tightened.

''I'm sorry for having been so brusque, Mr. Partridge. Your question startled me into speaking more curtly than I should have.''

He made a small, jerky gesture with his left hand. ''That's all right, ma'am.''

''No.'' She turned again, and smiled at him. ''I was rude, and I didn't mean to be.''

She had a very nice smile. It was as warm as Noah's insides were cold. She seemed to be a genuinely nice person, a person who, in former times, Noah would have liked. Hell, he might even have courted her. He'd been another man back then. Not like he was now. Now he was damaged goods. Nobody'd want him now, especially not this lovely, loving woman.

"I didn't mean to be so irritable, Mr. Partridge, and there's no excuse for it. As I said, your question surprised me."

"Um, I reckon nobody's ever asked you about selling that property before."

"No. No, they haven't."

Her smile seemed melancholy to him, and he didn't know if he was projecting his own unhappiness onto her, or if she was genuinely sad. He wondered what to say now. "Um, I, ah, reckon this is a new idea to you, ma'am, but do you suppose you'd be willing to think about it?"

She turned around again. Noah saw her hand, small-boned and delicate in spite of the rough work it was called upon to do, caress the polished arm of the medallion-backed sofa. After a moment, she said, "I'm sorry, Mr. Partridge. I wish I could encourage you to hope, but I plan to hold on to that land. It was Frank's dream to build a place for us out here in the Territory, and I aim to see it through."

"It'll be mighty hard, ma'am," Noah reminded her. Not, he expected, that she needed reminding.

"Oh, I'm used to hard work." She gave a soft chuckle that curled through Noah's insides like incense. "But I'm not going to sell that land. It was willed to me by Frank, and it's his legacy to our daughter. It's all she'll ever have of him, you see."

She looked at him over her shoulder, and he saw that her eyes were glittering, as if there were tears in them. His gut twisted painfully. Damn it all, why was she being so stubborn? What the hell did she think she owed her dead husband's memory, anyway? Hell, Julia had forgotten her promise to Noah before he'd been gone a month. All the soft feelings he'd been harboring for Grace Richardson died.

With more sarcasm than he intended, he said, "Wouldn't money provide her with a better legacy, ma'am? Money you could provide for her with? I aim to give you a good price for the land."

"Money isn't the same as land. Money is transitory. The land is solid. It endures. It lasts, Mr. Partridge. Money helps, but land is forever."

Exactly. That's why Noah wanted it. And he still couldn't understand her stubbornness. For the love of God, she'd never be able to work that place by herself. Even providing she could ever get anything built on it, what the hell would she do to support herself on it?

"What do you aim to do with it, if you don't mind my asking?"

"I don't mind your asking." She seemed to slump a little. "And I'm not sure what I'm going to do with it. Not yet. I'll think of something. But I'm not going to sell it."

Before he could think himself out of it, Noah blurted, "I think you're being foolish, ma'am."

He saw her mouth stretch down into a frown. He could tell she wasn't used to frowning. "You may think of me in any way you choose, Mr. Partridge. I still won't sell you the land. That's Frank's legacy to our child, and I won't sell it. That land was Frank's. Now it's mine. Someday it will be Maddie's. It's all we have left of her father, and I won't give it up. Not for any amount of money.''

"You'll never be able to work it on your own," Noah said flatly. It was the truth, dammit.

"What I do with my own land is not your concern."

She was getting mad at him, and her eyes had started to flash with ire. Under other circumstances—hell, even five minutes ago—Noah might have admired them. Not now. Now, she was simply frustrating the devil out of him. "Dammit, ma'am, you're being hardheaded. Why do you want to hold on to land you'll never be able to use?"

"I don't know that I'll never be able to use it. And you don't either. And I prefer not to be cursed at if you don't mind, Mr. Partridge."

Damn. He was such a fool. "I'm sorry, Mrs. Richardson.''

"I believe this discussion is at an end. I'm sorry to disappoint you, but I won't sell my land. Not to you, and not to anyone else."

She started to move away from him. He reached out to grab her, but stopped himself before he could commit another breach of etiquette. He'd already committed too many, and now she was mad at him. He was mad at her, too. Damned obstreperous, pigheaded woman.

"Listen, Mrs. Richardson, will you just think about it, please? I intend to offer you a fair price. More than fair. I didn't see any other land I liked anywhere near as well as yours."

She turned one last time and said coldly, "I like it

too. That's another reason I won't sell. Find yourself another piece of land, Mr. Partridge. That one's mine."

She left him standing there in the parlor he'd warmed up for her, in front of the fireplace he'd poked into life for her. He watched her go, feeling powerless and inept and furious. Rage caromed through him, thundered in his blood, pounded in his head. He turned and slammed a fist into the rough stones of the fireplace.

"Careful, laddie. Ye'll hurt yourself."

It was Mac. Of course. Noah turned around and scowled at the old man who, as usual, looked as calm as if he hadn't just walked into a room occupied by a madman. Noah couldn't make himself speak, couldn't think of a thing to say.

He wanted that land. With the tenacity of a coyote, the idea of owning that particular parcel of land had taken possession of Noah's being. He craved it. He needed it. He sensed something there that would be his salvation.

In a voice as mild as custard, Mac said, "Reckon your little chat didn't go the way you wanted it to, lad."

"No." Or did he mean yes? Well, Mac was a smart man; he'd figure it out.

The old man sank into his chair with a happy sigh and began to fill his pipe, peering up at Noah as he did it. "Grace thought the world and all of her Frank, y'know, lad. It won't be easy to persuade her to give up his land and the dreams they had together."

After he managed to pry his jaws apart, Noah said, "Evidently it's going to be impossible."

Mac's response was a grin, a twinkle, the snap of a

match. Noah was given a faintly ironic lift of a bushy white eyebrow as the old man drew on his pipe. Noah blinked when those damned sparkles puffed up in the smoke Mac released. He pressed a hand over his eyes. Damn, what was wrong with him? Stupid question. Noah knew what was wrong with him.

"You give up too easily, lad."

"Do I?" Noah didn't think so. If he gave up easily, he'd be dead by now. Of course, he'd probably be better off dead. He dropped his hand and watched Mac, sure he was going to say something more.

He did. "What ye need to do is get to know our Grace better, lad. Talk to her. Make friends with her. Walk out with her and Maddie. Maybe go on a picnic. Get to know them both. Then ye'll be able to figure out what to say to make her change her mind."

Noah stared at Mac, wondering if the old man had lost his mind, wondering if perhaps Noah wasn't the only madman in the room after all. The old Scot's shoulders shook, and Noah realized Mac was laughing at him. Again.

Peeved, he snapped, "Glad to know I can provide you with so much amusement."

Silent no longer, Mac's chuckles rolled out of his mouth and seemed to dance around the room. They played hide-and-seek with the smoke and sparkles, and Noah had to rub his eyes because the effect was jarring to his shaky nerves.

At last Mac gasped in a huge breath. "Ah, lad, I'm not crazy. No more are you, though ye won't believe me for a while yet, I'll warrant."

Frowning, Noah stared at the old fellow. What in blazes was he talking about?

Mac pointed his pipe stem at him. "I'm talkin' about you, laddie. And Grace Richardson. And little Maddie, who's hopin' for a merry Christmas."

A merry Christmas. How the hell had Christmas gotten mixed up in all this? Noah couldn't think of anything to say. He sat down in the chair that matched the medallion-backed sofa and studied Mac's face.

"Ye take my advice, lad. I mean it. Things will be fine if ye do as I say. Talk to Grace. Apologize for bein' too sharp with her." He paused and considered Noah thoughtfully. "If ye can find it in your heart to do it, explain why ye're standin' on shaky ground these days. Grace will understand, lad. She's not had the hard life you've had, but she's had to endure her share of unhappiness. She's got a heart as big as all outdoors, and she's capable of infinite love. She's been missin' havin' somebody to share it with. A man could do worse than to have Grace Richardson as a friend."

Befuddlement did a backflip into pique. "What the hell are you talking about?"

Another roar of laughter greeted Noah's question. Mac had to wipe his eyes, he was laughing so hard.

"Glad I'm so entertaining." Noah looked away, peeved.

"Aye, lad. Ye are that. Ye are that." Observing Noah's glower, Mac held out a hand to prevent an indignant outburst.

Noah watched that gnarled hand carefully, waiting for more sparkles to appear. They didn't. Wouldn't you know it? Every time Noah thought he had something figured out, the rules changed on him.

"It's only that when a body's seen as many years on this glorious earth as I have, laddie, he gets to ap-

104

preciating the way folks go about things." His voice changed timbre and became tender. "Aye, ye've been through hell, lad, and ye've survived. Nothing will ever be that bad again."

Noah swallowed. He tried to sound sarcastic when next he spoke, but couldn't do it. "*Now* what are you talking about?"

Mac didn't answer him. "This here's a great big, spanking new territory, lad. Ye can make something for yourself here without fearin' the past will find you out and take it all away from ye again."

He took a thoughtful pull on his pipe and blew out a series of smoke rings. Noah watched them, mesmerized, until he realized what he was doing and looked away.

"But y'see, lad, in order to do the thing right, you have to get to know Grace better. She's a fine woman. Ye took her by surprise this evening, but if ye get to know her, talk to her without mentioning how much ye want to wrest her own departed Frank's dreams from out of her grasp, you might be amazed by how well the two of you get along."

"I'd be amazed, all right." During Mac's little speech, Noah had been sitting with his knees apart, his elbows braced on them, staring at the floor. Now he glanced up at the old man. He hated to admit it, but the scenario Mac had just painted appealed to him. He could use a friend. He hadn't had one for years.

"Ah, lad, Grace won't hold tonight against you. She knows human nature too well to do that. She sees inside you almost as well as I do."

Lord, what an appalling notion. Noah started to say so, but thought better of it. He didn't want anyone to know what was inside of him. It was too awful. Too twisted. Too horrible.

"Ye're not the first old soldier to pass through my wagon yard, lad," Mac said in a velvety voice. "Ye're not the first man Grace has met who has seen too much and had too much done to him and too much taken away from him on account of the war. Don't know why folks think they always have to be fighting. Silly thing to do, if you ask me."

Noah couldn't get past the lump in his throat to agree. His eyes burned. Hell.

He didn't know how long they sat in the parlor after that. It seemed like hours, but it might have been seconds. It took a long time for his lump to melt and his eyes to quit burning.

"What are ye doin' out of bed, Maddie-lass?"

Surprised by Mac's soft question, Noah turned and saw Maddie standing in the doorway rubbing her eyes and staring straight at him. She hugged that same homemade rag doll to her chest, the one that looked like it was a hundred years old.

"I need a glass of water, Mac." She cocked her head to one side. "What's the matter, Mr. Noah?"

What was the matter? What was she talking about? Noah muttered, "Nothing."

"I'll fetch you some water, lass. You stay here and talk to Mr. Partridge.

Great. That was all Noah needed, to be stuck here with a little kid babbling at him. He glared at Mac, whose eyes twinkled at him. What a surprise.

All at once he felt a soft little hand on his cheek, and he almost jerked out of his skin. Before he could restrain himself he barked out, "What are you doing?"

"Petting you."

He stared at her hard, wondering what to say or do now.

"Mommy says sometimes when people are sad, it's nice to touch them because it makes them feel better. I feel better when Mommy holds me when I'm sad."

Noah tried to think of something to say that would make her stop and, at the same time, not crush her. He was unsuccessful.

"Don't worry anymore, Mr. Noah. Everything will be all right."

She sounded as if she was parroting lines taught to her by her mother. Noah still couldn't think of anything to say.

"It's almost Christmastime, Mr. Noah, and nothing bad can happen at Christmas."

Like hell. Noah bit back a retort. The kid was only five years old. Let her find out for herself how miserable life was.

Mac came back with Maddie's water, and she drank it down. "Thank you, Mac. G'night, Mr. Noah."

He forced himself to say, "Good night, Miss Maddie."

Then Mac carried her back to bed, and Noah headed out to his solitary stall at the back of the wagon yard. He kept from running only through a mighty effort of will.

Alexander McMurdo, a great one among of a race of beings who had for the most part deserted the earth long ago, stared moodily into the fire and smoked his pipe. Occasionally, for his own amusement, he made the flames assume human form and dance with each other. Once he created a cavalcade of circus animals and had them march around the parlor. Mac had always been fond of the circus.

Finally, though, he ceased his idle amusements and turned his mind to the problem of Grace Richardson and Noah Partridge. Noah had traveled a long way down a perilous path. Even though Mac was the mightiest wizard in a long line of mighty wizards, he wondered if he'd waited too long to call the boy here to be healed.

Mac didn't feel the disgust for humanity that the rest of his race did. He found human beings entertaining, occasionally amusing. Sometimes, as with Mr. Noah Partridge, they could be tragic.

He sighed and decided he was going to have to take a more active role in this matter. Still staring into the fireplace—it was naught but glowing coals now—he invoked a powerful spell.

Grace brushed out her hair and braided it with a hand trembling from hurt and anger.

"Imagine that awful man thinking I could give up Frank's land for money! Imagine him thinking for so much as a minute that I would even *dream* of selling the land Frank bought for us!"

Frank. Frank, Frank, Frank. Why had God seen fit to snatch him from Grace and Maddie so soon? It wasn't fair. Frank had been the most wonderful man Grace had ever known. She'd never meet another like him.

And Noah Partridge wanted to snatch the last token of her beloved husband away from her. *Buy* it away from her. She felt as if he'd offered her thirty pieces of silver.

Gradually her rage turned inside out. Her trembling didn't stop, but at last the rigidity that had held her upright as she stormed away from Noah, into her room, out of her clothes, into her night dress, and over to her dressing table, faded and she collapsed. Grace put her elbows on the table, sank her face into her hands, and cried.

"That poor man," she whispered through her tears. "That poor, poor man."

Noah stared at the sky, his mind whirling like a loose cog in a broken machine. What an ass he'd been. What a hash he'd made of his conversation with Grace Richardson.

Maybe he should just give up on trying to buy her property, and make an offer on one of those other pieces of land Mac had shown him. Hell, what difference did it make? As long as he had a place of his own, away from the company of his fellow man, a place where he could hide his infirmities from the world and live in peace, what did he care where that place was? Up there in the mountains near Capitan was kind of nice. Green, though. Noah didn't much fancy green. He preferred the dry, barren plains around Rio Hondo. They suited his dry, barren life.

He mulled the matter over in his mind for several minutes, mentally inspecting the other properties Mac had shown him, and building houses in his imagination where he figured they'd go. Unsatisfied, he scattered a few head of cattle around to see if they improved the pictures thus created. He added a herd of antelope. He tossed in a deer and three or four jackrabbits. He even sicced a coyote on one poor antelope just for the hell of it.

After a while he sighed heavily. It was no use. Those other places didn't do a thing for him. That one piece of land, the one with the Pecos River running through it, the one that belonged to Grace Richardson, was the only place he wanted.

He couldn't understand it. He'd never felt a craving this strong in his life, not even before the war, when he'd been a whole man.

"Hell."

All right. Noah acknowledged that Mac knew Grace Richardson a whole lot better than he did. If Mac thought she might change her mind if Noah became better acquainted with her, then that's what he guessed he'd have to do.

His insides knotted up and he had to take several deep breaths to tamp his panic down. If he kept his goal in mind, he could do it. He told himself so over and over as he lay there and stared into a sky that looked like a black blanket somebody had dumped a bucketful of diamonds upon. The stars reminded him of Mac's infernal sparkles.

He saw a falling star and made a wish, then wondered what had possessed him to do such a thing. Frowning at himself for being a sentimental lunatic, he muttered, "You can do it. You've done harder things in your life."

Offhand, he couldn't remember when.

Chapter Six

A few mornings later, Noah awoke to a shriek of joy. He pulled the blanket down from where it had covered his face, and squinted into the morning air. The sky was as gray as slate and overhung with fog. Fog? Here? How odd. The atmosphere was nippier this morning than it had been for the last several days. It was the first week in November, and Mac had told him several times that the weather could change any day. Noah guessed it had.

When he sat up, the blankets fell down around his waist, and cold air hit him like an arctic blast.

"Damn," he murmured when he saw the snow. It was only early November, yet a thin blanket of white covered the wagon yard. More flakes floated down from the sky like confetti, lazily drifting here and there in a slow meander to the earth. He'd never seen such a gentle snowfall. It surprised him, since he'd expected snowfalls to be rough out here where everything else, including the weather, was hard as rocks.

He realized the shrieks of joy were still going on, and he swiveled his head to see where Maddie was. He recognized her voice. A memory of the snows of his childhood tiptoed through his brain, and he smiled before he knew what he was doing. Then he saw her.

Maddie raced across the yard, swaddled from head to toe in a coat and mufflers and rubber boots, leaving a trough in her wake through the formerly pristine snow blanket. The only reason Noah knew that bundle was Maddie and not someone else was because she was so short. Then her mother came into view.

Noah held his breath, fascinated. Grace Richardson was laughing. He couldn't recall the last time he'd seen a woman in so unaffected and relaxed a mood. Or one so different from the mood in which he'd last seen her. She'd been furious when she'd stalked away from him after he'd asked to buy her property, and he'd kept to himself since.

She was a sight to behold right now, though. She was clad in heavy boots and, with a scarf wrapped around her head, only a little bit of her pretty hair showed under a Stetson hat. She wore mittens and a long coat, and had another scarf wrapped around her throat. The ends of it floated out behind her on the same mild breeze that made the snowflakes dance. She was almost as bundled up as her daughter, but Noah could clearly see her cheeks, pink with pleasure and exertion. He imagined her eyes were sparkling.

His sex began stirring to life, and he was ashamed of himself. Lordy, when was the last time *that* had happened?

112

He couldn't leave off staring at her, though, and when she glanced over and caught him, he got embarrassed. He saw her good humor slip for a second before she seemed to let go of restraint and waved at him, her cheery smile brightening the very air between them.

"Good morning, Mr. Partridge! What a surprise this snow is!"

He lifted his hand to wave and realized he was naked from the waist up. Quickly he grabbed a blanket and covered his chest, and then felt even more embarrassed. What a blockhead he was, to expose himself this way in front of a lady.

Grace laughed. Her laughter was as unaffected as her daughter's, and it held Noah spellbound. When was the last time he'd heard such a pure, joyful sound? He couldn't remember.

"Aren't you freezing to death?" she called. "My goodness, I don't know how you can stand to sleep out here in the cold. Why don't you come inside and bed down by the fire on these cold nights, Mr. Partridge?"

Noah cleared his throat. "I—" He stopped. His voice still sounded froggy, so he cleared his throat again. "I don't mind the cold, ma'am."

In truth, he craved the cold. In the summertime when the weather was hot, his thoughts crawled back to Georgia, to sweltering, starving and stinking in the prison camp. Then his dreams would be full of the stench of cholera and puke and death, the sight of skeletal men and rats and wormy biscuits and peanuts—if they were lucky—and misery and blood and death. Sometimes his mind's eye pictured the bodies. They'd pile up faster than the inmates could bury them in the hot months, and they'd begin to rot. The wardens had made Noah dig holes to put them in, and the stink would be so bad that Noah would actually send his mind away and leave only his body there in the hell that was the prison camp. Until his time in that camp, he hadn't known people could do that, detach their minds from their bodies.

He shivered. Not with cold, but with the soul-sickness that had been his closest companion for more years than he cared to remember.

"You're shivering," Grace said, laughing. "Let me bring you a cup of nice hot coffee."

No, his brain cried. Nothing came out of his mouth. He saw her whirl around, as if this first snowfall of the season had filled her, as well as her daughter, with energy and boundless gaiety.

Aw, hell. Noah scrambled out of his bedclothes, hoping Maddie wouldn't bounce back by and see him in his long underwear bottoms. Or see his back, scored deeply with hundreds of healed whiplashes. He didn't want to shock the girl.

He yanked on his shirt and trousers, and was tugging on his boots when Grace returned, a huge smile on her face and a tray in her hands.

"Here, Mr. Partridge. I brought you some break-fast." She handed him the tray, looking a little shy.

He took the tray, nodded, and forced out a muffled "Thank you."

She tucked her hands behind her back and turned her head so that she wasn't looking him in the eyes any longer. Thank God.

"Um, I don't want you to think I'm angry with you, Mr. Partridge. I apologize for losing my temper when we spoke last."

If Noah hadn't had his hands holding the tray—smells from which were kissing his nostrils and making his stomach growl—he'd have made a gesture of dismissal. "That's all right, ma'am. Reckon I caught you by surprise."

Mac had recommended that he tell her what was in his heart. Noah tested the idea, found his mind slamming shut against it, and knew he couldn't do it. Because he wanted to soften her up, he said, "I—ah—I'm not used to being around people much, ma'am. Reckon I was clumsy when I made my offer, and I apologize."

Even revealing that much made his intestines cramp. He held himself upright against the pain with an effort.

Grace laughed, apparently finding their mutual apologies amusing. "Well, I won't argue about who was wrong, but I hope you aren't miffed with me this morning for being so stiff-necked when last we talked."

"No, ma'am." He wondered if he'd just lied, then decided it didn't make any difference.

"Good. Well, then, I hope you enjoy your breakfast, Mr. Partridge. I promised Maddie I'd help her build a snowman this morning, and I expect we'd better get at it, because the snow will probably be gone by this afternoon."

Noah looked up at the sky, which remained as gray as smoke. Huge black clouds rolled across it as if the gods were angry and planned to do something destructive with them. "It'll melt? By the afternoon?"

She laughed again, joyously, naturally. Her laughter soothed his intestines, made an unfamiliar warmth settle in his chest, and made his groin stir again. Damn.

"My goodness, yes, Mr. Partridge. It's not unusual

to get snow this early, but it's rare to get a snow that sticks on the ground for long in November. Every now and then we'll get a white Christmas. Two winters ago we had snows that lasted for two weeks in February, but that's very unusual.'' She gazed at her daughter, who was busily making snowballs on the far side of the yard. ''That was the winter after Frank died.''

Frank. Everything in her life came back to Frank. The Frank who was dead and buried and to whom she remained loyal. Noah guessed Mac was right about her. She was staunch, he reckoned. He used to admire that quality in a person. This time it was making his life difficult, and his life was too damned difficult already.

''Yeah. Well, the snow looks pretty for now anyway,'' he said.

''Yes. It's beautiful.''

''Mommy, come and help me make the snowman!''

When he glanced her way, he saw that Maddie was looking much like a snowman herself, she'd gotten so much snow on her.

''Duty calls,'' Grace said cheerfully. ''Enjoy your breakfast.''

''Thank you.''

She turned and walked towards her daughter, and Noah added, ''It sure smells good, ma'am.''

He watched her until she got to Maddie. Then, because he figured he'd be embarrassed if she'd turned around and found him staring, he sat down and ate his breakfast. It tasted as good as it smelled.

Grace threw a snowball at Maddie, who gave another shout of laughter. ''Stop it, Mommy! We've got to finish our snowman before all the snow melts.''

"We will, sweetheart. It won't melt for hours yet."

She scooped some more snow onto the pile she'd built and rolled the bottom ball across the yard, picking up almost as many twigs and pieces of dried grass as she did snow.

"When I was your age, we could make a snowman that was all white because the snow was much deeper. And it would last for weeks and weeks."

"In 'Cago?"

"Yes. In Chicago. It would last for so long that we'd all get sick of it and long for spring to come and melt it all."

"I wouldn't get sick of it," Maddie declared with conviction.

"I bet you would. I think this fellow's bottom ball is big enough now." She rolled the ball to a stop and stood up, breathing hard and putting a hand to her back to straighten out the kinks. She'd forgotten how much energy playing took, and how hard it could be.

Maddie observed the ball with a critical eye. "All right," she said at last. "Let's make his middle now."

Grace almost groaned.

"Need some help?"

Both females turned to find Noah Partridge standing there, his face as stern and unsmiling as ever. Thinking she must have heard him incorrectly, Grace said, "I beg your pardon?"

He shrugged and gestured at the big snowball. "Need some help?"

Grace's mind went blank with astonishment. Thank heavens for Maddie, who didn't suffer from the same affliction.

"Oh, yes! Help us, Mr. Noah. You can roll a *big* ball. Bigger than Mommy's.''

Recovering from her amazement that this hard, icy man should be offering assistance in building so trivial a thing as a snowman, Grace said lightly, "Well, I like that! I almost broke my back rolling that snowball!''

Maddie giggled. Was it Grace's imagination, or did Mr. Partridge's eyes go soft? She couldn't tell. His expression didn't soften one iota. Poor man.

He'd dressed for the role, in a warm, fur-lined jacket and heavy gloves. He didn't wear a hat, and Grace saw silver glints in his hair.

He was going gray. Her heart gave a little flop. He couldn't be much more than thirty years old—scarcely older than she was—yet he was going gray. She understood that happened sometimes to people who'd lived hard lives. *Poor man,* she thought again.

She'd almost fainted dead away when she'd seen him this morning, sitting up in his bedroll. He hadn't been wearing a shirt. That was shocking enough all by itself, but what had really shocked her was the physical reaction she'd had to that bare chest of his, with the curly dark hairs covering it, and the muscles that had seemed to ripple under them. Mr. Noah Partridge was a hard man in more ways than one. There wasn't an ounce of fat on him.

Seeing his naked chest had brought back memories of Frank. Of course. Everything brought back memories of Frank. Frank's hair had been light, and his chest hadn't been nearly as hairy as Mr. Partridge's. This morning her fingers had itched to test Noah's chest hair, to compare it to what she remembered of Frank's. Good heavens, what was the matter with her?

118

The bitter thought occurred to her that if God were a fair divinity, it would have been Mr. Partridge who'd been struck by lightning and not Frank. Her husband had been as golden and happy as Mr. Partridge was dark and forbidding. She was immediately ashamed of herself for harboring the unkind thought for so much as an instant.

"Make a *big* ball, Mr. Noah! Bigger than that." Maddie pointed a fat, woolen finger at Grace's effort, and Grace said, "Hmph," to feign offense. Maddie giggled again.

When she glanced at Noah, he was nodding, his expression as sober as ever. She wondered if he'd always been serious. When he was a boy, had he been like this? Her curiosity was suddenly so intense that she very nearly forgot a lifetime's worth of good manners and asked him. She caught herself just in time.

"Well, since you two don't like *my* snowball, I'll just leave you to build his bottom and top and go into the house to fetch his eyeballs." She made a monster face at Maddie and wiggled her fingers at her.

Maddie said, "Ewww."

Wonder of wonders, Mr. Partridge gave her a grin. A very small grin, but a grin. Grace felt as if she'd conquered one of the Alps.

When they were finished, they had themselves quite a snowman. He looked a little dirty, and his snow body bristled with debris from the yard, but Maddie glowed with excitement, and Grace was happier than she'd been in months. All three of them had eaten more raisins than they'd used to make the snowman's mouth and eyes, and it had been Noah who'd suggested using an old dried yucca pod for his nose.

"There," he said after he stuck the nose in place. "He looks like he's been in a fight."

Maddie crowed with glee. Grace smiled.

Out of nowhere, Mac joined them with a pipe for their project's raisiny mouth and a straw hat for his head. Then he stood back and observed the snowman, his blue eyes twinkling.

"Poor lad needs some arms," he said at last.

They found some twigs and made him some arms with them. Then Grace had run inside to fetch a thin, striped Mexican serape, and they'd draped it over his humped shoulders. "There!" she said triumphantly. "He fits right in."

She couldn't believe her ears when Noah Partridge laughed.

Mac had been right, Noah decided. It was good that he'd made an effort to get to know Grace Richardson better, even if it had been difficult to stick it out at first.

Noah could hardly believe it, but he had actually—finally—enjoyed making that snowman with Grace and Maddie this morning. After the first several tense minutes, during which he'd had to wage a violent battle against his compulsion to run away and hide, his nerves had settled. He'd forgotten that he was unfit and no longer able to mingle with the society of his fellow human beings.

At one point he'd realized he was behaving almost like a normal man, as if nothing in the world was more important at that particular moment than finding twigs for a snowman's arms. For the sake of little Maddie Richardson, who lived in the remote New Mexico Territory with no friends her age to play with. And no father.

And then Grace and Maddie had laughed, and he'd experienced a sense of pride out of proportion to the accomplishment itself. He wondered if he could ever get used to that sort of thing again. He used to be a part of a community of people and hadn't thought anything of it. Now he was apart from the whole of humanity, and trying to belong was something else entirely.

He caught himself shivering and forced his mind back to the project he'd set out for himself. He'd survived mingling with Grace and Maddie this morning. He'd even accepted Grace's invitation to take lunch with them in Mac's house. He hadn't died. He hadn't had a nervous attack. He hadn't blown up and gone wild-eyed. And he hadn't run away. These were good signs.

So what he was going to do at lunch was take another step toward his goal. He was going to ask if Grace and Maddie would like to ride out with him on a picnic. When the weather cleared, of course. With luck, he'd have enough time to gird his loins to face the trip, but not enough time to go crazy again.

Just in case the weather stayed bad, he'd make an effort—something he hadn't done since his life had gone to hell—to talk to Grace every day, as Mac had advised him to do. Just one or two words at a time. That shouldn't be too hard.

Oh, God. Noah clutched a post supporting a wall to his stall, and held on while waves of panic crashed through him.

Who was he trying to fool? He couldn't do that. He

121

couldn't behave like a normal man anymore, could he?

He sucked in a deep breath and held it while he told himself to calm down. *Breathe,* he ordered his body. *Breathe.*

When his heart stopped thundering and his brain ceased shrieking, he sighed. All right. He was all right. At this one unique moment in time, he was all right, and he could plan a strategy by which to soften Grace Richardson up enough to sell him her land. The land was important; it might well be Noah's salvation—or, if not his salvation, at least his refuge. If he could keep his goal in mind, perhaps he could keep his lunacy in check.

So he would make an effort, and he *would* talk to Grace Richardson every day. Perhaps not much. But he could take small steps. A word or two. Three, if he could stand it. Maybe with practice he could build up into a longer conversation. He would be pleasant to her. If he could make himself do it, he would even smile. Since he knew that if he pushed himself too hard too fast, his mania would take over, he reminded himself he didn't have to force the smiles. If he could smile, he would. He would at least make an effort to be pleasant, to say more than one word at a time.

Since he'd become tense at the thought of what lay ahead of him, Noah forced his muscles to relax before he set out through the snow for Mac's house. He looked at the snowman at the far end of the yard as he did so, and smiled. He only realized what he'd done after he'd rapped on the door.

Two days after Noah helped build the snowman, somebody knocked at the door of Mac's house while

Noah was inside playing a game of hearts with Maddie and Grace. He'd discovered that playing cards kept his hands busy, his eyes occupied, and he didn't have to talk much. And if every now and then his hand brushed Grace's and he felt an urge to crush her to his chest and beg her to hold him, he suppressed it without too much difficulty. He considered this a good start. At the sudden noise, though, he jumped and had to hold on to the edge of the table to keep from diving under it.

Grace looked at him with compassion in her eyes, and he felt like ninety kinds of a fool.

Maddie patted his hand. "Don't worry, Mr. Noah. It's only someone at the door. I don't like sudden loud noises, either."

Mac, who had been sitting in his rocking chair, smoking his pipe, and gazing at the card game with the face of a benevolent gnome, chuckled. He heaved himself out of his chair. "Probably some poor soul has a wagon needs mendin'."

His footsteps clumping across the floor echoed in Noah's head like cannon fire. He tried to be inconspicuous when he took several deep breaths in an effort to fight down the panic that had burst, full grown, into him at that blasted knock. Hell. He'd been fine until that knock came. It had startled him and precipitated this crazy reaction. Some time ago, he'd decided he'd always be this way, but it certainly was inconvenient sometimes.

He didn't like Grace looking at him like that, as if he were a poor damaged creature that needed her pity— even if it was the truth. Shoot, Noah would bet money that the late, lamented Frank Richardson hadn't been spooky like this. Unquestionably, her Frank had been a splendid, whole, undamaged specimen of hearty masculinity.

After he'd swallowed his heart, Noah murmured, "Sorry. I've been, um, a little jumpy since, um, since the war."

Grace shook her head sadly. "Yes. I was very grateful that Frank didn't have to fight in that awful war."

Noah couldn't seem to tear his gaze away from hers. He wanted to say, *not fighting didn't save his life, though, did it?* He didn't, because it seemed too cruel.

"It's for you, lad."

Mac's announcement jerked Noah's attention away from Grace. He squinted at the door, sure he'd misunderstood, and saw a shivering, bundled cowboy standing behind Mac. Grace saw him, too, and hurried up from the table.

Maddie's little face lit up, and she cried. "Look, Mommy, it's Gus. Hello, Gus."

The man named Gus looked like he couldn't move his blue lips enough to smile. He lifted a swaddled arm in a stiff salute to the little girl.

Grace grabbed him and set a course toward the fire-place. "Good heavens, Gus, what are you doing out in this awful weather? You're frozen solid!"

"C-c-come t-to f-find Mr. P-P-Partridge, ma'am," Gus managed to get out through his chattering teeth.

"Well, you've found him, but you're not riding back again until you have some hot cocoa and dry yourself by the fire. Why, look at you!" Grace had started wrestling the gloves off the cowboy's hands. "I'm surprised Susan would let you ride all this way on such a freezing, windy day."

With Grace fussing over him, Gus made his way to

the fire. He held his hands, red with cold, out to the flames. "It was her made me come, ma'am." Already, his teeth weren't chattering so hard.

"*Susan* made you come?"

She grabbed the shoulders of Gus's frozen coat and tugged while he shrugged. Together, they worked it off, and Grace hung it on the corner of the mantel where it began to thaw and drip onto the hearth.

Their conversation had given Noah a chance to get his brain to form a coherent sentence. "You came to fetch me?"

Gus turned around and bent over slightly, as if to thaw out his frigid bottom. "Yes, sir. Mrs. Blackworth, she said to come and fetch you, because she wants you to fix that there piano she's got in her parlor."

Grace turned to gaze, wide-eyed, at Noah. The look of surprise suited her. Noah liked it. "You know how to repair pianos?"

Aw, hell. He shrugged and couldn't hold her gaze. "I, um, used to work in my family's piano and organ business, ma'am. Back before the war."

"My goodness."

When Noah forced himself to look at her, her expression had turned thoughtful.

Gus spoke again. "That's what Mrs. Blackworth said, ma'am. Said to come out here and fetch Mr. Partridge back so's he can fix her piano."

Thoughtfulness evaporated. Grace chuffed out an indignant breath. "Well, I swear. Sometimes Susan Blackworth is too autocratic for her own good."

Gus grinned. "For my own good, anyway."

She smiled and then laughed. "That's what I meant."

Their banter barely penetrated Noah's muddled brain. "She sent you out here—in the middle of this frigid spell—because she wants me to fix her piano?"

"Yes, sir." Gus apparently noticed Noah's look of incredulity, because he grinned again. He looked like a nice, easygoing sort of fellow. "She's like that."

Noah believed it. He squinted at the newcomer. "She aim to pay me? Last time I was there, she wanted to give me her reed organ if I'd repair the piano."

"Sounds like her, all right." Gus's grin made him look intolerably happy. "She said to tell you she aims to pay you in cash money, though."

Noah nodded.

"Mrs. Blackworth, she's kind of an old bully, but ain't no man on the spread wouldn't do anything she says, Mr. Partridge. She likes to pretend she's a mean old hen, but she ain't. Not really."

Grace huffed again. "Too bad the same can't be said of her husband."

Gus's smile faded. He looked as though he didn't care to get into that one.

"I'm sorry, Gus." Grace helped the cowboy unwind his long woolen muffler, and draped it out upon the mantel. "I didn't mean to say that."

Gus's grin came back. "That's all right, ma'am. Reckon I know pretty much what folks hereabouts think. Most of us hands'd just as soon keep mum on the subject."

She let go of her temper and laughed once more. Noah thought how nice it was that she could do that.

"Now you just stay right there and try to get warm, Gus. I'm going to fetch us all hot cocoa. After you've thawed out some, you take the rest of those wet things off, and I'll hang them up to dry.''

''Thank you kindly, Mrs. Richardson.''

She nodded and left the room. Noah noticed that he wasn't the only one who watched her go. Gus's appreciation was obvious, which only figured. Grace Richardson would draw stares even if she wasn't the only female within miles of the place. She was a fine figure of a woman.

Gus sighed when Grace left his sight. He turned to look at Noah again. ''Mrs. Blackworth, she said she wouldn't mind waitin' for the ice t'melt 'fore I set out to come here, but I didn't feel like riskin' it.'' Gus winked at Mac, who nodded his approval of Gus's sensible turn of mind. ''Besides, it gets mighty stale settin' in a cold bunkhouse with a bunch of bored cowboys with nothin' to do but play cards and argue with each other.''

Noah didn't doubt it, even if he still didn't buy the part about Mrs. Blackworth being secretly benevolent.

''Does she want me to go back to her ranch with you?''

''Yes, sir.'' Now that his limbs weren't frozen stiff, Gus began to shed several more layers of clothes, including his boots and two pairs of thick woolen socks. ''Sorry I'm drippin' on the hearth, Mac.''

''Think nothin' of it, lad. Worse things have fallen on that hearth than ice water.''

''Hope these here socks don't stink.'' He held one to his nose, sniffed, and said, ''Peeee-ew.'' Maddie giggled. Gus gave her a wink. Noah tried to recall if he'd ever been that easygoing around little kids. He thought he had been, once, but couldn't really remember.

Grace bustled back into the room bearing hot cocoa for everyone. "I'm not letting either one of you ride out to that place until every stitch of your clothing is dry, Gus Spalding, so don't even think it. In fact, I'm going to insist that you spend the night here. If the two of you are foolish enough, you can start back in the morning."

"Well—"

"Don't worry, Gus. I'll write you a note so Susan won't get mad at you."

Gus's grin creased his recently frozen cheeks. "Well, in that case, I ain't goin' to argue with you, Mrs. Richardson." They both laughed. Mac and Maddie joined in.

Noah wouldn't have argued with her, either. In fact, he'd have done anything she asked him to do. He watched the young cowboy grin at her, and the notion that the boy had a fancy for her solidified. Nothing to wonder at there. The wonder was that Noah's possessive instincts were so deeply stirred by the thought of the other man desiring her. Hell, he hadn't felt that tingle of jealousy for years.

"I don't have any tools with me," he said.

Gus looked over at him, surprised, as if he'd forgotten Noah was there. Something between cynicism and amusement curled inside Noah. He wondered how old Gus was. Maybe eighteen or nineteen, eight or ten years younger than Grace by Noah's reckoning. Hardly old enough to grow a beard. Noah couldn't remember ever being that young, although he must have been, once.

"Mrs. Blackworth, she says I wasn't to accept any excuses you might care to give me, Mr. Partridge." Gus grinned, and added confidentially, "She's like that, don't you see. Don't accept excuses from nobody. Most of us don't even offer her none anymore."

"I can understand that. But I still can't fix her piano without tools."

"She says she'll get you anything you need."

"But—"

"Go along with the boy, Noah lad. It'll be good for you to get out of the wagon yard. You've been cooped up in here for days. And it won't hurt you to get to know Susan Blackworth better, either."

Noah turned to peer at Mac, who grinned at him from the doorway. The old man sure was big on having Noah get to know people. Noah wondered if old Mac knew more than he let on.

"Yes," said Grace, sending Noah's attention swinging her way. "Susan Blackworth is definitely worth getting to know, Mr. Partridge. She's one of the local characters." She chuckled and handed him a cup of cocoa.

He took it with a nod, and thought about Mrs. Blackworth. "Seems to me most everybody out here's some kind of character, ma'am."

Grace burst out laughing. So did everyone else in the room, including Maddie. Noah glanced around, wondering what he'd said that was so damned funny.

"I expect you're right there, laddie."

"I expect you are." Gus took a sip of his cocoa and sighed contentedly. "If a man's not a particle strange in his upper works, he ain't going to leave his home and family and travel out here where life's harder'n

129

steel, and he's got nothin' but cows and hardcases for company twenty-three hours a day."

Noah hadn't thought about it that way. For the first time in years, he wondered if he wasn't more like some of his fellow men than he'd believed. At least the ones who'd braved this territory.

"And let us not forget the *women* in this territory," Grace said with a mock frown. "Any woman with half a brain would remain in civilization where she can attend church on Sundays and find playmates for her children. And schools."

She held out her arms to her daughter, who'd been following the conversation with interest. Maddie climbed down from her chair and raced straight into her mother's arms. Noah's heart did a painful calisthenic maneuver in his breast. Lordy, it must be hard on a woman to live out here where there wasn't so much as a convenience, much less a luxury, to be found within two hundred miles.

Grace gave Maddie a big squeeze. "But we manage." She settled Maddie back at the table with a cup of cocoa. Maddie looked awfully happy for a kid with no playmates, Noah thought to himself.

"Yes, ma'am. We manage." Gus's voice sounded almost syrupy. When Noah looked from Grace to him, he could swear the cowboy had tears in his eyes.

But all this sentiment didn't solve his own problem. On the one hand, ever since he'd seen that organ in Mrs. Blackworth's parlor, he'd itched to get his hands on it. If he went there to fix her piano, he knew he'd have a hard time leaving the organ alone. He supposed he could if he tried, especially with Susan Blackworth hovering over him like a bird of prey, ready to peck him if got out of line.

On the other hand, he feared that working on any instrument at all, even that old piano, would send him spiraling back into memories he didn't want stirred again. Hell, he had it hard enough just getting through one day at a time, sometimes one second at a time, without reminders.

What would happen if he opened that piano up and all the memories came flooding back? He hadn't had to think about everything he'd lost for some time now. He was pretty sure digging around in the guts of Mrs. Blackworth's neglected instrument would open barely healed wounds. Noah wasn't sure he could survive going through them a second time. He'd damned near perished the first time.

"Well—"

"I hope to God you're not going to say no, Mr. Partridge. 'Cause if you do, I reckon I'll just have to keep ridin' west from here, mebbe on out to Californy. It won't be worth my while to go back to the ranch and tell Mrs. Blackworth I failed. She don't hold with a man failin'."

Noah searched the young face, which seemed fresh and untouched by the world's badness. He decided the cowboy was only half-joking.

Taking refuge in his cocoa, Noah hoped inspiration would strike soon and hand him a good excuse for not going, because otherwise he was on the verge of capitulating to Gus's request. He had a shrewd notion that if he did give in, he was going to be in for some rough days.

Not to mention the fact that while he was playing

with Susan Blackworth's decrepit piano, wishing he could work on her organ, and tearing the scabs from his own old injuries, he'd be losing precious ground with Grace. Glancing at her out of the corner of his eye, he sighed. Not that he'd gained much ground in the first place. Hell.

"All right."

The words were out of his mouth before he knew he was going to say them. Then he silently cursed himself as a benighted simpleton.

Gus didn't seem to notice. His face lit up. "Thanks, Mr. Partridge. Sure glad I don't have to find me a new job."

"Can we go to Mrs. Backwort's and listen to the piano when Mr. Noah gets it fixed, Mommy?"

Noah's head swung around to observe Maddie, her big blue eyes shining as she smiled at her mother. Grace tilted her head to one side as she considered her daughter's request. "You know, Maddie, that sounds like fun." She turned to peer at Noah, and his gaze slid away. "Do you have any idea how long it will take you to fix that piano, Mr. Partridge?"

"No, ma'am." He was getting nervous about it already. He might not be able to fix it. Or it might need a part he didn't have and couldn't jury rig. Or he might get attacked by his goblins and have to run away before he finished the job. As Noah knew from unhappy experience, anything could happen, and seldom was any of it good.

Chapter Seven

Noah and Gus left the next morning, late. Grace made them eat a good, hearty breakfast before she'd allow them to set out across the windy plains.

"It's not icy any longer, ma'am," Gus pointed out. "It's a lot warmer than when I rode in here yesterday."

Noah, watching him from over the rim of his coffee cup, could tell the boy enjoyed being fussed over. He was making quite a show of being strong and manly. God, had Noah ever acted like that? He had a vague, shadowy recollection of once being young and alive and eager to please.

"Nonsense," said Grace, refilling Gus's cup. The boy stared up at her with worship in his eyes. "I'm not letting either one of you set foot out of this house until it's at least a couple of degrees warmer out there."

She knew she had Gus's puppy love. Noah saw her smile affectionately at the boy, like a mother bestowing a blessing on her son. Her easy, good-natured affection somewhat soothed Noah's overstrung nerves. At least she didn't look like she'd be succumbing to the young cowboy's adoration any time soon.

Not that Noah gave a rap, personally, if the two of them paired up. What he worried about was that Grace might marry one of the men out here, any of whom would probably leap at the chance to have her. Then her land would be lost to Noah forever.

Of course, if Noah married her himself, then the land would be his. He scowled into his coffee cup. Where in the name of holy hell had that notion sprung from?

For some reason, he glanced at Mac. It didn't surprise him when he found the old man grinning at him as if he could read every single twisted thought in Noah's head.

Lordy, maybe it'd do him some good to get away from these people for a while; maybe a little time off would save him from being seduced into total insanity. Marriages and mind-reading wagon-yard owners. Shoot. He had plenty of problems already without adding those two, thank you.

"Be careful, Gus. Be careful, Mr. Partridge."

Grace had made them take a huge bundle of food with them. It was lumpy, and bounced against the flank of Gus's horse. Noah hoped the poor animal wouldn't get a sore from it. He didn't say a word.

"Bye-bye, Gus. Bye-bye, Mr. Noah."

When Maddie's farewell filtered through the layers of fleece and wool he'd wrapped himself in, Noah had already hunched into his comfortable, keep-the-world-away mode. Her tone of voice, which seemed to indicate she expected a response, yanked him out of it momentarily. He didn't appreciate it. Nevertheless, since he'd never been a cruel man, no matter how crazy he was, he wouldn't allow himself to disappoint her. He straightened in his saddle, turned his head against the layers of bundling, and looked back at the porch.

And his heart stumbled in his chest. Grace stood there, in a dark skirt and white shirtwaist, that woolen paisley shawl caught around her shoulders to ward off the brisk weather, Maddie in her arms. The cold wind had nipped at her cheeks and nose until they glowed, and it had whipped her hair out of its carefully knotted bun.

A sudden blind longing struck him. With vivid clarity he recognized that it hadn't been merely his past that the great conflict and its aftermath had snatched from him. It had taken away his future too. He'd never have a woman like that to wave at him when he left home or to run and greet him when he came back again. He'd never have a sweet little girl like Maddie to call him Pa and sit on his lap and kiss his cheeks.

He gave Maddie a brief wave, which she returned with vigor, and glanced at his traveling companion. Those sorts of lives were for men like Gus Spalding— whole men, men who hadn't been ruined by a vicious and mercurial fate.

As a rule, Noah didn't feel sorry for himself. He knew what he was, accepted it, and tried his best to live with the devils that had been set loose inside of him. He knew he wasn't the only man in whom similar devils had been unleashed during that awful, bloody war.

Today, as he rode behind Gus out through the wagon

yard gates, Maddie's chirpy farewell singing in his
ears, his heart ached with a sickening sense of loss.

"You took your time getting here."

"Sorry, ma'am. I was froze by the time I got to
McMurdo's place. Mrs. Richardson had to dry my
clothes before she'd let me go again."

"Humph. A likely story."

Susan Blackworth's onyx eyes blazed with irritation.
Gus shuffled and fidgeted with the hat in his hands.

Noah didn't say anything. It was nothing to him if this
old lady was a shrew. He'd come at her request; he could
leave again in his own time if she aggravated him. Peek-
ing at Gus, he knew it would go hard on the boy if he got
fed up and left, so he determined to stick it out. Ex-
ternal events were nothing to Noah Partridge. He carried all of his own environment around within him.

He didn't like the way she bullied Gus, though.
"You got tools, ma'am?" His voice was rough from
the silent trip. He and Gus hadn't spoken a word on
their ride out here because they'd been too busy trying
to keep from freezing to death. Noah thought it was
interesting that he could get out of the habit of talking
so quickly. Must be because he hadn't exercised his
vocal chords enough in the short time he'd been at
McMurdo's to make up for his years of silence. For
the first nine or ten months, as he'd lain in that hospital
bed after he'd been carried out of the prison camp, he
hadn't spoken a solitary word. The mind he'd sent
away so that it wouldn't suffer with his body had a
hard time coming back again.

"You don't have the tools of your own trade with
you?" Mrs. Blackworth barked her question to let

136

Noah know she considered him an idiot at best and a shiftless wastrel at worst to have ridden out here unprepared.

Noah didn't like her. He lifted his gaze from where it had been idly inspecting the carpet at his feet and eyed her narrowly, keeping his expression blank. "It's no longer my trade, ma'am. I came out here at your request. You have tools or not?" He wanted her to know without a doubt that he'd be just as happy to go away again without looking at her damned piano. Happier.

He could tell she hadn't expected him to stand up to her. A wave of contempt dribbled through him. What a harpy.

"Humph. Well, come along. I'll see what I can find. I used to have the tools my father bought along with the piano."

He didn't answer, but followed her into the parlor. As soon as he did, he caught sight of her reed organ again, and he wanted it. Lord, but it was a beautiful old thing. And it was one his grandfather had made with his own two hands. Noah had loved that old man, loved him more than his father, which wasn't surprising. Noah'd heard it said once that grandparents and grandchildren always got along because they had a common enemy. Not that Noah didn't respect his father, but he had found it much easier to love his grandfather, who hadn't had anything to prove with Noah.

But no. He wasn't here for the organ. His business was with the piano. Fortunately, the piano stood in the opposite corner from the organ, so Noah's back would be to the organ and he wouldn't have to see it as he worked.

137

He brushed right past Susan Blackworth and went over to the piano without looking at her, although he was vaguely aware of her scrutiny of him. To hell with her. Let her look. Noah didn't care what she thought of him.

Somebody had dusted it. That was something, anyway. And she'd lowered the protector over the keys. By this time, they were probably sticky with dust and worse, but at least she'd done that much. He ran his hands over the finish. It looked like somebody'd taken some wax to it, too.

"How long since it's been played?" He didn't look at her.

"Years. I haven't played since the rheumatism twisted my hands up."

Noah suspected he ought to feel some compassion for her, but he didn't. She was such a bossy bit of goods. When he glanced at her again, he caught a look in her eyes that made him soften a millimeter. She was gazing at the piano with longing. Maybe she was cantankerous because of her own lost hopes, just as he was crazy because of his. Since he didn't much like her, he decided to wait a while before he changed his poor opinion of her.

"You got a child who wants to play the piano, ma'am?"

She snorted. "None of my sons would be caught dead doing anything so civilized, Mr. Partridge."

He looked up at that, into her dark, dark eyes. Again, he wondered if her caustic exterior hid a hurt she didn't want people to see. Lots of folks didn't like to exhibit their weaknesses to the world, Noah reckoned. He wasn't the only piece of broken merchandise wandering around loose in the world.

"Well? What do you think?" She folded her arms across her chest. Her posture seemed to challenge him, as did her tone.

Noah shrugged. "Can't tell until I open her up and poke around for a while, ma'am."

"What about the organ?"

His head jerked up of its own accord. "The organ, ma'am?"

"Yes. What if I decide to have the organ fixed? Can you do it?" Her voice was hard, challenging.

Noah swallowed, trying to tamp down the surge of hope in his chest. "Again, I'd have to open it up and look at it. If nothing's broken, and if the reeds are whole, I expect I can tune it. You might have to order pads and replacement reeds from back east."

"Oh? And just where does one get replacement reeds, Mr. Partridge, if your business has been burned to the ground?"

She asked the question as though she suspected Noah of trifling with her. He cocked his head and studied her for a few moments. She glared right back at him, unflinching. A tough old bird, Susan Blackworth. A reluctant appreciation of her grit began to steal through him.

It was funny how some people, when faced with hardships, developed a hide. Others, like Grace Richardson, remained vulnerable. Noah guessed it had something to do with their basic natures, and wondered if either reaction to adversity was better than the other. Maybe Susan Blackworth was better off than Grace. She had more money, at least.

None of that mattered. "The Estey Organ Works is still in business, ma'am. I expect you can write to them if you need to replace stops or reeds or anything."

Her eyes squinted up, as if she still didn't believe a word he said. He found her skepticism extremely irritating. "And where might this Estey Organ Works be located, young man?"

"Name's Partridge, ma'am," Noah said dryly. "Noah Partridge. And Estey's in Brattleboro, Vermont."

"Vermont! Why, that's at the end of the earth!"

He shrugged again. What the hell did she expect from him, anyway?

"How long would it take to get parts from them, Mr. Partridge?" Evidently recognizing his growing impatience, she made her tone not quite so sharp.

"I wouldn't know." He glanced back at the organ. Sadness welled up inside him. "You should have taken better care of it, ma'am. It's a fine old instrument and deserves care."

"Don't you presume to lecture me, young man."

Noah sighed, and decided that it wasn't even worth a response. He patted the piano. "Listen, Mrs. Blackworth, do you want me to take a look at this thing or not?"

"Well, of course I do! Why do you think I called you out here?"

"I wouldn't know. All I'm telling you is that your instruments have been neglected. As for the organ, it may need parts or tools that I don't have. You can get replacement parts in Brattleboro, Vermont. Now, do you want me to look at this piano or not?"

"Yes!" Her eyes were as hard as flint. "But don't

you go thinking I'm made of money, young man, because I'm not. My husband has seen to that.''

Hmmm. Was that her problem? Did she think he was
going to soak her for repair bills? Noah shook his head.
''I won't overcharge you, Mrs. Blackworth.'' He licked
his lips, suddenly frightened, and blurted out before he
could stop himself, ''Do you want me to look at the
organ while I'm here too? I've been hoping I could get
my hands on that thing, ma'am. I haven't worked on
an organ for years.''

Tilting her head to one side, she studied him, as if
gauging the veracity of his confession. Her lips pinched
up as tight as the knot on a noose, and wrinkles radiated from them. He wondered if she was as old as she
looked, or if her acerbity had dried her out and shrunk
her up and sapped the juice out of her. Noah wondered
if Grace might look like Mrs. Blackworth in a few
years, and rejected the notion immediately.

Grace didn't have Susan's acidity. Noah had a feeling that if Grace went through hell, she'd be more apt
to end up like Noah himself. Grace didn't seem to pos-
sess the natural internal defenses against the slings and
arrows life flung at her that this old woman did.

At last she said, ''Humph. Well, take a look at the
piano and tell me what it needs. Then you can look at
the organ and do the same thing. I'll have to decide
whether or not I can afford to have you finish the organ
repairs. I want the piano fixed.'' She eyed him keenly
for another second or two. ''Don't worry, Mr. Partridge. I'll pay you for your time.''

It sounded as though she expected him to protest,
although the notion hadn't even occurred to him. Hell,
if he told the truth, he'd work on this thing for free.

Music—pianos and organs—had once been his life. He could hardly wait for her blathering to cease so that he could begin work. He nodded.

Without another word, she turned and bustled away from him. Because the job was so intensely personal to him, he waited until she'd left the room before he turned to the piano again. He'd do it first. Then, if he still had an ounce of sanity left in him, he'd tackle the organ. Because he couldn't help it, he turned and gazed longingly across the room at it.

Lordy, it was a beauty. One of his grandfather's first and finest. A feeling of reverence the likes of which he hadn't experienced in years settled over Noah, and when he at last approached the piano, he did so with gratitude and respect.

Grace grabbed her daughter around the waist and laughed. "Don't bounce too hard, Maddie, or you'll fall right out of the wagon."

Maddie giggled at her mother's warning and calmed down. She crawled up onto Grace's lap and snuggled against her. The weather had warmed up some in the three days Noah had been gone from the wagon yard, but the winter wind felt as if Mother Nature were trying to blow them all away from her plains, as if she were trying to rid the land of usurpers. The wind was cold, too, and harsh, and Grace had to keep checking the bed of the wagon to make sure it hadn't dislodged anything. She'd baked several pies for the Blackworths, set them into a wooden crate, and covered the crate with a blanket. The ride was bumpy, and even though she'd snugged the edges of the blanket under the crate, she feared the crate would slide, allowing that pesky wind to whip under the edges of the blanket and coat her crusts with grit.

Mac, who was driving the team along a path only he could discern, chuckled.

"But, Mommy, I never heard a piano before!"

Grace's heart gave a sharp spasm. That's right. Born and reared out here in the middle of nowhere, Maddie's life had been circumscribed in ways Grace no longer even thought about half the time.

But it was true. Not only had Maddie never heard a piano, but she'd never been to Sunday school, she'd never met a grandparent, she'd never eaten ice cream, and she'd never had a friend her own age. Oh, Grace had let her play with the children of settlers who stopped in the wagon yard on their way through Rio Hondo to points west, but Maddie hadn't had a single friendship that had lasted more than a week or two.

Not for the first time Grace wondered if she should give up Frank's dream and move back to Chicago. Her parents would be thrilled if she did. Maybe she was only being selfish, keeping Maddie here. Maybe she was foolish to want to build something for the two of them on the land she and Frank had loved. She sighed, and then told herself to snap out of it.

If Maddie's life *did* have to be different from other little children's, the least Grace could do for her was give her a happy mother. "Well, you'll get to hear one today. Gus said that Mr. Partridge fixed it up perfectly, and it sounds like a choir singing."

"What's a choir, Mommy?"

A momentary feeling of despair rendered Grace speechless. She shook off the mood, and said calmly,

"A choir is a group of people who sing holy songs in church on Sundays, Maddie."

"Oh."

Grace and Mac exchanged a look over the little girl's head.

"We don't got us a church, do we, Mommy?"

"No, sweetheart." Grace hugged her. "But we will one of these days, I expect. When Rio Hondo attracts more people. More families."

"It don't take long for civilization to spread once it gets a toehold, Maddie-lass. You'll see. Pretty soon ye'll be longin' for the good old days." He chuckled and clucked at the mules.

Smiling, Grace said, "Well, maybe. I think I'll be just as happy as Maddie when a few more people decide to settle out here and raise families. It's—" She sucked in a breath, a stabbing pain having robbed her of words. "It's difficult, feeling so alone. I didn't mind so much when Frank was alive." She looked away from her companions quickly, so they wouldn't see the easy tears that had sprung to her eyes.

Grace often wished she was tougher. Like Susan Blackworth, who reminded Grace of a badger. Nothing soft and sentimental about *her.* Susan Blackworth didn't allow problems to sneak up on her; she attacked them head-on. But Grace had never learned to build defenses against the cruelties life flung at her—or to anticipate them. They invariably took her by surprise, and they always hurt.

"Ah, lass, life will get easier out here one of these days. And more folks will settle. And little Maddie will have friends her own age to play with." Mac gave Maddie a wink.

"I'd like a friend." Maddie sounded wistful.

Feeling guiltier by the second, Grace said, "Well, you'll get to see Gus again today. Maybe he'll let you ride on his pony."

"And Mr. Noah," Maddie said thoughtfully.

"Yes," said her mother. "And Mr. Noah Partridge."

Mac didn't speak again, but Grace took note of his rather sly smile.

They heard the music before they went inside. Grace's heart, which had been feeling lumpy and low with guilt and loss, lifted like a bird on the wing.

"Oh," she breathed. "Listen to that."

Maddie's eyes opened wide, and she looked up into the sky as if she expected to see a host of angels singing. "It's music!"

Mac chuckled. "It's music, all right, Maddie-lass. Pretty music."

It was lovely music. It wasn't a simple popular tune, either. Grace had to listen hard for a moment before she could place it. Then she recognized the tune as a lilting passage from Beethoven's sixth symphony. My goodness. She wondered who was playing the instrument. The *Pastoral* seemed too gentle, somehow, to have been selected by Susan Blackworth. Grace's conclusion made her smile. As little as she could imagine Susan Blackworth playing such a gorgeous piece of music, still less could she imagine the hard, cold, withdrawn Mr. Noah Partridge playing it. But it had to be him.

"Sounds like he got the thing tuned up pretty well," Mac observed.

"Indeed, it does."

"I can't wait to see it!" Maddie had taken to jumping up and down on the wagon seat again. Laughing, Grace restrained her gently.

The front door opened, and the music swelled in the air around them. Grace looked over to see Susan Blackworth standing there. She could hardly believe it when a smile creased those weathered cheeks, which she'd more often seen bent into a frown.

So it was Noah Partridge playing the beautiful music, as Grace had suspected. How perfectly astonishing. She called out a bright greeting. "Good morning, Susan! Cold today, isn't it?"

"Freezing," the older woman acknowledged in her rusty voice.

"Is that our Noah playin' so fair in there?" Mac climbed down from the wagon and stretched his old bones out before he walked to the other side to help Grace and Maddie.

"It is," said Susan, moving forward to greet them. She walked stiffly, as if every step pained her.

Grace's easy sympathy stirred. It must be hard for Susan, living out here. Grace understood she'd come from a wealthy and privileged family back east. In the Territory, wealth could provide a certain small measure of comfort, but no luxuries, certainly nothing akin to what Susan must have been accustomed to. With an internal giggle, Grace guessed that she herself was fortunate to have come from a plain, middle-class family with no pretensions to riches. She hadn't had so far to fall.

"I haven't heard any Beethoven pieces for years," she said, smiling.

"Don't expect you have," Susan acknowledged, her voice as tart as a crab apple. Of course, Susan Blackworth's voice was always tart.

"So our lad did a good job tunin' the old piano, did he?" Mac asked.

"I suppose he did."

Susan held out her arms, and Maddie went up and hugged her. It was a duty hug. Maddie was afraid of the wrinkled old woman who always dressed in black and smelled of camphor, and whose tongue could flay the hide from the toughest of cowboys. Grace was proud of her daughter.

She and Mac wrestled the crate full of pies to the back edge of the wagon. Over her shoulder, Grace asked, "Have you played it since he fixed it, Susan?"

The old woman opened and closed her hands a couple of times. "I tried." Her words were clipped.

Again, Grace's tender feelings stirred. "Rheumatism?" she asked sympathetically.

The older woman held up her hands. The knuckles were swollen, and her fingers gnarled. "It's hell getting old, Grace, and don't let anyone tell you otherwise."

Grace shook her head. "I'm sorry." She hoped Susan's arthritic fate didn't await her. She flexed her fingers experimentally. It would be difficult enough rearing her daughter and performing the tasks of a mother and father even if her health remained perfect. What would become of them both if nature played her a bad turn, as it had Susan Blackworth?

Well, she couldn't worry about that now. She could only do her best to fulfill Frank's dream. If she failed, she failed. The mere thought of failure made her heart ache. She feared the reality of such a prospect might kill her.

Grace, Mac, and Maddie, who clung like a vine to her mother's hand and dragged her feet a little, followed Susan Blackworth into the house. She led them past the tiled entryway and into the parlor, where they all stopped to watch and listen. The music flowed around them, filling the atmosphere with sound and beauty. Grace heard Maddie gasp and smiled down at her.

Her eyes as big and round as pie plates, Maddie whispered, "It's so loud."

Grace laughed. "Yes, sweetie, it is loud. It's pretty, though, isn't it?"

Maddie nodded solemnly. "It's beautiful."

"Do you like it?"

"Yes." Maddie gazed up at her mother. "Is this how Sunday school sounds?"

Grace knelt beside her daughter so she wouldn't have to shout. "Usually people play pianos or organs during church services, dear. Sunday school is when little boys and girls learn lessons from the Bible."

"I want a church," Maddie announced, and nodded decisively. "With a piano."

"That would be nice," Grace concurred, and sighed. When would the rough-and-tumble community of Rio Hondo ever have itself a church? Not until there were a lot more women out here. Right now, the tough men who struggled to gain a foothold in this inhospitable land cared about almost anything more than they did churches or pianos and organs.

When she glanced up, she saw Noah Partridge's back, slightly bent as he concentrated on his fingering.

She'd never in a million years have guessed that such a difficult, troubled man could have such magic in his fingers as he was creating now on Susan Blackworth's piano. She shook her head, wondering if the war had changed him from a man with music in his soul into the cold, emotional cripple he was today. How sad. How stupid of men to think they could solve their differences by fighting over them.

"He's got a gift."

Grace looked up to see Mrs. Blackworth staring at Noah's back too. A tear dripped down Susan's cheek, and she wiped it away impatiently. Grace wasn't sure if Susan's tear astonished her more than Noah's playing, or the other way around. Either way, this was a day full of surprises.

"Yes, he certainly seems to have a gift, all right." She rose and wondered what to do now.

Mac took the problem out of her hands. "What d'ye want me to do with these pies of Grace's, Susan?"

It seemed to Grace as if Susan gave herself a little shake. "Set 'em in the kitchen, Mac. Thanks, Grace. I don't make pies any longer. Juanita Valdez has been cooking for the lot of us for a couple of years, but she couldn't make a decent crust if her life depended on it." Again, she bent and straightened her crooked fingers as if trying to will them back into piano-playing shape.

Mac turned with the carton in his hands and headed out of the parlor.

"I hope you enjoy them."

"I'm sure we will. The boys like anything sweet."

Grace wondered if that was supposed to be a compliment, and then decided it didn't matter. She smiled at Mac when he returned, sans the carton of pies, to the parlor.

All at once the music stopped. The silence sounded like thunder in the house for several seconds. Noah Partridge stared down at his hands, as if amazed that they still worked, and then glanced over his shoulder. When he saw her standing there, he turned abruptly back to the piano. Grace saw him open and close his fingers as Susan Blackworth had just done. It looked to her as if he were testing them, as if they weren't used to the exercise they'd just been called upon to do. He didn't speak.

It was Maddie who broke the spell that seemed to have woven itself around Noah and his observers. She pulled her hand away from her mother's and ran up to the piano bench.

She stopped short of hugging Noah, although Grace noticed that he appeared to brace himself for an attack. Instead Maddie clasped her hands in front of her, and said, "Mr. Noah, that was the prettiest music in the whole world. It was the prettiest music I ever heard. Ever." She gazed at him in awe, as though she considered him some sort of magician.

Grace saw him swallow. "Thank you, Miss Maddie." His voice sounded funny, as if he had to force it past an ache in his throat.

Suddenly Maddie turned toward her mother. "Can you play the piano as good as Mr. Noah, Mommy?"

"Can I play as well as Mr. Noah Partridge?" Grace said, automatically correcting her daughter's grammar. She shook her head and smiled. "I'm afraid not, dear. Mr. Partridge is—he's a real musician. A gifted musician. I'm not nearly as good as he is."

Noah turned back to the piano and seemed to be studying its keys. Grace saw his hands—hard hands, callused, tanned—skim over them, almost caressing them. "I used to be." His voice still sounded funny.

"I'd say you still are, young man." Susan Blackworth's voice was as harsh and imperious as ever. "And that instrument sounds as good as it ever did."

Grace heard Noah clear his throat. "It's a fine instrument, Mrs. Blackworth. It just needed a little care and a few felts is all."

"My father bought me that piano from Partridge's in '27. I've had it ever since. Used to play it too. As well as Mr. Partridge there."

She sounded bitter. Grace wasn't surprised about that, although the information surprised her. "My goodness."

Noah stood abruptly, making Maddie jump. He glanced down at her. "Sorry, Miss Maddie."

She gave him one of her sunniest smiles, and he averted his face.

"Come here, Maddie," Grace said softly. She wasn't sure what was going on inside Noah Partridge, but she sensed it was powerful, and it was disturbing, and she didn't want her daughter anywhere near it.

Because she wanted to purge the odd atmosphere, she said brightly, "It sounds as if your grandfather's skill has been passed down to you, Mr. Partridge. That piece was beautiful."

She saw his back rise and fall as if he were taking and releasing a huge breath. When he turned to face her, his eyes looked as bleak as the weather. "Thanks," he said, and Grace felt like crying.

They took dinner with Susan Blackworth. Neither

Susan's husband nor any of her sons were there to dine with them. Grace wasn't sorry. They were a hard lot, the Blackworth men. She doubted if any one of them had a musical gift.

She wasn't sorry, either, when Noah elected not to ride in the wagon with them. He rode Fargo alongside the wagon when Mac drove it back to Rio Hondo. He didn't speak a word the whole way, and Grace got the feeling he wasn't really there except in the flesh. His spirit seemed to be visiting elsewhere, and his expression was as far away as summer.

Chapter Eight

He hadn't died. Noah awoke the next morning in his stall in McMurdo's Wagon Yard and felt almost proud of himself.

He'd tuned, oiled, and repaired the Blackworth piano, and even inspected the neglected reed organ, and he still lived. He'd tested the organ's stops and reeds and suggested what she needed to order from Estey's Organ Works in Brattleboro, and had managed to remain there the whole time. He hadn't blown up, broken down, screamed, cried, or run away. Not once.

Not that there hadn't been plenty of shaky moments, but he'd endured them. He'd even managed to hide the trembling of his hands from the sharp-eyed, sharp-tongued Mrs. Blackworth. At least, he thought he had.

Was that a step in the right direction? Noah wasn't sure. It would help if he knew what the right direction was.

With a heavy sigh, he thrust his bedroll aside and was immediately enveloped in a blanket of icy cold. Damn, he might have to start wearing both parts of his long underwear to bed. Ever since the war, he'd worn as little as possible at night because the terrors got him when he felt confined, especially when he was sleeping. But Lordy, when it got this cold, he supposed even his army of demons could use a little warmth. He looked into the sky and saw that it was a bright, brittle blue, with clouds like snowdrifts piled up at its edges. He breathed the frigid air and felt satisfied. How odd.

"I hope you'll join us for breakfast, Mr. Partridge."

Cripes. Noah jerked his head around, embarrassed that he'd been caught staring into the sky. There she was: Grace Richardson, looking like a winter angel, buttoned into her long gray coat, with her muffler wrapped around her neck, and holding a bucket. She gave him a smile as warm as the day was cold, and he felt himself begin to become aroused. Glory, this had to stop.

"I've been milking Betsy," she said with a laugh. "I'm surprised I didn't get ice cream out of her this morning."

He had to force himself to do it, but he smiled back. Recalling his near-naked state, he yanked a blanket over his chest. Damn, he wished he'd stop having these inconvenient physical reactions to Grace Richardson. He was hard as a rock. He didn't need to be reminded that he used to be a man. Life was difficult enough without knowing he was unfit ever to bed a woman again.

"Thanks," he said, surprising himself. "That'd be nice."

She took a few steps closer to him, holding the bucket in both hands. He saw that she wore those same woolen mittens she'd had on when they'd made the snowman, and that they'd been darned many times. "I really wish you'd sleep inside, Mr. Partridge. We all worry about you sleeping out here in the freezing cold."

"I like the cold, ma'am." It was the truth, but he was shocked to hear himself say it out loud. Telling the truth often provoked questions from others that he didn't care to answer.

"Really?" She tilted her head to one side, as if she were trying to understand. "Why is that, do you suppose?"

He knew why it was. Mac's suggestion that he tell Grace the truth filtered into his head, but he thrust it away again. He couldn't do that. Not yet, anyway. "Um, I reckon I had some bad experiences in the hot weather, ma'am."

Her head tilted the other way. She reminded Noah of a pretty, decorative bird. Except Grace Richardson was more than merely decorative.

"I'm from Chicago myself," she said. "We had some hard winters, and some awfully hot and humid summers back there. I'm not sure which I like better. I like them both, I guess, although I think I like fall the best, when the leaves begin to turn. Not that we have many trees to turn colors out here." She laughed softly. Noah thought he detected a measure of regret in her voice.

"No, ma'am." Her gentle laugh cut through him like a knife. He had a quick, impossible urge to rush off and find her a maple tree or something. He really was crazy.

She gave him another smile and turned to walk back to the house. "I fixed some buckwheat cakes for breakfast, Mr. Partridge. I don't know how he managed it, but Mac found some real maple syrup for the hotcakes. Better come in before we gobble them all down."

With a friendly wave, she was off. Noah watched until she'd entered the house before he shoved the covers down, dressed, took care of Fargo, and went to take breakfast with Grace Richardson. And Mac. And Maddie.

Lord, if he didn't watch himself, he'd begin to like this sort of thing, and then what would become of him?

Grace wished Noah Partridge would stop glancing at her and then jerking his head down again. He made her nervous, doing that. She couldn't tell if he was trying to get up his courage to ask her a question or stab her in the back.

Maddie asked him questions about music all through breakfast. He grunted monosyllabic responses for the most part, although he didn't appear to be impatient or bored. He mainly looked nervous.

Mac lifted his coffee cup and watched them all, his bright blue eyes glittering like sapphires. Grace got the feeling he was presiding over a drama of his own making. That made her nervous, too.

When her daughter paused in her chattering to drink her milk, Grace decided to take the bull by the horns and initiate a conversation of her own. "So, Mr. Partridge, how did you learn to play the piano so beautifully? You must have taken lessons for a long time."

His head whipped around so fast, Grace was afraid he'd hurt his neck. "My grandfather," he said, and swallowed. He took a deep breath, as if trying to get his galloping nerves under control. "My grandfather taught me, ma'am. He taught my sister and brother and me when we were just youngsters. The whole family played." He shrugged. It seemed to Grace as if he were apologizing for something. "It was our business, you see."

She smiled, hoping her smile conveyed what she couldn't say aloud: That he was safe here, that no one would hurt him, that he could relax his guard and allow whatever emotional bruises he carried around with him to heal here, in Rio Hondo. Then she admonished herself for being ridiculous. How could she know if he needed to heal? She didn't even know him. "My great-aunt Myrtle taught me to play. She was such a sweet old dear, and she always smelled of lavender and powder."

She thought Noah's lips might have twitched, but she couldn't be certain. He might have been offering her a smile of his own; it was difficult to tell with him.

"Mommy used to play the organ in church, Mr. Noah," Maddie said in her cheery way.

This time Noah did smile. It lasted perhaps a hundredth of a second, but Grace saw it, and it made her heart ache.

"Did she? I used to play the organ in church myself."

Maddie's eyes held wonder. "The same church?"

Mac and Grace laughed. Noah's smile lasted a fraction of a second longer than his prior one.

"No, Miss Maddie. My family lived in Falls Church,

Virginia. I think your mama is from Chicago.'' He lifted a brow and glanced in Grace's direction.

She nodded and turned to her daughter. ''That's right, sweetheart. Falls Church and Chicago are in two different states.'' And on two different sides of the great war that had just been fought. She wondered if Noah didn't like her because of it. Yet he didn't seem hostile, exactly—only remote.

Maddie looked confused. Grace was pretty sure she wasn't clear on what a state was. ''You see, Maddie, all of us live on a big continent. Part of that continent is called the United States.''

''I know that.'' She looked at her mother with scorn. ''I seen the globe in Mac's back room lots of times.''

Noah grinned again. Grace smiled too. ''That's right, you have. Why don't we study the globe after breakfast, and I'll show you where Virginia and Illinois are?''

Maddie brightened. ''All right!'' She loved playing with Mac's globe, and it gave Grace an opportunity to impart geography lessons without Maddie knowing she was learning anything. Sometimes Grace wondered why more schools didn't teach their students in a like manner. Maddie could already read quite well because she and Grace made up stories together. It was easy to teach reading and writing when a child had a stake in the results. It must be admitted, however, that Grace wasn't sure how to impart arithmetic and make it seem like a game. Every time they tried counting antelopes, the herd would scatter and leave Grace confused and Maddie frustrated. She sighed.

''Anything the matter, ma'am?''

She tried not to show how much Noah's question

had surprised her, but wasn't sure how well she'd succeeded. She wasn't accustomed to his being aware of her moods. "No, not really. I was just thinking about how nice it would be to have a real school and a real church out here in Rio Hondo."

Noah nodded, but Grace didn't detect much agreement in the gesture. It looked more like he was signaling his understanding of her wishes. "I get the feeling you aren't as eager for civilization to set down roots here as I am, Mr. Partridge." She gave him a big smile to let him know she didn't think badly of him for it.

He looked away nonetheless, as though he weren't pleased to have had his thoughts read accurately. "I, uh, like my privacy, I reckon."

"I can understand that." She'd said that by rote. She didn't really understand at all. Sometimes when she and Frank first moved to the territory, she used to think she'd go mad if she couldn't find another woman to talk to from time to time. She settled for Susan Blackworth, because there was no one else around.

Maddie tugged on her sleeve, and she smiled at her. "Yes, Maddie?"

"What's privacy, Mommy?"

Mac chuckled. Grace saw him twinkling and could tell he was eagerly awaiting her answer.

"Privacy is being left alone, Maddie. Not butting in when a person wants to be quiet by himself." Maddie would understand that part. So as not to make Noah seem like an oddity, she added, "Or herself. Some folks like to be alone more than others." She often wished she was one of them.

After contemplating her mother's explanation for a

moment, Maddie peered at Noah, a little frown creasing her youthful brow. "Don't you like people, Mr. Noah?"

Mac chuckled again.

"I, uh, I—" Noah's uneasiness was plain.

"Don't pester Mr. Partridge, Maddie," Grace said gently. "He's a man who likes his privacy." She smiled at Noah to let him know she wasn't being merely sarcastic, but was attempting to help him.

"I'm not pestering him!" Maddie sounded indignant. "I'm just curious, is all."

"Aye, lass, how's a wee bairn to learn these things unless folks explain 'em to her, eh?" He winked at Grace, then turned to Noah. "So, tell us: Don't you like people, Noah lad?"

The two men's gazes locked for a moment. Grace felt tension arc between them like electricity, and it startled her.

Noah broke the moment first. "Sure." The word was harsh, clipped. He threw his head back and gulped in a breath of air. "Sure, I like people just fine."

Mac winked at Grace again and turned to Maddie. "The lad's only out of practice, Maddie-lass. He'll get the hang of socializing one of these days."

"Yeah," said Noah, rising so quickly his chair bumped on the floor. "Yeah, that's right." He almost ran for the door, grabbing his hat from the rack before he stopped short and turned around. "Fine breakfast, Mrs. Richardson. Best I've eaten in years. Thanks."

And he fled. Grace stared after him with her mouth hanging open.

Maddie tilted her head. "Mr. Noah looks scared, Mommy. How come?"

Grace blinked at her daughter, then peeked at Mac, who grinned at her like a fox. Whole lot of help that was. "I, er, don't know, sweetheart."

Maddie said, "Hmmm."

Mac heaved an enormous sigh.

What a fool. What a blazing damned fool he was. Noah's heart thundered like a stampede of wild bulls, he couldn't catch his breath, his chest was so tight he could hardly stay upright, and his intestines were cramping as if his demons had taken hot tongs to them.

He didn't stop running, however, until he'd made it to the fence. There he doubled over for a minute, clutching his sides, until he was pretty sure he wouldn't pass out. He straightened slowly once his insides stopped hurting and his brain quit screaming. Then he took in several huge breaths of ice-cold air, hooked his arms on the top fence rail, and looked out into what he had begun to think of as his last hope on earth: The vast, empty, barren plains that stretched out beyond the tiny village of Rio Hondo forever and ever.

"Hal-lelujah!"

The words and music of Handel's famous chorus echoed in his head like a litany. He whispered them to himself, and they calmed him after a while. He noticed his fingers were moving, as if he were still sitting at Susan Blackworth's piano.

He'd played the "Hallelujah Chorus" on the pipe organ in church on Christmas Eve while the choir sang. When he was a boy, that service was probably the one he most looked forward to during the year. It had seemed to take eons before he'd been good enough that his father, who was the choir director, had allowed

Noah to play along with the choir. Noah remembered it well. He'd only been thirteen, and the congregation had been amazed and called him a prodigy. They'd even applauded, breaking into the silence that had echoed through the sanctuary when the last dramatic chords faded into the rafters. It had been his proudest moment.

"Cripes." Noah considered it a pathetic commentary on his life that its shining moment had occurred when he was thirteen years old.

No one in the congregation would even give him the time of day if they saw him now. He'd lost the respect of his fellow townsfolk, broken his parents' hearts, and alienated himself from his home forever when he'd joined the Union army instead of the Confederacy.

He'd believed he was acting upon his high ideals and firm moral principles when he'd determined to fight the good fight to eliminate the institution of slavery. Of course, his own family didn't own any slaves; they built and repaired pianos and organs for a living. What did they care about plantation owners whose businesses would suffer if slavery were abolished? Not that Noah condoned slavery for that reason; now, however, he understood what he couldn't understand in his youth: that folks fought change, no matter how good the cause engendered by it, especially if it hit them in the pocketbook.

What a dunce he'd been. Still was. The only thing his high-minded moral principles had earned him was the hatred of everyone he'd ever cared about. That and a stint in the foulest prison camp the world had ever known.

Andersonville.

He'd been—what?—nineteen when he'd joined up? Nineteen years old. What did a nineteen-year-old boy know about anything? He'd been twenty when he was captured, and he'd spent the next three years in prison, the last of that a year in the hell that was Andersonville. He was only twenty-seven today, but he felt like an old man. Looked like one too. He felt older than Mac, older than time, older than the ground he stood on.

In spite of the frigid weather, sweat crawled down Noah's back. He lowered his head until it rested on his folded arms and fought tears.

Would he never be whole again? Never? What was the use of living if he had to live like this, with demons forever running him?

He was out of practice. Everyone kept telling him that. Yeah, Noah was out of practice, all right. And no matter how much he tried, he didn't get any better. His father had told him that practice made perfect. Well, his dad had been right about music. Life was another matter entirely.

"Mr. Partridge?"

Noah whirled around, saw Grace Richardson standing there, and almost swore aloud.

Calm down, he ordered his frenzied nerves. *Calm down. This is the woman whose good will you need to earn if you ever expect her to sell you her land.*

He sucked in a deep, freezing breath. It was so cold it made his lungs ache, and he focused on the pain to distract himself from his unholy terrors. "Mrs. Richardson."

He willed himself to stand still and not run away. He'd already made an ass of himself in front of this woman once today. He didn't want to seal the impression in her mind that he was a lunatic, whether it was true or not.

Remember, he commanded himself. *You need her. You need her. You need her.* With those three words reverberating in his head like the "Hallelujah Chorus," Noah forced his lips into a grimace he hoped looked like a smile.

Good heavens, what could the matter be with the poor man? Was he mad? Grace didn't sense violence in Noah Partridge, at least not violence directed outward. His eyes looked wild, but he was trying to smile, trying to pretend he was all right. Grace recalled Uncle Henry, and felt a terrible sense of sorrow gnaw at her. This man reminded her so much of her uncle. It had taken Henry ages to get over the horrors he'd been through in the war.

"Is everything all right, Mr. Partridge? I'm sorry Maddie pestered you and chased you off this morning."

"Um, she didn't chase me off, ma'am."

"No?" Grace gave him a smile she hoped would convey her sympathy for his distress, even if she didn't truly understand what had caused it.

He shook his head and opened his mouth, but closed it again before he said anything else.

Take it slowly and gently, she cautioned herself. She didn't want to interfere, but she felt a compulsion to help this man if she could. Mac had told her he was troubled; Grace thought that was putting it mildly.

"Is there anything I can do for you, Mr. Partridge?"

His eyebrows lifted. "Ma'am?"

Blast. Grace chided herself for being maladroit.

She'd meant to be subtle. "I mean—" Oh, dear. She was so unused to subterfuge. She heaved an enormous sigh and decided yet again that she couldn't be anything but herself. "I mean, you seem so—so edgy. So restless. Nervous. If there's anything Maddie or Mac or I can do to help you to feel more at ease during your stay with us, we'd be more than happy to do it."

Good Lord, what if he was a vicious criminal on the run from the law? The startling thought frightened Grace for a split second. Then she remembered the magic he'd wrought with his fingers on Susan Blackworth's piano and took herself to task. Though she knew good and well that just because the man was talented didn't necessarily mean he *wasn't* a blackhearted scoundrel, it did tend to mitigate her fears. Besides, she trusted Mac implicitly, and Mac said Mr. Partridge was all right under his veneer of standoffishness and tension.

He uttered a short, humorless laugh. "You can sell me your land, ma'am. That's about all I can think of offhand that might help me."

Grace's lips tightened. "Anything other than that." The words came out tartly, and she regretted her tone. But she was annoyed that he'd turned her words against her when she'd been trying to offer him a measure of relief from his distress. "That land is all I have left of my late husband, Mr. Partridge. I'm sure you can understand what it means to me."

She felt like squirming under his penetrating gaze. Words bubbled up inside her, words she felt she needed in order to defend her position on the matter of her land. She almost gave in to the compulsion to say them until she recalled that she had no need to defend herself. That land was hers. Frank had bought it fair and square, and as long as she kept up the payments and taxes—admittedly a difficult prospect and one in which she was rather behind—it would remain hers. She needed no justification for wanting to keep what was already hers.

"Yes, ma'am. I reckon I understand."

He turned and gazed over the fence again, out into the empty plains. It seemed to Grace that he was doing his level best to thwart her good intentions to ease his worries. Was she being presumptuous? Probably. She huffed out a breath that billowed like whipped cream in the frosty air.

"Listen, Mr. Partridge, I don't know what's wrong with you. Maybe nothing is and you're merely a solitary, nervous sort of person, but please know that neither Maddie nor I would ever intentionally do anything to make you feel uncomfortable. Rio Hondo is—is a strange place. It's not like anywhere I've ever lived. Mac claims there's magic out here. I wouldn't know about that, but I do know that it's a lonely, isolated place and the people who live here need each other. I'd like to be your friend if you'd let me."

He muttered something Grace didn't catch. She decided not to let him off the hook. "I beg your pardon?"

For perhaps ten seconds Noah didn't move. Then he turned around so abruptly, Grace gave a start. "Mrs. Richardson, I know you're trying to be nice, but you don't know what you're saying. Hell, you don't know *me*. You might not want me for a friend if you did."

Annoyed, Grace snapped, "I believe you're being deliberately perverse, Mr. Partridge."

Noah shook his head. He looked about as frustrated

as she felt. "You don't know what you're talking about, ma'am, if you'll pardon my saying so."

Grace had never had so much trouble communicating with a person before. Even Uncle Henry had at least tried to appear normal. Oh, he'd been fidgety and as jumpy as a frightened cat. Loud noises had sent him into paroxysms of shivers and shakes, but when he was with the family, he'd at least attempted to relate.

"If you'll give me a chance, maybe I'll learn. I only want to help you."

"Dammit, Mrs. Richardson, there's only one way you can help me, and that's by selling me your land. I don't need any other help!"

"Oh, you're impossible!"

Stymied, Grace stared at Noah and stewed for several seconds, wondering if she should stand her ground and fight for his understanding or give up. It was unpleasant to have one's good intentions thrown back into one's face, especially when one was only offering friendship and a measure of compassion. She'd give anything to have more friends. It got intolerably lonely out here on the fringes of the frontier, where companionship was a luxury. But he was a tough nut to crack, was Noah Partridge. This morning Grace didn't have the energy to spare for him.

"Oh, never mind!" She whirled around, intending to stomp back to the house, and almost bumped smack into Mac.

"Mac!" She drew herself up short before she could run over him.

His smile was as benevolent and friendly as ever. Her heart registered appreciation, and she opened her mouth to greet him.

*　　*　　*

From the house, Alexander McMurdo had seen Grace and Noah at the fence. He shook his head. They were going at it, those two, and Mac could tell they were getting nowhere fast. Grace had no idea how much and what kind of damage Noah had sustained in the war. As for Noah himself, he was sure he was ruined forever and had given up on ever being whole again.

They definitely needed his help. Leaving little Maddie sleeping a magical sleep replete with happy dreams, he hastened outside to take care of things.

Grace almost bowled him over, but he lifted his hand, and she froze in mid-stride. Noah froze too, with an expression of anguish on his face, as if he wished he could do something to stop Grace from running away from him but didn't have the wherewithal to do it.

It was a useful tool, freezing people so he could work on them, although Mac used it sparingly. He was one of the ancients, and knew that most problems experienced by the human race worked themselves out— or didn't—in the natural course of time. But every now and then, as in the case of Noah Partridge and Grace Richardson, he liked to take a hand.

They were both good people, Noah and Grace. Mac loved them. They needed each other, too, as much as Maddie needed the two of them together.

Poor old Noah's inner workings were really knotted up, however, and his condition was getting in the way of any healing process. He needed more help than Grace did. Grace was still grieving for her lost Frank, but she was a basically sound woman. Noah needed work, and fast.

Very gently, Mac lifted Noah's hat from his head and waved his hand slowly over the young man's head three or four times. Nothing fancy needed here; he didn't bother with a wand or any of the other dramatic trappings of wizardry. Mac had graduated from needing the instruments of his discipline centuries before.

Sparkles like glittering dust particles filled the air, bathing Noah in shifting, shimmering light. Carefully, making sure he didn't skip an inch of the man, Mac dusted Noah with his healing magic. He paid particular attention to Noah's heart and his head, the two areas most severely damaged by years of hardship and bitter abandonment.

Mac's eyes filled with tears when Noah's memories became his. "Ah, ye poor lad," he whispered. "The things folks do to each other are mortal sad and hellish. But we'll get ye well again, lad. You just see if we don't."

It took a long time to finish with Noah. It would take longer yet, but Mac was willing to work with him for as long as the need remained.

Then he turned his attention to Grace. "Ye're a fine woman, Grace Richardson, but 'tis time to put your grief aside and let this poor man into your heart. Ye need each other, lass, and Maddie needs ye both."

Grace required much less time than Noah had. When Mac was through with her, he snapped his fingers and vanished into the house.

Noah blinked into the bright, harsh sunlight. He had an odd sensation in his chest, as if someone had lit a fire and thawed it out. He didn't want Grace to leave him.

Grace, feeling oddly as if she'd stumbled over a moment in time, caught herself before she could take another step. She turned around. "Oh, Mr. Partridge, I'm so sorry."

"No, ma'am. I'm the one who should be apologizing."

He looked impossibly uncomfortable. Grace's conscience smote her. "No. I have no business prying into your business. You obviously need solitude. I didn't mean to meddle."

"I, ah, guess I do need a lot of time alone, ma'am, but I don't necessarily like it."

Grace cocked her head, puzzled. She saw him lick his lips.

"I mean, I—I haven't been quite right since the war, to tell the truth, ma'am. I had some pretty bad times."

She nodded, her heart flooding with tenderness. "My uncle went through some terrible times, Mr. Partridge. I understand." She shook her head, annoyed with herself. "That is, I don't understand at all, because I've never been through anything so terrible, but I know how war can affect some men, because I've seen the results."

"It's hard for me to talk about it, Mrs. Richardson." He took an audible breath and looked away. "That is, I—haven't been able to talk about it yet. But that doesn't mean I don't appreciate your offer of friendship."

Grace was astonished when he smiled. He had such a beautiful smile, and he looked ever so much less forbidding when he smiled. She had a mad desire to see Noah Partridge as he might have been before the war got to him, to see him as a man who smiled as easily and as freely as he played the piano. She said, "Thank you," and wondered why.

"Um, if you're willing to put up with my moods and—and my craziness, ma'am, maybe you and Maddie would like to go for a ride one of these days. Maybe we can take a picnic or something out by one of the rivers."

He looked disconcerted, as though his offer had surprised him as much as it astonished Grace. "I mean, not alone or anything. We can all go. Mac too. When the weather's better and all." His words stuttered to a stop and he blushed. Grace could hardly believe her eyes.

How sweet. She smiled at him. "That would be lovely, Mr. Partridge. Maddie and I would both enjoy it. Thank you."

He nodded, and she got the impression he didn't know what to say now. This was silly. He couldn't remain outside on a day like this.

"Mr. Partridge, it's very cold today. Won't you come into the house? You don't have to talk to anyone. I'll be giving Maddie her lessons, and Mac is always busy in the store. There are lots of books in there, and it's warm. Won't you join us?"

He hesitated for several moments. Grace was surprised that his apprehension didn't annoy her. She reached out her hand and laid it gently on his arm. He looked down at it. Grace got the feeling he wished he dared touch her. She almost wished the same thing.

At last he said, "Thanks. I'd like that."

Mac watched them walk back to the house side by

side, closer together than either one of them realized. Even their steps were synchronized. Mac grinned and blew a series of smoke rings into the air. His touch remained sure. This was getting good.

He planned to make sure the weather was fine for a picnic very soon. He had one more trick up his sleeve before that, though. He looked forward to it.

Chapter Nine

At three o'clock the following afternoon, a family of settlers rattled into Mac's wagon yard. The weather remained cold. When Noah had awakened that morning, frost had covered his bedroll. When he'd sat up, he'd heard ice crystals crunch as his blanket wrinkled. The frost had melted by this time, but the air was like the inside of an ice house, and a strong wind cut through it like shards of glass. Inhospitable to most folks. It appealed to Noah more than he could say. He still harbored a faintly peaceful feeling left over from the day before, too, and he cherished it.

He watched the newcomers from his stall where he'd been reading *The Personal History of David Copperfield*, one of several books he'd brought to the Territory with him. As he watched, he wondered what it must be like for a family to pick up stakes and take off across this huge American continent to settle in new, unfamiliar territory. He'd left his home state and taken off across the country, but he'd had no stakes left at the time.

He heard the door to Mac's mercantile open and turned to see Maddie and Mac come out. He watched them head over to greet the newcomers, Maddie skipping along at Mac's side and looking as if this were the most exciting thing to happen to her since she'd heard that piano music the other day—which it possibly was.

Noah shook his head. His own desire to have her land aside, he couldn't understand why Grace Richardson wanted to put her own little girl, whom she obviously loved with all her heart, through the rigors of growing up out here in the Territory. Shoot, growing up was hard enough even when a kid had friends and family around.

But Maddie's upbringing should be nothing to him. What Grace did with her kid was her own affair. His only problem was how to get her land away from her. Roughly he told himself so when he realized his mind had taken to meandering fondly around thoughts of Grace.

"Welcome to Rio Hondo, strangers," Mac called to a bearded man driving a team of exhausted-looking oxen. The man seemed relieved to hear the friendly greeting.

"Good afternoon, mister. Understand you can help me repair this here wagon. She's got a wheel on her that's barely holding together."

"Aye," said Mac. "You've come to the right place for wagon repairs."

"Thank God." The bearded man turned and spoke

into the back of his covered wagon. "It's all right, Pauline. You and the children can get down now." He turned back to Mac. "The kids were taking a nap back there. Don't know where they found the room." He chuckled, sounding rueful. Noah didn't wonder at it. It must be difficult, carrying a family's entire belongings in so small a vehicle.

The bearded gent climbed down from the wagon. Faintly curious and figuring he might make himself useful, Noah wandered over to the strangers. Maddie and Mac greeted him as if they were happy to see him. He found himself enjoying their congeniality. Friendship. Is this what friendship used to feel like? Noah couldn't remember, but he warned himself not to get used to it, because it would end soon enough.

"It's my birthday, Mr. Noah!" Maddie announced eagerly. "And Mac says these new people are like a present!".

Cripes. Was it really the kid's birthday? Noah wished he'd known earlier. He'd have found or made something to give her. A present or something. That was what folks were supposed to do for kids' birthdays, wasn't it?

"Happy birthday, Miss Maddie. How old are you today?" He knew the answer, of course, but couldn't think of anything better to say.

"I'm six," she declared proudly. "And Mommy's baking me a real choc'lit cake."

"Sounds good."

Two children, a boy and a girl, both about Maddie's age, walked out from behind the back of the wagon. Noah watched Maddie's expression bloom into joy. She clasped her hands to her chest as if this were the happiest moment of her short life. His heart gave a painful spasm. What a life it was! Criminy, that little girl's life was even more circumscribed than his own.

"Oh, look!" Maddie sounded ecstatic.

"Aye, Maddie-lass. Looks like ye have some children to share your birthday wi' ye."

"Oh, yes!" Maddie raced over to meet the two children. "My name is Maddie Richardson. Who are you?"

The girl smiled uncertainly and hung back a bit from Maddie's exuberance. "My name's Anastasia," she said. "This here's my brother Paul. We're twins."

Maddie cocked her head as if this information were fascinating to her. "What's twins?"

Anastasia said, "Twins look alike. Sometimes you can't even tell 'em apart. You can tell Paul and me apart, though, 'cause he's a boy and I'm a girl. Twins are borned at the same time."

"Oh." Maddie nodded, accepting Anastasia's explanation easily. Noah grinned as he watched Maddie's attention transfer to Paul. "What's the matter with your brother? Is he shy?"

Evidently taking Maddie's question as a challenge, Paul straightened himself up and took a bold step forward. "I ain't shy," he asserted stoutly.

Unaffected by his show of bravado, Maddie grinned and said, "Good. I'm glad, 'cause it's my birthday, and I'm six, and my mommy's making me a real choc'lit cake and fried chicken for supper, and you can eat with us."

"Thank you," said Anastasia. "Happy birthday." She smiled a shy smile, and Noah's heart warmed up and got mushy. Cripes, if he didn't watch himself, he'd turn into some kind of maudlin soup here in this backwater of a territorial village on the edge of nowhere.

"We were six a long time ago," said Paul, obviously not wanting to be outdone by Maddie.

Maddie ignored him, which Noah thought was very wise of her, all things considered. "Want to see my dolly? My mommy made her for me. Her name's Priscilla."

"I've got a dolly, too," said Anastasia.

"Want to play together?"

Maddie's eyes were as bright as stars. Noah wished he could wave a magic wand and make the world beautiful for her. But he couldn't. The best he could do was buy her daddy's property and give her mama some money, if Grace would ever allow him to.

The children walked off toward the house, the two little girls chattering away as if they'd known each other since birth, the boy dragging his feet. It looked to Noah as if Paul didn't want to be seen playing with girls, but was hard-pressed to keep up his air of aloofness and superiority since there weren't any other children around. He must be lonely as the dickens for kids his own age to play with.

Noah suspected the boy's pretense of masculine pride would crumble soon enough, and he'd be playing with the girls before very much time passed.

He was right. Long before Noah had helped Mac and the newcomer, whose name was Claude Merchant, repair the broken wheel on his wagon, the three children were ensconced in Mac's store, playing together in the warmth of the potbellied stove like chums of long standing.

After the repairs were completed and the Merchants

177

had been ushered into Mac's store to meet Grace and purchase supplies, Noah went back to his stall, sat on his hay bale, and looked around. Now what could he give to little Maddie Richardson to make her birthday happier? He had no idea. What the hell did he know about children and, more particularly, little girl children?

Then, out of the blue, something occurred to him. He sat up straight on his hay bale and turned the notion over in his mind. He expected it to hurt, but it didn't, which seemed encouraging to him. Shoot, maybe this one tiny thing in his life was healing over.

Probably not.

Nevertheless, he got up, went to the neat pile of his belongings stacked in the corner of his stall, and reached for his saddlebags. From deep inside one of them, underneath the Bible his mother had given him when he was twelve, way down where he never had to look at it, he withdrew a small, decorative, heart-shaped gold locket on a short golden chain. He hesitated before he opened the locket, because he wasn't sure what his reaction was going to be, and he didn't fancy having another fit.

Finally he pressed the clasp, the locket opened, and there she was. Julia. She'd given him the tiny picture years and years ago—to remember her by, she'd said, when he went off to war. Noah recalled that day vividly. He'd felt so damned noble and so damned sad. Julia had had tears in her eyes.

He'd bought the locket to hold the picture somewhere in Washington right after he'd joined the regiment, thinking he'd give her the locket when he got home again, sure she'd still be waiting for him. Hell, she'd cried over him, hadn't she? He'd intended to get the back of it engraved with their initials, but now he was glad he hadn't had the chance to do so.

"What a damned dunderhead I was back then," he muttered, staring at the face in the locket. She'd sure been pretty, Julia had. Dark eyes, dark hair all shiny and cut and curled. She'd been a real belle. She hadn't waited, of course, but married another man not six months after she'd promised to wait for Noah. And now Julia was dead and Noah wasn't, and he still carried her picture around in this damned locket, a reminder of his youthful follies. He sighed.

"Ah, what the hell. At least Maddie Richardson's alive. She'll probably value it a hell of a lot more than Julia ever would have."

The truth didn't make him feel appreciably better. He stuck the small photograph of Julia into the Bible, shoved the Bible to the bottom of his saddlebag, snapped the locket shut, and wondered if he'd just made a big mistake.

Later that evening, however, when he joined the Merchants, the Richardsons, and Mac for Maddie's birthday dinner, he realized he felt freer somehow, as if by ridding himself of that last vestige of Julia's betrayal, he'd purged himself of a burden. He was probably just being whimsical again.

"I'm so glad you could join us, Mr. Partridge," Grace said with a warm smile of greeting. "I know you don't like to socialize very much." She blushed, and Noah suspected she thought she'd said something rude. As if the truth could be considered discourteous.

"Thank you for inviting me, Mrs. Richardson." He decided not to touch upon the subject of his lack of

179

social graces—or his lunacy. It was hiding out of sight at the moment, but he knew it was ready to spring out at him at the least provocation. If he went crazy and had to rush outside to escape the party, he trusted that Grace would make his apologies for him. At least now she knew what ailed him, sort of. She seemed to be good at gracious apologies, too.

Dinner was delicious. It didn't seem to Noah that Grace had been at all daunted by the prospect of feeding four more people than she'd originally planned on. He'd seen her earlier, heading out to the chicken coop with a hatchet in her hands, and guessed then that she aimed to sacrifice a second chicken for her daughter's sake and the sake of the strangers. At least Grace and her daughter didn't lack for food, thanks to Mac. Noah wondered how they'd have fared without the kind-hearted Scotsman's help.

"This is my favorite meal, Anastasia," Maddie confided to her new friend. "Fried chicken and corn and 'tatoes."

The two little girls had been giggling ever since Noah walked inside the house. If he'd been asked if he'd enjoy hearing a couple of six-year-olds giggling before he heard these two, he would have said he'd as soon skip it. However, he found himself oddly comforted as he listened to them. They sounded happy. Even Paul had fallen from his superior masculine pedestal—looked like he'd jumped off, actually—and giggled almost as much as the girls. Something warm snaked its way into Noah's heart and curled up there, heating him on the inside.

Grace looked like she was as pleased as anything to have another female to talk to. She and Mrs. Merchant were going at it a mile a minute. Mr. Merchant, a taciturn man, didn't speak much, but he kept casting tolerant glances at his wife and Grace, and Noah liked him for it.

Mac, of course, presided over the gathering as if he were Old King Cole himself, watching everyone's goings-on with a benevolent eye, and contributing a tidbit here and there to keep the conversation going. Noah didn't have to say much of anything, thank God.

The three kids sat at a table made of crates hauled in from Mac's store. Their special table was set apart from the adults because there wasn't enough room at the grown-up table. They didn't seem to mind at all. Noah remembered the tea parties his sister and her friends used to have. This reminded him of those long-gone days.

When supper was over, Grace and Mrs. Merchant cleared the two tables. Then Grace vanished into the kitchen and came back holding a masterpiece of a chocolate birthday cake for Maddie. Noah was impressed. He hadn't eaten a piece of chocolate cake for ages. He'd never eaten one that tasted as good as this one.

When they retired to Mac's parlor after devouring the cake, the room was plenty crowded, what with four more people in it than it generally had to hold. No one seemed to mind, though. Even Noah didn't get to feeling too crowded, although he did make sure he remained near the door, just in case.

Maddie modeled the new dress her mother had made her. "And see? She made Priscilla one just like it." She held up that old rag doll of hers—and rag pretty much described it—and her eyes danced with joy.

"That's so pretty." Anastasia held her hands together at her chest and didn't seem to notice Priscilla's deficiencies. Noah admired her for it.

He cleared his throat. This was the time, he reckoned, if ever there was one. "Uh, I have a little something for you in honor of your birthday, Miss Maddie."

Maddie's face lit up and her eyes widened, and she looked so happy, Noah got embarrassed.

Grace gaped at him. "Oh, Mr. Partridge, there was no need for you to go to the trouble of—"

"It was no trouble, Mrs. Richardson. I already had it." He shrugged. "Just thought maybe Miss Maddie here could use it. I sure can't."

That didn't sound altogether chivalrous, but Noah was out of practice. People kept telling him that. Well, he guessed they were right. He dug in his breast pocket and withdrew the locket. He didn't even feel a pang when he opened his hand and allowed the chain to dangle from his fingers. He took his lack of emotion as a good sign.

The golden locket glinted in the light from the fireplace as it twirled on its chain. Everyone in the room gasped as if he'd performed some sort of magic trick. That embarrassed him too.

"Ooooooh," Maddie breathed. She didn't step forward to take the locket, but only stared at it, mesmerized.

"That's much too fine a gift, Mr. Partridge," Grace said after an awed moment. "Much too fine. It's—it's beautiful."

He lifted his head and looked at her. Criminy, what was he supposed to do now? Take it back? He couldn't do that. He shook his head. "I don't think so, ma'am.

It's just a small locket, and it's something I already had. She can put a picture of—'' Of what? Inspiration struck. ''—of her daddy in it. If you have one small enough to fit.''

Damn. Noah hated even hearing about the saintly Frank. But Frank had been Maddie's father. He guessed she'd like a keepsake of him. She probably couldn't even remember what he looked like anymore.

He saw Grace swallow. ''Yes,'' she said. ''I do have one that will probably fit.''

Aw, hell, she was crying. He hadn't meant to make her cry.

Maddie slowly walked up to him. ''Can I really put a picture of Daddy in it? Does it have a place for a picture?'' Her tone was reverent, as if Noah were presenting her with a holy relic.

He blessed her for the question, because it gave him something to do other than stare at Grace and wish he could put his arms around her and wipe her tears away. ''Sure, Miss Maddie. Let me show you.''

So Noah sat on a chair by the front door, and Maddie promptly climbed onto his lap. He couldn't remember ever having a kid on his lap before. He didn't even feel odd about it. In fact, it felt kind of nice to know that Maddie both liked and trusted him. Him, of all people! Crazy old Noah Partridge. Wonders never ceased, he reckoned.

''Let me see that thing.''

Noah looked up to find Mac grinning at him. The old man walked over and stood behind Noah to watch while he fingered the catch to the locket. When Mac put a hand on Noah's shoulder, Noah felt a strange tingling sensation there. He wasn't altogether surprised when he saw sparkles in the air. Good old Mac. Up to his magic tricks again. He blinked and endeavored to ignore the glimmering dots floating in the air.

"See here, Miss Maddie? What you do, is you press this little latch here." He showed her. "Your fingers are real small, so it'll be easy for you to work it."

"It's so pretty, Mr. Noah. Thank you very much."

"You're very welcome." He returned her smile. Shoot, he couldn't recall ever having been smiled at like this by a little kid. He'd never known any kids except for Julia's bratty brother, and Noah'd never liked him. "Anyway, when you press that latch, the locket springs open. See?"

He pressed the catch, and Maddie squealed with joy when the locket opened up. There were spaces for two pictures in it, one on either side of the heart. Noah had once believed his likeness and Julia's would share the locket, fool that he was.

Maddie's little fingers indicated each space in turn. "There's a place for two pictures in here, Mr. Noah."

"Um-hum."

She lifted her head and stared straight into his eyes. "Can I have a picture of you to put in there? Along with my daddy's picture?"

Noah stared at her. She wanted a picture of *him?* What in blazes for? "I, ah, I don't think you want to carry a picture of me around with you, Miss Maddie. You need a picture of your mama to put in there with the one of your daddy."

"Oh." She frowned.

Noah got the feeling she was dissatisfied with his answer. He shot a glance at Grace and felt almost desperate to clear up any misunderstanding. He hadn't meant for this to happen. "I—ah—I mean, if you have a picture of your daddy in there, wouldn't you rather have a picture of your mama to go in there with it? I mean—I mean, they were married and all."

He heard Mac chuckle softly behind him and didn't appreciate it. Shoot, he could use some help here, not one of Mac's enigmatical bouts of hilarity.

"But I have mommy here all the time. She told me you might go away again and if you do, I want to be able to remember what you look like."

Stunned, Noah muttered, "You do? Why?"

" 'Cause I like you. 'Cause you're nice. And 'cause you gave me this locket and I love it. It's the prettiest thing I ever saw."

Out of the corner of his eye, Noah saw Grace lift a hand and brush it across her eyes. She looked like she was trying to pretend she wasn't crying, but she was, and he knew it. Cripes. He hadn't meant to make anyone sad here; he'd only been trying to give a kid a birthday present. He'd been improvising, for the love of God, like he used to do in church on the organ when there was too much time left over after the preacher finished his sermon.

"I, uh, don't have any pictures of myself, Miss Maddie."

"Oh." She sounded terribly disappointed.

"Maybe you can draw a picture of Mr. Partridge, Maddie," Grace suggested. Her voice sounded as if her throat was constricted.

"Good idea!" exclaimed Mac.

"But—but, you don't really want my picture in there, Miss Maddie." Criminy, she was just a kid. Noah kept reminding himself of that, because the idea of her wanting to keep his likeness in her locket was beginning to appeal to him way too much. He couldn't afford to get attached to anyone, much less a little child like Maddie Richardson.

"Sure she does," said Mac.

"I can help you, Maddie," said Grace. "We can draw a fine likeness of Mr. Partridge."

Noah looked up and his gaze got trapped in hers for a moment. Her expression was almost unbearably tender. He looked away first, unable to take in so much blatant caring. He wasn't used to it. It was like after they'd hauled him out of that prison camp, when he'd been nearly dead with starvation and illness and he could take in nothing but thin soups and dry bread for weeks and weeks. Anything rich would have come right back up again. That's the way he felt about Grace Richardson's expression. It was too rich. Too sweet. He couldn't tolerate it.

But, shoot! They didn't really want his ugly face in that locket with a likeness of Maddie's daddy. Did they? They couldn't possibly.

"That's just the sweetest thing, Mr. Partridge. Just the sweetest thing."

Noah jerked his head to the right and saw Mrs. Merchant wiping her eyes, too. Well, hell. He'd just been giving a child a birthday present.

"Thank you very much, Mr. Noah."

"You're welcome, Miss Maddie."

He was getting awfully itchy, being the center of attention this way. He could feel the pressure building up inside of him and hoped it wouldn't bubble over into an explosion of craziness. Not now. Not here. Not during Maddie's birthday party.

Then Maddie gave him a smacking kiss on the cheek, and any thought of cracking up flew right out of his head. She scrambled down from his lap and Noah was left to press his hand to his cheek and wonder why being kissed by a little girl should make his whole miserable life feel so much less miserable.

Grace watched Maddie and Noah and thought what a nice man he was, underneath all his nervousness and battle-scarred memories. She felt silly crying until she saw that Pauline Merchant was sniffling too, and then she felt a kinship with her rather than an alienation from the rest of the parlor-dwellers. Mac gave her one of his ever-ready winks, too, and she knew she wasn't being merely overwrought and emotional. The moment was genuinely tender, and Grace suspected she'd cherish it forever.

Imagine that hard man giving her daughter such a delicate, lovely gift! What a surprise. What an enigma he was. Not for the first time she wondered what Noah Partridge might have been like if he'd lived in easier times, if there hadn't been a terrible war to rip his life to tatters and spit him out as the damaged creature he was today.

She heaved a sigh, and was just in time to catch Maddie when she hurtled out of Noah's lap and into her arms.

"Look, Mommy! See what Mr. Noah gave me? Isn't it beautiful?"

"It certainly is, Maddie. It's perfectly lovely."

Grace's sentimental mood lasted for several more minutes, as Maddie showed everyone in the room her locket, how it opened, and exactly where she was going to put her daddy's and Noah's pictures. Grace caught Noah's eyes a couple of times, but he glanced away immediately whenever it happened. Poor man. Poor, wounded man.

Gradually the atmosphere lightened. Pretty soon, the two little girls began singing songs. Grace joined them, and so did Pauline. Then Paul's teetering reserve crashed and he sang, too, along with his father and Mac.

Grace's evening was complete when she heard Noah Partridge, very softly and looking as if it embarrassed him to do so, join in the happy group when they all sang "The Battle Hymn of the Republic." She very nearly teared up again, but didn't, and was proud of herself.

The Merchants stayed at Mac's wagon yard until three days after Maddie's birthday party. They set off again on a Tuesday, in spite of the icy wind blowing over the plains and the wall of black thunderheads hovering in the sky to the east like monsters about to pounce on the puny mortals who dared to live on the earth below them.

The Merchants were determined to make it to Pauline's brother's ranch near the New Mexico Territory-Arizona Territory border before Christmas, they said. Noah wished them luck.

He watched Grace and Mrs. Merchant embrace, tears streaming down their faces, and wondered why people chose to put themselves through the agony of uprooting themselves, tearing themselves away from friends and family, and starting over in precarious new settings. For the sake of cheap land? To make a new life because the old one was so rotten? He guessed he could understand that because it was the reason he was in Rio Hondo himself.

Still, it was hard for him to watch those two women bid each other farewell. They'd never see each other again; he knew it and they knew it, and the truth made them both sad. Truth had a way of doing that, in his experience.

Anastasia and Maddie, too, were sad to be parting company. Even Paul looked like he was having a hard time appearing bored with the females farewells. Noah knew exactly what Paul was feeling inside, though, and it was anything but bored. The poor lad was doing his level best to "act like a man," whatever the hell that was. Noah remembered doing the same thing when he was six, about a million years ago.

Grace and Pauline waved hankies at each other as the Merchants' wagon lumbered off. Both ladies were still crying.

"I'll write!" Pauline called out. "As soon as we get settled somewhere!"

"Please do!" Grace called back. "It will be so good to hear from you! I'll write back!"

Noah wondered if they'd ever hear from each other again. For all anyone knew, the Merchants might get wiped out by cholera or diphtheria or any one of a million other illnesses that preyed on the folks who traversed the hard trails west. Or they might be attacked by a roving band of desperadoes or Indians—although, Noah knew, Indians generally didn't bother settlers' wagons.

He admired the Indians for their forbearance. If he saw a bunch of people trying to take over his land,

189

Noah wasn't sure he'd be so tolerant. On the other hand, the army'd pretty much eliminated the Indians from the area. His heart felt heavy as he contemplated the Indian situation.

Oh, well, that was merely one more problem over which he had no control. Hell, more often than not, he didn't even have control over his own life.

The wagon trailed a huge cloud of dust behind it as it rocked over the bare, dry, cold land away from Rio Hondo. Grace, Maddie, and Mac stood outside and stared for a long time before they turned and headed back to the house.

Noah saw Grace and Maddie trying to be brave in the face of their latest loss. Then he looked after the retreating wagon, and he waved, too.

Chapter Ten

"My goodness, I know the weather out here is change-able, but I've never known it to change this fast."

"Aye," said Mac with one of his more mysterious smiles. " 'Tis a fine day for a drive out on the plains, lass."

Grace glanced up at him from the pot of hot lard in which she was frying doughnuts. He looked extremely self-satisfied, as if the weather were somehow his do-ing. She laughed. "Don't get any ideas in that canny old head of yours, Alexander McMurdo. Mr. Partridge and I are only trying to mend some fences." She frowned. "We had more words the day before the Mer-chants rode into the yard."

Mac raised his eyebrows. They were full and white and looked like the wings of a bird when he did that. "Did ye now?"

"Yes." Grace shot him a glance. She felt guilty

about having pursued Noah that day and forcing him to talk to her, especially now, since he'd been so kind to Maddie on her birthday. Maddie wore her new locket everywhere, and she was very careful with it. Grace sighed over her doughnuts. "I think perhaps I was too hard on him. A little bit. Maybe."

"You? Grace Richardson? Hard on a fellow?" There went Mac's eyebrows again. Grace grinned at his expression of incredulity.

"Yes. Can you believe it of me? I actually butted into the poor man's business and tried to pry his problems out of him. I thought that if he talked about them, he'd feel better, you see."

"Tsk, Grace, a crime, that."

Grace laughed. "Well, it wasn't very nice of me. After all, his problems are none of my business. But the poor man! He needs friends, Mac."

"Aye, lass, he does, and ye'll be a good one to him."

"Do you think so?" She was pleased to hear Mac's opinion on the matter. It made her feel not quite so much like a busybody and a bully.

"Aye, I do, if he can let himself accept ye."

Vaguely troubled by Mac's qualification, Grace lifted a doughnut out of the pot with a big slotted spoon. She laid it on a piece of butcher paper to blot up the excess grease. "He wants to buy Frank's land, you know."

"Aye."

"I wish you hadn't shown it to him."

"And why not? D'ye think he'll steal it from ye?"

She gave a startled laugh. "Heavens, no! But I know he thinks I'm being merely stubborn in not selling it to him. He told me it would be too difficult for me to work the land by myself. He got rather huffy about it, actually.''

''Mayhap the lad's right, lass. Runnin' a homestead in the territory's a hard business, ye know.''

''Mac!'' She was so alarmed by his words that she nearly dropped her spoon. ''That land is all I have left of Frank. It was Frank's legacy to our children—child! I can't give it up!''

''Don't take on so, lass. I'm not faultin' ye for your desire to cling like a bulldog to that land o' yours. But, lass, Frank's dead. He's been dead these two years and more.''

Feeling betrayed, Grace bowed her head. Tears filled her eyes. ''I know that. Do you think I can ever forget?''

''Nay, lass.'' Mac came over to her and patted her on the shoulder. ''But ye might consider movin' on one of these days.''

She sniffled and felt foolish when she had to pass the back of her hand over her eyes to wipe away her tears. She must have pressed too hard because stars swam before her eyes for a moment. That had been happening a lot since she came to live at Mac's wagon yard. Those sparkling dots were an odd, not unpleasant, phenomenon. Mac's words filled her heart with dread, though.

''What do you mean, I should think about moving on? Do you want us to move? Are we a bother to you?'' She didn't want to get in Mac's way. He'd been their most compassionate friend ever since she and Frank had moved out here. If he was tired of having her and Maddie living with him, Grace wasn't sure she could survive. She might have to move back to Chicago, and she didn't want to do that, because it would mean giving up.

He chuckled softly, and she felt better immediately. "Nay, lass, I don't want ye to be movin' on from here. But one of these days, ye'll have to move on from Frank. Ye know it in your heart, Grace."

She lifted her head and peered at him keenly, not best pleased by his assessment of her situation. "I'm not sure what you mean, Mac. If you think I'll ever forget Frank, you're wrong. I loved him."

"Aye, lass, I know that. And he loved you. You and your Frank had a happy life together. It was a crime when he was taken from ye so tragically. But ye have your Maddie, and ye have your health. Ye're a lovely woman, Grace Richardson. There's many a man as would be proud to take care of ye both."

Now Grace felt doubly betrayed. "I don't want another man."

Mac shook his head. "I know that, lass, and I'm not sayin' ye should take another husband merely to make your life easier. But I do think it's time ye opened your eyes and gazed about you."

She shook her head, unable to respond.

"Frank loved you, Grace. And he loved your little Maddie. He wouldn't want ye pinin' over his memory all your whole life long. He'd want better for you than that, lass."

Every one of Grace's senses rebelled. She whispered, "No." Even thinking about taking another husband made her heart ache. That would be deserting Frank, being false to his memory. She'd loved him more dearly than life itself.

"I don't want to talk about it, Mac," she said softly. "I'm sorry."

His smile conveyed deep understanding. Grace knew he understood—that's why his conversation this morning troubled her so much. She and Mac had talked hundreds of times about her marriage and her goals. Mac knew what she aimed to do; she couldn't comprehend why he seemed to be turning on her all of a sudden.

"Ah, lass, I'm not turnin' on ye."

Blast! Every time he did that, he startled her. She managed a tiny, tense smile. "There you go again, Mac, reading my thoughts."

He chuckled. "Forgive me, lass. I didn't mean to make ye sad."

She shrugged. "It's all right. I guess I'm a little touchy on the subject of Frank and marriage."

"Aye. A little, I'd say." He chuckled again and walked over to the back door.

When he flung it open, Grace saw Noah Partridge walking up to the door hand in hand with Maddie. Her mouth fell open in astonishment. It looked as if Maddie were leading Noah, whose face held an expression of absolute befuddlement, as if he couldn't quite figure out how he'd come to be holding a child's hand. Grace expected he'd had little to do with it. Maddie was a determined creature. The little girl saw her mother and waved. Grace waved back.

"Mr. Noah and I put the saddle and bridle on Old Blue, Mommy! We're going on a picnic, Mac!"

"Aye, lass. Your mother told me. She's making some doughnuts to take along wi' ye."

"Doughnuts! My favorite!" Maddie's eyes lit up as

if Mac had promised her the moon and stars.

Watching her daughter, a quick, unexpected shaft of defeat pierced her heart. Mac was right. She wasn't being fair to Maddie, keeping her out here in the Territory where simply the promise of a doughnut was exhilarating. Her daughter deserved better than what Grace could give her by herself. Maddie looked so happy walking along, hand-in-hand with Noah Partridge. She deserved a father. Playmates.

Maybe Grace should consider remarrying. At the notion, her blood ran cold.

Then she realized what Maddie had said. "Old Blue?" She looked questioningly at Noah, who shrugged uncomfortably.

"Mac said he thought Miss Maddie might like to ride by herself today."

Grace whirled on Mac. "Mac! Maddie can't ride well enough to sit a horse by herself."

"Calm down, lass. Old Blue isn't rightly a horse, ye ken. He's an old, placid mule, and he's as gentle as a summer breeze. I've led Maddie around the yard on his back countless times."

"But—but this is different." She was beginning to feel outmaneuvered and overburdened, as though they were all ganging up on her.

"I'll lead her, Mrs. Richardson."

She frowned at Noah. "I think it would have been appropriate to ask me first, Mr. Partridge." Her voice sounded strained to her own ears.

Noah looked at the ground at his feet. She didn't get the feeling he was abashed so much as annoyed. Irked in her own right, she snapped, "She's only a little girl."

196

"I'm six!" Now even Maddie sounded indignant. "I know how to ride a horse, Mommy."

Grace expelled a heavy breath. "Very well," she said ungraciously. "But you must promise me you'll be very careful, Maddie. Never let go of the saddle horn, and do everything Mr. Partridge and I tell you to do."

Maddie's face lit up like Christmas. "I will, Mommy! I already promised Mr. Noah I would."

Hmmm. Grace eyed Noah, who nodded without smiling. She entertained an odd, unpleasant feeling that she'd just been unreasonable. Still, Maddie was her daughter. It was up to Grace to protect her and guide her actions, not Noah Partridge or Alexander Mc-Murdo. The suspicion that she was jealous of Maddie's affection for these two men paid her brain a brief visit. She didn't thrust it aside, but she was awfully irritated that it sounded like the truth.

Well, there was no getting around it. Maddie would be riding Old Blue, and there was obviously nothing Grace could do about it. Feeling besieged, she muttered, "I'll finish packing the lunch."

"I'll help you, Mommy." Maddie let go of Noah's hand, pranced to her mother's side, and gave her a huge, happy smile. Grace felt much better about the day than she had only seconds earlier.

Noah couldn't remember the last time he'd held a kid's hand. Maybe he never had. He'd always tried to stay as far away from Julia's baby brother as he could because the kid been such an ill-behaved child. Now he was a dead ill-behaved child. Noah wasn't sure he'd

197

been enough of a brat to warrant that fate—but then, the war hadn't played favorites.

He hadn't wanted to hold Maddie's hand, either, but she'd given him no choice in the matter. She'd latched onto him like a clamp. Unless he'd wanted to shake her off and hurt her feelings—which he didn't—he'd had to go along with her. He was surprised he hadn't resented it more. Blamed kid presumed too blasted much. She bothered him. Just because he'd given her that stupid locket was no reason for her to take advantage of his good nature—not that he had one.

That being the case, he couldn't account for the desolation he felt when she let go of his hand and went to her mother's side. He shook his head, told himself he thought too damned much, and realized Mac was grinning at him. He frowned and turned toward the stable.

"I'll go saddle up a horse for Mrs. Richardson."

"You do that, lad."

Mac's chuckle followed Noah out of the house and into the stable.

Yet the day was fine, Noah actually felt almost human for a change, and he couldn't hang onto his irritation to save his life. In fact, when he, Grace, and Maddie waved good-bye to Mac and set out through the big gates of the wagon yard, his heart felt lighter than it had in years.

He watched little Maddie Richardson like a hawk. He'd already annoyed Maddie's mother once this morning. He didn't aim to earn her eternal enmity by letting her kid fall off that mule and hurt herself. He needed Grace Richardson. He needed her because he wanted her land. He kept reminding himself of that last part since it had a tendency to slip his mind.

It was because Mrs. Richardson was so blasted appealing. That's why he kept forgetting. It had been so long since Noah'd had occasion to appreciate human attractiveness that he'd forgotten how difficult it was to concentrate on other things in its presence. Even with that silly calico sunbonnet covering up her hair and shading her face, she was as pretty as a picture. In fact, he almost wished his old friend Bobby Garfield was here. Bobby had been a fine portrait painter. Until he'd had his right hand shot off in the war.

Noah wished he hadn't remembered that part.

In order to dispel the mood generated by his depressing recollection, he cleared his throat and spoke. "I'm sorry I didn't ask you about the mule, Mrs. Richardson. Mac and Maddie said it would be all right for Maddie to ride Old Blue. I thought they'd already cleared it with you." That sounded like he was making excuses, and Noah mentally chided himself. "I should have asked you first anyway." There. That was better.

Her smile lit up his insides. "I'm the one who should apologize, Mr. Partridge. I'm just so used to doing everything for Maddie, it—surprised me when the two of you took the decision about transportation out of my hands."

"Didn't mean to usurp your responsibility, ma'am," he mumbled.

"Don't be silly."

Grace laughed, a silvery, tinkling sound that feathered over Noah like a benediction. He even shut his eyes for a second and let it seep into his pores, imagining that her laugh could help cure what ailed him.

Fat chance. He didn't know what to say, so he kept quiet.

She took the burden of keeping the conversation going from his shoulders. "Did I hear Mac right when he said your family's piano and organ business was lost during the war, Mr. Partridge?"

Noah's insides cramped immediately. He made a valiant effort not to double over in his saddle with pain. He told himself that this was no time to be letting his soldier's heart play mean tricks on him, which did about as much good as his lectures to himself ever did. After he caught his breath, he said, "Yes, ma'am."

She shook her head, and he could see her genuine sympathy. "I'm so sorry. How did it happen?"

His cramps were easing up some, but Noah still wasn't sure he could talk much without groaning. "Burned to the ground."

"My goodness. Did you lose many instruments?"

"All of them."

"Oh, dear. How tragic. Do you know how it happened? Was it during a battle or something?"

Noah glanced sideways and saw her clear blue eyes wide with questions. Damn. She wanted an explanation.

Well, hell, maybe it was time. He could experiment with Grace Richardson, who seemed to have a warm heart. She'd already told him she had a crazy uncle. Maybe she'd understand if he had a fit when he tried to talk about what had happened to him.

He licked his lips and took an experimental breath. No cramp. Good. "Um, yes. I know how it happened. It wasn't in connection with a battle." There. That hadn't been so hard.

"Oh."

Noah darted another glance at her. She was frowning, puzzled. He couldn't make himself elaborate. Maybe if she asked him outright, he could force himself to explain.

"I'm sorry. That must have been awfully hard for your family."

He nodded again, unwilling to trust his voice to work right.

Maddie's voice piped up. "How did it happen, Mr. Noah?"

He jerked in his saddle. Even though he held Maddie's mule's lead rein, he'd forgotten the girl was there, her eager little ears picking up everything the adults in her life had to say.

Once again, Grace took the lead. "It's not polite to pry into other people's business, Maddie." She gave a short self-conscious laugh. "Although that's exactly what I've been doing, isn't it? I suppose we're both just curious, and I guess curiosity is a human failing. But I think Mr. Partridge doesn't like to talk about it, Maddie. It must have been a terrible thing for him to come back after having endured the deprivations of war and to find his family business in ruins." She smiled compassionately at Noah, who swallowed hard.

Maddie's big blue eyes, as round and pretty as those of her mother, radiated sympathy. "Is that what happened, Mr. Noah?"

He licked his lips. "Er, no. Not exactly. It was afterwards, you see."

"Afterwards?" Grace's eyes looked like deep blue pools under the shade of her sunbonnet. Lordy, he could get lost in those eyes of hers if he wasn't careful.

201

He nodded.

"Was it an accident or something?"

"No, ma'am, it was deliberate."

"You mean someone burned those pianos on purpose, Mr. Noah?" A perfect imitation of her lovely mother, Maddie's indignation on his behalf might have made him smile under other circumstances. "Who'd do a thing like that?"

Who'd do it? His neighbors. The people he'd grown up among. Unsure if he could make himself tell the truth, Noah remained silent for a long time. He knew it was too long a pause to be polite. The clop-clop-clop of the animals' hooves kept time to the thudding of his heart. His brain was in a scramble. He didn't know what to say. Everything he thought of sounded too harsh.

After several tense moments, Grace said, "I think Mr. Partridge feels very sad about it, Maddie. Maybe he doesn't want to talk about it." Grace gave her daughter a sweet smile. When she glanced at Noah, he read pity in her eyes and hated it.

"I fought for the wrong side, Miss Maddie. Most of the folks in Falls Church hated me. I was the only one left in my family after the war, and my neighbors burned me out when I opened up for business."

Brutal, brutal, Noah Partridge. Why did you say it that way? Why didn't you soften it for six-year-old ears? He shook his head hard, wishing he could live the last minute or so over again. He'd just keep quiet, whether they thought he was being rude or not.

"Oh, my!" Grace gaped at him, horrified.

"That's mean, Mr. Noah. That's mean and—and—and beastly." Maddie was clearly outraged on his behalf. He appreciated her very much in that moment.

In spite of himself, he grinned. "I thought it was pretty beastly myself, Miss Maddie."

"Just a 'cause a body don't like what you like doesn't mean you can burn his things." Maddie glared around as if looking for the perpetrators of Noah's tragedy so she could give them a good hot lecture.

"I agree with you there, ma'am." She was damned near as cute as her mother. Nice folks, Grace and Maddie Richardson. Maybe if he'd lived around them instead of the folks in Falls Church, his life would have been easier.

"What do you mean, you fought on the wrong side? What side did you fight on?"

Grace gazed at him in open curiosity.

"I fought for the Union, ma'am. I thought I was being noble." His cynical words and caustic laugh sounded a discordant note in the peaceful autumn morning air.

"Hmph. Well, I'm from Illinois, and if you ask me, you fought on the right side, Mr. Partridge. I can't even imagine people being so callous and unreasonable as to burn you out because they didn't approve of your choice during that awful conflict."

"I had a hard time imagining it myself, ma'am." Lord, he hadn't believed he could still sound so bitter.

"Hmph. I know animosities ran high, but that's carrying things much too far."

Noah nodded in agreement.

"Why, that war tore the whole country apart. I suppose it's not surprising things like that happened, although they're awful. Simply awful. The things people do to each other!"

"Yes, ma'am. I couldn't agree more."

"Of all the nerve!"

Noah saw Grace's hands knot into fists around her reins.

"Of all the nerve!" Maddie sat on Old Blue as if she had a poker strapped to her back. She looked every bit as incensed on his account as her mother did. The two Richardson ladies made a fine Greek chorus. Noah was glad they were on his side.

"I appreciate your sympathy," he said, and meant it.

"I can't believe the ghastly things people can do to each other," Grace repeated.

"Me, neither. I can't b'lieve it neither." Maddie nodded firmly. Cute as a button, she was.

"That sort of thing is why Frank and I decided to move to the Territory, Mr. Partridge. Emotions were running so high before the war. He didn't want anything to do with it. I mean, it was bad enough that people hated each other because they had a difference of opinions, but they wouldn't let each other rest in their own beliefs. They had to be arguing all the time over who was right and who was wrong. Neither Frank nor I could tolerate it, and we decided to get out."

Noah nodded. Although he didn't see that Frank Richardson had benefited much from his neutrality— he was dead, after all—he could understand his sentiments. If anything like that happened again, Noah'd be inclined to escape it as well.

"How come people fight wars, Mommy?"

Both Noah and Grace turned to stare at Maddie. Noah didn't know about Grace, but he thought that was an interesting question. He wished he knew the answer.

He nodded to Grace, silently letting her know that the answer was her responsibility. Maddie was her kid; she could answer the tough questions.

"I—I don't know, Maddie."

Noah thought she'd quit without even trying to answer the question. When she glanced at him to gauge his reaction, he lifted an eyebrow to tell her so.

Little Maddie tilted her head to one side, as if she were mulling over her mother's non-answer. "But there must be a reason."

Grace sighed audibly. Noah's lips twitched into a grin again. When he looked at her this time, he saw her mouth the words, *It's your turn.*

Great. He'd always wanted to offer answers to ponderous philosophical questions in language a six-year-old could understand.

Well, hell, why not? "Sometimes people have different ideas about how the world should run, Maddie. In the Southern states, the economy was based on an agricultural system that depended on the labor of slaves to keep it going."

"But slavery is bad!" Maddie looked up at him, righteous outrage on her face.

"Lots of folks would agree with you on that issue, Miss Maddie. I know I do. But it's hard to get folks to change their whole way of life because other folks—folks who live hundreds of miles away—think it's wrong."

"You din't live hundreds of miles away, and *you* think slavery's wrong too."

He couldn't argue that one. He nodded, ceding the point and wondering what to say now. Maddie didn't give him a chance.

" 'Sides, slavery *is* wrong! How come they wouldn't change if something's wrong?"

Ah, the mind of a child! Noah could hardly remember a time when things had been all black and white to him, his entire life had been gray for so long. Too long. Much too long. He sighed, contemplated explaining the economic implications in changing a system that had been working for a hundred years and more, and decided that it was too big a job for him. Like Maddie's mother before him, Noah opted for the easy way out. "Well, I reckon I wondered the same thing, Miss Maddie. That's why I joined the Union army. That, and because I didn't want the nation to be split in two."

Maddie swiveled in her saddle and peered up at her mother. "We were for the Union army, weren't we, Mommy?" Noah held his breath, fearing for her safety. But she was a good little rider, and she didn't so much as wobble.

"We believed in the Union cause. Yes, dear." Grace's voice was so benevolent, Noah wished he could bottle it and take it out on those occasions when he was feeling particularly worn down.

"And the Union won, didn't it, Mr. Noah?"

Now Maddie's clear gaze was upon him, and Noah bit off the retort he'd been about to spout. He'd been going to say that no one ever won a war, but Maddie was too young and innocent to understand that. He compromised. "Yeah. I guess."

Maddie didn't like his equivocation. She turned back to her mother. "We did win, didn't we, Mommy?"

"Yes, dear."

"How come Mr. Noah said that, then?" She cast an accusatory glance at Noah, who sighed.

Grace smiled at her daughter. "I think Mr. Partridge is trying to tell you that the cost of war is very high, Maddie, and that even when one side emerges victorious, the losses of war far outweigh the benefits, both financially and in human suffering."

"Yeah," Noah said. "That's right." He wondered if it was. Then he decided that he really, really didn't want to think about the war any longer.

The weather was lovely—at least thirty degrees warmer than it had been for a week or more. He was actually enjoying the company he was in, and the war was long over. At least for most people, it was. If the memory of it occasionally paid Noah visits at inopportune moments, it wasn't doing so now, and he didn't want to chance inviting it in.

"So, where are you leading us, Mrs. Richardson?"

She gave him one of the smiles that went through him like a tiny ray of sunshine and warmed his cold insides. "I thought it was time you saw the lakes, Mr. Partridge. There are several of them a few miles off. They're quite pretty, and they're very deep. I believe some of Mr. Chisum's cowboys have tried to find the bottoms of a couple of them by tying lengths of rope together and dangling them in the water, and no one's hit bottom yet."

He lifted his eyebrows. "They sound awfully deep, ma'am."

"Indeed, I expect they are. Although Mac says they're probably fed by underground streams, and the current moves the rope, making them appear deeper than they actually are."

207

"Makes sense." Hell, Noah reckoned the rainwater had to go somewhere. It sure didn't stick around on the surface out here. This land was as hard as flint. Like him. He was liking it more and more every day.

"Yes, it does. Anyway, the cowboys have taken to calling them the bottomless lakes. I don't know about that, but I do know that they're pretty, they're deep, the fishing is good in them, and Maddie loves to wade in the shallows." She glanced up into the blue, blue sky. "And the weather's warm enough today for some wading."

"Yes!" Maddie's face beamed up at him like sunshine.

"Maybe we can catch some fish for lunch."

"Maybe so."

Grace heaved a big sigh. Noah glanced at her, wondering if she was upset about something. She looked happy, though, her clear eyes gazing about with eagerness, and he guessed maybe her sigh had been one of contentment. It seemed odd to him that anyone would be content in his company. He liked the idea, though, and he looked around too, admiring the beautiful landscape that he was growing so fond of so quickly.

Chapter Eleven

Noah leaned back against a boulder. He didn't know beans about geology, but this particular rock was striped with layers and layers of different colored strata, and he expected a geologist would have a field day out here. Maybe even find some fossils.

Grace had been right about the beauty of these lakes. There were several of them, and they all sat in hollows that looked as if water had carved them out of the surrounding cliffs thousands of years ago. The cliff sides were so sheer in some places, he didn't think they could be scaled without mountain-climbing equipment, even though they weren't very high.

A buzzard floated over the top of one of the cliffs, lazily riding the breeze and making Noah envious. He'd like to be able to float away on the wind. He was surprised to see the bird because he'd assumed the buzzards had flown south long since. It was pretty, though, soaring way up there like that. Really pretty. Strange that a carrion-eater should add such a fine, peaceful touch to a beautiful day.

This was the oddest country he'd ever seen. Near as Noah could tell, there wasn't a tree within a hundred miles or more that hadn't been planted by settlers. He didn't count the scraggly mesquite bushes; they didn't properly look like trees, although their red wood added a bright note to the relentlessly beige landscape.

He wondered how this place would look in the springtime. Would it still be tan and brown, or would greenery liven it up? Mac claimed that flowers bloomed after the rains came, but Noah somehow doubted that the land would ever, even in the rainiest of springs, resemble his native Virginia. But still, he was glad of that.

"Wonder how long it'll take folks to plant trees around here and for the trees to grow big enough to shade their picnics."

Grace looked up from the pan in which she was frying the perch Noah'd just caught. Actually, he and Maddie had caught them together. He'd had to help her, of course, but it hadn't been the burden he'd anticipated. She'd been eager as anything, and happy as a clam. Her cry of joy when she pulled out the first one, a whopper that wiggled and fought for its freedom, had lit him up inside. He'd had to help her land it. Grace had been right about the fishing; those were some of the biggest fish he'd ever caught, and they smelled heavenly as she tended them over the fire he'd built from a bunch of dried mesquite branches they'd gathered.

His stomach growled, and even his hunger pleased

him. Made him feel human, connected somehow with the rest of his fellow creatures on this earth. The feeling was a pleasant novelty.

"I don't know. Frank and I planted some willows and cottonwoods on our land, but they're still very small." She shot him an apprehensive look, as if she wished she hadn't mentioned her land.

Noah sighed, and wished she hadn't mentioned it, too. But he wouldn't spoil this picnic by bringing up his desire for her land. He'd lull her into forgetting about it, that's what he'd do. Immediately his cynical side reared its ugly head and he thought what a damned imbecile he was. As if he still had the wherewithal to lull a lady into any kind of complacence about anything at all. Cripes, who did he think he was? He was a lunatic, for God's sake. Well, he'd not talk about Grace Richardson's land today in any case.

"Yeah," he said. "I saw them."

"Mac's planted trees too. Some oaks and willows, and even some cottonwoods by the swamp. Did you know there's a swamp close by his property, Mr. Partridge?"

"A swamp?" In spite of himself, Noah chuckled. A swamp! In this desert?

Grace nodded. "Indeed, there is. You'd never believe it, would you? But it's no more than half a mile north of his wagon yard, where the Spring River flows through Rio Hondo. It's quite green in the springtime and summer, and the fishing's good there too."

"I'd never have guessed."

"Maddie likes to hunt for tadpoles there during the summer."

"I bet she does. I remember doing that when I was

a kid." He looked at her from under his hat brim. When she wasn't messing with the fish, she sat with her back against another boulder, her knees drawn up and her arms around them. She looked relaxed. Approachable. As if she might not slap him silly if he were to go over there, put his arms around her, and—

Lord above, where had that thought sprung from? He jerked his head in the other direction and looked at Maddie.

Grace and he were both keeping an eagle eye on the little girl, who had shucked her shoes and stockings, hiked up her skirt around her waist, and now waded in the clear water of the lake. Noah could hear her singing "There Is a Balm in Gilead" at the top of her lungs from where he sat. She was a tuneful little kid, Maddie Richardson, and he wondered, when she sang "to heal the sin-sick soul," what possible sins could lie within her blameless breast. She was only a kid, for the love of God. She couldn't have racked up enough sins to fill a thimble.

"Bet that water's freezing," he said, thinking of Maddie's toes and trying to forget his recent, indiscreet thoughts concerning Maddie's mother.

"I imagine it is, but the weather is so fine, I'm sure she won't take cold."

"No, I'm sure she won't. It must be seventy-five degrees today."

Grace looked up, as if gauging the temperature from the looks of the sky. "I do believe you're right, Mr. Partridge. Isn't that something? Why, only week or so ago, it was snowing."

"Reckon the weather's unpredictable out here, ma'am."

She chuckled. "It certainly is. It might snow again tomorrow. We can get some tremendous thunderstorms too."

"Yeah, I can imagine."

"We generally only get the thunderstorms during the summertime."

He nodded.

"The winters aren't as hard here as the winters in Chicago, though, even if the landscape isn't as friendly."

"They call Chicago the windy city for a reason, I expect."

"They certainly do." She laughed again.

Grace lifted the fish pan from the fire and conversation lagged. Noah twirled a grass stalk in his fingers and watched Maddie. She was having the time of her life out there in the shallows of the lake. It must be nice to be a kid and to be able to entertain yourself by doing nothing more than collecting shiny rocks and singing hymns at fish.

"Ever eat frog legs, Mrs. Richardson?"

"Sometimes. They're quite tasty, but I don't like to cook them. They jump out of the pan if you're not careful, and I always feel sorry for the frogs." She gave him a sheepish grin, as if she expected him to consider her a fool. He didn't. He'd always felt sorry for the frogs too.

"My mama used to cook up a mess of frog legs every now and then. I liked them a lot."

"I prefer fish. They don't jump so."

"I reckon not." He gave her a smile, to let her know he understood. "What about the jackrabbits I see around here? They any good to eat?"

213

She sighed. "Not very. They're tough as old boots, actually. There are cottontails out here, though, and they're pretty tasty. Mac made Maddie a blanket out of cottontail hides sewn together. She loves it because it's as soft as feathers. It's her favorite blanket. Won't go to sleep without it at night."

"I can imagine." Noah shut his eyes for a moment and tried to envision sleeping with something as soft as rabbit fur. He'd rather sleep with Grace. His eyes popped open, and he blinked, annoyed by his sudden fantasy. Criminy, he hadn't thought anything like that in years until he met Grace. Now he could hardly think of anything else. He was damned near a virgin reborn, if men could be virgins.

Grace transferred the cooked fish to a dish and put another cleaned fillet on to cook. As the fish sizzled, they watched Maddie for a while. She seemed to be collecting a fine pile of shiny, water-polished stones. Noah couldn't offhand recall the last time he'd felt so completely at peace with himself and the world. This picnic had been a good idea on somebody's part.

"And then there are the antelopes. There are lots of herds out here."

"Yeah, I've seen several. Deer too."

"I understand some folks eat mountain lions, although I don't think I'd like to try them."

Noah shrugged. "Reckon a body does what he has to do when it comes to food. If all you had was a cougar, I expect you'd eat it." A few years ago, Noah himself would have killed for a piece of meat. He wouldn't have cared what animal it had come from.

"I suppose."

He saw a soft smile play at Grace's lips and felt an

unexpected compulsion to kiss her. Damn, he'd gone loony as a March hare. He looked away quickly and his gaze fastened on Maddie once more.

They didn't talk again until Grace said, "I think this is the last of the fish. If you'll get Maddie, I'll serve up our lunch."

"Sounds like a fair swap to me." Noah sighed, heaved himself to his feet, and walked the twenty or so yards to the lake.

Lunch was delicious. Grace had noticed before that fish tasted better when freshly caught. And there was something about eating them in the open air on a beautiful, clear day that perked up one's appetite too.

Company counted a lot toward the enjoyment of meals as well. She glanced at Noah Partridge once in a while and marveled that she should be taking pleasure in his company. He was such a hard, aloof man, yet from time to time his humanity showed, and he seemed almost friendly. Grace found herself wanting to tempt his sociable qualities out into the open, to pamper them so that they would surface more often and and stick around longer.

Don't be foolish, Grace Richardson. She knew good and well that people never changed in essentials. If Noah Partridge was an unfriendly, reserved individual, there was nothing she could do to draw him out.

Of course, if he had merely been damaged by circumstances, like Uncle Henry, and her friendship could help him, she'd be glad to oblige. He had given Maddie that locket, after all. He must have some finer qualities, besides being quite the handsomest man Grace had ever seen—in a hard, chiseled sort of way.

Bother. There she went again. She shook her head and wished she could get her mind to dwell on things other than Noah Partridge. Her thoughts seemed to linger over him entirely too much.

"Delicious fish, Mrs. Richardson."

As if answering her mind's probing, Noah's voice penetrated her thoughts. She glanced up from her plate. "Yes, you two caught some good ones."

He grinned. "I think it's the cooking makes them taste so good, ma'am."

There was no reason for her to be blushing. Grace was annoyed with herself. "Fish always taste better fresh," she said, snapping the words out curtly. She felt even more embarrassed when Noah's eyebrow lifted. To cover her befuddled state, she fussed with her daughter. "Do you want another fish, Maddie?"

"No, thank you."

It was a point of pride with Grace that Maddie was such a polite little girl. There weren't many folks to practice on in Rio Hondo. It would have been easy for Grace to let her daughter's manners slide, but she didn't do it.

"If there's enough, I'll take another one, ma'am."

Grace glanced up to find Noah holding out his plate as if in offering. She scooped up another fish and plopped it down. "There's plenty. You two caught enough for an army."

Maddie giggled. "The Union army."

Grace shot an uneasy look Noah's way, and was relieved when he smiled. Good. She didn't want Maddie's innocent comment to stir up old memories. She could tell he hadn't enjoyed their chat about the war earlier in the day.

"Can I have another pickle, Mommy?"

"May you have another pickle? I should say you may." Grace speared a stalk of dilled okra out of the jar and put it on Maddie's tin plate. Mac and Maddie both enjoyed her pickled okra. Grace preferred cucumber pickles herself. "There are dried-apple tarts for dessert."

"Yummy!"

Noah's deep chuckle was music to her ears. Almost as soon as they'd finished the last fish, Maddie began to rub her eyes.

"Let's find you a shady spot, Maddie, and I'll lay out a blanket so you can take a nap."

The little girl didn't object. She yawned hugely. Grace walked her behind a big boulder, helped her with her underdrawers, and let her relieve herself before she led her back to the blanket. She was intensely aware of Noah's gaze on them both when Maddie settled down on the blanket. His dark, brooding scrutiny made her nervous, so she sat on Maddie's blanket too, leaned back against a rock, and let Maddie rest her head on her lap.

"Sing me a song, please, Mommy."

"All right, sweetie."

"You can sing, too, Mr. Noah."

Grace felt Maddie's head turn in her lap and realized her daughter was smiling at Noah. She gave her shoulders a little shrug, trying to let him know that he didn't have to sing if it embarrassed him to do so.

She nearly dropped her teeth when he said, "Well, I reckon I could do that, Miss Maddie." Then he launched into a rendition of "Barbara Allen" that took her breath away.

217

Merciful heavens, he had a beautiful voice. A rich, clear baritone, it would have done any choir in the world proud. He was musical through and through, Noah Partridge. It seemed a shame to Grace that he had to live in these terrible modern days, when civil war could shatter a musician's life and soul to pieces. He should have been some aristocrat's son during the Renaissance, when his talents could have been nurtured and allowed to bloom unhampered.

The lovely old song had always stirred tender sentiments in her breast. Today, when Noah's deep voice caressed the words and tune, she wanted to cry. Because she didn't fancy him knowing how moved she was, she bowed her head, stroked her daughter's silky hair, and hoped her sunbonnet hid the tears in her eyes. His voice seemed to echo over the lake when he finished. Maddie heaved a big sigh.

"That was real pretty, Mr. Noah."

"Thank you, Miss Maddie."

Maddie yawned again. "You sing one now, Mommy."

"I'm afraid my voice is nowhere near as good as Mr. Partridge's, Maddie, but I'll try."

Because she didn't want to spoil the mood Noah's sad love song had created, Grace chose to sing "Jeanie with the Light Brown Hair," only she changed *Jeanie* to *Maddie*. By the time she'd sung the second verse, Maddie was sound asleep. She finished all the verses she could remember anyway, because she was uneasy about what to say to Noah without the safety net of Maddie's scrutiny to fall back on.

There were only so many verses to the song, though, and they didn't last forever. When she'd sung the last note, she looked up to find Noah watching her. His eyes were half-closed, and he had a crooked smile on his face. He looked handsome and awfully appealing, in his lean, hard-edged way. She wished she hadn't noticed.

After several moments of quiet, he said softly, "You have a very pretty voice, Mrs. Richardson."

"Thank you." She laughed nervously. "I used to sing in the church choir back in Chicago. I've, ah, seldom heard a man sing so beautifully, Mr. Partridge. Did your father teach you to sing too?"

She and Frank had met at church when they were children; Grace had considered it an auspicious beginning. Frank's reedy tenor voice had been nowhere near as refined as Noah Partridge's baritone, but Frank had had a fine voice. A wonderful voice.

Noah's smile broadened fractionally. "No, ma'am. My father was the church's choir director, but my mother was really the singer in the family. She sang to us kids all the time when we were little."

A topic! Grace grabbed it with both hands. "I remember you've mentioned a sister and a brother. Where are they now?"

"She died of typhoid when she was seventeen. My brother died in the war."

"How tragic for you and your family."

"It was, yes."

He glanced away, and Grace saw his lips tighten. Drat it, wasn't there anything on the face of the earth she could talk about that wouldn't remind him of some awful incident in his past? Church sounded neutral. She'd try church. She hoped to heaven he wasn't a Catholic or she'd be at sea without a compass.

"Did, er, you sing in church with your father's choir?" Why did she feel so nervous all of a sudden? They'd been chatting together all day long. There was no reason for her to have developed a case of the jitters now.

"Yes, ma'am. Before I became the organist, I sang in the choir. Shoot, I must've started when I still sang soprano." He laughed softly.

She decided she might as well ask. "What church did your family attend, Mr. Partridge? We were Presbyterians. My family, that is." Good grief, what was the matter with her?

He nodded. "We went to the Presbyterian Church too."

Common ground! Grace could hardly believe it. Unfortunately, she couldn't think of how to expand on Presbyterianism without sounding like a priggish proselytizer. Music. She'd go back to music; music was good. "I think it's wonderful that your family gave you such a fine legacy of music, Mr. Partridge." Considering what had happened to that legacy, Grace wondered if her comment had been less than tactful. Drat! "I mean, if the war hadn't ruined everything." Oh, dear. There she went again. Conversing with Noah Partridge was certainly a ticklish business.

He looked away and his smile faded. "Yeah."

She licked her lips, jumpy as one of the frog's legs she hated to cook. "It's a shame there aren't more families out here yet. You might be able to set up a music business again if there were."

"I don't expect I'll do that again, ma'am."

"No?"

He shook his head.

"That's too bad."

"You think so?" He smiled again, only this time his smile seemed hard, ironic, and it made Grace's heart hurt.

"Yes, I do think so. I think it was awful of your fellow citizens to burn your family's business, Mr. Partridge. After enduring the horrors of battle, at least you should have been able to expect peace when the war was over."

He didn't speak for a minute. "Actually, I didn't see too many battle horrors, ma'am."

Her hand stilled on Maddie's head, and she stared at him, surprised. "You didn't?" Why was he in such terrible shape, then? She'd assumed he'd been in the thick of the fighting—had been wounded, perhaps. "Oh."

"No. I was shot and captured during my second fight, in '61, and sent off to prison camp."

Shot and captured? Prison camp? Good heavens, from what Grace had read, some of the prison camps were even worse than the battlefields. No wonder he looked as if he'd been half-starved and hadn't recovered yet. "My goodness. I'm sorry, Mr. Partridge. Which prison camp were you held in?" Should she have asked that? Well, it was too late now.

Again, he was silent for several seconds. Grace wished she'd kept her mouth shut.

Then he turned again, looked her in the eye, and said distinctly, "Andersonville."

Andersonville? Grace's mouth dropped open. She whispered, "Andersonville!" endowing the word with every ounce of the revulsion it deserved. "My God."

She'd read an account of what they'd found at Andersonville after the war ended. Horrors heaped on horrors. Acres of graves. Pits, really, into which bodies had been dumped, unnamed. No one knew who'd died there, whose bodies remained there, whose families would never know where their loved ones lay buried. They only knew that there had been hundreds of men who hadn't made it out alive. Starvation, illness, cold, heat. Perhaps her sister Eleanor's husband's bones were there. They'd never know, unless Miss Clara Barton's humanitarian organization had better luck in the future than they'd had so far.

She'd cried through the entire article about the vile place, but she'd made herself finish it, sensing that it was somehow her duty. This was what her fellow countrymen had done to each other, and she needed to know, to understand, how they could have done it.

It hadn't helped. She didn't understand to this day. In fact, she suspected that if she'd read that account a thousand times and a dozen more like it, she still wouldn't understand. Perhaps she was a better person because her mind couldn't comprehend how people could perpetrate such grotesque, regrettable things upon one another; she didn't know, but she doubted it.

All she knew for sure is that she no longer wondered that Noah Partridge was such a strange, unhappy man.

She had to swallow before she could get her voice to work. "And you say you were wounded when they took you there?"

He nodded.

"How—how awful."

"It was pretty bad."

"Did, um, they tend to your wound?"

There went that caustic smile again. "Sort of."

Sort of. What did that mean? She couldn't make herself ask.

He chuffed out a short breath and gave her a half-answer to her unasked question. "It healed eventually."

Well, she was glad of that. She swallowed. He absently rubbed his thigh as though he were remembering. A leg wound. It must have been a leg wound.

"I'm, ah, surprised you survived."

He gave a short, humorless laugh. "Yeah. I was kind of surprised myself." He sucked in a deep breath. "I had to bury a lot of men who didn't, and I wasn't in very good shape when they took me out."

"I can imagine."

He was leaning back on an elbow, his posture relaxed, casual. His eyes belied his pose. They were as bleak as winter, and they frightened Grace. He might have realized it, because he shifted his gaze to the lake as if seeking answers there. Grace suspected there were no answers anywhere.

"I was in the hospital for eight months afterwards, in Washington. I couldn't walk—too weak from starvation and malaria. There was no food at all towards the end. We ate acorns, peanuts, slop, anything we could find. There weren't even any rats left alive there by that time. We were better than cats at getting rid of vermin."

She shuddered and didn't trust herself to speak.

"It was—pretty bad."

She had to wipe tears from her cheeks and cursed herself for her wretched emotions. What a weakling she was. This poor man had lived it, and she couldn't even bear to hear about it. "I'm very sorry, Mr. Partridge."

"Thanks."

She sensed he meant it, although she knew her sympathy was pitifully inadequate compensation for what he'd endured.

Maddie made a little mew in her sleep and turned over, rolling from Grace's lap. She was sorry to lose the security of her daughter's weight, but decided her time could better be used in cleaning up the dishes and repacking their picnic trappings. With a sigh, she rose to her feet.

"Let me help you, Mrs. Richardson."

Noah got up too. It was the first time Grace noticed he favored his left leg the slightest bit. All at once the idiocy of men infuriated her. She turned on him abruptly and could tell she'd startled him.

"You know, Mr. Partridge, if Frank and I had ever had a son, I think I'd leave the country before I'd let him fight in a war. Wars are stupid. They're uncivilized. They're horrid! They don't solve anything, and only make people hate each other."

Tears had built in her eyes again, and she dashed them away, embarrassed. But what she'd said was the truth, and she wouldn't retract it. His grin caught her off guard.

"Don't reckon I'd try to stop you, ma'am. Not today, I wouldn't. When I was a young buck and my mama told me pretty much the same thing, I had arguments enough."

She blinked at him, trying to hold back her tears. "You did?"

"Yeah."

He shook his head. Grace read bitter irony in his expression. She got the feeling he was mocking the boy he'd once been. All at once she thought she understood what his motivation might have been. "You were idealistic, weren't you, Mr. Partridge? You really believed that fighting for the Union's cause would bring about changes for the better in the world, didn't you?"

He picked up and stacked the three tin dishes they'd used for their lunch. "Yeah, reckon I had my head stuffed all full of chivalrous nonsense back then. I was a damned fool." Glancing up, he murmured, "Sorry, ma'am. Didn't mean to swear."

Grace cast aside his apology. She didn't blame him for swearing. Feeling indignant and furious on behalf of all the young men—she didn't consider them young fools—who'd fought and died—and worse—in the conflict that had torn the country apart, she stooped and gathered the fish pan and spatula. She wished she could konk the leaders of this country over their heads with the cast-iron skillet. Maybe it would knock some sense into them.

"It's not your fault you believed what people told you, Mr. Partridge. If I were a man, I'd probably have done the same thing. They make you believe you're fighting for a good cause, don't they? They pretend your life matters to them." She wanted to shriek her rage to the skies, for whatever good that would do.

"I expect so, ma'am."

"But they don't really care about anything but their own pocketbooks, do they?"

He shrugged. "I'm not qualified to answer that one, I'm afraid."

She sniffed angrily. "If women had the running of things, you wouldn't see any more wars, I'll warrant. Women aren't so eager to send their men off to die."

Her mood was black. She wanted to punish someone for Noah Partridge's sake, and for the sake of all the women who'd lost fathers, husbands, sons, and brothers in the wars of men.

He chuckled, and she didn't appreciate it. "Maybe you're right, ma'am."

"Yet men won't give women the vote. I wonder if it's because the old fogies who run the country are afraid that if they did, the young men might live long enough to take their places. I guess war eliminates a lot of the competition."

Grace couldn't recall ever before saying anything so clearly hateful, and the words embarrassed her once they were out in the open. She glanced at Noah, wondering if she'd shocked him. He merely smiled, his face looking much softer than it usually did. She got the feeling he might actually agree with her.

Frank and she had never talked about serious issues. They hadn't needed to, really, because they were so attuned to each other. In a way, she appreciated this opportunity to stretch her reasoning and flex her mental muscles.

At least Mr. Partridge didn't laugh at her. Every time she'd mentioned anything the least outré to Frank, he'd chuckled and told her ladies didn't need to worry their heads about those things. She'd never resented his saying so, and she'd never have dreamed of arguing with him. Right now, though, she wondered if Frank might have been wrong. Women had every bit as much business thinking as men did. More, if men's thoughts led them to war, she decided defiantly.

She didn't like to think of Frank as being anything but the most perfect man in the world, so she didn't linger over her doubts. Rather, she got her scrub brush and a bar of lye soap out of her pack and walked to the edge of the lake. Noah walked with her. There she knelt and began scrubbing the utensils, using the heavy-bristled brush on them the way she'd like to use it on a couple of politicians. She'd like to scrape their precious skin raw for a while and see how they liked it!

Noah rinsed and wiped, as quietly as he did everything. Today, now, his silence didn't seem sullen to her, but merely natural. After enduring what he'd endured, what was there to say? Grace expected she'd be silent too. Idle chatter must seem ridiculous after Andersonville.

When she was through, she stood, stretched out her back, and smiled at him. "Thank you. That didn't take long at all with both of us doing it."

"Yes'm. My mama used to make my brother and me wash dishes at home. Said there was no such things as men's work and women's work, but only work that needed doing."

She laughed. "Your mother sounds like a woman after my own heart, Mr. Partridge."

"Yes'm. I think the two of you would have liked each other."

Grace looked up into his eyes, and seemed to get caught there for a moment. He was such an intense man. Frank hadn't been nearly as intense as Noah Partridge. Frank had been rather happy-go-lucky, actually. He hadn't been hard and lean and ragged like this, on edge, as if he might break apart any second.

Noah Partridge frightened her. He made her nervous. She felt funny inside, as if she'd stood up too fast and her head was swimming. His powerful gaze made her remember how it had felt to have Frank's arms around her. She'd felt treasured, protected, loved. Mr. Partridge's gaze made her long to feel those things again.

Good heavens, what was the matter with her? With an effort, Grace broke eye contact and turned away. She rubbed her hands up and down her arms where gooseflesh had sprung up. She felt foolish.

"I won't hurt you, ma'am."

Noah's soft assurance startled her. She whirled around. A response danced on her tongue. She wanted to tell him that she hadn't thought he'd hurt her, but the declaration died before she could speak it because she got trapped by his eyes again. His intense, brooding, beautiful green eyes.

As if of its own accord, her hand reached out to him. He caught it in his and drew her to him.

When he kissed her, Grace felt as if a firecracker had been shot off in her veins.

Chapter Twelve

So long. It had been so long since Noah had lost himself in the arms of a woman. He'd been a boy, an innocent, no more than a child, the last time.

Grace Richardson yielded to the soft pressure of his lips as if she and he had been made for each other at the beginning of time, separated by accident, and had only just found each other again. She was perfect. She fit exactly. She filled his senses and his arms, and he knew he could lose himself in her and forget all the bad things in his life with her, if she'd only let him.

His tongue met hers in a slow, delicate dance. She clung to him, her fingers digging into his shoulders as if she, too, felt the rightness of their kiss. He felt her lush body under his hands, limber, sweet, and he knew that if he allowed her to, she could help cure him. Already he felt her sweetness penetrating his dark places and shining healing light on them, illuminating his dark caverns, bringing soothing rays of sunshine into his blighted life.

She felt like his sanctuary, his refuge, his deliverance. He knew a moment of hope for a life that, until now, he'd believed was irredeemable. The most he'd hoped for in years was perhaps, one day, to salvage a tiny space for himself in the world where he could hide away and protect his raw wounds from further damage. He'd never dared hope that he might find real peace. But he felt peaceful now, with Grace in his arms.

Grace. Was she his grace? His salvation? She felt like it. Desire blossomed like a spring bud in her sunshine alongside a blessed peace of mind he'd never hoped to experience again. By God, he felt like a man. For the first time in years, he felt like a man.

"Mommy? Mommy, why are you kissing Mr. Noah?"

Noah's brain felt muzzy, and he uttered a soft cry of distress when Grace wrenched herself away from him, turned, and pressed her hands to her burning cheeks. It took him a moment to orient himself; his head was addled, full of Grace and passion and hunger. He stared at her, blinking, wondering why she wasn't in his arms any longer. He needed her there.

Then Maddie's voice came again, sleepy, confused. "Mommy?"

"My God, what did I do?"

Grace's voice was a mere whisper, filled with consternation. It jolted Noah out of his trance. He felt as if the newly grown bond between them had just been hacked apart. The split left him bleeding inside.

Damn, what an idiot he was.

He turned and forced himself to grin at Maddie.

"Did you have a nice nap, Miss Maddie?" His voice was gravelly, hoarse with shattered hopes.

The little girl nodded. She sat on her blanket, rubbing her eyes and looking troubled. He gave her what he hoped was an encouraging smile. Little kids didn't know anything; they weren't responsible for the state of the world—the state of Noah Partridge. Maddie was guiltless. It wasn't her fault she'd interrupted the most significant experience of his life. The most significant pleasant experience, rather.

Turning to Grace, he mumbled, "You all right, ma'am?" He needed to say more, but couldn't make himself apologize. Not yet. Maybe later, when he could coerce a lie out of his mouth, he'd say he was sorry. At the moment, the only thing he was sorry about was that their kiss had been cut so short. He wanted her back in his arms so badly that he ached with the yearning.

"Yes. Yes, I'm all right." She turned and began walking toward her daughter. "Did you have a nice nap, Maddie?" Her good cheer sounded forced.

The little girl nodded and watched her mother somberly. "Why were you kissing Mr. Noah, Mommy?"

Great. Kids never let things just slip by, did they? Noah felt guilty for putting Grace in an uncomfortable position with her daughter, even if he'd never regret that kiss.

"Um—" Grace shot him a look over her shoulder. Thank God it wasn't accusatory. She actually looked kind of helpless, as if her imagination wasn't good enough to tackle this situation, and she hoped he'd help her.

Noah grinned, feeling marginally less like he'd been

231

abandoned on a desert island. "I was thanking your mommy for a nice day and a delicious lunch, Maddie. That's all." That's all! What a blasphemy.

Grace appreciated it, though, and that's what mattered. She shot him a grateful glance and scooped Maddie up from the blanket. "Yes. Sometimes grown-ups kiss each other for thank-you's, dear."

Maddie seemed to accept the feeble explanation from these two adults in her life, although it took her a minute. Noah wasn't sure he'd survive her speculative scrutiny.

With his mind's eye, Mac observed the picnickers and shook his head. He was both glad and sad about Grace and Noah finding passion and relief in each other's arms. Not that they didn't need it. If they'd only let themselves, they could be happy as a couple of nesting doves with each other, but Mac suspected they both needed a little more time.

Every now and then, Mac wished human beings weren't such a stubborn, foolish lot. Maybe his kin were right about 'em. But no. Mac liked these two, Grace and Noah. They were good people, both of them, and there was certainly no denying they needed each other, for their own sakes and for the sake of wee Maddie.

Aye, but they were an obstinate lot, the two of them.

Grace, for instance, continued to labor under the misapprehension that Frank Richardson had been the be-all and end-all of the human male. And there was no denying that Frank had been a nice enough fellow. He'd loved his wife and daughter, which proved to Mac he'd had more than common sense.

But Frank was dead.

Besides, no matter what Grace thought, Frank wasn't the only good man in the world. If Grace would only allow herself to recognize Noah Partridge's fine qualities through the wall the memory of her sainted Frank had erected, she'd find another good man who'd love her and Maddie as much as Frank ever could. And, although Mac would never say so to Grace, Noah Partridge was more attuned to her basic nature than Frank ever had been or ever could have been.

She and Noah were alike in so many ways, if they could only work past their personal anguish to see it.

Then there was Noah. Mac puffed on his pipe, sympathy for Noah Partridge making his eyes sting. The poor man. A poet and a musician, truly, if ever a man had been born one. And then he'd had his life and all of his good intentions torn apart in that terrible, unforgiving war.

Mac heaved a big sigh. Noah wasn't the only one who'd suffered, not by a long shot. But there was a cure here, if Noah could make himself accept it. Mac intended to see that he did.

With a grin, he decided to recruit Susan Blackworth to help him. Susan was as hard as nails, but she knew what was what. A smart woman, Susan. Mac liked her.

Grace was alternately ashamed of herself and defiant when she and Noah packed up their picnic things, Noah saddled the horses and strapped everything in place, and they set out for home. Because she wasn't sure how to make conversation with the man who'd shattered her composure, and with that astonishing kiss fresh in her memory, she fussed over Maddie until her daughter objected.

"I can ride Old Blue, Mommy! I rode him all the way to the lakes." Indignation brightened her eyes and made her cheeks burn pink.

Grace sighed. "I'm sorry, Maddie. I know you can ride Old Blue. You did a very good job riding out to the lakes."

Maddie sniffed and continued glaring at her mother.

"You're a good little rider, Miss Maddie."

Grace glanced at Noah. He smiled at her, and she got the impression he felt as rueful and uncomfortable as she did. That was something anyway. Suddenly she had what she considered a brilliant idea.

"Would you like to stop by the Blackworth place, Mr. Partridge? We can pay our respects to Susan, and you can see if your piano repair work has held up."

Was that less than diplomatic? Well, no matter. It was out in the atmosphere now and couldn't be re-called.

He shrugged. "All right by me."

Good. She could chat with Susan Blackworth, and maybe the memory of her indiscretion would fade by the time she, Noah, and Maddie started back to the wagon yard. Grace wasn't sure how she was going to face Noah Partridge in the days to come with that kiss between them. What an idiot she was. And what an unfaithful, unnatural wife to Frank she'd proven herself to be. The knowledge sat like vinegar in her stomach.

Oh, Frank, I didn't mean it.

But she had meant it. When it happened, she'd meant it, anyway. Grace hadn't known herself to har-bor such weakness of the flesh until that episode with

Noah Partridge. She'd mildly enjoyed carnal relations with Frank, although she'd always craved the intimacy of the act more than the act itself. She had seldom felt real lust.

Had she felt lust with Noah? Grace didn't know, although she had a sinking feeling that she had, and that she still did. If Maddie hadn't stopped them, Grace had a shrewd notion she herself wouldn't have stopped them, either. She was so upset and confused by her own behavior, she couldn't even bear to think about it now. Maybe tonight, in her bed, she could contemplate her shortcomings, figure out why she'd weakened, castigate herself, and formulate a plan to make sure it never happened again.

"I don't want to go to Mrs. Backwort's."

Surprised but glad for the diversion, Grace asked, "Why not, Maddie?"

The little girl's mouth set into an uncharacteristic pout. "I don't like her."

Maddie's stout declaration cut across Grace's mental recriminations like a splash of acid. The girl must still be sleepy, or she'd never have made such a bald statement.

"My goodness, Maddie, that's not a very nice thing to say."

Her daughter's little chin lifted defiantly. "Well, I don't. She's all dark and wrinkled, and she smells funny."

"Maddie! That's a very harsh judgment, and quite disrespectful." Grace frowned. "What do you mean, she smells funny?"

"She does."

Unsure how to combat this unusual, sullen rebellion

on her daughter's part, Grace wasn't encouraged when she saw Noah grin.

"I think that smell's from camphor, Miss Maddie," he said. "Folks use camphor balls to keep the moths from eating their clothes."

"Mommy's clothes don't smell like camper," Maddie said, as if that in itself was sufficient indictment against Mrs. Blackworth and her funny smell.

"I don't like to wear woolen things unless the weather's very cold, because wool makes my skin itch, Maddie. It's wool that the camphor protects. The moths don't like the smell either. People don't have to use camphor to protect calico and other cottons, because the moths don't eat those fabrics."

"Oh." Maddie scowled. The expression looked so out of place on her pert face that even Grace smiled at the incongruity of it. "Well, I still don't like her. She never smiles."

"Do you like folks who smile, Miss Maddie?"

"Yes. Smiles make people look nice."

"I don't smile much, Miss Maddie. Do you not like me?"

Noah's question surprised Grace, who hadn't realized he knew how grim he always appeared.

Maddie shrugged. "You're just out of practice and sad. Mac told me so. You'll get better one of these days."

"He did, did he?" Noah eyed Maddie slantways. His hat shaded his face, but Grace saw his quick grin. He looked awfully handsome, and she wished she hadn't noticed.

"Yes. Mac knows all about stuff like that."

"I see."

Uncomfortable with the conversation, Grace said, "Mac's a pretty wise old fellow, all right, but little girls still mustn't say unkind things about their elders, Maddie. Mrs. Blackworth is an old lady, and she deserves your respect."

Maddie's sigh was so huge, it nearly lifted her out of her saddle. Grace knew exactly what she was thinking, because she remembered thinking pretty much the same thing when she herself had been a little girl and had been made to be polite to people she didn't like. She forced herself not to smile. Noah, she noticed, didn't try anywhere near as hard as she did. His grin softened his grim face like magic. She wished she hadn't noticed that, too.

Conversation lagged until Maddie tilted her head to one side and said, "Why do moths eat wool? Doesn't it taste all dry and icky?"

Maddie looked resentful when both Grace and Noah laughed, but Grace appreciated her daughter's lightening of the atmosphere more than she could say.

Taking in the full glory of Susan Blackworth, who looked like she was all set to attend a funeral in her signature black garb, whose face was wrinkled into a permanent scowl, and who clutched her black cane in gnarled fingers as if she intended to lift it and smack someone with it, Noah guessed he could understand why Maddie found the woman intimidating. He kind of did, too. And she did smell of camphor. Kids. They were so honest.

Like his being out of practice in smiling, for instance. Every now and again, honesty could be a mighty uncomfortable commodity to hang around with.

237

He banished the thought and tipped his hat to Mrs. Blackworth, who had hobbled outside to greet them. "Afternoon, ma'am."

"Good afternoon, Mr. Partridge." She eyed Grace and Maddie. "And what are you doing with the Richardsons, if I might ask?"

"The weather was so lovely after all that snow and cold that Mr. Partridge was kind enough to take Maddie and me out to the lakes for a picnic, Susan."

"A picnic, eh?" Mrs. Blackworth gave Grace a brief hug and held out her arms to Maddie. Maddie didn't look very happy as she walked into the old woman's embrace. It appeared to Noah as if she were holding her breath. "Sounds like a damned fool thing to do in the middle of winter."

The shocked expression on Maddie's face—Noah guessed she didn't approve of a lady swearing—was comical, and Grace laughed cheerfully. Noah admired her for being able to do so in the face of the older woman's black frown. Shoot, Susan Blackworth gave him the willies, and he was a grown man.

"It's a beautiful day, Susan. Just because it's getting on towards Christmas doesn't mean we can't enjoy the fine weather while it lasts."

"It won't last much longer."

Mrs. Blackworth snorted after her pronouncement, but Noah realized her black-olive dark eyes twinkled appreciatively. Evidently Grace wasn't merely tolerant of the older woman's eccentricities, but had noticed something worthwhile in her. Maybe Mrs. Blackworth wasn't really such an old crone. He decided to withhold judgment. When he'd worked on her piano, she hadn't had three kind words to say to him in as many days.

She seemed to like Grace Richardson, though, and that showed she possessed some sense.

They entered the house and went to the parlor. Because he knew where to look, the first thing his gaze landed on was that gorgeous old reed organ standing neglected in the corner. His fingers curled in anticipation, and he straightened them deliberately. That organ was nothing to him, he reminded himself. He'd told the old bat what parts to order, and she could do it or not as she chose. He had nothing to do with it, and wouldn't have unless she asked.

"I don't suppose you've come to give me back my money, have you, Mr. Partridge?"

Mrs. Blackworth's voice sounded like old papers rustling together. Her words brought him up short. "Bring your money back?" He stared at her, open-eyed with astonishment. "Doesn't the piano still work?" Hell, he'd done his best. He knew he'd repaired it properly. Tuned it, replaced worn-out felt pads. Cleaned it of years' worth of caked-on grime.

"Oh, it works, all right. I've even been amusing myself by picking out a few tunes when my hands don't hurt too badly."

The sly old witch squinted at him as if she knew something he didn't. Which she undoubtedly did. Her attitude annoyed him. "Well then, why should I give your money back?" His tone was curt.

She chuckled like a bin full of rusty nails. "My bargain still stands, Mr. Partridge. That old reed organ your granddaddy built for the repair of my piano. But you'd have to give me back the money I paid you for fixing it."

Noah let out a breath. Oh, yeah. He'd mercifully

forgotten her bargain; he didn't appreciate her bringing it up again. "What the hell do I need with a reed organ?" If he recalled correctly, he'd asked her that the first time she'd made the offer.

Her bony shoulders lifted with her shrug and her teeth glittered in her weathered face. The damned old bat seemed amused about something. "I wouldn't know."

He felt a tug on his hand and glanced down to see Maddie's bright face smiling up at him. "You can give it to Mommy for Christmas, Mr. Noah!"

"Oh, yeah?" He could, could he? His gaze shifted to Grace, who looked mortified.

"Maddie! Mr. Partridge doesn't want to give me an organ for Christmas."

"How come?"

Yeah, Noah thought. *How come?* What the hell else did he have to do with his money besides buy expensive Christmas presents for Grace Richardson?

He had land to buy, is what he had to do with it.

"Maybe another time, Miss Maddie."

Susan Blackworth let out with another rusty-hinged laugh. "I think you're missing out on a golden opportunity, Mr. Partridge. Where else can you get one of your own grandfather's best—and first—instruments for so low a price? They don't make 'em like that anymore, you know."

He eyed her and wondered if she was trying to be funny again. "Yeah," he said. "I know."

Grace gave a small, indulgent mew, as if she sympathized with his losses. Whole lot of good that did him.

"Can you play us something on the piano, Mr. Noah?"

He glanced at Maddie again and fought a frown. He didn't want to play that instrument. Playing the piano brought back too many memories, memories that made his heart and head ache and were liable to bring his demons back. He realized with something of a shock that he hadn't had a bad attack of nerves for several days.

Oh, hell, maybe this would be a test to see if he was getting better. He could play a little tune on that blasted piano, and if he had to run screaming from the house, he'd know for sure he wasn't cured. Mrs. Richardson already knew he was crazy, and he didn't give a rap about Susan Blackworth. If he scared poor little Maddie, so be it. Her mother would just have to deal with her.

"Reckon I could play a song, Miss Maddie, if it's all right with Mrs. Blackworth."

"I think that would be lovely, Mr. Partridge."

Noah jerked his head around. Damned if the old witch hadn't sounded almost courteous.

"Let me get Mrs. Valdez to fetch us some tea and gingerbread."

Maddie clapped her hands. "Oooh, a tea party! Can I have a cup of tea, Mommy?"

"I suppose so, dear."

"With sugar and milk?"

"Of course, with sugar and milk, Maddie. I know how you like it."

Grace's face held an expression of such affection that Noah could hardly stand to watch it. And Maddie ... Hell, the kid sounded like tea and gingerbread was some sort of special treat. Cripes, he guessed it was. He shook his head. What a life this territory was for women and children. Noah thought Frank Richardson had been a blasted numskull to bring his wife out here.

Although, he must admit, she didn't seem to resent old Frank for it. Rather, she loved him as much today as she ever had, if Noah was any judge. But then, what did he know about women and love? Or faithfulness?

There he went, letting his spite get him down. Frank Richardson had clearly been a paragon; he'd surely deserved Grace's love and loyalty. Unlike Noah Partridge, who had deserved hardship and gotten it. Aw, hell.

He forced himself to smile. "What do you want me to play first, Miss Maddie?"

"Play some Christmas songs! It's going to be Christmas pretty soon." Maddie turned to her mother. "Isn't it, Mommy?"

"Yes, it is, sweetheart."

Hell. Christmas. The season Noah hated most in a year full of hateful seasons. The season in which he'd lost his family, his livelihood, and the woman he'd loved. Even if she had already deserted him and married someone else, he'd loved her. Julia had died giving birth to her husband's child on Christmas Eve. If he recalled correctly, that was the last time he'd cried. He wished he hadn't remembered.

"Sure. Why not?" He walked over to the piano, prepared to meet his fate.

Juanita Valdez brought a plate of gingerbread and a pot of steaming tea into the parlor after he sat down and played the first notes of an old Christmas tune. As gingery fragrances kissed his nostrils, Noah Partridge played "We Three Kings."

Maddie sang along, in between bites of gingerbread and sips of tea, as if she hadn't a care in the world. For Maddie, Noah remained seated on that piano bench. For Maddie, his fingers kept moving over the keys. For Maddie, he didn't scream, and he didn't run away.

He considered it a minor triumph.

"Um, may I talk to you for a minute, ma'am?"

Grace looked up from the tub of sudsy water in which she'd been washing the supper dishes. Supper had been an easy meal tonight, consisting of bread and butter and cheese and apples, since she and Maddie were both tired from their adventurous day.

Mr. Partridge looked nervous as he stood there twirling his hat in his fingers. Grace hoped he wasn't going to apologize for kissing her. Thanks to Mac's cheerful questions and humorous supper-table conversation, she'd managed to forget that torrid kiss as they'd eaten. Now the memory of it came crashing back into her mind like a herd of Chisum's long-horned steers.

She decided not to borrow trouble. "Of course, Mr. Partridge. Let me dump this water outside."

He lurched forward, consigning his hat to the table. "Here. Let me do that, ma'am. That tub looks heavy."

She bit back the retort that she was fully capable of doing her own chores. He was trying to be nice. At least she guessed he was.

With a grunt, he lifted the washtub and carried it out back. She heard the water slop out onto her garden, and was pleased he'd thought to empty it there even if she hadn't told him to. Out here, one didn't waste water, even leftover soapy dishwater.

He wasn't going to ask her to marry him out of some misguided sense of southern chivalry, was he? Heavenly days, that's all Grace needed. She tried to cast out the notion that she'd be awfully flattered if he did. But that was foolish thinking, and Grace wasn't foolish. Besides, she didn't want to marry anyone. Most particularly, she didn't want to marry a hard-edged, brooding man who made her nervous, even if he did play the piano and have a lovely voice and seemed nice despite his burdens.

It was his problems that worried Grace the most. Andersonville, for heaven's sake. Even if she managed to forget about how much she loved and missed Frank, she didn't feel up to coping with both Noah Partridge's blue devils and her own. The combination was more than any woman should have to cope with

Of course, if he got better—but, no. Grace was ashamed of herself when she realized the direction her thoughts were taking. It was wicked of her even to think about marrying again. Disloyal. And marriage to Noah Partridge? Why, he wasn't anything like Frank. And Frank was the only man she'd ever loved and ever would love. Ever could love.

Troubled, she took the tub from Noah's outstretched hands. "Thank you." She tried to sound grateful.

With care, because he made her edgy, Grace hung the tub on its proper hook on the wall, scooped out a fingerful of Mac's special lanolin cream, and rubbed it thoroughly into her hands. Only then did she feel settled enough inside to allow herself to look up and smile at Noah.

"Now, Mr. Partridge, you wanted to talk to me. Would you care for a cup of coffee?"

"No, thank you, ma'am."

"Well, I do believe I'll have one. Coffee never keeps me up at night, because I'm so worn out it doesn't have a chance." She managed a little laugh, and was proud of herself.

"Reckon that's true, ma'am."

His voice sounded harsh, and Grace glanced over her shoulder at him from the stove, where a pot of coffee always stood. He didn't look any different than he ever did—which wasn't friendly and certainly wasn't easy. There didn't seem to be one single easy thing about Noah Partridge.

At the moment Mac was reading Maddie a bedtime story. Grace didn't expect it to last long, since Maddie was so worn out from her happy day that she'd probably be sound asleep before Mac finished the second page. She supposed she should thank Mr. Partridge for the day. Leaving out the kiss, of course.

"Maddie had a very good time today, Mr. Partridge. Thank you for taking us—her—on that picnic."

He brushed aside her thanks. "You're the one who did everything, Mrs. Richardson. I only tagged along."

Hmph. Grace sat and motioned him to take a chair on the other side of the kitchen table. He complied, and began fiddling with his hat again. She sipped her coffee and wondered what to say now. With luck, he'd take it from here.

He did. "Um, have you given any more thought to selling me your land, Mrs. Richardson? I mean, have you reconsidered? Thought it over, I mean?"

For a second, Grace felt like he'd punched her in the

stomach. It took a mighty effort for her to set her coffee mug down on the table and not splash its contents into Noah Partridge's face.

Was that why he'd kissed her? Had he believed she'd succumb to his fleshly lures and weaken in her resolve not to sell him Frank's dream? Her eyes squinted up, her heart hurting, and she felt as helpless as if he'd shoved her from a high precipice. Her nerves jangled, and her throat tried to close up on her. Her eyes burned.

Pinching her lips tightly together, she managed to keep from yelling at him to get out of her kitchen. It wasn't even her kitchen. It was Mac's kitchen, and Mac had invited this man in. Grace only worked in it, and in Mac's mercantile. She had nothing in the entire world to call her own.

Except that one plot of land out there beside the Pecos River, where Frank himself had planted two willows and three cottonwoods. Where he'd aimed to build them a house one day, and run some cattle, and have some pigs and chickens and sheep. Perhaps they'd have had more children and reared them there, on that plot of ground that Noah Partridge wanted to take away from her. That land belonged to Grace, and it would one day be Maddie's. It was all either of them had left of Frank.

"No, Mr. Partridge. That is, yes, I have thought about it. And no, I won't sell you the land." Her voice was amazingly level, considering the state of her nerves, which were tangled up in knots and jumping around like spring lambs.

His brows lowered over his green eyes. Grace glared into them, refusing to look away. He didn't speak immediately. Grace wondered if he was surprised by her continued refusal or merely peeved. If he was, he certainly didn't know her very well. According to Grace's mother, Grace Richardson was the most stubborn female ever born. And perhaps her mother was right. Why else would she have agreed to brave the Territory with Frank—or, even more to the point, without Frank.

"Quite honestly, I'm surprised you're still interested in it," she went on. She could hear the anger seeping into her voice and didn't care. "There's a whole lot of land available for purchase or claim out here in this part of the Territory. Why do you insist upon that particular parcel?" Maybe he was one of those competitive men who always wanted what other people owned, like Susan's husband, Hugh Blackworth.

He was furious; Grace could tell. There was nothing he could do to her, though, no matter how mad he got. She owned that land. It was hers to do with as she chose, and she chose to keep it.

"Damn it, ma'am—beg pardon. Didn't mean to swear."

Grace huffed softly.

"But, if you'll pardon me for saying so, I think you're being pigheaded about this whole thing. There's no way you'll ever be able to work that spread yourself, Mrs. Richardson. Why do you want to hold on to something you can't use?"

She was so angry, her teeth didn't want to unclench and allow her to respond. With some difficulty, she pried them far enough apart to say, "My plans are no concern of yours, Mr. Partridge."

Noah averted his eyes. She could see fury radiating from him in almost palpable waves. Too bad.

"To tell you the truth," she continued, "I resent your continuing to pester me about it. I won't sell that land. If something happens and I lose it, it won't be because I haven't done everything in my power to retain it." She sucked in a deep breath and wished she hadn't said that. "You can ask me from now until kingdom come, and my answer will remain the same. That land was bought by my husband, it was left to me, it will belong to our daughter someday, and no amount of asking or arguing on your part will change my mind."

Her heart pounded like an artillery barrage. She wished she weren't too well-bred to tell him to go to hell.

"Dammit, you're being foolishly obstinate! There's no way you can use that land, Mrs. Richardson!"

She stood, pressed her hands on the table, and leaned over until she was within an inch of his face. "That's neither here nor there! That land is mine, and I won't sell it. Not to you, and not to anyone else!"

Noah stood, too, so precipitately that his chair tilted and almost fell over backwards. He caught it awkwardly. She saw his cheeks flush—with rage, she was sure.

"That piece of property is perfect for what I want, dammit, Mrs. Richardson."

"It's perfect for what I want too, Mr. Partridge. That's exactly why I won't sell it!"

"But what are you going to do with it?"

"That's none of your business!"

"But you can't even *use* it!"

"So what?" Grace snatched her cup from the table, whirled around, and marched to the sink. She almost cracked the mug when she set it down. "I don't care to talk about it any more."

"Damnation!"

She turned again and practically shouted at him, "And I would appreciate it if you would stop swearing!"

A soft chuckle from the door brought them both up short. Grace felt her own face flame when she saw Mac, his eyes gleaming like sapphires, grinning around the pipe clenched in his teeth. He removed the pipe, blew out a smoke ring that danced in the kitchen air, and shook his head.

"Tut, tut, you two. What a row ye're havin'. I'm surprised wee Maddie can sleep through it."

Grace pressed a hand to her cheek. "Oh, dear, did we wake her up?"

"Nay, lass. 'Twould take an army to wake the bairn up tonight. The two o' ye showed her a fine time today."

Noah grunted. Grace swirled around. "Too bad it didn't last." And with that, she flounced from the room.

Chapter Thirteen

Noah was mad enough to spit horseshoe nails when he stomped out to his lonely bed in the stall that night. Damned recalcitrant female. Why the hell was she being so stubborn about that parcel of land? It wasn't as if she could ever do anything with it. She needed a man to help her if she expected to build anything out there, or plant crops, or raise cattle or sheep. Hell, she'd even need help raising chickens unless she aimed to build a coop by herself.

He kicked the ground at his feet and sent a shower of dirt onto his neatly stacked bedroll. Cursing, he shook out his blankets, figuring this was a fitting end to a frustrating day.

It took a while to rearrange his bedding comfortably, during which period of time he fumed. Then he lay back on the rolled-up saddle blanket he used for a pillow and stared into the night sky. It looked like a million stars were twinkling down at him, but he didn't appreciate the serene beauty of the heavens. He was still too furious to appreciate anything but the bull-headed obstinacy of certain females he could mention.

He'd been fuming in his bedroll for a good fifteen or twenty minutes when something Grace had hollered at him penetrated his anger.

If something happens and I lose it. What the hell had she meant by that? Noah frowned at the stars, his head cradled in his clasped hands. The night had turned nippy, but he didn't mind. He was glad of the cold. Besides, he was plenty warm in his bedroll and long johns and temper.

He wondered where the nearest land agent was, and if there was a telegraph office in Rio Hondo somewhere. Susan Blackworth had mentioned that she was going to wire to the Estey Organ Works about parts for her organ, so there must be.

He hoped to hell Rio Hondo's telegraph operator wasn't Mac, because what he planned to do might be construed as sneaky.

"A telegraph? Aye, lad, we have us a telegraph in Rio Hondo." Mac waggled his bushy eyebrows at Noah. "Plannin' a coup, are ye, lad?"

Noah had been slumped in front of the old potbellied stove in Mac's mercantile, drinking the coffee Mac had pressed upon him. He looked up from his mug and frowned. What the hell had the old man meant by that? "A coup?"

Mac chuckled. "Never mind, lad. Aye, we got us a telegraph. It's down the road a piece, in what passes for the courthouse. That's where the circuit judge sets up when he comes through, which isn't often.''

"Thanks." Noah was sure he heard Mac laughing as he stomped out of the mercantile and headed toward the wagon yard gates.

Mac was right about the courthouse. It sat next door to the Pecos Saloon, and looked like it had been slapped together out of two-by-fours and glued into place. Noah shook his head and wondered if Rio Hondo would ever be a grown-up town with the real trappings of civilization. He hoped not.

The telegraph operator, Percy Wiggins, chomped on his cigar and eyed Noah with distaste. Pompous little bastard. Noah hadn't hardly met him yet, and he didn't like him already.

"I can't tell you how long it'll take to get an answer, Mr. Partridge. I ain't responsible for answers to the wires I send out, just the wires themselves. For all I know, the Comanches will cut the lines, and you'll never get an answer."

Of course. Noah knew that. He resented the self-important little man for being snippy with him anyway. "How'll I know when an answer comes in?"

Wiggins blew out a ring of gray smoke and looked irked. "You'll have to come in and ask, I reckon, just like ever'body else does."

Noah tugged his hat brim down lower over his forehead. He wanted to punch the insolent man, and knew the impulse to be unhelpful. So, what else was new?

Without succumbing to violence, he wrote out his message, paid Percy Wiggins the appropriate fee, and waited until Wiggins had clicked it into his machine. Noah didn't trust him to do it out of his watchful eye.

"There," said Wiggins when he was through. "I've sent your message." He smirked.

Noah didn't thank him. He merely nodded and left the depressing building.

Because he didn't want to see Grace Richardson even more than he didn't like Percy Wiggins, Noah stopped in at the Pecos Saloon before he returned to the wagon yard. He hated drinking, and he had no interest in whores. The two times he'd used a whore, he'd felt dirty afterwards. Today, when Miss Aggie rubbed her bosom against his arm, he almost succumbed, not because he felt any lust toward Miss Aggie, but because his frustrations were running so high.

In the end, he couldn't make himself do it. It might be pleasant to lose himself to passion for a few minutes, but there was something about buying all that pink-and-white flesh that set his teeth on edge.

Grace Richardson, now . . . Hell, he could make love to her from now until ten years hence and consider himself a lucky man. Miss Aggie's hard, painted face, overblown body, and undoubted laudanum habit—every whore Noah'd ever met had drug habits—seemed grotesque by comparison. Miss Aggie cursed him when he left the saloon without even buying her a drink. He figured his luck with females was running true to form today.

That night, for the first time in two weeks, Noah awoke in the middle of the night shaking and sweating and hollering. In his dream, he'd been back at Andersonville, listening to the sounds of distant cannon fire and digging graves for the bodies of his fellow prisoners. The cannon fire didn't quite muffle their groans and whimpers, and there was nothing he could do for those men except dig graves to hold them when they finally stopped whimpering.

Thank God he still slept outside. He'd almost given in to the lure of Mac's fireplace. He'd have felt like even more of a dolt than he already did if he'd woke up yelling in Mac's parlor. He'd probably scare poor little Maddie to death.

"Damn." He sat up, shivering. The sooner he got that property, the better. He'd find himself a dog and buy himself some cows and a couple of pigs, build a chicken coop, settle down, and never have to think about Grace Richardson again.

His mood didn't lighten any when Gus Spalding made an appearance at the supper table a couple of nights later, for Thanksgiving. Noah had forgotten all about Thanksgiving, but Grace wasn't one to forget things like that, he reckoned. She had prepared a fine meal, considering the pickings were pretty slim for a traditional dinner out here on the frontier.

From somewhere, Mac had found a turkey. Noah was beginning to think of Mac's powers of supply as almost magical, although he didn't believe in magic any more than he believed in the inmate goodness of man. This bird wasn't one of those skinny prairie-chicken varieties, either, but a plump hen that weighed at least twelve pounds and tasted like Noah remembered from his childhood. Grace roasted it with corn-bread stuffing, and she served it up with potatoes and gravy and string beans, and she'd made a pumpkin pie for dessert. She was a better cook than Noah's mother had been. There wasn't so much as a sliver of pie left when the meal was over.

During the entire evening, Gus looked like a lovesick

calf, gazing at Grace Richardson as if he were starved for a word from her. She gave him plenty of words. She was as warm to Gus as she was cold to Noah.

It was obvious that Maddie and Gus were buddies of long standing. The young cowboy and the little girl had built a rapport Noah envied. Maybe if he could get on Maddie's good side, Grace would soften her attitude towards him. Given Noah's state of mental health, such a proposition seemed unlikely, more's the pity. Noah was as tense and standoffish as Gus was friendly and easygoing, blast it. It was no wonder that Maddie liked Gus. The wonder was that she'd been friendly with Noah.

Mac looked like a benevolent gnome, taking in everything and grinning at them all, presiding over the table and directing the conversation with the ease of a master. Noah always got the impression Mac knew the answers to everybody's questions, and was keeping them to himself.

Damn it all to hell and back again. Noah wished to heaven that the old man would share. He needed some answers bad.

After Thanksgiving dinner, replete and sleepy, they sang songs in front of the fireplace. Gus Spalding turned out to have a rich, albeit untrained, tenor voice that blended well with Grace's soprano. Maddie, fingering her locket and smiling at Noah, said she wished they had a piano so that Mr. Noah could play it. Noah pretended to enjoy himself.

"Are you mad at Mr. Noah, Mommy?"

Grace looked up from the cinnamon stick she was twisting. Maddie liked them curly. The dried-apple pie

255

baking in the oven filled the kitchen with a tantalizing aroma that the fragrance of cinnamon enhanced. Grace's stomach growled in anticipation. Turkey sandwiches and apple pie for supper. Life could get a lot worse than this, she guessed. She couldn't account for why she'd felt so sad ever since her last argument with Noah.

"No," she lied. "I'm not mad at Mr. Partridge."

"How come you don't talk to him anymore?"

Grace realized her mouth had tightened into a flat line of frustration, and she made herself relax it. None of this was Maddie's fault. "We still talk, dear." Leftover indignation at Noah made her add, "I guess we just don't have much to say to each other, is all."

Maddie scowled as her little fingers—scrubbed with plenty of lye soap—patted out her own piece of pie dough. She planned to cut pumpkins from the dough when it was flat enough, in honor of her mother's tales of autumns back east. Grace realized with something of a shock that Maddie had no personal experience with the oranges and golds of autumn foliage, with trees baring their branches to the season, with the crunch of dried leaves underfoot and the smell of loamy soil. Maddie had never watched squirrels scurrying to hide nuts and acorns in preparation for winter.

Had Maddie ever even seen a real full-grown tree? Once or twice, perhaps, when they'd trekked up to Lincoln and Capitan, in the mountains to the southwest of Rio Hondo. How long ago had their last trip been? She couldn't recall, but she knew it had been before Frank died. Maddie probably didn't even remember it now.

Tears burned Grace's eyes. Was she depriving her daughter of a happy childhood? Of fall harvest festivals and Halloweens and Christmases full of laughter and food and fun and relatives? That one spindly pumpkin vine growing on a mound in back of Mac's house and its crop of skinny pumpkins seemed pathetic compared to Grace's memories of autumns back home when Thanksgiving had truly been a festival of God's bounty. She thought President Lincoln had done a good deed when he'd declared a national day of thanks back in '63.

The land was so hard out here, it took mountains of soil amendments and hours of backbreaking labor to grow so much as a tiny crop of carrots. At least they had access to scads of manure—which was a good thing, since they had to use it for fuel sometimes.

Life was a perilously makeshift affair in the Territory, where everything was just shy of the edge of disaster. Oh, dear. Suddenly Grace missed her family with such fierceness, she almost cried out with pain.

"Well, *I* like Mr. Noah," Maddie said with resolution. "And I'm gonna give him one of my punkins."

"I'm sure he'll like that, sweetheart."

"I'll put extra cimmon and sugar on his, 'cause he needs to sweeten up."

In spite of the turmoil raging in her heart, Grace laughed. "He does, does he?" She agreed, although she'd never say so to Maddie.

Maddie nodded. When she did that her shiny braids bounced up and down. Grace pulled one for fun, and Maddie giggled.

"As soon as we put your pumpkins in the oven to bake, why don't you go and fetch Mac and Mr. Partridge for supper, Maddie."

"All right!"

So the apple pie came out of the oven, and the pumpkins and cinnamon sticks went in, and Maddie skipped outside to do her chore. Grace stared after her, her heart heavy.

The wind shrieked like a soul in torment across the plains outside Mac's small house. It reminded Noah of himself. The weather had turned cold again, but it wasn't like the cold of the winters with which Noah was familiar. This was a hard, dry cold that sliced through a fellow and made him wish for things that could never be. Like sanity, for instance. Or a few moments of comfort in Grace Richardson's arms.

Noah frowned at his hot apple pie, and silently called himself fifty kinds of fool. He'd already eaten his cinnamon-and-sugar-covered pumpkin and pronounced it delicious. Maddie had been pleased.

"Ye're lookin' a little peaked, Grace," Mac said. "You feeling all right?"

Noah, who'd been trying to stay out of supper-table conversations lately because he didn't want Grace any more mad at him than she already was, looked up from his plate.

Damn, she did look tired. His heart gave a sudden twinge. There was no reason for him to feel anything in the least proprietary about Grace Richardson. If she were sick, however, he'd ride to hell and back to fetch a doctor. When had that happened? What did it mean? He shook his head and returned his attention to his pie. It didn't matter when it had happened, and it meant nothing, unless it was another symptom of his overall madness.

"I'm fine, Mac, thank you," Grace said with one of

her usual smiles, the ones she reserved for the people she liked. Noah hadn't received one since the last time he'd asked her to sell him her land. When she smiled at him these days, usually because Maddie was watching, her smiles were brittle travesties of the ones she gave to her friends.

Noah sighed.

"Everything all right back home?"

Back home? Noah glanced up again.

"Mommy got a letter from my Grandma Baxter," Maddie explained in her piping voice. "That's my mommy's mommy."

At least Maddie still liked him. Of course, that might change if she knew he wanted her mother's land. He gave himself a mental shake and told himself to snap out of it.

"Oh, everything's fine back in Chicago."

In spite of her words, which she took pains to speak gaily, Grace looked troubled. Noah experienced a fierce urge to take her burdens away. Jeeze, he really was a lunatic!

Mac chuckled. "Let me guess. Your mother's askin' ye to go back home again, eh?"

"You guessed it, Mac." Grace heaved a huge sigh, and speared an apple slice out of her pie. "She just doesn't understand."

Before he could stop himself, Noah asked, "What doesn't she understand?" He cursed himself as a jackass when Grace turned her head and peered at him with an expression colder than the weather.

"She doesn't understand my determination to make a life for Maddie and myself out here in the Territory. Not unlike some other people I could name."

259

Right. No subtlety there. Feeling defeated, Noah nevertheless pursued the matter. "Well, ma'am, she's probably read about how hard a life it is for settlers in this part of the country."

Mac nodded and grinned. It didn't look like agreement to Noah, but as if he were enjoying the show. It figured. Ever since he'd ridden into Mac's wagon yard, Noah had felt like a specimen under a microscope of Mac's design and operation. Every now and then, it could be a damned uncomfortable feeling.

"Yes, I know all about your opinion of women who try to make a go of their lives without the help of men." Grace sniffed with immense hauteur.

"It's not that I don't think women are as smart as men," Noah explained patiently.

Grace grunted and stabbed another apple slice. Noah had a feeling she'd rather be stabbing him.

"It's just that men are stronger than women. Physically." Definitely not mentally, although he'd not say so. "Out here, it takes a lot of brute strength to wrestle the land into submission."

She eyed him coldly. "You've made a study of it, I suppose."

"Well—" He thought about lying, then decided *to hell with it.* "Yes, ma'am. I read up about all the territories and newly developed lands out west when I decided to move away from Virginia. I chose the New Mexico Territory because it was harder than any of the others."

"And so are you." It was an accusation. She obviously thought she'd said something that would cut him. As if he were still capable of being hurt by words.

"Yes, ma'am. I am." *And I don't give up, either.*

He spared her that part. She'd find out. Hell, if he were a quitter, he'd have been dead years ago. As he'd admitted to himself before, he'd probably be better off, but he was stuck with himself now and that was that.

"Well, neither you nor my family back in Chicago are going to make me give up my land, Mr. Partridge."

"Yes'm," he said meekly. He hadn't received an answer to his wire yet, and was through arguing with her about that land for the time being. Depending on what the territorial government said, he might try again. Fighting with Grace Richardson made him sad, though, and he'd just as soon not if he could avoid it.

This time it was Mac who sighed. "You two," he said, and shook his head.

Maddie looked merely puzzled.

After supper, stuffed with good food and feeling lazy, Noah joined Mac for a chat in the parlor. He'd begun to anticipate these evenings before Mac's fire with something akin to pleasure. It had been so long since Noah had taken pleasure in anything that it had taken him a while to recognize the sensation.

One of the reasons he enjoyed these evening visits so much was that Mac didn't make him talk. Hell, half the time he didn't even make him listen. They both just sat there, Mac in his easy chair, Noah on a stool in front of the fire, and they stared into the flames.

Sometimes he imagined he could see things in the fire. Once, he could have sworn he saw a whole circus parade, with elephants and lion tamers and ladies in fancy costumes riding high-stepping horses. But he knew that was merely a manifestation of his craziness. He might well see things like that in a simple after-supper fire. Still, he liked to watch it, and his fireplace visions didn't trouble him.

Almost hypnotized by the flames, he would allow his mind to wander undirected. More often than not, it wandered of its own accord to Grace Richardson.

It did so tonight.

"She's worried about ye, lad," Mac said, his soft voice intruding so gently into Noah's consciousness that it had begun to travel down Noah's mind's path before he was even aware of it.

"I didn't mean to make her worry," he said, lulled into honesty by the spell of Mac's parlor. "But I feel a powerful attraction to that land of hers."

"Aye, lad. So does she."

"Yes. I know." Noah was unhappy about it too. It seemed like, whatever happened, either Grace or he would be wounded.

"It's magic, that land of hers."

"Magic?" Noah smiled, finding Mac's assessment pretty funny.

"Aye." The old man chuckled as if he found the whole thing funny too. " 'Tis magic, all right. There's a lot of enchantment in these wild plains."

"Is there?"

"Oh, aye. The Indians knew that."

"I expect." He'd heard stuff like that before. Noah was reserving judgment on the issue.

"Takes a certain kind of person to tame the magic and use it."

"It does, does it?"

"Aye. Grace—well, now, she has it."

Noah glanced at Mac. The old man appeared dreamy as he sat there, holding his pipe to his lips and gazing into the fire. His eyes were bright, though. Mac's eyes were always bright. They were the twinkliest blue Noah had ever seen. Not gray-blue like Grace and Maddie's eyes, but a bright, robin's-egg blue. Grace and Maddie's eyes might be serene—when Grace wasn't wishing Noah dead. Mac's eyes were anything but.

"But, Mac, how does she, a woman alone and without a husband, expect to be able to use that land of hers?"

"I don't know, lad. But she's got the spirit for it."

Noah shook his head. "I wish I'd seen another plot of land I liked as well. I really don't want to take her land away from her. But it doesn't make sense that she's so set on keeping it when she can't use it."

"Oh, lad, anything can happen in this wonderful life. Who's to say what a body can or can't do in it?"

"But . . ." Noah didn't know what to say.

Mac chuckled again. "I think the two o' ye ought to go out alone and look at that plot of land together. Tell each other what ye'd do with it if you could do anything you wanted. Who knows? Maybe ye'll come up wi' a plan for it between you."

Noah frowned, troubled. He didn't want to be alone with Grace Richardson. He didn't trust himself. Even his dreams—the ones unplagued by rotten memories of the war—had begun to feature her. "Well . . ."

"I don't think that's a very good idea, Mac."

Noah jerked his head up and saw Grace standing in the doorway. She was staring straight at him and scowling fit to kill. Damn.

"Why not?" Mac shared his grin equally between Noah and Grace. "It'll give ye both a chance to see what the other finds so appealin' in that one parcel of land that ye're willin' to hate each other over it. Maybe ye'll both decide it's not worth hanging on to or fighting over.''

Hate each other? Noah only wished he could hate Grace.

Her lips pinched up tight. Noah could tell she felt both angry and betrayed by Mac's sensible suggestion. He guessed she'd expected more loyalty than this from her old friend. Truth to tell, Noah was kind of surprised himself. On the other hand, Mac was probably subtly implying that Noah himself should back off.

Well, cripes, maybe the old man was right. Maybe Noah'd made more of that land than was really there. Maybe he only wanted it because he couldn't have it. He wouldn't put it past his brain to pull a stunt like that.

''Actually,'' he found himself saying. ''That doesn't sound like a bad idea.''

Grace stiffened up like a spike. ''It sounds like a terrible idea to me.''

Mac laughed. Noah rose from his stool. ''I promise not to pester you about selling it, Mrs. Richardson. But maybe Mac's right. Maybe if we went out there together and looked it over, we might come up with some kind of compromise.''

Offhand, he couldn't think of one. He didn't want the parcel divided. He wanted the whole thing. He'd gone out there by himself and ridden the perimeter. It was perfect for what he had in mind for his life.

Still, he didn't think a trip to the Pecos with Grace would hurt. It might even help, especially if he could get her talking about how she planned to do whatever she planned to do. Maybe if she said it out loud, she'd finally understand how stupid it was to believe she could make anything out there by herself.

Of course, the experience might just drive her into the arms of the young Gus Spalding. Noah would bet his last dollar that Gus wanted to marry her, although Grace seemed to be determined to remain true to her damned dead husband, the saintly Frank. Still, Noah was willing to take a chance that the trip would open her eyes to the futility of her dreams.

Noah's dreams were infinitely simpler than Grace's. All he wanted was to get away from everything. And stay there.

"I don't see what purpose it would serve," Grace said, obviously nettled. "Besides, we can't just ride out for the day and leave Maddie alone and Mac with no one to tend the store."

"Ach, lass, I'd watch Miss Maddie for ye. And there's no one to visit the store. Everybody in the area stocked up before Thanksgiving, and won't be back until Christmas."

Grace didn't look at all pleased to have these truths pointed out to her. She huffed indignantly, sat in a fluff of calico and petticoats, yanked her embroidery out of the basket that sat beside her rocking chair, and began stabbing her needle into the cloth trapped in the embroidery ring. Again Noah got the impression she'd rather be stabbing him. He remained undeterred. Suddenly Mac's proposed trip seemed like the only solution to a tricky problem.

"Please, ma'am? I'll renew my promise not to badger you about buying the land. I just want to see it, to look at it through your eyes. I'd like to hear what your plans for it are." If she had any; he doubted it. "And I'll tell you mine." Why the hell had he said that? There was no way he'd confess to being so sick of life that he wanted to hide away from it, to lose himself out there on the prairie, where nobody could ever get at him again.

She looked up from her embroidery, squinting at him as if she didn't trust him an inch. Noah fought his impulse to take exception to her skepticism. He guessed she deserved the emotion.

"You really mean it?"

"Of course I mean it!"

Noah didn't appreciate it when Mac laughed again.

"Oh, very well."

Noah stood and held his hat in front of him. "Thank you, ma'am."

"I'll pack us a lunch. I don't care to starve while we're pursuing this foolish nonsense."

She sounded less gracious than Noah had ever heard her, even when she was screaming mad at him. He did his best to remain humble. "Thank you, ma'am."

She gave him another harumph. Noah figured not much had changed. It seemed that no matter how reasonable he tried to be, the females in his life always turned on him.

Nevertheless, when he saddled Fargo and Grace's mare the next morning, he discovered he was anticipating their upcoming ride together with satisfaction. Even if Grace hated him, he couldn't find it in his heart to dislike her—no matter how stubborn she was, and how inconvenient that stubbornness was to him.

Maddie skipped outside with her mother, her elfin countenance a sunny counterpoint to Grace's stormy expression.

"I wish I could go with you, Mr. Noah," Maddie said wistfully. "But Mac says I gotta stay here and help him mind the mercantile."

"That's an important job, Miss Maddie."

Grace sniffed. Noah peered at her and then back at Maddie, and he sighed.

"I reckon. That's what Mac says, too." Maddie didn't sound altogether convinced, but she was too well-behaved to object to the decisions the adults in her life made for her. Noah wondered how long that would last. He wondered if Maddie would grow into adolescence and resent this lonely life. It would break his heart if he ever heard of her running away to some big city like some kids did, in order to get away from these lonely, isolated plains.

Cripes, he was being crazy again. He told himself to stop thinking crazy thoughts.

Mac came out to bid them adieu, as friendly and jovial as ever. He held Maddie by the hand when Noah and Grace set out, and they both waved after the two of them. Noah wondered if it was the crisp winter air that made sparkles seem to fly from the old man's fingertips. Nah. He was just nuts, was all it was.

Grace remained stiff as a board through the first leg of their journey. It didn't look to him as if she aimed to thaw out a bit during this little expedition; it was as if showing him a modicum of friendship might weaken her position and send her straight to perdition and Noah into possession of her property. He guessed she aimed to show him by her frigidity of posture and attitude exactly how useless this trip was.

Well, maybe she was right. And maybe she wasn't. All Noah knew was that as soon as Mac had proposed it, this jaunt had sounded right to him.

Chapter Fourteen

Much to Grace's surprise, they didn't freeze to death on their ride out to the Pecos River. She'd thought Mac was out of his mind when he suggested this trip, but now—and in spite of the company she was in—she discovered she was enjoying herself. There was something very pleasant about getting away from her responsibilities for a little while and knowing they'd be taken care of in her absence. With Mac minding Maddie, Grace knew she didn't have to worry about her daughter.

The landscape in these parts never varied. The flat, rolling plains went on forever. Dry grasses, flattened by icy wind, rippled like fields of stringy gold. The caprock, as level as a pancake, stretched on for miles to the northwest, and it was still early enough in the season for flocks of geese and cranes to pass above them. Grace loved those graceful, elegant birds.

She almost even managed to forget that Noah Partridge, her enemy, rode beside her. He was such a silent man, even when he was at his most chatty, that she didn't feel obliged to initiate a conversation or pretend friendship. In truth, she feared him more than she'd ever feared anyone.

She didn't think he could get Frank's land away from her, but he did dreadful things to her peace of mind. She couldn't stop thinking about him, even when he wasn't around. As much as she told herself she hated him, still more did she have to fight the strange attraction he held for her. She felt like a traitor.

He was nothing like Frank. He was nothing like sweet Gus Spalding who, Grace knew, had a crush on her. Noah was dangerous. Not that Grace feared that he'd hurt her physically. He didn't seem violent in the least. But he cut up her peace. Destroyed the calm placidity she'd made of her life. Disrupted her thoughts—even her dreams. He annoyed her. And he wouldn't give up. She considered his obstinacy particularly trying, especially since she wasn't confident she could hold on to that land even without Noah looming over her like a buzzard, ready to snatch it up if she lost her hold on it.

Blast that mortgage!

But Noah Partridge didn't know about the mortgage. How could he? She'd sure never tell him. And she was catching up. Every penny she made went to cover the back payments. She even denied her daughter toys and new shoes to pay for that land.

Guilt pricked at her. The land was more important to Maddie than toys and new shoes, even if Maddie couldn't know it. Even if Grace's own mother thought

Grace was a bullheaded dolt. She chuffed out an irritated breath.

"You all right, Mrs. Richardson?"

Grace lifted her head and saw Noah watching her, his eyes hooded, his granitelike countenance impassive. She snapped, "I'm fine, thank you."

She heard his heavy sigh, and it irked her. What reason did *he* have to feel exasperated? All he had to do was turn his head, and he'd see acres of land. He could have just about any of it he wanted. The only piece of land he couldn't have was the few acres Frank had bought for his family. For her. She didn't think she was being unreasonable at all.

"I'm hoping we can have a nice day, Mrs. Richardson. It would be easier if you didn't demonstrate how much you hate me with every breath you take."

She was surprised that he could sound so annoyed. She'd begun to think he didn't care enough about anything to have emotions. Except when he thought about the war, of course. Or her land.

"I don't hate you." Her voice was tight and hard. She wouldn't have believed herself if she'd been him, even though it was the truth.

"I'm glad," he said, surprising her again.

She expected him to say more, but he didn't. After a minute, she glanced at him. His expression looked slightly sad, unless she was reading things into it that weren't there. She probably was. He was a cold, detached man, and she'd better remember that or she'd be inclined to start caring about him. Any woman who began to care about a man like that would be no better off than she ought to be.

Men like Noah Partridge were the kind who ruined

271

innocent girls; Grace had seen such things happen. She remembered pretty little Lanita Gracechurch, who'd been seduced and abandoned by a gambling man, a man as cold and hard as Noah Partridge ever could be. Poor Lanita's mother had tried to say the baby was her sister's, but everyone had known better. Lanita still couldn't hold her head up; Grace knew it, because her mother had taken pains to write about Lanita in her letters from home. Grace suspected her mother's reports had been meant to serve as a warning to her. As if she needed one!

Then too, again back in Chicago, Grace's best friend had married a man named John Grant, a man she knew to be irresponsible, thinking he'd change after they were married. He hadn't, and now poor Meribel was suffering for it. Grace got the occasional letter from Meribel, and Grace wrote to her on a regular basis, but their lives had diverged so much since their marriages that they might have been speaking to each other in tongues. Poor Meribel. In spite of the hardships Grace faced every day, she considered herself luckier than either Lanita or Meribel.

If there were any justice in the world, God would have taken John Grant or that wretched gambling man and spared Frank Richardson. *Justice,* Grace thought with contempt. There was no such thing as justice anywhere, for anyone. If one needed proof, one needed look no farther than Frank Richardson. Or Noah Partridge.

Andersonville. Grace shook her head and wished she didn't feel such intense sympathy for this frozen man who coveted her land.

Of course, he wasn't so *very* cold. Not any longer,

he wasn't. It had taken him a while to thaw out, but he seemed much less alienated from the rest of the human race than he'd been when he'd first arrived in Mac's wagon yard. Grace remembered when she'd seen him for the first time; she'd worried that he was a criminal because he looked so hard. She hadn't realized then that his hardness wasn't that of a vicious man, but a wounded one. Like a wild animal that had been caught in a trap.

He seemed almost friendly around Maddie these days. Grace smiled. Who wouldn't be friendly with Maddie? She was such a sunny, happy child. She was like her father in that regard. Grace occasionally brooded. Maddie took after her daddy; she didn't have a brooding bone in her body.

"To tell you the truth, Mrs. Richardson, I thought that seeing that piece of property again might make me not want it so much. Maybe hearing your plans for it will make more sense to me than my own."

She shot him a sharp look. "It doesn't matter one way or the other, Mr. Partridge. I'm not selling it."

He sighed heavily. Again, Grace resented it.

"Listen," he said. "I'm sorry I brought it up. Let's not talk about the land, all right? I'm interested in how folks live out here, though. It's a rough place."

She hesitated, pondering his comment, wondering if he planned to use any response of hers against her. She didn't see how he could, but she wasn't a subtle thinker. The ways in which people undermined each other always caught her off guard.

Frank used to honor her integrity and openness; he'd told her more than once that she'd have been lost from word one if she'd gone head to head with that sneaky

Emma Craig

Italian fellow. What was his name? Machiavelli—yes, that was it. Now *he* was a real sneak. Not Grace. Grace was as open as the day was long; she couldn't have perpetrated a subterfuge if her life depended on it. Now she wished she weren't so blasted candid.

Yet she didn't see much point in disagreeing. Anyone could tell by looking that the land out here wasn't hospitable. Feeling like she was being forced to walk on eggshells with excruciating care, and resenting it, she murmured, "Yes. It is."

"Is it easy to grow a garden out here? A kitchen garden, I mean. You know, vegetables?"

She uttered a short laugh. "No. It isn't easy to grow anything out here but greasewood and cactus."

"You seem to have a pretty fair garden at the wagon yard, though."

"Yes. Mac started it before Maddie and I moved there. Before Frank died."

"Yeah."

She wished she hadn't mentioned Frank aloud. Every time she did, Noah Partridge seemed to shrink into himself. Not that he was ever very forthcoming. But he seemed to be making an effort to be expansive today, and she was sorry to have nipped his effort in the bud.

On the other hand—as she kept reminding herself—she was what she was. And Grace Richardson was a good-hearted, unsubtle woman with a keen interest in her fellow man. Propping herself up with that thought, she decided to be bold.

"Were you ever married, Mr. Partridge?"

He was so startled by her question that he started in his saddle and had to calm his horse down. Grace

274

hadn't expected such a strong reaction to her innocent question, and wondered if she should have kept silent.

He answered her, though. Perhaps he didn't consider her merely nosy. "No. I was engaged once."

She gazed at him for a moment, but he didn't seem inclined to expand on his comment. Since she didn't know the circumstances, she wasn't sure what to say now. She opted for a brief, "Oh."

He peered at her out of the corner of his eye. She tried to look sympathetic and not merely inquisitive. But she was inquisitive. Intensely.

After a moment, he huffed out a breath. "She married somebody else when I was gone off to war. Reckon she didn't want to wait, and she was probably right. I wasn't exactly prime husband material when I got back."

"You mean she didn't wait for you even though she'd agreed to marry you? Were you formally engaged?"

"You mean, had I given her a ring? Yeah."

Grace's indignation was profound. She didn't hold with two-timing people, male *or* female. And a promise was a promise. Especially such an important promise as an engagement. She muttered, "Well, I never," under her breath.

Noah's laugh offended her. "It's not funny, Mr. Partridge! I think that's a terrible thing to do to someone. She might have been able to help you through a miserable time in your life. That's what commitment means, after all. It's not merely savoring the good times, but helping each other through the hard ones. A woman who won't wait for her man isn't worth your time."

Oh, good grief. Grace and her big mouth. She *really* wished she hadn't said that, especially when Noah seemed to stare daggers at her. But she'd meant it. She lifted her chin very much the way Maddie lifted hers when she was feeling defiant. "Well, it's the truth. I certainly wouldn't want any man who wasn't willing to wait until I'd fulfilled my commitment to my country, or one who wasn't willing to help me if I'd been injured." She added, "If women did things like that, of course."

"You didn't know Julia." His voice was hard, and the words sounded like an accusation.

She gave a soft snort but recognized the justice of his observation. Inclining her head in a gesture meant to be apologetic—and although the words nearly choked her—she said, "You're right. I beg your pardon, Mr. Partridge. Perhaps there was a good reason for her to have broken her promise to you." Grace couldn't think of one. She did, however, know herself to be blind when it came to shades of gray. Black-and-white Grace, Frank had used to call her.

"Anyway, she didn't approve of my joining the Union army. I reckon she had her reasons."

"She had strong political views, did she?" Grace's skepticism sang out loud and clear in her question.

Noah shrugged. "I reckon. I don't know."

Humph. *I'll just bet she did,* Grace thought indignantly. "Didn't she write and tell you her reasons for breaking her promise to you?"

"No."

No elaboration there. Grace thought she knew why. Prissy Miss Julia had probably been embarrassed by Noah's conscientious choice and was too weak-willed to tell him so openly. She might even have been wishing he'd die and spare her of ever having to face him. As for Grace, even if she hadn't been firmly on the side of the Union during that horrible conflict, she didn't think she'd have broken an engagement to a man just because his conscience had led him in another direction.

In fact, she couldn't think of very many reasons good enough for a woman to break her promise to a man. Perhaps if Noah had been a drunkard or a criminal, she could understand. Or if Julia had been a politician's daughter and she feared for her father's career. Still and all, if a woman truly loved a man enough to allow him to father her children, to give him the keeping of her life . . .

"Did she come from a political family, Mr. Partridge?" She tried to sound polite.

"No. None of her kin cared beans about politics, although her older brother fought for the Confederacy."

That's what Grace had figured. In other words, Julia Whoever-She-Was had no good excuse not to have waited for the man who'd loved her and given her his ring. Grace's heart began to hurt for Noah. Actions like those of his precious Julia gave the whole female sex a bad name. She'd probably been a delicate Southern belle who'd thought she was too good to wait for a man who'd followed his conscience.

Noah's chuckle surprised her. "You're right, though. I reckon she wasn't worth it. She was a spoiled child when I left Virginia." His smile lasted only a moment. "She died not long after I came back."

"Oh! I'm so sorry." Now Grace felt guilty for having thought such evil things about her.

"Yeah. She died in childbirth."

"My goodness. How tragic."

"Her husband thought so."

Grace got the feeling Noah Partridge thought so too. "I was very fortunate, I guess. I had no trouble with Maddie." Suddenly she wondered if Noah wished he could trade her for his lost Julia, as she sometimes wished she could trade him for Frank. No—that was a wicked thing to think. She really didn't mean it.

She expected the conversation to end on that gloomy note since she didn't feel up to keeping it going, but Noah surprised her yet again.

"She died on Christmas Eve, the night my grand-daddy's business went up in flames."

"Mercy sakes. What an awful combination of tragedies for you, especially after what you'd endured during the war."

"Yeah. I guess."

"You *guess?*" Grace had been so angry with Noah herself lately, that her anger now, on his behalf, surprised her. "I should say you should guess! First the woman you loved died, and then those wretched people burned your business."

"Yeah, well, there's not much of that sort of thing going on these days anymore, so I guess I shouldn't dwell on it."

She didn't understand at first. When his meaning hit her, it made her sad. "Oh. I suppose not. I suppose today people are too busy trying to rebuild and heal the wounds to tear things down."

"I reckon."

Their horses clopped on for a few minutes while their riders pondered the mysteries of life.

"You know," Grace said after a moment or two, "losing Frank hurt me more than I have words for, but I'll never be sorry I loved him." She glanced sideways at Noah, hoping he felt the same way about Julia.

After another short pause, Noah said, "Lucky for you."

She got the feeling he didn't share her sentiments. If Julia was as coldhearted and self-centered as Grace figured she had been, she didn't blame him.

Good grief, what was the matter with her? She didn't even know Mr. Partridge's precious Julia. For all Grace knew, Julia had been a treasure. Maybe he'd been as cold and aloof then as he was now. After darting him another glance, she didn't believe it.

Noah felt a bitter sense of defeat when they rode up to the boundaries of Grace Richardson's property along the Pecos River. The land her estimable Frank had bought extended for acres on each side of the river. There'd never be any question about water rights here, unless someone tried to dam the river upstream. Since the land in this area was perilously dry, that was an important consideration.

They dismounted. Noah unsaddled the horses and let them drink deeply of the mineral-rich water of the Pecos. It was a good thing these two horses weren't anything fancy. Some of the thoroughbreds raised by plantation owners back in Virginia would have keeled over in a colic if their delicate constitutions had been fed this water. It was hard as iron. As hard as Noah Partridge.

"Do you want lunch now, Mr. Partridge, or do you want to wait a while?"

Emma Craig

"I'm not hungry yet, ma'am. Unless you are."

"No. I'd just as soon wait a little bit. I love coming out here and looking around." She sounded pensive. Noah took that as a bad sign.

He still wanted this land. He'd seen hundreds of miles of land since he'd arrived at Mac's wagon yard. He'd ridden out with Mac and without Mac, and looked at every inch of ground from Rio Hondo for seventy-five miles in any direction, and this was the land he wanted. Right here. This piece of property where the Pecos River twisted like a snake, and Frank Richardson's trees were beginning to grow.

Noah nodded his head toward a small willow. "When'd he plant those, ma'am?"

She sighed. "Three years ago. They're about twice the size they were then. It'll take another ten years before they provide much shade." Her gaze drifted away from the willows, following an invisible path. When it stopped, Noah knew exactly where she and her cherished Frank had planned to build their house.

"He was going to plant some oaks and mulberry trees over there."

It was a good spot. On a rise, it would be protected should the river happen to overflow its banks during heavy rains, which Noah understood happened sometimes. Cattle occasionally drowned when they got caught in dry washes during flash floods. The East and West Berrendo Rivers, bordering Rio Hondo, were notorious in that regard, according to Mac.

But that rise—well, that gently swelling hill would keep a house and its occupants safe and dry. Noah could picture a pretty white house there, shaded with mulberries and oaks.

He cleared his throat and dove in head first. "What kind of house did you plan to build, Mrs. Richardson? I understand lots of folks build sod houses, at least at first." Hell, now he remembered that she'd already told him Frank had ordered lumber for a frame house.

"Frank had planned to build a wooden structure, Mr. Partridge. He had it budgeted down to the last penny."

Maybe she didn't remember their earlier conversation. It probably hadn't been important to her. Noah couldn't imagine anything he said being important to anyone—except when he'd said he wanted her land. That was important to her, damn it. "I see."

"It would have been small at first. We figured three rooms. Then Frank could add on to it as our family grew and the business prospered."

If the business prospered. Noah spared Grace the qualification. "What business did he propose to go into?"

"Cattle and sheep. They aren't necessarily compatible, but Frank thought he could raise them both, since we had land enough. The sheep chew the grass up by the roots, so they ruin cattle pasture land, but Frank's father has a seed business back east. He planned to help us out."

"Fortunate," Noah murmured. Maybe Frank hadn't been as much of a dunce as Noah'd at first believed him to be.

Grace smiled slightly. "Very fortunate. Without help, I'm sure Frank would never have considered sheep. But there's a big market for wool."

"Cattle too, I understand."

"Oh, yes. Of course, the most profitable cattle ranchers—Chisum and Blackworth—they run their own

281

cows to market and have beef contracts with the Indian Agency and with the government to supply beef to the forts. Frank wouldn't have done that. He'd have sold his stock to Chisum, probably, and Chisum would have taken care of the marketing.''

"What about Blackworth?"

As Noah watched, Grace's mouth flattened. He gathered that she didn't much like Mr. Blackworth, even if she did seem friendly with Blackworth's wife.

"Neither Frank nor I cared for Mr. Blackworth's business ethics, Mr. Partridge.''

"A rascal, is he?"

She laughed, and her expression brightened a hundred percent. Noah was glad to have made her laugh. Hers was a nature made for laughter, unlike his.

"You might say so. Frank called him an unscrupulous son of a—well, I'm sure you can finish that one for yourself.''

He grinned too. "Yes, ma'am, I think I can.''

"Anyway, Frank didn't have as many qualms about Chisum, although his reputation is far from spotless, and I understand he can be ruthless to small ranchers who get in his way. But Frank was willing to cooperate with Chisum and sell him his cattle. I guess he figured he'd be treated more fairly by Chisum than by Blackworth.''

"Would that have made any money for you, ma'am?"

"Oh, yes. Beef is a very profitable crop. Of course, out here, you need acres and acres more land than you do back east, where the rain is plentiful and the grass is lush.''

"Yeah. I studied up on cattle ranching before I left Virginia."

"That's right. I remember you saying so."

"Yeah. When I decided to move west, I had to figure out how to make a living. Didn't think there's be much call for piano tuners here in New Mexico."

She honored his sarcasm with a sunny smile. "But there's enough land here for cattle-ranching." Grace waved her hand to indicate the land she owned. The land Noah wanted.

There was, indeed, enough land here. It was perfect.

They walked along the bank of the Pecos. Noah realized how close they were to each other at one point and considered standing off a little, but he didn't. He liked being close to Grace. She was soft and sweet and smelled good and made him feel not quite so alone in the world. He knew the sensation was an illusion, but he allowed himself to appreciate it while it lasted.

"It's a sluggish river," he remarked at one point.

Grace skipped a flat rock across the placid surface of the water. She was good at it—must have practiced when she was a kid. "It is now. When the rains come, it'll stop being sluggish, believe me."

"Rains pretty hard out here, does it?"

"Oh, my, yes. Especially during the summer, we get tremendous thunderstorms. People are always getting hit by lightning." Her voice hitched. "That's what happened to Frank."

"I'm sorry." He was, too. No matter how much he resented Frank Richardson for having secured the love and fidelity of this special woman, he still regretted her loss of him. If he'd been married to her, she'd probably have been glad to get rid of him. He didn't allow himself to dwell on that cheerless probability.

She skipped another rock and looked sad. He wanted to wipe that look off her face because it hurt him to see it.

"Does it flood much around here?" He knew the answer to his question. He only asked it to get her mind off her dead husband.

"Yes, indeed. That's why Mac built his mercantile and house up off the ground, so they wouldn't flood every time it rained. He's close to the Spring River, you know. There are rivers all over the place out here, although you'd never guess by looking." She laughed.

Noah was glad to hear her. "Smart man, Mac."

"He certainly is." Her voice held utter conviction. "Sometimes it rains so hard, soddies will melt clean away. That happened to a couple of settlers last spring. I felt sorry for them. They decided they couldn't stick it out here, and moved back to Vermont."

Noah shook his head. He didn't care about other settlers. In truth, he was glad those Vermonters were gone. The fewer people who settled out here, the better for him.

"What about fences? Did your—did Frank plan to build fences?" He'd heard cattlemen didn't hold with fences, but he wasn't sure about sheep pens.

"Frank aimed to fence in the sheep. They're remarkably stupid animals, you know."

"I've heard."

"The cattle could roam free, though. People live so far apart out here, it's not profitable to build many fences. Of course, you run the risk of getting your cows rustled, but that happens anyway."

Noah lifted his eyebrows. "Have a lot of trouble with rustling out here, do you?"

Grace's forehead wrinkled up when she frowned. Noah fought a compulsion to smooth his fingers over it. Hers was a face made for smiles, not frowns. "Yes, it happens too much. We're a lawless community here in the southeastern part of the territory. It used to be the Apaches who stole cattle. Now most of the Indians have been rounded up and taken to the Bosque Redondo Reservation out by Fort Sumner, although there are still a few renegade bands around. But it's the neighboring ranchers you have to watch out for."

Noah had a hunch. "Blackworth?"

She shot him a grateful grin, as if she were happy she didn't have to propound the slander. "Frank thought so."

"How do you combat that sort of thing?"

"Well, you have to decide on a brand that's not easy to alter, for one thing. Chisum's jingle bob is well known in these parts. Frank was designing a brand for us when he died."

Noah offered a short, "Hmm."

She laughed again. "Mac found a cow wandering outside his wagon yard once that had more brands on it than any animal should ever be forced to wear. There was a jingle bob and a running B—that's Blackworth's—and, oh, I can't even remember. That poor beast had been branded at least five times, though. I guess she was a victim of wanderlust or something and kept meandering onto other people's range lands. Of course, no one bothered to return her. They just branded her again."

Noah shook his head and wondered if there were

285

some other business for a man to go into out here that wouldn't put him into conflict with his neighbors. He didn't want trouble. He didn't want any human contact at all, if he could get away from it.

At least, he thought that's what he still wanted. As he peered at Grace's pretty profile and read the varying emotions on her face as they chatted, he was no longer sure about his desire for solitude. In fact, he had a sudden bright vision of Grace Richardson and her daughter at the door of a little white house on top of that rise, waving to him as he came home in the evening.

As if he could ever win Grace Richardson. She could never love him. He'd be willing to marry her anyway, but he had a shrewd suspicion she'd never marry any man she didn't love.

Shoot, he was getting crazier and crazier with each passing day. He cleared his throat. He'd promised not to pester her, but he was curious. "Um, I'm not trying to annoy you, ma'am, but I'm just wondering. Now that your husband's gone, what do you plan to do with this land? I mean, do you still want to run cattle and raise sheep?"

She shot him a keen, questioning glance. He tried to maintain a serene expression, one that conveyed mere interest and not avid greed. Noah didn't think of himself as greedy. Not really. He just knew what he wanted out of life—and what he wanted out of life was *out* of life.

He had evidently succeeded in setting her mind at rest, because she answered him with a fair degree of civility. "I don't know. That is, I'm not sure what to do."

"Do you think you'll be able to set up a cattle operation on your own?"

Again, she shot him a look, and again she seemed reassured by his expressionless expression. She heaved a sigh and said, "I don't know that either. All I do know is that I'll never give up this land." She smiled at him, but he heard the steel in the words and saw it in her eyes.

From out of nowhere, he heard himself saying, "I reckon that young buck Spalding would be happy to help you set up, ma'am. He'd like to marry you."

"Gus?" She sounded shocked. "Gus Spalding is a child, Mr. Partridge."

He looked down at her, puzzled. He didn't understand her attitude. "He's not a child, ma'am."

"He can't be any older than eighteen."

Noah shrugged. "Eighteen's old enough." Hell, he'd been not much older than eighteen when he'd become engaged to Julia.

"Good heavens, I'm almost thirty. I can't marry a boy that young!"

Her cheeks had turned pink. Noah couldn't tell if she was embarrassed or offended. Damn his tongue. He didn't know how to talk to anyone any longer, much less a woman.

"I'm almost thirty, too. Want to marry me?"

Chapter Fifteen

Grace opened her mouth, then shut it before she said anything. How could she say anything? She couldn't believe her ears hadn't deceived her, yet she thought sure she'd heard Noah Partridge ask her if she'd like to marry him. It had rung out as clear as a bell.

But, honestly, had he asked her to *marry* him? Asked *her* to marry *him?* He couldn't have said that. Could he? Impossible. Ridiculous. Absurd!

The truly ridiculous aspect of this embarrassing situation was that his suggestion sounded good to her. If she'd heard him right. Her hearing had always been keen, but she really couldn't credit such a question issuing from this man's mouth.

"I—I beg your pardon?"

Noah was looking off into the distance, up the Pecos, as if he were pondering the answers to various questions in his head: How long is this river? How many

acres do I need to do what I want to do? If she won't
sell, can I get this land another way? By marrying her,
for instance?

He shrugged. "Stupid question. Forget I asked it."

Forget he'd asked it? How was she supposed to do
that? Annoyed with herself and him both, Grace
snapped, "I don't think that was a very funny joke,
Mr. Partridge."

His sigh sounded intolerably sad. "I didn't mean it
as a joke, Mrs. Richardson."

Grace tried to work up some indignation, but discovered her heart had taken to aching, and she felt
more like crying than getting mad. Marry Noah Partridge? Forget Frank? Never!

Yet she couldn't shake off the strange, shivery sensations that the notion of marriage to Noah Partridge
had fostered inside her. A father for Maddie. A husband for her. No more solitary nights, lonesome and
worried in her bed. More children. More children?
With Noah Partridge?

She stared at his profile and could read nothing in
his expression. He looked as far away as Capitan,
standing cold and alone to the west of them. Noah was
every bit as aloof and cold. As lonely? How could anyone tell?

"I don't even know you, Mr. Partridge."

He glanced down at her. A smile made the right side
of his mouth kick up. He didn't look amused. "I'd say
you know me better than most folks do, Mrs. Richardson. I've never told anybody some of the things I've
told you."

Oh, how sad! Grace swallowed the lump in her

throat and whispered, "That's still not very well, Mr. Partridge."

He shrugged again. "Reckon not."

"You seem such a—oh, I don't know. You're not like Frank." She wished she hadn't said that, especially when Noah flinched as if she'd struck him. "I didn't mean you're not a nice man," she hastened to add. Even as she said it, she didn't know if it was true.

"Yeah."

"I mean—I mean, I can imagine marrying you. I mean—not me. I mean, I can imagine some woman marrying you."

He said, "Yeah?" again. This time he sounded amused.

"I'm sure you'd make someone a fine husband."

His grin broadened, and he looked as cynical and hard-edged as she'd ever seen him. Oh, dear. What was wrong with her, that she kept blundering on like this? She hadn't meant to hurt his feelings. If he had any.

Before she could think of anything else to say, Noah turned abruptly. "How about that lunch now, ma'am? I'm getting hungry."

She didn't believe him, but she appreciated his changing of the topic. "Good idea."

While Noah spread a blanket out on the dry grass beside the river, she fetched the bundle of food. At least they had a good lunch to eat. Noah's offer of marriage didn't seem too awfully silly in light of her cooking skills. She was a good homemaker, and could keep a household going, even out here in the Territory where life was difficult and precarious. Frank had always praised her cooking, and so did Mac, although

Mac was more encouraging than Frank ever had been when it came to her other talents.

"Females have to be twice as smart as men," Mac would tell her with one of his endearing winks. "They not only have to keep life going, but they have to put up with men at the same time."

Grace did love Mac so well. He was better than a grandfather to Maddie, and he had been her own saving grace, without whom she'd have gone mad, ever since Frank's death.

And he'd told her it was time for her to get over mourning. Easy for Mac to say. She glanced at Noah Partridge and found him methodically going about his business, gathering fuel for the fire so they could have tea with their meal. His movements were economical, spare, like him. He didn't waste energy fussing and fluttering like Frank used to do.

The thought seemed treacherous, and Grace tried to dismiss it. What was the matter with her, comparing Frank to that man? Why, Frank had been as warm as the sun; Noah was as cold as the dark side of the moon. How could she even think of marrying him?

Unfortunately, she could hardly think of anything else. She wished he hadn't mentioned marriage.

Suddenly he looked up from his task. "Look, Mrs. Richardson, please forget I said anything. I didn't mean to spoil the day."

So he regretted his rash offer as much as she did, did he? There was no reason for Grace to feel miffed, but she did. "An offer of marriage, however much it was meant in jest, is difficult to forget, Mr. Partridge."

"It wasn't meant in jest," he said through gritted teeth.

Grace sniffed, but she felt better that he'd denied her assertion. If, of course, he were telling the truth. It was so difficult to tell with him, although she had no reason to believe him to be a liar. He certainly wasn't in the habit of making jokes. She didn't say anything.

Noah had been adding some small, twisted mesquite branches to the fire as kindling, but he straightened and turned to look at her again. "Listen, I know I'm crazy. I've been crazy since the war. No woman in her right mind would have me. I know that. I don't know why I asked you that. It was stupid, and I'd appreciate it if you'd just forget it." He squatted down, scratched a sulfur match on his boot heel, and held it to the tiny, brittle branches he'd piled in the middle of the firewood. Even though a noon sun shone down upon them, light from the flames licked his face, emphasizing the harshness of his features. "Just forget it. Please."

Grace's heart flooded with compassion. She set down the bundle of food and knelt beside him. "I can't forget it, Mr. Partridge. And you're not crazy. You're *not.*"

He watched her out of the corner of his eye. His gaze caught hers, and its intensity startled her. Maybe she was wrong; maybe he was crazy.

No. He'd been through hell in the war. Like poor Uncle Henry, who, according to Aunt Blanche, still had terrible nightmares—and Uncle Henry had been wounded and sent home during the first year of the terrible conflict. Noah Partridge, who'd been sent to the vilest prison camp the world had ever seen, must be in much worse shape than Uncle Henry.

She put a hand on his arm. He'd shucked off his jacket because the weather had turned so warm. She felt his muscles beneath the fabric of his shirt, and wanted to run her hands over them. He was so very hard. Frank had been lean and wiry, but not rock-solid-hard, like this.

"I, ah, wouldn't touch me if I were you, ma'am."

His voice shook. Good heavens, did her touch affect him so much? Or was he experiencing some sort of vision? Uncle Henry had night visions; he woke up screaming from them, according to Aunt Blanche.

"I think you need to be touched, Mr. Partridge," she whispered, knowing it to be the truth, although she didn't know how she knew.

He shut his eyes. "Please, ma'am. I can't guarantee my reaction to you. I don't want to hurt you."

She peered at his face closely, trying to determine what lay behind his strained expression. Violence? Toward her? She didn't believe it. Toward himself? That seemed more likely.

Perhaps it wasn't violence. Perhaps it was some kind of other strong emotion trying to get out. Love? Grace wished she knew.

He took her in his arms so suddenly, she hardly knew what had happened to her. Then his lips were devouring hers, and she was crushed against him, fighting for breath. The sensation was not unpleasant. It had been a long time since she'd felt a man's desire, but she felt Noah's, hot and hard against her hip. And she felt it in his arms, which were strong around her. She felt it in his lips as they moved against hers.

What astonished her more than his passion was her own. When he'd kissed her beside the lake, she'd felt the stirrings of desire as shocking and shameful. Today, she clung to him as if to life itself, and the power of his hunger for her thrilled her.

She'd never considered herself anything special. Oh, she knew she was pretty, but there were pretty women all over the world. She was certainly no prettier than thousands of other females.

She and Frank had met in Sunday school when they were children and had grown up together. She'd accepted his love as a natural extension of their mutual affection for each other. As she'd grown, she'd expected his passion, because people had told her that's the way men expressed their love. She wasn't sure about that any longer, after learning about those females at the Pecos Saloon. What men did with them didn't have much to do with love, as near as she could figure, but it was the same thing they did with women they claimed to love.

But she'd known Frank's passion and his love were as strong and as enduring as the earth itself. It had been natural and pleasant and it hadn't surprised her.

This desire Noah Partridge had for her was as surprising as it was obvious. She'd never considered herself the type of woman who could inspire passion in the male animal. Oh, she knew Gus Spalding had a crush on her, but she figured that was only because there weren't any young, pretty girls around. If there were, Gus wouldn't look twice at Grace Richardson, a middle-aged matron.

But Noah . . . Noah was a man with a man's experiences behind him, and a man's heart in his chest. He'd loved a woman once, and lost her, as she'd loved and lost Frank.

And now Noah wanted her. And, no matter how

much she wished she didn't, she wanted him. It had been two years since she'd felt a man's passion. Sweet heaven, it felt good!

Somehow, they had sunk down onto the blanket. He was now holding her in his arms, and his callused hands were moving over her back in long, tender strokes. He flung one leg over her, pinning her down. She didn't feel trapped. Not at all. Rather, she moved closer to him, rubbing her thigh against his arousal, relishing the feel of him, hard and wanting her.

Was she a wanton female like those poor creatures at the Pecos Saloon? Grace caught glimpses of them sometimes, and always tried neither to stare nor to turn away in disgust. The poor things. They looked pathetic in the clear light of day, with their rouge and white rice powder covering the signs of dissipation on their unhappy faces. Mac had told her most of them had terrible problems with drink and opium. She'd shuddered, glad she hadn't been forced into such a degrading life—and she had no illusions about those women being innately worse than Grace Richardson. She'd lived out here long enough to know that most women on the frontier were only one man away from disaster— or from the Pecos Saloon.

Her thoughts shattered when she felt Noah's fingers fumbling with the pins in her hair. Her fingers burrowed into his hair, too. She was fascinated by his hair, as she was fascinated with the rest of him. It was silky, his hair, even the silver streaks. Grace knew from experience that often gray hair grew in wiry. Noah's hair wasn't wiry at all. It waved a little bit, but even the silver was soft.

"Your hair is beautiful, Grace."

His voice was husky. And he'd called her Grace. She smiled at him, and knew for the first time that she wasn't going to stop him today. She didn't know what that said about her. Or him. Maybe he wanted to make love to her only to get her land, but she didn't think so.

She murmured, "Thank you." Then she shut her eyes and gave herself up to sensation.

His gentleness surprised her. Frank had been gentle, too, but not nearly so desperate. Well, Frank had no reason to despair. He hadn't lost anything, or fought for anything, or risked anything.

That was a disloyal thought, and Grace banished it. Just because Frank hadn't had to endure the hardships Noah had undergone didn't mean Frank hadn't been a wonderful man. He *had* been wonderful. The most wonderful man in the world.

It was no sin for a woman to feel desire for a man who wasn't her husband. Grace knew it in her heart and in her body. It wasn't uncommon for a woman to marry again, even, if her husband died.

Grace didn't want to think about that. She decided to concentrate instead on the pleasures of the flesh. Did that make her a scarlet woman? She didn't know. At the moment, she didn't care.

Her breasts ached for Noah's touch. Faint recollections of how much Frank had enjoyed her breasts sneaked into her mind. She rubbed her bosom against Noah's chest and heard him groan. Good. She seemed to be doing the right thing.

She'd never kissed any man but Frank until Noah Partridge had thrust himself into her life. She hadn't realized the kisses of two men could be so different, yet so wonderful. Noah's lips were softer than Frank's had been. And they seemed almost frenzied as they kissed her throat. Then she felt his mouth at her breast, and sighed deeply as her head fell back. It seemed almost wicked that this sensual pleasure could feel so near to heaven, but it did.

Noah mumbled something. She couldn't make out the words, but she heard the desperation in his voice, and she knew he was asking for permission. She gave it to him.

With trembling hands, she unbuttoned her bodice. She heard him suck in a breath and hold it while she revealed herself to him. A modest woman, she wore a corset and chemise under her dress, but she still felt herself blush when she exposed her naked shoulders to the mild autumn air and Noah's avid gaze.

She watched him watch her and felt beautiful for the first time in her life. Slowly she lifted her hands to her corset hooks and unlatched them. She never corseted herself tightly, because she considered such affectations as a wasplike waist senseless out here where one's life depended on things other than beauty. Nevertheless, she felt vulnerable and exposed when the corset fell away and she wore nothing but her chemise.

She looked into Noah's eyes and read the pleading there.

''Are you sure?''

His voice was as ragged as his face. She nodded, afraid to talk lest she cry and humiliate herself. But she was sure. This might well be a dreadful mistake, but she wouldn't stop now. She couldn't do that to him; she couldn't do it to herself.

He reached for her. Grace expected him to draw her

to him, but he didn't. Instead, he rested his hands lightly on her shoulders and feasted his eyes on her body. He looked at her as if he'd never seen a woman before, as if the sight of her body was precious to him somehow. For a moment, she felt like some kind of holy icon.

The feeling made her uncomfortable. There was nothing holy about this thing they were going to do. At least, she didn't think there was.

In her confusion, she became desperate to do something, so she reached for his shirt buttons. In a moment, she had his flannel shirt open. He wasn't wearing his undershirt today. Evidently, Mr. Noah Partridge didn't mind the cold as much as other people did.

His chest rippled with muscles. And scars. He had scars. Everywhere. Grace's eyes filled with tears when she ran her fingers over a scar that ran diagonally across his stomach. "Oh, Noah," she whispered. She felt foolish when her tears overflowed.

Either her voice or her tears nudged him. His hands slid down her shoulders and he reached for her at last. She flung her arms around him and hugged him hard. Her hands splayed over his back, and she felt the ridges of more scars. Shocked, she pulled away and looked into his eyes.

They burned with emotion. "Whip," he murmured.

Whip? "They whipped you?"

He nodded.

Grace swallowed. They'd whipped him. Like a dog. Like a felon. Lord, what this man had endured. Grace couldn't stand it. "Kiss me," she said. And he did.

His body was beautiful to Grace, who had never considered that a man's body—especially one as damaged

298

as Noah's—could be beautiful. She could see every muscle on his chest. Soft hair covered his muscles. The hair on his chest, like that on his head, was turning gray. He hadn't eaten enough since his release from prison camp to flesh out very much. She felt his ribs, and she had the mad impulse to take him into her life and feed him good things until his ribs could no longer be delineated like that. Of course, what she really wanted was to make him forget what he'd been through.

She caressed the scar on his leg, the one that made him limp sometimes, and knew her wish was an idle one. There was no way he could forget. That scar was huge. It looked to Grace as though his wound hadn't been tended properly and had become infected. Well, of course it hadn't been tended properly. It had probably been left to heal or fester as it would while Noah languished in Andersonville, wishing he could die.

"I don't know how you survived," she murmured at one point, gazing at his violated body and feeling such a combination of sadness and rage as she'd never experienced before.

"I don't either sometimes." He kissed her again. Grace got the impression he didn't want to be reminded of his ordeal.

It was her great pleasure to help him forget, however briefly. He took her almost savagely at first. She arced like a bow under him, feeling more like a woman than she'd ever felt in her life. Then, with a groan, he calmed himself, and became gentle.

They established a rhythm immediately, Grace moving with him as if they'd been accustomed to doing this for ages and ages past. It had taken much longer for her to get used to making love with Frank. But she'd been so innocent then; so had he.

There wasn't a hint of innocence about Noah Partridge. Or Grace, either, any longer. They'd been weathered by life. Maybe that's why she appreciated Noah so much in those few minutes of passion they shared together on the bank of the Pecos River. He made her feel wonderful. He took her to a place she'd never been before, and then he joined her there.

She cried when it was over, not with regret, but with wonder at how delicious life could be.

Fierce joy shook Noah when he spilled his seed into Grace, a joy both physical and mental. For the first time in years, his brain turned off and ceased tormenting him. The heaven of sexual fulfillment and physical exhaustion left him weak. It was all he could do to roll to Grace's side and draw her into his arms. She snuggled up against him as if she cared about him, as if he weren't the wreck of the man he'd once been.

He realized he loved her, and his joy faltered. Then he told himself to forget it, to forget everything. He would allow himself to enjoy this moment for however long it lasted. It wouldn't be long. Nothing good in his life lasted long.

The day was surprisingly warm, considering it had snowed less than a month before. The sun shone down upon them like a blessing. Noah told himself to stop being fanciful. The sun was the sun. It shone or didn't shine as the weather gods saw fit, and it didn't offer blessings to anyone, much less to the likes of him.

But Grace Richardson had. She'd given him the greatest gift of his life, if she only knew it. He wished he had words to tell her so, but he didn't. He'd talked to her more than he'd talked to any one person for six years or more, but he couldn't tell her this.

He wanted her to marry him. To hell with her land. He wanted her because he wanted *her*. And her kid. Hell, he loved little Maddie almost as much as he loved Maddie's mother. How had this come to pass in so short a time?

Noah sighed, wishing he were whole once more so that he could win Grace's affection. He was too wise by this time to expect he could ever achieve her love. Asking her to marry him now, as he was today, had been a stupid thing to do. He wasn't the kind of man a woman like her would ever want. He was damaged, ruined. The best thing for him to do would be to disappear from this woman's life so he wouldn't ruin her, too. She needed someone like her excellent Frank, who hadn't been wrecked by forces beyond his control.

The thought of releasing her, even momentarily, filled him with dread. Why had he allowed this to happen?

He felt her fingers stroke his cheek and closed his eyes, savoring the softness of her body against his. God, how he wished things could be different.

"Noah?"

Her voice was delicate, almost tender. He was afraid to look at her, although he knew he'd have to do it sometime. It took almost more energy than he had to open his eyes, turn his head, and gaze at her. His heart turned over. She was so lovely, so sweet. She was exactly what he needed. He wished he was what she needed. He wasn't, and he knew it.

Words floundered around in his head. What was he

supposed to say now?*Thank you?* He did thank her. She'd made him feel human for the first time in years. Yet it seemed inappropriate somehow, as if he were thanking her for her sexual favors when that's not what he meant. Or, rather, he meant more than that. *I love you?* That was the truth, but he couldn't imagine her wanting to hear it from his lips. She wanted her damned Frank back, is what she wanted, and he was only a very poor substitute.

At last he said, "Are you all right?"

Her smile was like a benediction. It was all he could do to keep from closing his eyes against it. He didn't deserve it.

"I'm fine. How are you?"

He nodded. "Fine, thank you."

What a damn-fool conversation. She was still smiling at him, and her hand caressed his cheek as if he felt good to her, as if he were something worth touching. He grabbed her hand and kissed her palm. Oh, Lord, if only they could stay here, like this. Together.

A cloud crossed the sun and he felt her shiver. Damn. It was getting on towards winter, and they were lying here buck naked in the middle of the high plains of New Mexico Territory. What was wrong with him? He knew the answer to that one. He was crazy.

With a huge sigh, he pushed himself up onto his elbow. Her body glistened with sweat. Rays from the sun crept out from behind the cloud and bathed her in light. She looked like a madonna basking in the sun's rays. Noah wondered if that thought was a blasphemy. It didn't feel like one.

He watched his dark, callused hand reach out and splay against her stomach. Her skin was as white as parchment, and it was soft under the roughness of his palm. He wished he could stroke and pet her for the rest of his life. He wished he could keep her with him, to give some delicacy and beauty to his ravaged life.

Hell. He withdrew his hand and pushed himself to his feet. "I'll heat some water so you can wash up." He struggled into his trousers. His leg ached. It hadn't been called upon to prop his body up in that way since before he was wounded.

He and Julia had never made love. She was saving herself, she said. He guessed it was just as well, as it turned out. She wouldn't have wanted the man he was when he finally came back, even if she'd waited for the boy he'd been when he left.

Grace murmured, "All right, thank you," and he saw that she had sat up, too, and had wrapped her arms around her knees, which she'd drawn to her chest. She looked like the picture of a sprite—whatever the hell a sprite was—that he'd seen in a fairy-tale book once.

He didn't look back when he went to the river and filled the pot. He wanted to. He wanted to look at her the way she was now, and to sear the image of her into his brain so that he'd never forget it, so that he could watch her in Mac's kitchen or in the mercantile and always remember that they'd shared this one experience together, and that it had been beautiful. She deserved her privacy, though, and he didn't intrude. He knew ladies needed to tidy themselves up after—after—afterwards.

Damn him to hell. He lugged the full pail back and set it on a rock beside the fire. "It should be warm in a minute." He squatted down, held his hands out to the fire, even though they weren't cold, and still didn't look. When he felt her hands on his shoulders, he started with shock. Then he looked, and found her smiling down at him.

"Don't look so worried, Mr. Partridge. I won't make you marry me."

What? What was she talking about? "I wish you would," he muttered, because he meant it.

Her hands left his shoulders, and he heard her laugh softly. When he looked again, she was making her way toward the river. She'd flung on her chemise, and he sighed with regret. What a lovely woman she was. Even her body was pretty, slender and well-rounded. Soft and curvy, not all hard planes and angles and ridges of scars like his. He wondered if she'd let him brush her hair. Then he shook his head and told himself to snap out of it.

In the end, she did let him brush her hair. He enjoyed the job. Then she twisted her hair up into a bun and pinned it into place, and she looked as if he'd never touched her.

Mac frowned out of his front parlor window and puffed on his pipe, deep in thought.

He'd been reading in his chair when he became aware that the relationship between Noah Partridge and Grace Richardson had achieved a new level. He wasn't sure what it was at first. He'd contemplated the deep emotions he was receiving on his wizardly antennae, and after contemplating matters for a while, decided this new level was a good one. They were learning more about each other—and discovering the excellent qualities they could share with each other. Good. That was good.

His plan was working out well. Quite well. All things considered, his plan was going better than he'd anticipated. It wasn't until after he'd drawn Noah Partridge here that he'd truly understood how hurt Noah had been by life. But the poor lad was on the road to recovery now, thanks to Grace.

And Grace was getting better, too. She'd never forget her Frank, but she might, one of these days, come to understand that Frank hadn't been the only good man on earth Not by a long shot.

Now, if only Mac could think of some way to keep those two from feeling guilty about what they'd done, perhaps the cure could continue for both of them. As Maddie slept an enchanted sleep, full of the happy dreams Mac had created for her, he contemplated Noah Partridge and Grace Richardson.

"At least the lass is fair to understanding him now. If he could forgive himself for what other people have done to him, they might have a fine life together. Hmmm."

Since fantasy often helped him think, he conjured a troupe of actors out of the clouds. He used to enjoy traveling with theatrical companies in Will Shakespeare's day. Even back then, most of his kinfolk had gone away from the world. Wizards, as a rule, never had liked people much, and they'd resented them like fire when they'd begun to multiply and take over. Mac liked people just fine. He only wished they weren't so hard on themselves and each other.

Since Noah and Grace had endured enough tragedy, Mac decided to stage *A Midsummer Night's Dream* for himself. As he watched Puck disport himself in the cloudy garden of the heavens, he had a good idea.

If those two had something to worry about other than what Grace might come to think of as their sin by the river, Mac could probably have them back here and under his care before they knew it. Then he'd make sure they were both so busy that they'd have no time to fret.

It was almost Christmas, after all, and Christmas, even in Rio Hondo, on the edge of the American frontier, was a busy time. Grace would be writing letters to the folks back home, and she'd be baking pies and such and taking goodies to Susan Blackworth and to a couple of her other friends in the area. She and Maddie would have a wonderful time decorating the Christmas tree Mac planned to conjure for them.

Mac knew exactly what Noah would be doing as well. The old man grinned around his pipe. The poor fellow still had some learning to do, but he'd do it before Christmas. Mac guaranteed it. Christmas was a magical time. A holy time. It was a season during which miracles should occur if they were ever going to occur at all. Noah and Grace both deserved a miracle. And so did little Maddie.

Yes, indeed. With luck and timing and Mac's magical interference, Mac would have the two of them hitched and set up in housekeeping before either one of them realized Grace was carrying Noah's child.

Chapter Sixteen

Noah squinted up at the sky. "Damn, I've never lived any place where the weather changed so fast."

Grace laughed. She'd been doing that a lot since they'd made love. She'd laughed during lunch, and as they'd packed up the blankets and leftovers, and then she'd laughed while he saddled the horses and strapped everything back on. Every time she laughed, Noah felt his heart melt a little more. He wasn't sure that was a good thing.

"Yes. Frank used to say that if you didn't like the weather out here, all you had to do was wait fifteen minutes."

Noah glanced at her. She was smiling as if she believed her precious Frank had thought that one up all by himself. Noah had heard it said about every place he'd ever been in. Folks always thought they were being clever when they said it, too.

Well, no matter how much he wished Frank's revered memory could be wiped from Grace's mind, he wouldn't sully it. He'd only make her hate him if he did, and she was going to do that soon enough anyway.

"Yeah," he said. "Reckon he was right."

She pulled her woolen shawl more tightly around her. Noah wished she'd brought along something heavier; she was so small, and she didn't have much extra padding to keep her warm. Hell, she looked like a strong wind might blow her away. He worried about her. When had he started doing that?

He had his sheepskin jacket tied on the back of his saddle. "Let's stop for a minute, Grace. I've got something you should be wearing now that it's gone cold again."

He unstrapped the lunch bundle and reached for his jacket. They'd had a very pleasant lunch after they'd made love. Grace was a damned good cook. If he could keep eating her good cooking for a few months, he might stop looking like a scarecrow. He wondered if he'd still feel like one, or if his extra padding would protect him. Stupid thought. He scolded himself for being preposterous.

Noah wondered briefly if Julia had known how to cook, and then decided he no longer cared. Hell, he hadn't cared back then. All he'd known was that he'd loved the image Julia had projected of a delicate Southern belle. And all the men in town had lusted after her. He'd considered it a major coup when she'd singled him out of the pack and agreed to marry him. It was only later that he realized she'd done so because his family had money and a good business.

He shook his head as he unstrapped the jacket. He

had to stop thinking about the old days. They were gone; he was here; he had a goal to achieve, and he had another woman with him, however briefly. Grace was worth a dozen Julias.

"Here." He shook out the jacket.

"My goodness. That looks like it would keep anyone warm."

"Sheepskin. It is warm. Too warm for me." He grinned up at her. His cheek no longer felt as though they were splitting every time he smiled. Grace had done that for him. Noah guessed it was an improvement. He grinned inside when he remembered little Maddie Richardson telling him all he had to do was practice, and his smiles would come easier. She'd been right. The wisdom of children amazed him.

"Thank you. If you're sure you won't need it . . ."

"I won't need it." Hell, he couldn't get enough cold weather to suit him. Maybe he should have moved to Montana. He understood the winters sometimes lasted nine months up there. No. Montana was too damned green. Noah wanted the desert. He needed the harsh barrenness of this land. This is where he belonged.

After he'd made sure she was bundled up, they rode on. They hadn't gone far when Grace's exclamation broke into Noah's dark contemplation of the landscape.

"Good heavens! Is that thunder I hear? In December?"

Thunder? Cripes, they'd just been naked in the sunshine. Noah squinted at the rolling black thunderheads mounding up overhead. Where had those things come from?

A thick, jagged streak of lightning cut through a

cloud to the west of them. "Criminy, I think you're right."

". . . Eleven-one thousand. Twelve-one thousand. Oh, there it is."

A sharp explosion of sound shook the air around them. Shoot. That was close. He looked over to see how Grace was taking this change in the weather. Her adored Frank had been struck by lightning, after all. Noah could understand how it might happen out here. There was sure nowhere to hide away from it. He could see nothing but low scrub, dead grass, and a few creosote bushes for miles.

She looked nervous. "You all right, Grace?"

"I guess so. It's awfully close. I can't remember how many miles each second means, but it was only about twelve seconds from that bolt of lightning to the boom of the thunder. I think that's pretty close."

"It's close, all right. We'd better speed it up some."

"All right, but we have to watch out for prairie-dog holes, too, so the horses won't stumble and break a leg. That won't help us get home any quicker."

"I expect not." He grinned to show her he appreciated her common sense. She'd worn that silly Stetson hat again today. Now she yanked it resolutely lower on her head, and pulled the strap up under her chin. The gesture tickled Noah, who hadn't been tickled by anything in a long time. She was game for whatever life threw at her, Grace Richardson. It was a good quality to have, especially out here. He admired her for it.

"But if we keep our eyes open, I suppose we can go a little faster." She shot him a huge smile. "This should be fun."

It should? Her attitude astonished Noah, who was used to females who whimpered and screeched every time thunder dared assault their ears. He wondered why he was surprised. Grace was as stubborn as a mule; he supposed she must like adventure, or she'd have run home to her family when her husband died. Hell, she wouldn't have come out here in the first place.

"If you say so," he murmured.

She laughed again, a big laugh, one that threw her head back and almost dislodged her Stetson. She slapped a hand on it to keep it on her head. "When we get to the road to town, we can go much faster, because the path has been beaten down. No self-respecting prairie dog would dare dig a hole on the road, because he'd be squashed like a bug every time a wagon or a herd of cattle rolled into town."

"Well, then, let's get to the road." Noah discovered he was laughing, too.

The wind picked up until it was a fierce, cold presence trying to impede their progress. The horses' manes and tails flew out behind them, and twice Noah turned to check on the bundle strapped to Fargo's saddle.

Grace looked like a fuzzy lump on the saddle of her mare, hunched over in his sheepskin jacket and gripping the reins in her gloved fists. But she never stopped smiling. She was enjoying this. Damn, maybe she should have gone to war instead of him. He'd known men like her, men who became exhilarated and fearless in the face of danger. Noah'd always wished he'd been one of them. Maybe he could learn from Grace.

They saw the rain before it hit them. It hung like a gray sheet suspended from the clouds directly in front of their horses. Noah hadn't ever seen rain like that. The rain in his old neck of the woods was less concentrated. He'd heard Mac talk about "local showers" once or twice, but he hadn't understood what the old man had meant until now. He had the whimsical thought that God had decided to water ten square yards of the earth at a time with a giant watering can, and that He was moving the can around as it suited Him.

"You think we can outrun it?" he asked Grace, who was squinting into the wind.

She laughed again, and his insides lit up as if one of those lightning bolts had struck his chest. "I don't see how, since we're aiming directly at it."

"Maybe the wind will blow it off our course?" Noah suggested, mostly to see if he could make her laugh again.

She did. "I doubt it. The wind's blowing straight from the southwest, as usual, and pushing the storm right smack into our path. I expect we'll be as wet as drowned rats before we get back home."

Back home. Didn't that sound nice? Noah guessed he'd better not dwell on it.

A sheet of lightning lit up the entire sky in front of them. "Lordy. I've never seen lightning like that."

"We get it here most often in the summer. Folks call it heat lightning, although it sure isn't hot today. It comes not in forks, but blankets. It's strange, isn't it?"

"It is."

"Oh, look! There's the road. I guess we can speed up now."

"You sure?" Noah glanced at Grace just as huge, fat drops of rain began to pelt down on them.

She gave him a smile that nearly knocked him out of his saddle. "Sure as anything!"

"All right, then." He nudged Fargo, thinking he'd take his cue from Grace as to how fast she thought speeding up meant. He was startled, but not surprised, when she kicked the old swaybacked mare she was riding, and the animal sprinted ahead of Fargo. He laughed out loud and nudged Fargo into catching up.

They were riding on the well-beaten road into Rio Hondo, but it had begun raining fit to kill. Grace knew what that meant. She made them slow down when the road started to run like a river with the rainwater the ground was too hard to absorb.

"It's dangerously slippery." She had to shout to be heard over the roar of rushing water and the pelting rain. "Around here, the ground's clay, you know. Even horses and cows slip and fall sometimes."

"Yeah, I reckon they might."

Noah looked happier than Grace had ever seen him. She felt happy too, and their respective good humors seemed strange to her under the circumstances. After all, they were caught in the middle of a deluge, and might very well catch their respective deaths with pneumonia if the lightning didn't get them first. She didn't think so, though, and she was having more fun than she could remember having since she'd grown up. Imagine, that. She was having fun and playing like a kid with Noah Partridge, of all people, and in a dangerous rainstorm, of all things.

By the time they rode through Mac's gates, which he'd obligingly left open for them—Grace presumed so they wouldn't drown trying to open them—they were so full of giggles, they could hardly sit in their saddles. She was soaked to the skin, too, in spite of Noah's sheepskin jacket. He must be freezing to death in his flimsy duster. He didn't look it, though. He grinned from ear to ear, as if he'd just heard the funniest joke in the world.

She shouted, "If you take care of the horses, I'll run inside and make us some hot cocoa."

"Fair exchange."

To the boom of thunder, Noah slid off Fargo's back and made his way to Grace's side. He skidded on the slippery soil and almost fell on his butt helping her to dismount. The near accident precipitated another bout of laughter, and Noah had to hold on to her tightly to keep them both upright.

Sopping wet, Grace looked up into his eyes, and her heart melted. The wariness he wore like armor had disappeared somewhere during the day, either out there by the Pecos or during the last hectic minutes as they rode through the rainstorm. For the first time, Grace got a glimpse of the man he was underneath it.

"Oh, Noah." The wind carried her whisper away on a flurry of raindrops.

"May I kiss you?"

"You don't have to ask." And even though her feet were wet and cold and she was standing in three inches of mud, Grace lifted herself onto her tiptoes and gave Noah Partridge a kiss from her very heart. She suspected she loved him, knew it to be false to Frank's memory, and at the moment couldn't make herself care one whit.

Mac and Maddie had made popcorn balls in her absence, and Mac had a pot of cocoa already steaming

314

on the stove. After she changed out of her dripping clothes, Grace prepared some cinnamon toast. When Noah came in, he changed too, and they sat at the parlor table to consume their afternoon feast.

Then the two of them replayed their wild ride through the storm to the accompaniment of many excited questions from Maddie. This mode of entertainment lasted until suppertime, when they dined again— this time on some of Mac's famous stew and corn bread. After supper, they played hearts until Maddie's yawns became too big to ignore. Noah and Mac helped Grace tuck her into bed.

As far as Grace could tell, Noah was truly happy for the whole rest of that day. He slept in the parlor that night, out of the rain. When she went to bed, she wished he could join her there.

She prayed that God—and Frank—would forgive her.

Noah received an answer to his wire to the territorial government in Santa Fe the day after he and Grace picnicked on the Pecos.

Because he felt his demons ganging up on him, he excused himself from breakfast, and fled out of the house at first light. He decided to visit the telegraph office, but he took care of his horse first, and ate some of the jerky he'd packed, because he was hungry. It tasted like dry wood, and he wondered if he was punishing himself by not eating breakfast with Grace. Probably.

The jerky left him still hungry. He could have eaten another strip of it, but he couldn't quite face the notion.

His growling stomach accompanied him down the street.

By that time, the prior day's events had begun to seem remote to him, as if he'd only heard about them from someone else. Those good things couldn't have happened to Noah Partridge.

Could he have made sweet love to Grace Richardson by the banks of the Pecos River? Could he have laughed with her through a treacherous thunderstorm as they raced home? Could he have played hearts with her, an old man, and a little girl? Could he have joked and laughed some more as they ate popcorn balls and cinnamon toast and drank hot cocoa?

An anomaly. Yesterday had been an anomaly, and a cruel one. He walked through the muck and mud to the telegraph office and brooded. It wasn't really fair of the fates to have given him yesterday. They had evidently decided he wasn't suffering enough, because they'd taken to taunting him by showing him fleeting peeks of what he was missing in his life.

As if he needed reminding.

Percy Wiggins was as sour and sarcastic as he ever was. Sourer, perhaps, because his office had flooded during the storm, and he'd had to shovel a ton of mud out of it that morning. Noah got the feeling Wiggins didn't enjoy manual labor very much.

"Yes, you received an answer to your telegram." Wiggins scowled as he slapped it onto the counter. Noah wondered if the answer was that terrible, or if Wiggins merely disliked having to perform the duties for which he was being paid.

"Thanks."

Percy Wiggins snorted. Noah presumed it was his version of "You're welcome."

He took the wire outside and opened it while he stood in mud baking under the sun's rays. The sun shining down on Rio Hondo hadn't made the weather warm today. A frigid wind almost ripped the message out of Noah's hands.

When he read it, his heart fell to his boots and he cursed. It looked like he could get that land after all.

Noah pondered his options long and hard as he walked back to McMurdo's Wagon Yard. He could do the honorable thing and leave—take this wire and high-tail it out of Rio Hondo and forget the whole thing. He could make another offer for the land without bringing up the news contained in the cabled message. He could renew his offer of marriage.

The last option made him snort sarcastically and tell himself not to be any more of a damned fool than he could help being. Grace Richardson would be an idiot to marry him. Even if she would lower herself to take him, Noah wasn't sure he wanted to compete with the angelic Frank for the rest of his unnatural life. No matter what he did, he was sure to come up short when compared to a damned martyred saint.

"Aw, to hell with it."

If he was destined to live and die alone and despised by the rest of the world, he might as well do it where he chose. He might hate himself forever, but he figured the chances of that were better than even, no matter what he did.

This way, at least he'd know exactly when Grace's good opinion of him—if she had one—changed to loathing. He was going to go to her right now, in fact, and watch it happen.

Grace looked up from where she sat behind the counter of Mac's mercantile, and gave him a beautiful smile. Noah tried to smile back, but wasn't up to it. The freezing wind whistling through the fence slats outside the snug store had nothing on him. He felt as cold as it was, and then some.

"Good morning, Noah. We missed you at breakfast."

He tried to discern accusation in her expression or her words, but didn't. He wouldn't blame her if she hated him already. After all, he might be said to have seduced her and then run out on her. At any rate, he guessed that's what he had done. Yesterday's events were mixed up in his mind, and he wasn't sure. However they'd ended up naked there on the bank of the Pecos River, and he was sure it had been all his fault.

"Good morning, Grace. I was—" He was what? He decided to tell her the truth. "I was feeling a little shaky this morning, so I ate with my horse."

Telling the truth seemed to free him, and he discovered he could smile after all.

"I'm sorry, but I understand." She looked down at the counter, and Noah realized she was reading a book. "At least, I don't really understand—not what you went through. But I understand your need to get away sometimes. Your need for solitude."

"Thanks."

Good glory, it was a Bible. She was reading the Bible. Shoot, what did that mean? Was she looking for a chapter and verse that would excuse what they'd done

318

yesterday? Noah didn't think there were any passages in the Bible rationalizing fornication, although his knowledge of the Good Book was limited. He nodded at the book.

"Reading that for fun?"

She gave him another smile. Lordy, one of her smiles could last a man for months. Which was a good thing, in his case. "I feel the need to commune with the apostles every now and then. Although, I must say I wished they'd used plain old language. I find this very difficult to understand sometimes." She tapped the book.

"Reckon that's the translation, ma'am."

She chuckled. "I imagine you're right. Do you suppose anyone will ever translate the Bible into language a plain, modern-day person can understand, or will we be forever doomed to read it the way King James did two hundred and fifty years ago?"

"Can't offer an opinion on that one. I'm no theologian."

Grace put a pretty, lacy bookmark in the book and closed it with a sigh. "No, I'm not either." She folded her hands together and rested them on the thick Bible in front of her. "Did you need some supplies, Noah?"

He loved it that she'd started using his Christian name. He'd never cared one way or another about his name before, but she made it sound good. He forced another grin.

"Well . . . I don't suppose you've changed your mind about that land out there? I'm willing to offer you a fair price. More than fair. I'll give you more than the land's worth, because—because—"

Because why? He couldn't think of anything to say

that didn't sound insane. Because he loved her? Shoot, she'd really go for that. Because he was crazy? She already knew that. He shrugged and decided to quit while he wasn't behind yet. "I'll give you a dollar an acre more than the asking price." That would pay the late mortgage fees, the back taxes, and she'd have plenty left over for whatever she wanted to do. Hell, he'd even pay the back taxes. The insurance from his burned-out business had left him well enough off for that.

Her smile flickered and died. She shook her head. "No. I'm sorry. I won't sell that land. It's Maddie's only link to her father, you see."

"Yeah." Noah couldn't look her in the eye any longer. His gaze faltered and shifted to the shelves of Mac's store. He'd lived here long enough to know that supply wagons rumbled in from Amarillo and Santa Fe every week or so, but he still marveled at some of the things Mac stocked.

"Tins of milk," he muttered, taking in the sight of a dozen or more cans of milk stacked neatly on a corner shelf. "There much call for tinned milk out here?"

"People buy it for their children sometimes."

His gaze flicked to her again. "Their children? Are there other children in Rio Hondo?"

"Settlers pass through sometimes, like the Merchants did, often with small children. An Indian woman needed milk for her baby not long back." Grace's brow creased, and she looked troubled. "The army doesn't treat them very well at the reservation, you know. Mac sent over a crate of tinned milk for the children, but not even Mac can feed all the Indian children at the Bosque Redondo."

"Doesn't the Indian Agency see that they get food?"

Grace heaved a heavy sigh. "Well, there you have to contend with the Indian agents and the ranchers in the area, you see. Some of them are honorable, and I guess some of the Indian agents are honorable too. Not very many, however. It's pretty well known in these parts that Blackworth sends his worst stock and worst beef to the Indian Agent. Of course, the soldiers at Fort Sumner eat pretty well. It's evidently all right to give the Indians rotten meat, but not the soldiers."

Noah couldn't think of anything to say. The situation sounded hopeless to him, and he was past wanting to fight for causes, good or otherwise.

Grace chuffed indignantly. "Why, you'd think they didn't even consider the Indians human, the way they treat them. It's a crime, Noah. It's a real crime, and I hope somebody takes care of it someday."

"Do you think that will happen?"

Her indignation faded into sadness. Noah was sorry to see it. "I don't know. If women had the vote, I'll bet you anything we'd at least try to rectify the situation. Women aren't as happy to see babies starve to death—even Indian babies—as men seem to be."

Noah bowed his head. "I watched men starve to death in Andersonville. It was—terrible."

Grace slid from her stool, opened the counter, and rushed to Noah's side. "Oh, Noah, I'm sorry. I didn't mean to bring up unhappy memories."

Were there any other kind? Noah took the hand she held out to him and kissed it. Yes, there were other kinds. He'd always remember their picnic by the river yesterday, and Grace's precious body in his arms. He

321

released her hand and shut his eyes. "Maybe you'd better read this, Grace."

He handed her the cable. She looked up at him, surprised, then unfolded the paper and began to read. Noah wondered if it was his imagination that made her seem to pale.

She took a step back, staggered, and he knew it wasn't his imagination. He caught her before she fell.

"Grace, I—"

"No!" She shook him off and steadied herself. "So you went to all the trouble of telegraphing Santa Fe for this information, did you?"

He nodded. "I like that land, Grace."

"You like that land." She made it sound like a curse. "Well, so do I."

He waved his hand toward the paper in her hand, feeling helpless. "But you're about to lose it."

"Not if I can help it."

He let a second or two slip by as he wondered what to say next. "Can you help it?" he asked at last. His heart hurt when he saw tears building in her eyes.

"I don't know, but I'm doing everything I can."

"What happened, Grace? Did your husband mortgage the land? It says here you haven't paid the taxes since he died."

"I'm working on it. I'm trying my best. I've even sold preserves, taken in washing, and knitted shawls for those poor women at the Pecos Saloon to supplement the money I make in Mac's store."

"Will it be enough?"

She took in a gigantic breath and held it for a moment before she let it go in a whoosh. "I don't know. I don't know! But I'm trying with every ounce of strength I have in me to keep that land. It's Frank's legacy to our daughter, Noah!''

This was the clincher. He knew she'd hate him now. ''Yeah. Well, if I pay the back taxes and catch up with the payments, I can take it over, Grace. The government will let me have it and not give you a cent.''

She refused to look away from him. ''I know. Will you do that?''

He looked away first. ''I don't know. I want that land.''

''And you're willing to get it that way?''

All at once, her attitude chafed at him. ''What way?''

She waved the wire under his nose. ''This way! You're willing to take the only thing my daughter has because you want it, and you can?''

''It's legal. And, damn it, Grace, you won't be able to work that land even if you can hang onto it! Don't you think your daughter would rather have pretty dresses and friends than a piece of dead land?''

''It's not dead!''

Before he heard her today, Noah would have said Grace Richardson didn't have a scream in her. But she screamed at him. Then she dashed a hand across her eyes, furiously wiping away her tears.

''It's not dead! There are trees growing there that Maddie's father planted! That's her legacy! It's all she has left of Frank! It's all I have left of Frank!''

''You have Maddie,'' Noah said, feeling worse than he'd felt since he was carried out of Andersonville on a stretcher and deposited in the army hospital in Washington. He'd been too weak to feel much of anything then. Now his whole body ached with remorse and determination.

"I can't believe you're going to do this to us." Her voice had sunk to a whisper.

He couldn't believe it either. But he wouldn't back down. Her plans were flat stupid. Sooner or later she was going to lose that land. At least if he had it, it would sort of still be in the family. Noah would love her for the rest of his life; he knew that without having to think about it. He'd will it to her, free and clear, so that if they all got lucky and he died young, she and Maddie could still have their precious land, bought by their precious Frank. And mortgaged by him so that she couldn't hold on to it. Damn Frank Richardson.

Because he felt so awful, he muttered, "Yeah, well I reckon I'm just a son of a bitch."

"Yes," she said. "I guess you are."

She whirled around too fast for her balance. Noah guessed she was still reeling from shock because her knees buckled. He caught her before she could fall, and held her tight.

God, he loved her! He hated himself in that moment more than he'd believed possible. He'd thought he'd sunk to the lowest level a man could sink years before, in Andersonville, but he realized now he'd been wrong.

When he kissed her, he put every ounce of his love into the kiss. And all the apologies he couldn't force himself to speak. And every good wish for her and her daughter.

He nearly keeled over himself, from shock, when she kissed him back.

* * *

Shaken and terrified, Grace clung to Noah as if he were her last hope on earth. He felt like a refuge to her in those few seconds—until she realized she was kissing the enemy, the man who was determined to take her refuge away from her.

She wrenched herself out of his arms and reeled backward, her knees knocking. Pressing the back of her hand to her lips, she whispered, "How could you? How *could* you?"

He shrugged. The gesture didn't look insolent so much as helpless.

"You don't know?" Her laugh rang out bitter and brittle, and it didn't sound like her at all. "You don't know how you can do what you aim to do? You don't know how you can destroy a little girl's only link with her dead father? You don't know how you can ruin my life forever? Well, I don't either."

"You can still marry me."

Grace stared at him, openmouthed. She couldn't believe he'd said that. Of all the hollow, empty, miserable things people said to each other every day, those words of Noah's rang hollowest in Grace's ears. Noah's green eyes seemed to burn in his haggard face. She had no words with which to respond. He held out a hand. Grace saw that it was scarred too. At the moment, Noah Partridge's wounds meant nothing to her.

"Grace, I—"

"Oh, spare me, please! I don't want to hear it."

"Listen, maybe—"

"No!" She whirled around. Never in her life had she felt so alone or so forsaken. Even when Frank died and she'd felt abandoned, she'd known he hadn't meant it. For heaven's sake, no man would wish to be struck and killed by a bolt of lightning.

But there was no excuse for Noah Partridge. He was deliberately and maliciously planning to strip Grace and Maddie of the land she and Frank had worked so hard and so long for. Noah Partridge was going to take it away from them with no more compunction than he'd feel if he swatted a fly.

He'd made love to her, and now he was going to ruin her.

"Grace, can we talk about—"

"No!" She swung around again, bracing herself on the counter so she wouldn't fall. She felt light-headed, and her heart pounded so hard her ears rang. "No. I don't want to listen to anything else you have to say to me, Noah. And to think I thought I loved you."

She balled up the telegram and flung it at him, and had the satisfaction of seeing the shock on his face before she ran out of the mercantile and into Mac's house. Thank God, she saw neither Mac nor Maddie, but was able to make it to her room and throw herself onto her bed before she burst into tears.

Chapter Seventeen

Noah discovered he was trembling. And his emotions were running wild. He couldn't sort out which emotion predominated, but he could distinguish shock, lust, rage, sorrow, and compassion. They were mixed up in such a potent blend that it took him three tries before his shaking hand could pick up the crumpled telegram from the floor and smooth it out.

She'd thought she loved him? Him? Noah Partridge? He shook his head, certain he hadn't heard her right. No one, least of all a woman like Grace Richardson, could love Noah Partridge. Hell, she loved her damned Frank. There was no room in her heart for the likes of him.

He stared at the door out of which Grace had just rushed, and ran her last words over and over again in his brain. They didn't make sense to him.

When Maddie entered the room holding her blasted

rag doll, he scowled before he could stop himself. If there was one thing he didn't need right now, it was to confront the little six-year-old girl whose daddy's legacy he was about to take away. Noah hated himself. It wasn't a new feeling, but it hurt worse today than it generally did.

"H'lo, Mr. Noah."

As much as he didn't want to deal with Maddie, Noah couldn't make himself be unkind to her. Hell, he loved her. He tried to smile. "Good morning, Miss Maddie."

"You din't eat flapjacks with us this morning at breakfast."

"No. I—ah—had business in town."

Maddie nodded solemnly. "That's what Mac said."

"He did, did he?"

She nodded again.

"How'd he know I had business in town?"

She shrugged. "He just knows things."

He just knows things. Noah had observed that before. Today he noticed that Maddie seemed to take Alexander McMurdo's "just knowing things" in stride. He wished he still had even an iota of the easy acceptance of childhood left in him.

"See my dolly?" Maddie held out the doll for Noah's inspection.

As before, to Noah it remained a paltry excuse for a doll. His sister had been given beautiful dolls with wax heads and fancy clothes when she was a kid. This one had obviously been made by Maddie's mama, out of scraps, yarn, and love. Noah understood now, as he hadn't before, that Grace wouldn't spend a dime on anything but keeping that damned land in her life. She surely wouldn't spend money on a wax-headed doll for her daughter. He didn't know whether to applaud her persistence or condemn her as a fool. She'd taken care to embroider a happy face on the thing, but she must have done so a long time ago. It looked as if Maddie had loved that doll almost to death.

"Yeah, it's a real nice dolly," he said, wishing it were true.

Maddie heaved a sigh too big for her six-year-old body. If Noah hadn't been feeling so bad, he might have grinned because the sigh made the little girl sound like a junior adult.

"Oh, I know it isn't store-boughten like the kind you're prob'ly used to. Mommy says we can't afford store-boughten dollies. But I love this one, and I think she's pretty. Her name is Priscilla."

"Priscilla, huh?" He remembered that from when Maddie had met Anastasia Merchant.

Maddie nodded. "I wish my name was Priscilla, but Mommy says Daddy and her named me after my grandma. Daddy's mommy, Madeline Richardson. She lives in 'Cago, like Grandma and Grandpa Baxter."

"In Chicago, does she?" He couldn't figure out why she was bothering to explain her family history to him today of all days, when the only thing he wanted was to be alone so he could contemplate his many sins in private.

Another nod. "So I named my dolly Priscilla, 'cause that's what I want my name to be."

"Makes sense." Noah was astounded to realize it did. Did that make him more or less crazy, that he understood the reasoning of a six-year-old?

"And Mommy makes Priscilla new clothes whenever she can."

"Yeah. Like on your birthday."

"Uh-huh. Mommy has to work in Mac's store, you know, so she doesn't have a lot of time to sew."

"Yeah. I know."

Maddie brightened. "But sometimes she sews dolly dresses while she's waiting for customers to come in. She makes Priscilla dresses out of the same material she makes my dresses. And matching sunbonnets too, though I don't like sunbonnets. I'm s'posed to wear them so's I don't get sunstroke."

"Sounds like fun."

Maddie gazed up at him, her expression critical, as if she detected the false note in his voice. "You don't have to lie, Mr. Noah."

"I'm not lying, Maddie." He almost crossed his fingers behind his back as he used to do when he was six and told a deliberate fib. He and his chums had believed crossing one's fingers negated the sinfulness of the lie. Ignorance was such bliss.

"Hmm. I know Priscilla isn't as pretty as storeboughten dollies, Mr. Noah, 'cause I seen a storeboughten dolly once in a wagon."

"Priscilla is a fine dolly, Miss Maddie." He felt pressured, and he didn't like the feeling. His lips still burned from Grace's kiss, his mind raged, and his innards were doing backflips. He didn't want to be talking about dollies with Maddie Richardson, especially since old Priscilla was about the sorriest excuse for a kid's toy he'd ever seen.

Why the hell wouldn't Grace just give up, as any sane woman would do? She wasn't doing herself or her kid any favors, remaining out here, living on love. Living on love. The expression made Noah feel queasy.

"You're just saying that," Maddie announced with a firm nod. "You've seen much nicer dollies than Priscilla, huh?"

Noah glared down at her and wondered how she'd gotten so damned smart all of a sudden. He didn't feel obliged to answer since she was doing so well on her own.

"But it's not true, you know." She kissed her doll on the top of her yarn hair. "Priscilla is the best dolly in the world because Mommy made it for me with love. Mommy says that love can make anything beautiful."

"She does, does she?" Noah wondered if he was having a seizure. Suddenly his heart hurt like a coyote had just bitten a chunk out of it.

Another nod from his pint-sized conscience. "I keep praying to God in heaven that love can give my mommy a reed organ." She grinned up at him like an imp. "And me a daddy. If Mommy could have an organ and I could have a daddy, Priscilla and me would be real happy."

She bounced off, humming, holding Priscilla like a baby. Noah watched her go, feeling like a two-thousand-pound draft horse had just kicked him in the gut.

Mac took the pipe from his mouth when he saw Noah stomping over to him, and blew out several smoke rings. He'd been expecting this.

People. They made things so hard for themselves. As much as Mac loved human beings, he sometimes didn't wonder that the rest of his wizardly race had given up on them. They were an obstinate lot, humans. And here came Noah Partridge, one of the most obstinate of them all, looking like he was upset enough to spit poisoned darts.

With delicious irony, Mac gave Noah the sweetest smile in his repertoire. "Good morning, lad. Ye're lookin' fit today." He looked like he was about to pitch a fit, is how he looked.

"Yeah?"

"Aye. Grace's cooking is doin' ye a world of good, lad."

"Is that a fact?"

"Oh, aye." Mac winked, and was amused to see Noah's mouth flatten out into a rigid white line.

"Listen, Mac, I have to go away for a while. I'll be back sometime, I reckon."

"You will, will you?"

"Yeah. That all right? I mean, do I owe you any money or anything?"

"Nay, lad. Ye're all paid up. Ye don't owe *me* a thing." He figured Noah was smart enough to understand what he'd left unsaid. He knew it for certain when Noah's frown intensified. Mac didn't laugh, because he knew how seriously people took themselves. Noah, especially, wouldn't appreciate having his misery laughed at.

In truth, Mac's amusement wouldn't have been meant as a criticism or a mockery. He only wanted to laugh because it seemed an absurd shame to him that the poor lad had to go through this terrible crisis. Yet Mac knew that people needed their crises. Crises somehow helped them come to appropriate conclusions. Humans weren't wise, like Mac's race of wizards. They did things by trial and error or by instinct, neither of which was very reliable.

"I'll need a bag of grain to take with me for Fargo."

"Of course. Is Grace in the store? She can take your money for it." Mac knew very well that Grace was crying her eyes out in her bedroom, poor lass.

"Er, no. No, she had to leave the store for a minute."

"All right, lad. I'll fetch ye a bag of grain."

So he and Noah walked back to Mac's mercantile, Noah as frigid as an icicle beside him. Even his walk was stiff. His leg must be paining him, Mac reckoned, because his limp was more pronounced today. Well, such was life if one were a human. Too bad about that, but there was only so much a wizard, even one as old and wise as Mac, could do.

He heaved a sack of grain onto the counter and took Noah's money. Then he walked back outside with him and watched him saddle up his horse. "Got food for yourself, lad?" he asked gently.

Noah lifted a shoulder. "I'll kill something."

He sounded as if he were looking forward to it, and Mac grinned. "Aye. There's plenty of game around if you know where to look for it."

Noah didn't answer. He pulled Fargo's cinch tight, flipped the stirrups down, laid the bag of grain evenly across Fargo's back so that the horse would be balanced—which made one of them, Mac thought with an internal grin—strapped down his bedroll, and swung himself into the saddle. He didn't speak another word, but pulled the brim of his hat down in Mac's direction by way of farewell. Mac nodded pleasantly.

Then Noah was off, looking like his last friend had died. Mac sighed.

"Poor lad," he murmured. "Poor lad."

"He's gone?"

Grace's eyes were red-rimmed and puffy. She'd laid a cold rag over them, but she didn't have time to pamper herself for very long. Her head ached, too. Crying always gave her a headache. At Mac's words, her heart plummeted to her shoes.

"Where'd he go?" Maddie asked after she swallowed a bite of the dumpling she'd been chewing. She was so very polite for a six-year-old. Grace thought defiantly that at least she'd done that much right in the rearing of the little girl.

"I don't know, Maddie-lass. He didn't look very happy when he left, though."

Maddie frowned as she carefully spooned up a bite of chicken and gravy. "I hope I didn't make him sad when I told him about Priscilla."

"Priscilla?" Grace turned to stare at her daughter. "What did you tell him about Priscilla?"

"Only that you made her for me and I love her better than any old store-boughten dolly. I could tell he didn't think she was as pretty as some dollies he's seen."

"Oh." Grace's eyes filled with tears again. What was the matter with her, that she was getting emotional at the supper table? "That was very nice of you, Maddie. I'm glad you like Priscilla." She'd made that doll with every ounce of love she'd had in her. That didn't make it as fine as any of the wax-head dolls her family could buy Maddie in Chicago.

She wanted to fold her arms on the supper table, lay

her head on them, and give herself up to another crying jag. She was depriving her daughter, whom she loved more than anything else in the entire world, for a dream. What's more, it was a dream destined for failure. She knew it, and she kept fighting for it anyway. What an idiot she was.

Maddie's smile was as bright as the Christmas star. "You know what I think?"

Grace couldn't force any words through her aching throat. She shook her head and willed herself not to bawl out loud. She couldn't quite force a smile.

Mac said, "What do you think, Maddie m'lass?"

When Grace looked at him, he winked, and she knew he was aware of her distress. She turned her head away and tried to wipe her eyes without Maddie seeing.

"I think Mr. Noah has gone away to get Mommy's reed organ."

"Oh, Maddie!" Grace got up from her chair so fast it nearly tipped over. She ran to the kitchen sink so her daughter wouldn't see how her perky comment had devastated her mother. She braced her hands against the sink and commanded herself to take control of her rocky emotions.

"Why'd Mommy get up, Mac?"

Maddie sounded puzzled—justifiably so. Grace hadn't even excused herself from the table. What kind of example was that? She pressed a hand against her abdomen, where even now another baby might be growing, and wondered about her priorities. Speaking of examples, what kind of example would *that* be for her daughter? If Grace had been alone in the house, she'd have howled in frustration.

"I think she went to the stove to get the cobbler, Maddie m'lass."

"But we aren't done with the chicken and dumplings yet."

Grace heard Mac laugh gently.

"Aye, lass, but you know your mama. She's an organized thing, your mama."

An organized thing, was she? Well, Grace guessed Mac was right. She'd organized herself into a job at his store, and she was working herself blamed near to exhaustion, and for what? For a piece of land that was likely to be the death of her. She'd refused a perfectly good offer for it, an offer that would have paid her and Maddie's way back to Chicago with money left over. Or she could have bought another parcel of land here, if she was determined to stick it out, a smaller stake, one she could handle, perhaps in town, where she could at least get work for wages. And she'd refused. Thrown it back in Noah's face.

Frank used to tell her that she could out-stubborn a mule when she put her mind to it. And he'd been right. And Frank was gone. And now so was Noah.

He was gone. He'd just taken off, without even saying good-bye. Of course, she'd as much as told him to go to hell. Maybe that's what he was doing. At least if he did, he wouldn't get her land.

"Oh, my heavens," she whispered. If Noah didn't get her land, so what? Someone else would soon. What a monumental, blazing ass she was!

"I think I'll save room for some clobber," Grace heard from the table. "I like Mommy's clobber."

She sounded so grown up, except for her mispronunciation. She was growing like a weed. Soon, Grace knew, she'd be old enough to know what she was missing. Grace wondered for the first time if Maddie would hate her when she realized that Grace's determination to fulfill Frank's dream had condemned her to a life alone, on the empty plains of New Mexico Territory, without family or playmates or luxuries. Luxuries? Without even many common necessities.

If only Frank had lived, they would have made out all right. Frank would have seen to it. They'd have both seen to it that Maddie went to Chicago for visits. And, with luck, they'd have had more children. Grace hadn't had any trouble giving birth to Maddie. They'd wanted more children.

"Your mommy's a good cook, Maddie-lass."

Her daughter didn't answer, but in her mind's eye Grace could see her nodding as she chewed another bite of chicken. Or maybe a carrot. Maddie liked carrots. *Oh, Maddie, Maddie, I was doing it for you!*

Grace stared into the kitchen sink, a fancy galvanized metal model Mac had managed to come up with from somewhere. He found the most amazing things. Must be because he had connections he'd met through running his mercantile. She and Frank had determined to make do with zinc buckets and wooden tubs for the first few years. It would have been hard, but they'd been up to it. They'd been up for anything, together.

Why was she struggling on alone? This evening, with Noah's absence gaping like an unbridgeable chasm in her mind's eye, she couldn't think of any answer that didn't sound stupid.

Mac's gentle hand on her shoulder startled a squeal out of her. She saw what looked like millions of sparkles in the air when she jerked around.

"He'll be back, lass. You'll see."

Mac looked at her with such a kindly expression on his face that Grace couldn't be strong for one second longer. She uttered a sob, and fell into his open arms. He patted her on the back and clucked softly, and a feeling of peace seemed to permeate her body from where his hands touched her, through to her insides, and even to her fingers and toes. She didn't cry long—which was a good thing, since the headache from her emotional fit this afternoon was vicious.

When she pulled away from him, she saw that he was dangling a handkerchief in front of her. She managed a shaky laugh. "Where did that come from?"

He gave her another wink and grinned. "Ah, lass, I have me ways, y'know."

"Yes," she said as she took the handkerchief and mopped her face. "I know." She made sure her cheeks were dry before she blew her nose. She didn't want Maddie to know her mama was such a deplorable weakling. "Thank you, Mac. You always know what a body needs."

"Aye, I have me ways," he said again. "Are ye all right, lass? Do you need to be alone for a while?"

"No, thank you, Mac. I'm fine. Fine." Fine, was she? As Grace went back to the kitchen table—holding the pan of cobbler so Maddie wouldn't suspect anything was amiss—she wondered if she'd ever be fine again in this life.

Maddie's happy smile when she spotted the cobbler almost broke her heart.

Noah rode until his bones ached. He rode until his head pounded. He rode until he feared for Fargo's health, and then he rode some more. He let Fargo lead the way and didn't know where they were going until they got there.

He eyed the sweep of the Pecos River as it twisted through the scrub. He saw those blasted little trees sitting there, just waiting for Grace Richardson to come live beside them and charm them into life, and he muttered, "Damn it, Fargo, why'd you bring me here?"

The horse, winded and hanging his head, didn't answer. Noah swung down from the saddle. His bum leg almost buckled under him, but he refused to let it. Damn it, he was in charge of his body; if he couldn't control his heart or his mind or anything else in this rotten world, he could at least control his body.

He glanced at the river again, remembered the few short hours he'd spent with Grace here beside it, and knew that even his body ruled him more often than not. He kicked the dirt at his feet, startling a jackrabbit out from under a low-growing mesquite bush and sending it bounding away across the plains. Noah thought about shooting it, but he didn't have the heart. He'd find something else to eat for supper, if he ever got hungry. He probably would. His luck wasn't running high lately.

"Criminy, Fargo, what am I supposed to do now? Take Grace's land away from her or stick around, buy another parcel—one that I don't want—and watch her lose the land we both want anyway? What purpose would that serve?" He glowered at the river, his hands stuffed into his jacket pockets.

Another alternative occurred to him, but he rejected it savagely. "She sure as hell doesn't want to marry me now. She hates me."

Fargo had wandered over to the river. Noah felt a stab of guilt. Guilt wasn't an unusual emotion for him, but he generally didn't feel it for his horse. He'd been used to treating the animals in his life much more gently than he treated himself. With a sigh of remorse, he walked over and took up the trailing reins.

"After you drink yourself sick on that mineral water, I'll take care of you, boy. I'm sorry."

Lordy. He was talking to his horse! Well, why not? There weren't in any people around who wanted to talk to him.

"Criminy," he muttered. "Now you're feeling sorry for yourself."

He told himself to snap out of it, and proceeded to remove Fargo's saddle and rub him down. Then he gave him a few extra oats to make up for the harsh treatment the horse had endured since they'd left Rio Hondo. Only after Noah had cared for his horse did he catch some fish for himself. They were pretty tasty, considering everything in Noah's life seemed to have turned to ashes in the last few hours. Not that anything had been particularly appealing before.

Knowing Grace Richardson hated his guts hurt, though. It hurt more than Noah had believed anything would ever be able to hurt him again. He'd believed all his sensitivity had been used up years ago. He was terribly unhappy to discover the truth.

Noah and Fargo camped that night beside the Pecos River, on the property owned by Grace Richardson. Noah's dreams were filled with odd images and sensations. Grace was in them, and Maddie, and more children. Noah awoke with the strange conviction that they had been his children. His and Grace's. He rubbed his eyes, trying to wipe the dream away. It wouldn't be erased. Damn it all, how many more kinds of a jackass did he have to prove himself to be, anyway?

The dry grass and scrub shimmered with frost. The silvery glitter went on forever until it disappeared over the horizon. The effect of all that silver sparkling under the hazy sunlight was peculiar. Noah'd never seen anything like it. He tilted his head back and stared into a sky as gray and hard as steel, as gray and hard as his own soul. The moon still hung up there in the western sky, a translucent, mottled, yellowish pearl. Capitan stood like a sentinel guarding its barren treasure, the Pecos Valley.

When he walked to the river to wash, crunching the frosted grass underfoot, Noah got the impression he was treading on slivers of icy silver. When he dipped his hands into the frigid water and drew them out again, not only did the water drip from them like sheets of crystal, but he discovered two pinkish quartz stones, unique to the area and that people hereabouts called Pecos Valley diamonds, resting in his cupped hands. He had the fanciful thought that, what with his strange dreams, the weirdness of the frosty landscape, and those crystals, God was giving him a sign.

"Shoot, you're even crazier than usual this morning, Noah Partridge."

Try as he might, however, Noah couldn't shake the feeling that there was something magical about this dawn. The impression made no sense to him. He kept glancing over his shoulder to see if Mac were anywhere about. Strange things happened in Mac's vicinity. Mystical things. Things Noah couldn't explain.

Mac was nowhere in sight, of course. "He's in Rio

Hondo, for God's sake, man. Snap out of it!'' He was embarrassed about his outburst when Fargo lifted his head, turned, and blinked at him.

Still, after he fed Fargo his morning meal and as he himself dined on fish for breakfast, he realized what he had to do. Knowing he was a being a blockhead even as he did it, after breakfast he saddled Fargo and rode toward the southwest.

''I'm crazy, Fargo,'' he muttered. ''I'm flat-out crazy.''

This morning, for the first time since the war, he couldn't make himself care two hoots about the loss of his godforsaken sanity.

Mac smiled with satisfaction as his mind's eye pictured Noah Partridge and his horse.

''The lad's coming around,'' he murmured to his frosty window, which remained as silent as ever.

''Who are you talking to, Mac?''

He turned to see Maddie Richardson, holding her dolly, Priscilla, knuckling her eyes and yawning at him. She was about the cutest little tyke on earth, and Mac loved her very much. He gave her a happy-morning smile.

''I'm just lookin' out at the day the good Lord's given us, Maddie m'lass, and thankin' Him for it. 'Tis a fine, fine day.''

Maddie walked across the cold parlor floorboards and her mother's warm, braided rugs to Mac's side and peered out the window with him. ''It looks cold out there to me.''

''Oh, aye, it's cold all right. It's gettin' on towards

Christmas, lass, and out here the weather's cold at Christmas."

Maddie reached up and put her soft little hand in Mac's hard big one. "Isn't it cold everywhere at Christmas time?"

"Nay, lass. In the Southern Hemisphere it's warm this time of year."

"Was it cold where Jesus was born?"

Mac smiled down at her, feeling his old heart go warm with tenderness. "I don't know, lass, but I do know that the land where Jesus was born is a lot like this. It's as dry and desert-like in Bethlehem as it is here in Rio Hondo. Dryer, maybe."

"Really?" Maddie looked up at him, her blue eyes wide with surprise. "How come Christmas pictures always have snow in them, and sleds, and stuff?"

"I think that's because people remember Christmas as the time they were the happiest, Maddie, and for most of the folks in Europe and America, the weather's cold and often snowy at Christmas."

"Oh."

Mac was pretty sure she didn't understand what he was talking about, but she didn't press the issue. Instead, she stood there, holding his hand and Priscilla and staring out into the day with him.

Noah Partridge was out there, somewhere, doing what Noah Partridge had to do. Mac was pleased he was doing it. He couldn't very well tell Maddie or Grace what it was. They'd find out soon enough.

"Mr. Noah's gone to get Mommy's reed organ, hasn't he, Mac?"

Mac gave her hand a squeeze. "We'll find out pretty soon, I reckon, Maddie, m'lass."

"Mommy doesn't think that's what he's doing, but he is, isn't he?"

"Ah, lass, I can't tell you that."

"How come?"

Mac laughed softly. "Now how should I know what a man is going to do before he does it?"

"I don't know, but you always do."

He couldn't get out of it. Maddie was smarter than most folks Mac knew. "Well, maybe sometimes I do, but I can't tell, 'cause that wouldn't be fair, now, would it?"

"How come?"

"Ah, lass, folks have to find things out for themselves, and then do what they have to do. If everyone knew ahead of time what was going to happen, life wouldn't be fun anymore, would it?"

A frown creased her perfect little forehead. "I guess."

They were quiet for a minute. Mac could hear Grace moving about in the kitchen, and he could smell the pleasant aroma of fresh coffee brewing and bacon frying. Grace was a good woman, one of the best. It was a shame she had to be going through this unsettled time now. Mac sighed.

"I wish Mommy would believe Mr. Noah's going to help her," Maddie sounded sad. "But she doesn't. She doesn't say so, but I can tell. I keep telling her he's going to bring her the organ, and she always says not to get my hopes up. She thinks he isn't coming back."

Mac murmured a sympathetic noise for Maddie's benefit.

"But he is coming back, isn't he, Mac?"

344

"Ah, lass, I can't tell you that, either."

"I hope he does. Every night I pray for him, you know."

"Aye, that's the best thing ye can do for a body, child, is pray for them. I hope you add a prayer for your mama when you're prayin'."

She nodded solemnly. "Oh, yes. And I pray for my daddy too, even though he's dead."

"Ye're a good lass, Maddie."

"Oh, but Mac, I hope so hard that Mr. Noah will come back. And that he'll bring Mommy a reed organ. She wants one bad. I know she does, even though she never says so."

"Aye, well, perhaps it's best not to hope too hard for things, Maddie. It's best to accept things as they come, I reckon."

When he glanced down, he found Maddie frowning up at him as if he'd shattered a cherished illusion. She'd learn soon enough that life held all sorts of things, good and bad, for folks. She'd already learned that good men could die, poor fatherless thing.

"But I can guarantee," he said to make her feel better, "that your life will hold lots of happy times, Miss Maddie."

"That's what Mr. Noah calls me," she said softly.

"What's that, lass?"

"He calls me Miss Maddie, like you just did. Mommy says that's because he's a Southern gentleman, and Southern gentlemen say things like that."

Mac chuckled again. "Aye, I reckon she's right about that, Maddie m'lass. Your Mr. Noah's a gentleman, all right. To his toes."

"It's time to get dressed, Maddie. Breakfast is almost ready."

When Mac and Maddie turned around, Mac was sorry to see that Grace's face was wan, her eyes had dark circles under them, and her expression was mournful. She looked thinner too. He'd noticed that she'd only been picking at her meals lately. He shook his head.

"I'll help Maddie get her shoes and stockings on, Grace. You finish breakfast."

"Thank you, Mac." She gave him a sad smile. "I appreciate your help."

"I know ye do, lass. I know ye do."

With another sigh for the state of things, Mac led Maddie to her room and helped her dress.

Breakfast that morning was a very quiet meal.

Chapter Eighteen

On the second Monday of Noah's absence from Mc-
Murdo's Wagon Yard, Grace told herself she was glad
he wasn't coming back. The only reason she still felt
like crying all the time was that Maddie missed him.
Grace resented Noah Partridge fiercely for having wea-
seled himself into her daughter's good graces and then
abandoning her. She refused to allow herself to resent
him on her own behalf.

"It's not as if she hasn't already suffered enough
loss in her short life," she growled as she slammed her
bread dough onto the floured board. Loose flour puffed
up in all directions, and she uttered a short, sharp,
"Damn!"

Grace was shocked when she heard herself. She
couldn't recall ever having sworn out loud before. Mut-
tering under her breath, she grabbed a damp rag, knelt
down, and began cleaning up the flour. When Mac

came through the door, she looked up and brushed hair out of her eyes. She'd forgotten that her hands were coated with flour until she felt her hair stick to her gluey fingers.

"Oh, botheration! Now look what I've done!"

"Aye, lass, ye're a rare mess."

She almost hollered at Mac before she caught herself. Good heavens, what was the matter with her? Grace couldn't remember the last time she'd been so short-tempered. She forced a smile.

"I'm making cinnamon rolls for breakfast tomorrow."

"Yum. Sounds like heaven."

Sounded like heaven, did it? Grace's idea of heaven encompassed a lot more than cinnamon rolls, but she let Mac's assessment pass without comment.

"Do you have any objection to Maddie ridin' out with me to see Cody and Arnold this morning? I have some mail for them from Georgetown." Cody O'Fannin and Arnold Carver were a pair of cousins who ranched a few miles out of Rio Hondo. Cody was a particular favorite of Maddie's. "Last time Cody came to town, he said they were going to be busy buildin' onto their cabin, so I don't expect they'll get to town before Christmas, and I suspect these are Christmas messages from their family."

Grace had finished sponging up the mess she'd made on the floor. She guessed she'd better wash her hair out, too, before she finished rolling the dough, or the wet flour would dry and harden into paste and she'd have to cut it out.

"That would be nice." She didn't mean it. She hated it when Mac and Maddie went off together and left her alone, because she tended to brood when she was by herself. But Maddie loved visiting. Well, why shouldn't she? There were so few people out here that even visiting two bachelor ranchers was a treat for her. Grace sighed inside. "Let me get a package I made up for them. It's just some fruitcake, and a tablecloth I sewed out of some checked material."

Mac laughed. "Tryin' to civilize 'em, are ye, lass?"

Grace couldn't help it. She laughed too. "I suppose so. But I feel sorry for the poor men who have to live out here without any of the comforts of home around them."

"Aye, I know what you mean, lass. Although I reckon there are some men out here who don't have many comforts to remember from home."

Like Noah. Grace glanced keenly at Mac, but his countenance was as serene as an angel's. She didn't believe that innocent expression one tiny bit. "I suppose so." Her tone was clipped. Mac laughed again.

Annoyed with him, Grace maintained her dignity as she left the kitchen and went to her bedroom. There, with so much force that she poked a hole in it, she snatched up the package she'd put together for Cody and Arnold. "Bother!" She'd been in such a state these past two weeks, she hardly recognized herself.

"Here," she said, thrusting the package at Mac. "Better be careful with it. That fruitcake is protected only by the tablecloth and some paper."

"I'll be careful with it, lass. You be careful with yourself."

Mac patted her cheek as if she were a two-year-old. Grace had to wipe tears from her eyes.

She had more or less composed herself when Mac

and Maddie started on their journey. And she'd managed to wash all the flour out of her hair without dripping water all over the floor.

She stood on the porch and waved good-bye, feeling as if her last link to life were deserting her and wishing she could just go to sleep for a hundred years like a fairy-tale princess. Humph. Some princess *she* made.

When the truants returned later that afternoon, they brought with them a package from Cody and Arnold to Grace and Maddie, and a small Christmas tree. Grace took the package and attempted to be happy that Maddie was bouncing up and down with enthusiasm. Lord knew, her daughter deserved this present.

"Mac says we can dec'rate the tree tonight after supper, Mommy!"

"We certainly can," she said, trying to sound cheerful. "I'll fetch those garlands we made last month. They'll look pretty on the tree."

It was already a pretty tree, really, even if it did seem a trifle small. It stood only about four feet tall, but that was a good thing, Grace told herself. If it were any taller, Maddie would have trouble reaching. Because she knew she should, she said, "Thank you, Mac. Where did you get the tree?"

He winked at her. "I have me ways, lass."

His insistence on mystery irked her, but she didn't snap at him. "Yes, I know that, Mac. But I am curious." She heard the vinegar dripping from her words, and regretted it. She really had to get her emotions under control. This would never do. Mac had been her kindest friend for years now; she had no business being short with him.

Fortunately, he didn't take her mood amiss. He never

did. His tolerance made her want to burst out shrieking. Good grief!

"Ah, lass, I'm not tryin' to tease you. Maddie and me, we stopped by the Blackworth place on our way home. Gus Spalding and another of Blackworth's cowboys had gone up to the mountains and brought back a few trees. Susan Blackworth gave us this one. Said it's just Maddie's size."

Now Grace felt terrible for having been snappish. "She's right. It is. And it's a very pretty tree. I'm sure it will look lovely when we've decorated it."

"Aye. I'll fetch some of the boxes off the top shelf in the back room. I think there are some Christmas things in there." He winked again.

Since Grace had been home alone with no one visiting the mercantile and nothing to occupy herself with but her own black thoughts, she'd prepared a bigger supper than usual. Mac and Maddie appreciated her efforts. She guessed that made them worthwhile.

After she and Maddie had washed the supper dishes, she went to their room and hauled out the Christmas garlands and the little angels she and Maddie had cut out and pasted together

Mac had moved the furniture in the parlor to accommodate the Christmas tree. He'd cleared one entire wall, in fact. Grace wondered if he expected lots of Christmas presents to arrive by carrier pigeon, but didn't ask because she knew the intemperate thought to be the product of her worried mind. Then Mac set up the tree in a bucket of sand and brought a box of Christmas things from the back room.

Grace and Maddie had just wound the first garland around the tree, and Grace was finally getting into the spirit of Christmas, when Maddie piped up, "Mrs. Backwort said that Mr. Noah was at her house until yesterday, Mommy."

Grace's heart swooped, and she dropped the angel she'd been about to hang on a branch. She swallowed painfully and managed to say mildly, "Really? I wonder what he was doing there."

Maddie shrugged, nonchalant. "I don't know, 'cause she didn't say. I wish he was there when we visited, though, 'cause I miss him."

Damn Noah Partridge to the eternal pit for leaving Maddie like this. Grace sucked in a big breath and kept her mouth shut. Out of the corner of her eye, she saw Mac sitting in his big old chair, puffing on his pipe and watching her, his eyes twinkling like sapphires. She wondered what was going on in that old head of his, then decided she was better off not knowing.

"Mrs. Backwort played some Christmas carols on her piano, though, and they were pretty," Maddie chirped happily.

"Did she? Her rheumatism must be better."

"It is. She said so. It's 'cause of Mac's limment."

"His limment?" Grace peered at Mac, who blew out a perfect smoke ring and grinned back.

"My extra-special, super-effective horse liniment, is what our Maddie's tellin' ye, Grace m'lass. Works on people's knuckles and ankle bones, too."

He offered another one of his winks. Grace didn't resent this one as much as she had the last several. She considered it a major dispositional improvement on her part. "I see. Well, Mac's as good as a doctor in these parts, and he knows what people need."

"That's what Mrs. Backwort says. She said she was

sending Gus over here on Christmas Eve, 'cause she's got a present for you.''

''Does she? That's nice of her. If I'd known you were going out to Susan's, I'd have given you the shawl I knitted for her.''

Not that Susan Blackworth couldn't afford to send to New York or Baltimore or anywhere else she chose—Paris, even—for better shawls than Grace Richardson could knit. Grace reminded herself that expense wasn't the point. The point of giving Christmas gifts was to honor the spirit of the season by acknowledging friendship. The good Lord had given His Son, for heaven's sake. And if all Grace could afford to give her friends were handmade goods, that's what she'd give.

Where was Noah? Why had he been at the Blackworths'? Was he ever coming back?

When she perceived the track her thoughts had taken, Grace very nearly forgot herself and swore out loud for the second time in her life.

''You just missed Mr. McMurdo and Maddie Richardson, Mr. Partridge. Your timing is impeccable.''

Noah scowled at Susan Blackworth. She was the most sarcastic damned woman he'd ever met in his life. ''Yeah? Sorry I missed them.''

She cackled like a witch. ''I'm sure you are. Grace wasn't with them, though, so you don't have to be too sorry.''

His scowl deepened, and he didn't bother to respond.

''Did you get the papers you were after?''

''Yes.''

Noah brushed past her and headed for the back room

he'd been using for the past two weeks. His work here was almost done, thank God. Then he'd be able to find out what was in store for the rest of his life. The possibilities scared him, but he wasn't about to quit now, damned fool that he was.

He'd been both surprised and glad when the wire he'd sent to Santa Fe had produced such quick results. He'd expected to have to wait until well into the new year before he could finish up his job at the Blackworth's spread and head back to Rio Hondo. But now, maybe he'd be able to get everything done by Christmas Eve. The timing seemed appropriate to him, probably because he'd hated Christmas for so long. If his luck remained unchanged, he'd lose again. He didn't look forward to it.

He heard Susan's cane on the hardwood floor as she hobbled after him. "Wait up there, Mr. Partridge. Mac left something for you."

Noah turned and frowned at her. "He left something for me? How the hell'd he know I was staying here?"

"Oh, Mac has his ways."

"Yeah, I guess so. And I suppose you confirmed what he'd already figured out on his own."

"I told him you'd been staying here for a couple of weeks. I didn't tell him what you're up to."

That was something, anyway. He didn't say so.

"Maddie was sorry she missed you."

Her smile was a work of black art. Damn. Trust Susan Blackworth to muddy the waters of his life. As if they weren't cloudy enough already. He hadn't wanted anyone from Rio Hondo to know where he was. He elected not to waste his breath telling her so. If Susan knew how irritated he was, she'd probably send for

Grace for the simple pleasure of riling him. Her eyes glittered like black diamonds, and her grin was diabolical.

"Yeah," he said. "I'm sorry I missed her too."

She cackled again. "I'm sure you are. Here." She thrust a small package at him. "Mac said this was to encourage you."

"What did he mean by that?"

She shrugged. "I have no idea."

He took the package and ripped the paper from around it.

"Aren't you going to wait until Christmas?"

Noah glanced up at her, and realized she wasn't being sarcastic for once. He shook his head. "No." Damn, he hated Christmas.

"You're a hard man, Noah Partridge."

"Yeah." The paper fell away to reveal a very small scrap of wood upon which was painted, in pretty gold script, "God, I thank thee, that I am not as other men are. Luke 18:11."

Noah stared down at the plaque. "What the hell is that supposed to mean?"

Susan Blackworth peered over his shoulder and shrugged. "That's what Jesus said in one of His parables. Didn't you ever go to Sunday school, Mr. Partridge?"

"Yeah, I went to Sunday school. That was a long time ago."

"Well, I think the point of the story was that we're all alike under our skins. And maybe that going through the motions of piety or whatever doesn't make us right."

Noah squinted at her and thought hard. "What does

that have to do with me?'' He peered down at the plaque again.

"I have no idea. That particular sentence Mac plucked out of the parable has you pegged, though.''

He lifted his head and glared at her. "And what the hell is *that* supposed to mean?''

She gave him another one of her witchy cackles. "Just what it says. You cling to your isolation from the rest of the human race like other folks cling to life, Noah Partridge.'' She gazed at him with her shrewd black-olive eyes until Noah felt like squirming. "I expect Mac's trying to tell you that you're all right in spite of yourself. Of course, I have no opinion on the matter.''

He discovered he couldn't speak for a minute. Then he forced a brief, "Of course you don't.''

Her wicked laughter followed him down the hall. He was relieved when the door shut behind him, cutting off the noise. What a strange woman Susan Blackworth was. She was damned near as strange as Noah himself.

He picked up the plaque and gazed at it some more. It was small enough to fit into his shirt pocket, and he wondered if that's what Mac had intended. But why?

" 'God, I thank thee, that I am not as other men are.' What in blazes does that mean? Damn, I hate being crazy. I'd give anything to be like other men.''

Perplexed and annoyed, Noah opened the top drawer of the dresser beside his bed. He'd put his spare clothes in there—two shirts and two pairs of trousers—when Susan had told him he could stay at her house, and he'd discovered an old, worn Bible in the drawer. He thumbed through it until he came to Luke, and read the entire parable. It was about a Pharisee, for Pete's sake. It still didn't make any sense to him, so he read further.

By the time he'd finished Luke, he decided he'd go ahead and read John. He remembered he'd used to like John because the language was so pretty.

Still feeling unsettled when he'd finished John, Noah decided to flip to the beginning of the New Testament. Hell, why not? Christmas was coming. As much as he loathed the season, he couldn't very well avoid it.

He hadn't read Matthew for years. Decades, maybe. By the time he'd finished the first two chapters of Matthew, Noah did something he hadn't done since before the war ripped his life to shreds. He got down on his knees and prayed.

On Christmas Eve, Maddie knelt on Mac's medallion-backed sofa and stared out the window into the bleak and barren wagon yard.

The day before she and her mother had opened a big package that had arrived a week earlier from Chicago. Maddie had taken great pleasure in guessing what might reside in all the boxes inside the package.

"Do you think Grandma Richardson got me a store-boughten dolly, Mommy?" she asked, holding out a big box wrapped in brown paper and twine.

Grace had hesitated, wondering if Maddie wanted to replace Priscilla. She wouldn't have blamed her if she had. Even though Grace had made both Maddie and Priscilla pretty new Christmas dresses out of green-and-red plaid calico, the doll looked pathetic. The least she could do, Grace decided, was stuff some more cotton wadding into her and perk up her embroidered face.

Even then, she'd still look like a poor girl's doll—which is exactly what she was.

"I don't know, Maddie. Would you like a new doll?"

Maddie had considered her mother's question with great seriousness of mien. "Yes. Yes, I think I would."

Grace had felt minimally better when Maddie added, "If there is a store-boughten dolly in here, I'll still love Priscilla best." She'd set the box with a carefully printed label reading, "To Maddie with much love from Grandma and Grandpa Richardson," under the tree.

Now Maddie stared out of the window, searching the empty plains for Christmas-Eve visitors. Grace, setting a plate of Christmas candy on the table beside Mac's chair, saw her, and her heart hitched painfully. Maddie was still hoping for Noah to come back; Grace knew it, and she knew her little girl was destined to be disappointed—again. She went over to her and laid a hand on her shoulder.

"What are you looking for, Maddie? Mac said Gus was coming for dinner this evening. Are you watching for Gus?" She hoped so, even though she didn't allow herself to hope too hard. She'd learned a long time ago that hopes and dreams led one only to disaster.

Maddie lifted her head and peered up at her mother. "Mr. Noah isn't coming back to us, is he, Mommy?" She sounded intolerably sad, and Grace's heart ached for her.

She shook her head. "I don't think so, Maddie. I'm sorry." Because her sympathy seemed inadequate, she asked, "Would you like a piece of candy?"

Maddie's eyes widened. "Before supper?"

"It's Christmas. Things are special at Christmas."

"Are they?"

Grace grieved when she saw the doubt in her daughter's eyes. Blast Noah Partridge! He'd done this to her. In her suffering heart, Grace knew she was being unfair. It was her fault that Maddie lived out here in the New Mexico Territory. It was her own fault that one man coming into her daughter's life had meant so much—because she had so few other people to care about.

If they lived in Chicago, with Grace's own family and Frank's family to supplement her supply of acquaintances, Maddie's life wouldn't be nearly so circumscribed. If they lived in Chicago, Maddie would have friends, playmates, and relatives to brighten her days.

She gazed out the window at the darkening day. The wagon yard gates stood open, and Grace saw the plains stretching out forever beyond them—dry, windswept, and bare as a bone today, in the dead of winter. Dust churned up by the bitter wind hit the fence like tiny, sharp spikes. The boards were already pocked with small holes from prior dust storms. The whole world looked tan and lifeless outside Mac's window.

When she turned around, even the decorations she and Maddie had arranged in the parlor looked meager and pathetic, as if they were only one inadequate woman's feeble attempt to disguise the truth of an empty life. Which is exactly what they were, Grace acknowledged with a shaft of pain in her middle.

She hoped Gus would arrive soon. He was always cheerful, and he was a good friend to Maddie. Gus wouldn't go away and leave them; Grace was sure of it.

During the past week, she'd been thinking about Gus Spalding a lot, had even considered marrying him if he'd have her. She refused to let herself think about why she was contemplating doing such a rash thing—and why, if he ever asked, she couldn't. She did press a hand to her abdomen for a second before she told herself she couldn't be sure. Anyway, even if she was with child, anything could happen. Women lost babies every day. Especially out here, in the territory, life was uncertain.

She told herself to stop thinking about it or she'd begin to cry. That was no way to be on Christmas Eve, in front of her daughter and her friends.

Oh, but it was hard not to worry. Grace wished life could be different. Easier. She wished—

"Somebody's coming!"

She swung around, saw Maddie pressing her nose against the window pane, and smiled in spite of her underlying misery. "Who is it? Is it Gus?"

As Maddie squinted hard, Grace joined her at the window. It was about four-thirty in the afternoon, and the overcast day had begun darkening into night. Whoever it was had himself well bundled up, and she couldn't make out his features. She supposed it could be Noah, although . . . No. Her heart plunged sickeningly when she recognized the horse. That is to say, she didn't recognize the horse, and she would have recognized Fargo from any distance. It must be Gus.

Maddie confirmed her suspicion a moment later when she said, "Yes. It's Gus." She sounded disappointed.

Mac made it to the front door before Grace and Maddie got there, and swung it wide, revealing Gus, stamping the dust from his boots and looking cold. "Welcome, Gus. Happy Christmas to ye!"

Maddie rushed up to him, took him by the hand, and dragged him inside the house. "C'mon in and get warm, Gus. Mac says it's as cold as a witch's behind out there."

Even Grace laughed at her daughter's appropriation of one of Mac's less respectable expressions.

"I reckon he's right there, Maddie." Gus let Maddie help him unwind the long woolen muffler he'd wrapped around his neck and lower face.

"Your nose is all red, Gus. Is that from the cold?" Maddie reached up to feel his nose, which he wrinkled obligingly.

"I expect it is, Maddie. It's real cold out there."

The cowboy's wide grin made Grace think of the young men she'd known back home in Chicago. It made her think of Frank, and her heart felt constricted. Gus looked happy, pleased with life, eager to experience the world and everything in it. He looked as if he hadn't been tested yet. Not like Noah Partridge, who'd been tested so hard he'd broken.

With a sigh, Grace told herself yet again to stop thinking about Noah. She'd just have to deal later with whatever consequences her foolishness brought her. And Maddie. Oh, how she wished Maddie hadn't become so attached to him.

But that was neither here nor there. At the moment, Gus was looking at her like a puppy eager for a petting. She reminded herself that this was Christmas Eve, that Gus was a good friend, that he cared about her—at least as a friend—and that he deserved her best wishes and goodwill. She hurried to him with her hands outstretched.

"Merry Christmas, Gus. It's good to see you, and I'm glad you've come to take Christmas dinner with us."

"Thank you for having me, Mrs. Richardson. It sure smells mighty good in here."

"That's the ham, Gus," Maddie told him. "Mommy and Mac and me made dinner, and I was a big help with the yams. Mac said so."

"Aye, Maddie-lass, ye were a big help."

"And we have pinto beans, too. Mommy said they didn't have pinto beans in 'Cago, but we gots a lot of them out here, so we eat them all the time."

Gus laughed again, and the atmosphere seemed lighter. "I expect pinto beans are about a cowboy's best friend in these parts, Maddie."

Maddie's bright braids bounced with her nod. "And I helped soak the beans too."

"You did, did you? And is soakin' them beans a hard job for such a big gal as you?" Gus's laugh was genuine and hearty, and even Grace felt herself cheer up a little bit.

"Naw. It was easy." Maddie grinned, enjoying the joke on herself. "It was just the pot that was heavy."

"You're a good helper, Maddie-lass," Mac repeated, grinning around his pipe.

"It sure sounds like it," said Gus. "And I have a couple of things here that maybe you can help me set under that pretty Christmas tree over there."

Maddie's eyes twinkled like the candles Grace's German grandmother used to put on the Christmas trees of her childhood. They couldn't use candles on the piñon trees out here because the branches were bushier, and they'd catch fire.

"Is there something there for me?" The little girl sounded breathless with excitement. She skipped over to the tree with Gus.

"Why, I do believe there is," he said with another laugh. "You seem pretty happy this evenin', Maddie. You like Christmas, I reckon."

"Oh, yes!" She sobered almost instantly. "But Mr. Noah didn't come back, Gus. I felt sure he would, but he didn't. I'm sad about that."

Gus, kneeling beside the tree, shot a quick glance at Grace and Mac. Mac shrugged. Grace hurt too much to do anything but maintain her smile, which almost killed her. Gus's gaze lingered on her for only a moment, but it felt like forever. "Well," he said at last, "maybe he'll still get here, Maddie. The evening's young yet."

Maddie heaved a sigh that seemed too big for her small self. "I don't think so, Gus. Mommy told me not to hope too hard, but I did anyway, and now I'm sad about it."

Grace swallowed and refused to give in to her emotions. Her throat ached with the effort.

"Aye, well, how's about I fetch us all some holiday eggnog," Mac suggested cheerfully.

"I'll help," Grace forced out through her aching throat.

"Thank'ee Grace, m'lass."

For several minutes, it seemed to Grace that Mac was the only happy person in the house. She prepared Mac and Gus's eggnog with a shot of brandy for the sake of the holiday. She sprinkled nutmeg on her own cup and Maddie's. Mac carried the tray into the parlor, and Grace handed the drinks around.

Mac lifted his and smiled at the small assembly of Christmas revelers. "To the season! May it shower its blessings on us all!"

Grace bit back a bitter rejoinder and raised her cup. "To the season." She wished she'd tried harder to sound happy.

"Merry Christmas to y'all," said Gus, looking as if he meant it.

"Merry Christmas!"

"May the good Lord smile upon us," Mac added, and they all drank their eggnog.

The rich drink tasted like brine in Grace's mouth. Nevertheless, she managed to choke it down and even smile afterwards.

"Well, I'll leave you three to ponder the joys of Christmas while I get dinner on the table." She set her cup back on the tray.

"Do you need any help, Mrs. Richardson?"

If there was one thing Grace didn't need at the moment, it was to have a lovesick Gus Spalding help her lay out their Christmas dinner. She gave him what she hoped was a gracious smile. "No, thank you, Gus. You just rest in the parlor with Mac and Maddie. I'll set the supper out. I'm sure you need a rest after your long ride from the Blackworth place."

"Thank you, ma'am." He looked disappointed, but he didn't argue. Grace appreciated him very much in that moment.

She had just opened the oven door and moved the

ham to a big platter when Maddie's shrill voice nearly startled her into dropping it.

"It's somebody else! It's somebody else coming, and he's in a wagon! Oh, Mac, look! What's that in the wagon?"

Grace set the ham platter on the kitchen table with a clank. Someone else was coming? Who on earth could it be? Mac hadn't told her to expect anyone but Gus for dinner. Not that there wasn't plenty of food, but—

"Well, by golly." That was Gus, and he sounded impressed. "It looks like he did it."

It looks like he did it? What was Gus talking about? Puzzled, Grace puffed a lock of hair out of her eyes and set the cloth she'd used as a hot mitt over the back of a chair. Still in her apron, she decided she was too curious to finish laying out supper until she knew who had invaded the wagon yard.

She'd almost made it through the door into the parlor when she heard Maddie cry out with delight, and then call, "Oh, look, Mac! It's Mr. Noah!" Grace's knees gave out, and she had to grab the door jamb and brace herself or she'd have fallen flat on her face.

"Aye, lass, it looks to be Mr. Noah, all right. And it 'pears to me as he might just have that reed organ you were talking about in the back of his wagon there."

A reed organ? Grace pressed her other hand against the door jamb opposite. Otherwise, she feared she'd slither into a lump on the floor.

"I wasn't sure he'd be finished in time," Gus said, sounding not altogether happy that Noah had succeeded in whatever it was he'd finished.

Grace couldn't move from the doorway. She gaped at the three people standing at the open front door and peering out into the gloomy yard.

"Reckon I'd better go help him. He ain't gonna get that thing in here by himself."

"I'll help ye, too, Gus m'lad."

And while Gus and Mac went outside to help Noah Partridge carry Susan Blackworth's old reed organ into Mac's parlor, and Maddie skipped at their heels, Grace stood in the doorway, quivering like Great-aunt Myrtle's cranberry jelly.

Chapter Nineteen

Noah still wasn't sure this was a good idea, even when he and Gus Spalding and Mac carried the beautiful old resuscitated reed organ into Mac's parlor, and he saw that Mac had cleared a place for it before Noah'd even arrived. He wondered how Mac had known, but didn't dwell on it. He'd learned a while ago that Mac just knew things.

When they'd settled the organ gently into its place, Noah stood back and gazed at it. "It looks pretty good there, don't you think?"

"Aye, lad. It's looks right lovely there next to the Christmas tree and all."

Noah squinted at Mac and wondered if the old man knew how much Noah hated Christmas. Mac's countenance was as cherubic as ever, and Noah decided he did know.

Maddie bounced around like an India-rubber ball,

clapping her hands and making joyful noises. Noah grinned at her. At least Maddie seemed pleased to see him. "You like that organ, Miss Maddie?"

"Oh, Mr. Noah, I *love* it."

"I'm glad. I fixed it all up for your mommy."

"I *knew* that's what you'd do!" she cried. "Din't I say so, Mac?"

"Aye, lass, ye did."

Now was the time. Noah hadn't dared do more than locate Grace's position in the room when they'd carried the organ into the house. He was frightened to death of what her reaction would be to what he had to propose to her. Holding his breath, he turned. She still stood there in the doorway, her hands on the jamb as if she needed it in order to keep herself upright. She looked awfully pale—too pale. Noah wondered if she'd been ill. He whipped his Stetson from his head and cleared his throat.

"Grace?" His voice sounded strange. Strained. Hoarse.

Her eyes looked huge and dark against the pallor of her face. She didn't answer, but remained silently clinging to the door. Crap, now what? Well, he reckoned he'd just better blunder on. Then he could get the hell out of there if that's what she wanted. He expected that's what she'd want.

He took a step in her direction and held out his hand. "I—ah—have an offer for you."

She blinked and said nothing. Good Lord, was his presence that unwelcome to her? Noah's heart, which had been behaving very unlike its old, cold self in recent days, plunged violently.

"Um, may I talk to you for a minute?"

Grace stared at him as if he were some odd and unseemly thing that had suddenly sprung up from the atmosphere to haunt her. Noah found the sensation most unpleasant, and he wished she'd say something. He glanced at the other people in the room. Shoot, they didn't seem to be going away. They looked damned curious, in fact. He guessed he'd have to do this in public.

Grace still said nothing. He licked his lips.

"Listen, Grace, I've been doing a lot of thinking these past three weeks."

Finally she spoke. She said, "Three weeks." Her voice sounded as strained as his.

He waved the hand holding his Stetson. "I know, it's a long time. I'm sorry. I shouldn't have just gone away like that. I reckon I haven't been, um, altogether sound these past few years. I've gotten out of the habit of thinking about other folks."

Damn, this was hard. He wished Mac and Gus would leave the room, at least for a minute or two. Noah didn't expect little Maddie would know what the hell he was talking about.

"I didn't mean to run off and leave you. I had—a lot of thinking to do and a lot of decisions to make."

She jerked a nod. To Noah it looked as if she were a puppet being yanked around on strings by a drunken puppet master. Her movements were short and choppy. She still hung onto that blasted door.

"Um, I guess you know I was pretty crazy when I got out of Andersonville."

Behind him, Noah heard Gus breathe, "Andersonville?" He spoke the name with shock and revulsion.

"And I reckon I'm still crazy, Grace. I still have

369

times when I wake up hollering with nightmares, and I still have times when I feel like there are devils running me from the inside, and I have to go away and be by myself or explode. These past three weeks have been pretty rough.'' Guilt whupped him upside the head, and he swallowed audibly. ''I guess they have been for you, too.''

Another jerky nod.

''And me, too,'' Noah heard in a high, piping voice at his right elbow.

He glanced down at Maddie. ''I'm sorry, Miss Maddie. I didn't mean to make anyone feel bad.''

She nodded. Her expression was sober, judicious, much too old for a six-year-old. ''I know it, Mr. Noah. That's all right.''

''Thank you, Miss Maddie.'' He felt properly humbled by the little girl's forgiveness. He turned back to Grace and took a deep breath.

''I reckon what I'm trying to say is that I'm no great shakes as a fellow. I used to be all right, I guess, but the war—the war—well, I expect I didn't handle being locked up very well.'' He had to look away. Her eyes looked too pained, and he couldn't stand staring into them any longer. ''Anyway, I know I'm no bargain. I've got a lot of problems, in other words.''

He heard a movement behind him, but didn't dare turn to see what it was because he was afraid if he moved he'd run away, and he had to say this. He had to say it now, or he'd never drum up the courage again.

Grace didn't even nod this time; she only stared at him as if she thought he was a dangerous lunatic, and she was afraid he'd suddenly pick up his gun and shoot her. As if he could ever hurt her. He might be crazy, but he couldn't hurt her.

He drew in another audible breath. "Anyway—aw, hell, I'm not doing this right." Criminy, what was the matter with him? Just because he wasn't used to proposing to females didn't mean he had to go and be a total idiot in front of this one, did it?

"Anyway, I guess you already know I'm kind of crazy sometimes. And I'll understand if you don't want anything to do with me, because—well, who would?"

This time, Noah was almost sure he heard a soft chuckle from behind him. It was Mac, damn his eyes. He frowned, but didn't waver or turn around. He had to get through this.

"Aw, hell, I know you think I'm crazy. I think so too, for even asking, but—well—damn it all, I love you. And if you'd marry me, I'd be the happiest man on earth. And the luckiest." Jeeze, that sounded trite. Noah couldn't believe he'd said it, no matter how true it was. "And the most surprised," he added because it was true.

Grace's mouth fell open, but she still didn't say anything. Noah thought he heard Gus Spalding utter a soft, "Drat," behind him, but he didn't dare break eye contact with Grace. He took another step toward her. At least she didn't shrink away from him. Of course, that might be because she was hanging for her life on to that damned door.

"I, ah, bought up your land, Grace. And I have the papers here. I figure I'd sign 'em over to you. That way, if you'll consent to marry me, you'll still own the land. It's yours free and clear." He waved in the direction of the organ. "That's for you, too, because I know you don't have much by way of music in your life, and I reckon you love music as much as I do.''

Damn it, he was babbling like a drunken sailor on shore leave. What the devil was the matter with him? Nerves. Only this time, for the first time in years, Noah figured he deserved to be nervous.

He took one last deep breath and said in a rush. ''If you'll have me, I'd love to marry you. And adopt Maddie, if you'll consent to me being her daddy. I don't reckon I'm much of a replacement for your Frank, but I'll try. And if you don't want me, I'll just go away again, and leave you with the land.'' He ran out of breath, but managed to gasp, ''And the organ.''

Then he could only stand there, his Stetson in his hand and his heart in his mouth, and wait.

He heard Grace's teeth clink together when she finally forced her mouth shut. Then she licked her lips. Noah held his breath.

''You—you love me?'' she asked as if that were the most astonishing piece of news she'd ever heard.

Noah wondered why she seemed so surprised. Shoot, any man would love her. He nodded and squeezed a raspy, ''Yes, ma'am,'' out of his lumpy throat. He swallowed, and added, ''Very much.''

Oh, criminy, she was going to cry. Noah saw the glitter in her eyes and felt like a brute. Then he saw her begin to slide down the wall as if her legs wouldn't support her a single second longer, and he dropped his hat, surged forward, and caught her before she hit the floor. She was as light as a feather pillow. He figured he should, as a gentleman, carry her to the sofa or something, but she felt too good in his arms, and he didn't.

So he stood half in and half out of the parlor door-way, staring into her drowning blue eyes, and couldn't think of a thing to say. *I'm sorry* sprang to mind, but he wasn't sure an apology was appropriate in these circumstances. Hell, he'd just handed her Frank's damned dream, free and clear.

Her fingers dug into his arms and she clung to him now much as she'd clung to the door jamb. Noah guessed he and a piece of nailed carpentry had as much in common as any other two things he could think of.

The air around him almost crackled with tension, and he wished someone would say something. He was re-signed, but not surprised, when he saw the parlor sud-denly swimming with those blasted sparkling dots. He felt a tug on his shirt sleeve and looked down to see Maddie gazing up at him. Her eyes were as big as her mother's, but they weren't filled with tears. Instead, they looked to be filled with awe. That seemed prom-ising to him.

"Mr. Noah?"

"Yes, Miss Maddie?"

"Did you just ask my mommy to marry you?"

He had to swallow again. "Yes, ma'am. I did."

"Did she say yes?"

"Not yet."

Maddie's eyebrows dipped. "How come?"

Noah couldn't quite make himself laugh because the truth hurt too much. "I suspect she has lots of reasons, Miss Maddie. And I'm sure they're all real good ones, too."

"No."

That was Grace, and it made him transfer his attention from Maddie to her. No? Had she said no? What did that mean?

"Um, I beg your pardon?"

She ducked her head and wiped her eyes on his shirt sleeve. That was all right with him. She could use him as a towel any old time she wanted to.

"I mean no, I didn't refuse your offer of marriage."

She hadn't? Noah didn't allow himself to hope, because his hopes had been dashed too often in his life already. He didn't allow himself to ask her to elaborate, either, because he wasn't sure he could stand it if she made it plain that she was going to refuse him.

"So," little Maddie said, sounding extremely curious, "does that mean you're going to marry him, Mommy?"

Grace nodded. Noah didn't believe his eyes. Then she whispered, "Yes," and he didn't believe his ears. He stared at her hard, trying to decipher a veiled refusal in the set of her countenance. This was some kind of cruel joke—he knew it. Noah was past believing anything good could ever happen to him.

"I'm glad," Maddie said.

Noah peered down at her. She looked as if she'd meant it. How very strange.

"So then," the little girl continued, "that means you'll be my daddy, doesn't it, Mr. Noah?" She gave him a huge smile.

Tongue-tied didn't half-describe Noah's condition. Dumbstruck came close.

It was Grace who finally answered her daughter's question. "Yes, Maddie. If he'll have us, Noah will be my husband and your daddy from now on." Her voice shook as if the wind outside was blowing it.

If *he'd* have *them?* Noah's own knees were beginning to feel rubbery. He staggered back a pace, and then thought he'd better sit down before he fell and killed the both of them.

With an enormous, mischievous grin on his wrinkled old face, Mac swept his hand aside as if ushering Noah into the parlor. Noah blinked through another swarm of sparkles and finally made it to the rocking chair Grace always sat in beside the fire, directly across from the Christmas tree. And the reed organ. His knees gave out at the last instant, and he fell rather than sat in the chair. Grace bounced onto his lap. He tightened his arms around her and finally found his voice.

"You mean it? You mean you really want to marry me?" No, that was stupid; of course she didn't *want* to marry him. He amended, "I mean, you'll have me? *Me?*"

She smiled at him, sending rays of heat burrowing more deeply into his heart and melting the last few remaining stubborn icicles lodged there. When she reached up and pressed a palm to his cheek, he leaned into it and felt Grace's warmth and softness steal into his body. He felt as though her touch were healing him at last.

"Yes, Noah. I'll have you. I *want* to marry you. I love you."

He stared at her, unbelieving.

She repeated, "I love you. I've loved you for weeks and weeks now."

He opened his mouth and shut it again.

"You're a good man, Noah Partridge, no matter what you think you are. You're an honorable man, a noble man."

Honorable? Good? Noble? *Him?* Noah blinked because his eyes had begun to burn. When Grace reached up and brushed his hair gently away from his forehead, he realized with acute embarrassment that he'd begun to cry.

Then she kissed him, and all his surviving barriers broke apart at once. Crying and laughing, in a state alternating between absolute ecstasy and perfect disbelief, he kissed her too, and kept kissing her until Maddie's high voice finally penetrated his befuddlement.

"So you *will* be my daddy, Mr. Noah?"

He sat up and stopped devouring Grace's lips. Panting, he held out an arm and Maddie obligingly walked into it. He lifted her up onto his lap too. What the hell, he might as well get used to it. His two females sat there hugging each other and looking so happy, he could hardly believe his eyes. They were happy to have him. They were happy to have *him.*

When he finally managed to tear his gaze away from Grace and Maddie, he saw Mac leaning against the new-old organ, his pipe in his mouth, his arms crossed over his chest, and looking as satisfied as if he'd arranged this whole affair himself. With something of a shock, Noah wondered if perhaps he had.

No. That was crazy thinking, and Noah was finished with craziness if he could help it. Then his gaze slid over to Gus Spalding, who nodded and half-grinned at him as if ruefully acknowledging a fair win on Noah's part. Noah nodded back and silently thanked Gus for taking his defeat with such good grace.

Noah understood. But Gus Spalding was a young man, and a whole, undamaged one. He'd find another woman someday, one closer to his age and temperament. Noah had thought for several weeks now that Grace Richardson had been made for himself alone, that she was some sort of balm sent to heal his devastated soul. He simply hadn't allowed himself to hope that Grace would ever think so.

Yet she evidently did. She loved him. He still couldn't quite take it in. He gave her and Maddie another squeeze and cleared his throat.

"I'd, ah, like to adopt Maddie, Grace, if that's all right with you. I mean," he hurried to explain before she could object, "I don't want to take her father's place or anything, but legally, I'd like to adopt her so that if anything happens to me, both of you will be protected under the law."

"Oh, Noah." Grace stroked his cheek again. When she did that, he wanted to purr like a cat. "It took me a long time to realize it, but there's an abundance of love in the world. There's plenty to go around, you know. Maddie and I loved Frank. And we love you now, too. We'll never stop loving Frank, and we'll never stop loving you."

"I do love you, Mr. Noah," Maddie confirmed, sounding rather shy about admitting it out loud.

Damn, he was going to cry again. Noah swallowed resolutely and said, "I love you too, Miss Maddie. And I love your mama." Then he decided to quit before he started blubbering.

Shoot, this was getting maudlin. Noah was as grateful as he was startled when someone pounded on the front door. Grace and Maddie turned in alarm and stared at Mac, who shoved himself away from the organ.

"My, my," Mac said, sounding not at all surprised. "Now, I wonder who that could be on Christmas Eve and all." He left them with a wink and walked to the door. Gus appeared ill at ease and as if he felt left out, and guilt pummeled Noah. He was sorry about that, but guessed it couldn't be helped. He caught Grace's eye. She nodded and stood up. He set Maddie on her feet too, and got out of the rocking chair. Thank God, his legs held him upright.

"Well, I'll be blessed," said Mac. "It looks like we have ourselves a preacher come to sup with us on Christmas Eve, children."

Noah, Grace, and Maddie held hands and gaped at the door. Gus stood up straight and tugged at his bandanna, tidying up, Noah figured, in reaction to the word "preacher."

Grace whispered, "A preacher?"

"Thank you kindly, sir. My name is Joshua Horgan, and I am a minister of God, although I don't know how you guessed. I was attempting to find my way to my sister's ranch, but my horse came up lame. It was just luck that brought me to this little village. I slept last night at the ranch of Mr. Grover Baldridge, and set out early this morning." The Reverend Mr. Horgan held his black hat nervously in his gloved hands as he peered past Mac into the parlor. He looked as if he expected one of them to grab up a gun and shoot him. Noah figured he'd been reading yellowback novels. "Er, I hate to interrupt you, especially on this, one of the holiest nights of the year."

"Not at all. Not at all. Come right in, Mr. Horgan. Ye're most welcome in our house." Mac ushered the man in, took his overcoat, and Noah saw the distinctive collar he wore. "What's more, ye're just in time for Christmas-Eve dinner. And ye can perform a great service for three of our little group after supper, if ye're willin'."

The minister beamed at Mac, obviously relieved to be welcomed so heartily into this house full of strangers. "I'd be happy to perform any service in my power. And you are?"

"Alexander McMurdo, Mr. Horgan, proprietor of this wagon yard." Mac performed introductions all around.

Grace was her usual gracious, genteel self. As she shook Mr. Horgan's hand, she asked, "What denomination is your church, Mr. Horgan?"

"I'm a Presbyterian minister, my dear."

Grace shot Noah a glance over her shoulder, and he shrugged, as amazed as she. Fancy that: three Presbyterians in the same room in Rio Hondo, in the New Mexico Territory of all places. Right strange coincidence, that.

Mr. Horgan was a friendly looking fellow with rosy cheeks and a well-fleshed-out form. There was something familiar about him. Noah couldn't decide what it was until the minister sat on the sofa in the parlor, glanced around the room, and suddenly jumped up again as if he'd been goosed.

"Why, isn't that my sister's organ?"

Noah, Grace, Gus, and Maddie stared at the newcomer as if he'd lost his mind. Then Noah recognized those eyes, gleaming, black-olive eyes, this time set into the Reverend Horgan's plump face and appearing not at all witchlike in the more genial setting.

"Susan Blackworth!" he exclaimed.

Mr. Horgan turned and fairly glowed at him. "Indeed, Mr. Partridge. Susan is my older sister, and she invited me out to her ranch for Christmas. Since I'd never been to the Territory before and I've read a lot about it, I decided to accept her offer. I must say it's a vast, rather difficult place to maneuver about in, even with directions and maps. There were times when I was sure the wind would blow me off my horse."

"I'll say," muttered Noah, flabbergasted. This man bore no resemblance whatever, personality-wise, to Susan Blackworth. Why, he seemed like a real nice fellow. Jovial, even. Susan Blackworth might know the meaning of the word, but Noah had a feeling she would sooner be caught dead than jovial. This fellow must be a good twenty years younger than she was, too.

"That looks like the organ our parents gave to her. Years ago, it must have been."

"It's the same organ, Mr. Horgan. I fixed her piano, and she gave me the organ."

Horgan peered at Noah, an odd light in his friendly eyes. "Partridge," he said. "Partridge. Say, you aren't related to—"

Noah nodded. "Yes, sir. The Partridge Piano and Organ Works in Falls Church was established by my grandfather."

"Well, isn't that something? It's a small world, isn't it?" Horgan seemed extremely happy about it.

Noah guessed the world was mighty small. Inconveniently so at times. Blessedly so at others. He glanced back at Grace, whose smile rained down another blessing upon him.

Grace and Mac went to the kitchen for more eggnog. Since the preacher didn't look like he was any too familiar with horses and what to do with them, Noah and Gus took care of his horse. They stabled him next to Fargo, who greeted him with a friendly whicker. Neither man spoke a word during the operation.

When they were walking back to the house, Gus spoke. "I'd like to offer my congratulations, Mr. Partridge." He held out his hand. His voice was gruff.

Noah shook his hand gladly. "Thank you, Mr. Spalding." He needed to say more. Damn, as much practice as he'd had lately in conversation, he did come up mute at the most inopportune times. Struggling, he finally said, "I'll treat her as well as any man ever treated a woman, Mr. Spalding."

Gus looked him straight in the eye for a few seconds. Then he gave him a sharp nod. "I believe you will, Mr. Partridge. I believe you will."

Noah felt as if he'd passed some kind of test. It made no sense to him, but he returned to the house with a light heart.

Mr. Horgan accepted a cup of eggnog with pleasure. "Thank you very much. I'd begun to think I'd have to spend the night on the prairie out there. I wondered if I'd freeze to death before morning."

Mac laughed. "Nay, Mr. Horgan, ye won't have to freeze to death now. We have plenty of room here."

They did, did they? It would have served Noah better if they'd had a good deal more room. He'd wait for Grace forever—already had, for that matter—but he'd really like her to himself tonight. Mac's sly grin alerted him.

"In fact, I have the back room behind my store all fixed up for a bedroom. And I think it would be a right good thing if, after Mr. Horgan performs the marriage rites for Noah and Grace here, they were allowed to retire there for their first night together as man and wife.''

Grace blushed adorably. Noah might have blushed too, although he knew that if he did, he looked considerably less adorable than she. Since there weren't any mirrors handy, he didn't know. What he did know was that Alexander McMurdo was the smartest man he'd ever met in his entire life.

Noah helped Gus and Mac put the extra leaf in Mac's dining room table while Joshua Horgan fluttered around uselessly, picking things up and putting them down where they didn't belong, and chatting amiably the whole time. He seemed like a very nice, good-natured man, wholly unlike his sister, and as bumbling as Susan was efficient. Grace and Maddie set two more places at the enlarged table. Grace's heart felt so buoyant, she was surprised her feet even touched the ground as they moved.

Noah had come back. And he loved her. And he wanted to marry her and adopt Maddie.

She watched her daughter skip around the table, setting out the knives, forks, and spoons, and felt truly blessed. She also wondered how she, Grace Baxter Richardson—nobody in particular, really—could have been so fortunate as to have secured the love of two good men in one lifetime. Some—no, most—women, weren't nearly so lucky. With virtually every breath she took for the rest of the evening, she sent up prayers of thanks.

And to think she'd doubted Noah. She ought to have known better. He might still harbor terrible scars on his body and in his heart, but his goodness remained. Grace kept having to blink to hold back her tears.

"I'm real happy, Mommy. I'm glad Mr. Noah is going to be my daddy."

"I am too, sweetheart."

"It's like the best Christmas present of all."

"It is, isn't it?"

A pang twisted her heart as Grace thought about Frank. She loved him no less today than she had yesterday or last week or last year. She had told Noah the truth, though. There was enough love in the world for everyone, and she loved Noah Partridge today every bit as much as she'd ever loved Frank.

She hoped Frank, if he was watching her from his new home in Heaven, would understand that she still honored his memory. But Mac had been right: It served no purpose to cut herself off from life because the man she'd loved was no longer with her. She'd been given a second chance, one she hadn't anticipated—hadn't even believed was possible—when Noah Partridge rode into her life.

Grace and Maddie would be part of a real family again now. And they would be happy. With their love, Grace was sure Noah's wounds would heal. She knew he'd never forget his horrible experiences during the war, any more than she'd forget her wonderful ones with Frank. But together they could forge an unbreakable bond. They could build a new life, a strong, healthy one, one with deep roots and sturdy branches. And if the good Lord blessed them with more children ... Grace paused and smiled a secret smile. There would be more children. She knew it already.

If she'd ever been this happy before, Grace couldn't

recall when it was. It wasn't when she and Frank had been together, because she hadn't been tried back then; she hadn't understood that joy could grow from tragedy, or that deep, painful emotional bruises could mend. The lessons she'd learned seemed miraculous to her this evening. Well, she supposed, if there was a season for miracles, Christmas was it.

Dinner tasted more delicious than any other meal she'd ever eaten. Of course, her life had suddenly been filled with unexpected love. Love added a special spice to everything.

After dinner Maddie distributed the packages. Grace helped her, thinking all the while, *Mrs. Noah Partridge. Grace Partridge.* She was going to be Noah's wife. And he'd saved her land. If she hadn't already lost her heart to him, she'd have loved him forever for that alone.

When all the packages had been distributed and opened, and Maddie had finished squealing with delight over the top Mac had given her, and the cradle Noah had built for Priscilla, and the two pretty dresses her mother had sewn for her, and the several books her grandparents had sent her from Chicago, Noah persuaded Grace to play some Christmas carols.

''I think Christmas music is some of the most beautiful ever composed,'' he said, and then looked astonished that those words had come out of his mouth.

Grace cocked a questioning eyebrow and was surprised to see his cheeks flush with color. ''What is it, Noah?'' Because she couldn't seem to stop herself, she touched his cheek. She loved touching him. He was so very lean and rugged. She hoped one day, she'd be able to help soften him up a little—at least put a bit of flesh on his bones. The poor dear man had been starved for much too long.

"I, ah, didn't used to like Christmas much."

"You didn't like *Christmas?*" Maddie looked up from her cradle, where she'd just tucked in Priscilla.

Noah shrugged uncomfortably. "I, ah, had some bad experiences at Christmas, Miss Maddie."

"Oh," said Maddie. "How sad." Her expressive face showed her distress. "I'm sorry, Mr. Noah. Mommy told me Christmas should be a happy time, and a time for forgiveness."

Noah peered at Maddie, an odd light in his eyes. Then he knelt down beside her and gave her a quick hug. "You're right, Miss Maddie. And if I lost some things in Christmases past, this Christmas I've been given my heart's desire, and that makes up for everything."

"Good. I'm glad." Maddie reached up and kissed his cheek. Grace pressed a hand to her own cheek and told herself to stop this foolish crying.

Noah pushed himself up from the floor. "And now I think it's time your mother took a turn at her Christmas present. Want to sing some carols, Miss Maddie? I brought a book of them from Mrs. Blackworth's place."

So for an hour or more, Grace and Noah took turns playing Grace's wonderful new reed organ while Mac, Maddie, Gus, and Joshua Horgan joined them in singing Christmas carols. Grace noticed that Noah's voice, which at first sounded dry and rusty, gained strength the longer he sang. When they finally sang "Silent Night," his voice had become rich and beautiful, and she loved it as much as she loved him.

After all the presents had been opened and all the carols sung, and right about the time Maddie began rubbing her eyes and yawning, the Reverend Mr. Joshua Horgan performed the ceremony uniting Noah Partridge and Grace Richardson in holy matrimony. From somewhere, Mac produced a bouquet of flowers. Maddie held it as her mother and Noah exchanged vows, and Maddie grinned so hard, Grace wondered if the expression would be permanently plastered to her daughter's face. She hoped so.

They both tucked Maddie into bed that night. Then, while Mac, Gus, and Mr. Horgan discreetly chatted in the kitchen, Grace and Noah made their way through the frigid winter wind to the back room in Mac's mercantile establishment.

Grace gasped when Noah opened the door. "Good heavens! It looks as if he'd anticipated this!"

Chapter Twenty

Noah pushed his hat back and stared at the room. Mac had decorated it for Christmas. There were even red-checked curtains at the windows, a red-and-green-striped bedspread on the bed, and a fire smoldering in the fireplace. The outdoor chill that had followed them from the house and through the store stayed in the store when they shut the door on it. The bedroom was as warm as toast. As warm as Noah's heart.

He went over and poked the fire into life. He added another log from the stack waiting in the brass fireplace basket—which was decorated with a big red bow—standing beside the fireplace. "I wonder how he knew."

She shook her head, obviously as puzzled as he was. "I don't know."

"Well, there's no point in pondering imponderables, I reckon."

He took her in his arms, and was sure he'd never be this happy again. He'd sure as the devil never been this happy before. He was also sure he didn't deserve her—but he'd try his best for the rest of his life to do so.

"I love you, Mrs. Partridge."

"And I love you, Mr. Partridge."

He almost believed her.

There was a lot to be said for maturity and experience, Noah decided. Grace had obviously learned a lot about giving and receiving marital pleasure from her years with Frank. Noah guessed he owed the poor dead fellow a debt of gratitude.

He was more gentle this time than he had been the first time they made love, out there beside the Pecos River. He marveled at the fine texture of her skin. His hands were rough and callused, and he worried about hurting her, but she didn't seem to mind.

"You're so beautiful, Grace." He gazed at her nakedness, and his heart filled with awe. "I can't get over your having me."

Her smile was tender. "I love you, Noah."

He couldn't get over that, either.

"And I'm glad you think I'm beautiful," she whispered. "You're beautiful, too, Noah Partridge."

Her comment caught him off guard, and a harsh, startled laugh escaped his lips.

"Your soul, Noah. Your soul is beautiful."

His soul. His scarred, battered soul. She loved him, and she thought his soul was beautiful. Noah laid his face against her breasts and breathed in the essence of her.

Great God in heaven, until he met her, he hadn't believed he still possessed a soul. He'd thought his soul had been starved and beaten out of him in Andersonville. He'd thought his soul had dried up under that relentless Georgia sun when he'd been digging graves for men who, Noah was sure, had deserved to live more than he did.

But he hadn't died; he'd survived. For this. He knew it in his heart. He'd survived for Grace and Maddie, and he'd never fail either one of them if it was humanly possible.

They made beautiful, sweet love in that little room. He felt Grace stiffen and then seem to shatter in his arms as she reached the pinnacle of ecstasy. Delight filled him, and he joined her in her pleasure. And then, as he lay exhausted beside her, sated and happy for the first time in years, he had an astonishing thought.

His eyes popped open. He might have gasped aloud, because Grace laid her head on his chest, snuggled up closer, and whispered, "What is it, Noah?"

"You know, Grace, everything that's ever happened to either one of us in our lives, good and bad, has led us to this."

She didn't speak for a minute. Then she said, "I do believe you're right."

"I mean, if I'd never fought for the Union, if I'd never gone to Andersonville, if my business hadn't been burned out, if I hadn't gone crazy—"

"You're not crazy."

He smiled and kissed her shoulder. "Well, if none of that had happened, I'd never have come here, and then I'd never have met you."

"And if Frank and I hadn't decided to leave Chicago and make our way west, and if Frank hadn't ridden out in that storm, and if he hadn't been struck by lightning, I'd never have met you.''

Noah wished she hadn't brought that up—yet it was true. He cleared his throat. "Do you still miss him, Grace?''

She hesitated. Noah wondered if she was merely gathering her thoughts or if she was thinking up a good lie. He didn't really care much, although he hoped he knew what her answer would be.

"You know something?'' she said at last. "I don't think I've really missed him for a year or more. I mean, I did love him. Very much. But a body gets used to things, you know, and I got used to living without him. It was so gradual that I didn't notice when it started to happen. Looking back, I can see that I thought I missed him long after I didn't any longer. It had just become habit. It's—it's funny. I'm not sure I'm explaining it right.''

Noah considered her confession for a minute. "I think you're explaining it fine. I know what you mean. I had a bad time during the war and afterwards, and I'd come to the conclusion that I didn't want anything to do with people anymore. The truth was that the people who hurt me didn't hate me, they hated what I stood for. And I didn't hate people in general, but only the ones who had used me as a symbol for their hatred.''

Grace didn't say anything. Noah laughed. "Cripes, I'm getting philosophical in my old age.''

She laughed, too. "So am I.''

Then she told him about the baby, and Noah thought he'd never been given a finer Christmas present. Grace,

Maddie, and his own new baby child. If life got any better than this, he wasn't sure he could stand it.

Christmas morning dawned bright and cold and white with the magical snow that Mac had produced during the night. He produced a fine breakfast for his guests, as well—without the benefit of magic—and welcomed them all to eat it in his small house at the back of his wagon yard.

He could have built himself a palace, of course, but it would have looked absurdly out of place here on the bleak, barren plains of southeastern New Mexico Territory. A wizard as wise as Alexander McMurdo knew better than to overdo things.

"Well, Mr. McMurdo, I must say I appreciate your hospitality. I was quite worried for a while there yesterday after the sun began to set."

Joshua Horgan's dark eyes gleamed with jollity. Mac grinned, and was amazed all over again that two human siblings could be as different as Susan Blackworth and Mr. Horgan here. Although he knew Susan had a good heart down deep. Ah, he did love humans. They could be unpredictable at the strangest times. Irritating, they might be, but they never failed to amuse Mac.

"Aye, well, it's a big place, the Territory," he said with a wink. "And I'm right glad ye made your way to us, Mr. Horgan." He didn't mention that he, Alexander McMurdo, had drawn him to this house. No one other than Mac needed to know that. Things had worked out well, and that's what mattered.

Noah and Grace entered his house hand in hand, looking as much in love as any two people Mac had ever seen. Aye, the lad was on his way now. He'd been in such bad shape when he'd ridden into the yard a month and half back that even Mac had wondered for a while if he'd been too far gone. But he'd come back. He wasn't whole yet, but he was on the mend. With Grace and Maddie to see to him, and with the new wee bairn on the way, the lad would soon look back on the war as if it had only been an especially terrible nightmare.

It amazed Mac how strong some folks were. Take Noah, for instance. Why, the lad had survived against overwhelming odds—and then blamed himself for it. As if he didn't deserve to live! Ach, human beings were such an odd lot. But the lad might one day learn that his strength, the strength that had brought him out of that vile place, wounded and scarred and sick almost to death, had helped hone him into the fine man he truly was.

Grace knew it. Mac was proud of her for recognizing Noah's sterling qualities underneath his brittle shell.

Maddie knew it too. Now, there was a lass who was worth her weight in diamonds. He watched her race into the parlor to greet her mother and new daddy, and grinned around his pipe stem. She and Priscilla were wearing matching Christmas dresses today. Grace had made them for her, of course.

Noah swung Maddie up and gave her a kiss on the cheek, and Mac blew out a series of satisfied smoke rings. For fun, he made two of them twine into a lover's knot, then decided he'd best not do too much of that sort of thing.

Anyway, Christmas was magical enough all on its own. It needed no help from Alexander McMurdo.

After breakfast, Gus said he'd be honored to guide

Mr. Horgan to his sister's ranch. He was another good lad, Gus was. And he'd find his own woman one of these days. Grace had been meant for Noah. Poor Gus's heart was aching now, but he was made of resilient stuff. These disappointments in life helped to strengthen people. Gus would heal, and he'd toughen up, and he'd grow wiser, and he'd be fine. Just fine.

Grace, Maddie, Noah, and Mac went out to the wagon yard gates to wave Gus and Mr. Horgan off. Cries of "Merry Christmas" rang in the crisp morning air and blended beautifully with the scent of wood smoke and the clean, fresh atmosphere of the Territory.

Mac loved this wild and empty land. It was a strange place, a land full of enchantment and promise. As he watched Grace, Noah, and Maddie shout with laughter as they made angels in the snow, he was glad its enchantment had worked so well on those three. Together, they'd fulfill their own promises.

IT'S A DOG'S LIFE ROMANCE

Stray Hearts by Annie Kimberlin. A busy veterinarian, Melissa is comfortable around her patients—but when it comes to men, too often her instincts have her barking up the wrong tree. So she's understandably wary when Peter Winthrop, who accidentally hits a Shetland sheepdog with his car, shows more than just a friendly interest in her. But as their relationship grows more intimate she finds herself hoping that he has room for one more lost soul in his home.
___52221-7 $5.50 US/$6.50 CAN

Rosamunda's Revenge by Emma Craig. At first, Tacita Grantham thinks that Jedediah Hardcastle is a big brute of a man with no manners whatsoever. But when she sees he'll do anything to protect her—even rescue her beloved Rosamunda—she knows his bark is worse than his bite. And when she first feels his kiss—she knows he is the only man who'll ever touch her heart.
___52213-6 $5.50 US/$6.50 CAN

Dorchester Publishing Co., Inc.
P.O. Box 6640
Wayne, PA 19087-8640

Please add $1.75 for shipping and handling for the first book and $.50 for each book thereafter. NY, NYC, and PA residents, please add appropriate sales tax. No cash, stamps, or C.O.D.s. All orders shipped within 6 weeks via postal service book rate. Canadian orders require $2.00 extra postage and must be paid in U.S. dollars through a U.S. banking facility.

Name
Address
City   State   Zip_____
I have enclosed $.   in payment for the checked book(s).
Payment <u>must</u> accompany all orders. ❏ Please send a free catalog.

TIMESWEPT

Christmas Carol
FLORA SPEER

Bestselling Author of *A Love Beyond Time*

Bah! Humbug! That is what Carol Simmons says to the holidays, mistletoe, and the ghost in her room. But the mysterious specter has come to save the heartless spinster from a loveless life. Soon Carol is traveling through the ages to three different London Yuletides—and into the arms of a trio of dashing suitors. From Christmas past to Christmas future, the passionate caresses of the one man meant for her teach Carol that the season is about a lot more than Christmas presents.

_51986-0 $4.99 US/$5.99 CAN

MONTANA
Angel

THERESA SCOTT

Amberson Hawley can't bring herself to tell the man she loves that she is carrying his child. She has heard stories of women abandoned by men who never really loved them. But one day Justin Harbinger rides into the Triple R Ranch, and Amberson has to pretend that their one night together never happened. Soon, the two find themselves fighting an all-too-familiar attraction. And she wonders if she has been given a second chance at love.

___4392-0 $5.99 US/$6.99 CAN

Dorchester Publishing Co., Inc.
P.O. Box 6640
Wayne, PA 19087-8640

Please add $1.75 for shipping and handling for the first book and $.50 for each book thereafter. NY, NYC, and PA residents, please add appropriate sales tax. No cash, stamps, or C.O.D.s. All orders shipped within 6 weeks via postal service book rate. Canadian orders require $2.00 extra postage and must be paid in U.S. dollars through a U.S. banking facility.

Name_____
Address_____
City_____State_____Zip_____
I have enclosed $_____ in payment for the checked book(s).
Payment <u>must</u> accompany all orders. ❏ Please send a free catalog.
CHECK OUT OUR WEBSITE! www.dorchesterpub.com

SUPERSTITIONS

ANNIE McKNIGHT

Beautiful young Billie Bahill is determined. Despite what her father says, she knows her fiancé won't just leave her. So come hell or high water, she is going to go find him. So what if she rides off into the deadly Superstition Mountains? Billie is as good on a horse as any of the men on her father's ranch, and she won't let anybody stop her—especially not the Arizona Ranger with eyes that make her heart skip a beat.

___4405-6 $5.50 US/$6.50 CAN

Dorchester Publishing Co., Inc.
P.O. Box 6640
Wayne, PA 19087-8640

Please add $1.75 for shipping and handling for the first book and $.50 for each book thereafter. NY, NYC, and PA residents, please add appropriate sales tax. No cash, stamps, or C.O.D.s. All orders shipped within 6 weeks via postal service book rate. Canadian orders require $2.00 extra postage and must be paid in U.S. dollars through a U.S. banking facility.

Name_____
Address_____
City_____ State_____ Zip_____
I have enclosed $_____ in payment for the checked book(s).
Payment <u>must</u> accompany all orders. ❏ Please send a free catalog.
CHECK OUT OUR WEBSITE! www.dorchesterpub.com